TIL DEATH DO US PART

The Thomas Potts Mysteries by Sara Fraser
from Severn House

THE RELUCTANT CONSTABLE
THE RESURRECTION MEN
THE DROWNED ONES
SUFFER THE CHILDREN
TIL DEATH DO US PART

TIL DEATH DO US PART

A Constable Thomas Potts Mystery

Sara Fraser

This first world edition published 2013
in Great Britain and in the USA by
SEVERN HOUSE PUBLISHERS LTD of
19 Cedar Road, Sutton, Surrey, England, SM2 5DA.

British Library Cataloguing in Publication Data

Fraser, Sara.
Til death do us part. -- (A Thomas Potts mystery)
1. Potts, Thomas (Fictitious character)--Fiction. 2. East
India Company--Fiction. 3. Police--England--Redditch--
Fiction. 4. Detective and mystery stories.
I. Title II. Series
823.9'14-dc23

ISBN-13: 978-0-7278-8254-7 (cased)

Typeset by Palimpsest Book Production Ltd.,
Falkirk, Stirlingshire, Scotland.
Printed and bound in Great Britain by
MPG Books Ltd., Bodmin, Cornwall.

ONE

Lincolnshire
Wednesday, 2nd January, 1828
Afternoon

The skies were dark grey and rain gusted on the bitterly cold north wind, but in the gloomy sheltered porch of the isolated ancient church, Walter Courtney's smile radiated benign warmth.

'This has been a stroke of unexpected good luck, Cousin Sylvan. I never expected the auction to gross so well, what with the house fabric needing so much attention.'

'No more did I, Cousin; it was a bloody wreck if truth be told. But even the furnishings are fetching almost double the prices we estimated.' Sylvan Kent chuckled. 'It makes the memory of the old bitch almost bearable. But I've still got the stink and taste of her turning my stomach, so I need to gorge on a sweet scented young dish.'

'And so you shall, Cousin; you shall feast on the sweetest, juiciest young whore you can find,' Courtney assured him, then frowned as he saw someone pass through the churchyard gate and head towards the porch. 'Who's this coming?'

Kent looked round and hissed with annoyance. 'It's the damn busybody parson.' Then he called out to the oncoming man, 'Good afternoon, Reverend, I trust you are hale and hearty despite this inclement weather.'

'Indeed I am, I thank you, Sir Henry, and I truly hope that your own health is bearing up, despite the tragic loss you have suffered.' The elderly clergyman entered the porch and squinted short-sightedly at Walter Courtney. 'Greetings to you also, Sir. Have I had the pleasure of your acquaintance before?'

'To my regret thou hast not, Reverend. I am merely a wayfarer who has taken shelter here from the rain, and have had some conversation with this other gentleman concerning his recent tragic bereavement. My name is James Gibson. I give thee greeting,

Reverend, and with all respect I must ask thee not to address me as "sir". We of the Society of Friends are addressed by our names only.'

The clergyman moved closer and squinted for long moments at Courtney's traditional Quaker dress of low-crowned wide-brimmed black hat, pocketless coat, knee breeches and stockings, plain white linen shirt and stock, totally without any type of adornment.

'I beg your pardon, James Gibson. I confess the correct usage of speech when addressing those of the Quaker persuasion had slipped my mind. The Society of Friends are indeed true Christians whom I hold in the deepest respect.'

'I most humbly thank thee for thy kind words, Reverend, and do assure thee that in return we of the Society of Friends hold the established church in the deepest respect.'

They exchanged bows then the clergyman turned to Sylvan Kent.

'Are you come to inspect your lady wife's gravestone, Sir Henry? The sexton informed me that it was mounted only yesterday afternoon.'

'Indeed that is the very reason I am just arrived here, Reverend. I've taken lodgings in Lincoln, but until my return to Ireland I shall come here every day and pray over my beloved wife's last resting place.'

'Be assured, Sir, that the Good Lord sees your pain and will bring comfort to you as time passes. Remember always that when it is your time to pass on you will most assuredly find your lady wife awaiting you in Paradise. Now I must leave you for I have work to do inside. I bid you both a good day and may God's presence be always with you.'

'Amen,' both Kent and Courtney intoned with feeling.

As the church door creaked shut behind the clergyman, Kent winked and jerked his head, whispering, 'I'd best be seen to be saying a prayer over the sour bitch's gravestone before I leave.'

Courtney nodded and whispered. 'I'll keep you company.'

The newly erected gravestone bore the glittering gilt words:

In Memory of Fanny.
The beloved Wife of
The Honourable Henry Kinleary. Bart.
Died November 16th 1827. Aged 48 years.
''Til Death do us Part'

Courtney pointed at this last sentence. 'That don't scan well, Sylvan. Death has already parted you, has it not?'

Kent grimaced as though he had a bad taste in his mouth. 'Listen, Cousin Walter, I was wed to that nagging old cow for four long months, and she kept telling me every day . . .' His voice became a querulous, high-pitched tone. '"May the Good Lord have mercy on me, because I'd never have married you if I'd known what a wicked, brutal, drunken wastrel you are! And now I must live with you in misery because we're man and wife 'til death do us part!"' He grinned savagely. 'In fact she was shouting those very words when I dosed her tea with that powder you gave me, and released her from her life of misery! So I thought she would appreciate having them on her gravestone.'

Courtney chuckled. 'What a kindly and considerate gesture on your part, Cousin, in return for her being kindly and considerate enough to leave us in handsome profit.'

'Have you made preparations for our next venture?' Kent wanted to know.

'Of course I have, and very thorough ones as regards our new identities. They are both real people. Your man was kicked out of the East India Company Army some years past, and has not been heard of since; and mine is apparently incarcerated in a private lunatic asylum down in Kent.

'We shall be fishing Warwickshire and Worcestershire and my postal drop is in Redditch Town on the county border between them.' Courtney radiated self-satisfaction. 'I've placed a series of notices in the Birmingham and Worcester news sheets, and already have a prospective client. A widow in Warwick by the name of Adelaide Farson.'

He took a sheaf of papers from his inner pocket and handed it to the other man. 'Here's the script for your next role. You are now Major Christophe de Langlois of the Honourable East India Company's Madras Native Infantry Regiment; and I am the Reverend Geraint Winward.'

Courtney produced a miniature portrait from his inner pocket and chuckled as he displayed it to the other man. 'I've had this likeness of you altered somewhat. As you can see, instead of a dreary black scholar's cap and robe, you are now clad in splendid scarlet and gold.'

Kent shook his head doubtfully. 'But I don't know anything about soldiering.'

Courtney frowned irritably. 'Then study the script closely and learn all you can about military matters, and about India, instead of wasting all your time drinking and gambling. Now there's the parson just come through the door, so let's make a show of it.'

They stood with bowed heads and hands clasped as if in prayer while the clergyman walked past them and disappeared through the lychgate.

Then Courtney announced, 'Well, our business is all but done here. I'll leave you to finish the odds and ends, while I establish myself in the Midlands. Behave yourself, study the script, and keep sober.'

He turned and walked away.

Sylvan Kent scowled resentfully after him, and muttered, 'You're not my boss, you cunt, and the first thing I'm going to do now is get as drunk as a fuckin' Lord.'

TWO

Beoley Village, Worcestershire
Tuesday, 8th January
Morning

Sitting in the drawing room of her spacious home, Phoebe Creswell's imagination soared, and her heartbeat quickened, as she read and re-read the advertisement in the *Worcester Herald* newspaper.

> Matrimony. An Officer of the Honourable East India Company, who notwithstanding his warlike profession possesses a most tender heart and gentle nature, is greatly desirous of finding a soul mate to share his life and fortune.
>
> Preferably this Lady should be of similar social standing and have power of property, which may remain in her own possession.
>
> Should any Lady find this advertisement worthy of notice she may reply by letter (post paid) to 'XYZ', care of Mr Charles

Bromley, Stationery Emporium, High Street, Redditch, Worcestershire.

Honour and Secrecy are guaranteed to any replies.

'India! How I would love to sail to India and see all the wonderful sights there.' She sighed wistfully, and then hastily folded the newspaper as an elderly, bent-bodied man shuffled into the room leaning heavily on his walking cane and complaining petulantly.

'Damn it all, girl, why didn't you tell me that the lad had fetched my *Herald*? Why do you always keep me waiting for it? It's damnably bad of you, it really is.'

'I'm sorry, Father; Jack only came a couple of minutes past and I was about to bring it to you.'

She rose and went to him, took his arm and led him to the tall-backed armchair beside the brightly burning fire.

'Don't drag me so roughly, you brutal wretch! I'm not a dog on a leash, damn you!' he scolded angrily.

'I'm very sorry, Father, I don't mean to drag you at all, it's just that I'm anxious to see you comfortably settled in your chair,' she apologized.

'Not half as anxious as you are to see me settled in my grave!' He glared accusingly. 'I know very well that you only see me as a burden that you wish with all your heart to be rid of!'

'That's nonsense, Father, and you know well it is.' She sighed dispiritedly.

'I know well that you blame me because you're an ugly old maid that no man wants to marry. But that's no fault of mine.' He scowled. 'I'd gladly have given you to any man who asked me for your hand. It's you who is the burden that I've been cursed to carry all through your useless life!'

He held out his hand. 'Now give me my paper and get out from my sight. I can't bear to look at your miserable ugly face a moment longer.'

She silently obeyed and went from the room closing the door quietly behind her. She stood for a moment drawing long deep breaths, then crossed the central corridor which bisected the large house and went into the dining room where the family cook/housekeeper was clearing the breakfast dishes from the table.

The woman's broad features were flushed with anger and she exclaimed, 'I don't know how much longer I can put up with his bloody nastiness, Phoebe, I surely don't. Does you know what he said to me this very morning? I've a mind to give me bloody notice, I have!'

Phoebe could only shrug helplessly. 'I'm sorry if he's upset you again, Pammy, but he's somewhat out of sorts this morning. I'm sure he really didn't mean whatever it was he said to you.'

Widow Pamela Mallot indignantly shook her mob-capped head. 'He said that I ought to be a pig keeper because me cooking was only fit for pig swill and that me kitchen stunk like a bloody pigsty. I tell you truly, if I'd had me ladle in me hand I'd have cracked it over his bloody head, so I 'ud. I'm going to give in me notice, so I am. This very day!'

'Oh no, Pammy!' Desperation flooded through Phoebe and she pleaded, 'Please don't do that! I don't know what I'd do if you were to leave me! I couldn't bear to see you go! I beg you not to leave me!'

Seeing the distraught expression on the younger woman's thin sallow face, the cook's strident voice softened. 'There now, my dearie, don't upset yourself so.'

Tears stung Phoebe's eyes and her voice became choked. 'Don't go, Pammy. I beg of you, don't go. You're the only friend I have in this world, and having you here is my only comfort. Please don't leave me here by myself with him, I couldn't bear it!'

For some moments Pammy Mallot regarded Phoebe's distress with troubled eyes, shaking her head and clucking her tongue. Then finally she nodded.

'Alright, my dearie. Because I've known you ever since you was a little mite, and been as fond as if you was me own flesh and blood, then I'll stay for your sake. But I tell you truly that from now on whenever that old devil speaks to me harsh, he'll get the rough side of me tongue, and he can like it or lump it because I don't give a bugger for him.'

Absolute relief shuddered through Phoebe, and despite her tears she smiled and blurted, 'Oh thank you, Pammy. Thank you from the bottom of my heart.'

The other woman smiled back at her. 'Let me give you a piece of advice, my dearie. You start looking about and find yourself a decent, kindly man to wed, and leave your Dad to stew in his own nasty juices.'

Phoebe shook her head regretfully. 'I'm too worn and ugly to find a man who'd want to wed me. I'm destined to remain an old maid.'

'That's only what that old devil keeps on telling you, aren't it? Well pay him no mind, because you'm still the right side o' thirty, and though you might not be a beauty, you'm presentable enough in your face and figure to get yourself a husband.' She pointed to her own gapped decayed teeth, ran her hands down her fat body and chortled. 'Look at the state o' me and I've managed to marry and bury three husbands, and Joey Stokes the carter tells me every time he sees me that I've only to give the word and he'll be me number four.'

Her infectious good spirits lifted Phoebe's own and she laughed. 'I'll bear what you say in mind.'

Even as she voiced the words the recollection of that advertisement in the newspaper flooded into Phoebe's mind, and she suddenly thought, 'Dare I do it? Dare I reply to that soldier? What an adventure it would be!'

'Phoebe? Phoebe? Goddamn and blast you, get in here! Get in here this instant!' George Creswell's irascible shouts caused Phoebe to twitch nervously and she started to go to him.

'Where are you, you useless ugly bitch? Get in here now, damn you!'

In the corridor Phoebe suddenly became filled with an all-consuming, flaring defiance. Then quite deliberately she walked on past the closed door, ignoring the man's commands.

'Goddamn you! Come here, you ugly bitch! I wish to God I'd drowned you at birth! Come here!'

Up in her bedroom she sat down at her writing desk, arranged note paper, checked the inkwell was full, sharpened a fresh quill pen and, face still hotly flushed with defiance, came to a momentous decision.

'I really am going to write and send this letter, and I'm going to do so this very day!'

> Sir,
>
> I am writing in answer to your notice in the *Worcester Herald* newspaper . . .

The letter was quickly finished, and as she shook the fine drying powder across the wet ink she looked at the clock in her bedroom. 'The Bellman should be doing his rounds right now.'

She put on her bonnet, wrapped a shawl around her shoulders and with the letter hidden in her bodice hurried from the house.

As befitted the representative of His Majesty's Royal Mail, Harry Pratt was resplendently uniformed in a red frock-coat with grey collar and cuffs, blue knee-breeches, white stockings, black shoes and a grey top hat emblazoned with a gilt Royal Cypher. Slung from his shoulders was a large leather letter-bag, securely padlocked with a slit on its top through which the letters were posted.

Now he came marching down the hill into the village with the ramrod-straight bearing of a veteran soldier, ringing his large brass bell, and bellowing, 'Bring me your letters! Bring me your letters!'

The upper casement of a house opened and a man's voice shouted, 'Just you hold right where you am, Bellman. I'll be damned if I'm going to chase all over the village to catch you up.'

Harry Pratt scowled as he halted and waited impatiently until the man eventually came out from the house.

'I've got two for Birmingham and one for Cheltenham.' The man proffered the folded and wax-sealed sheets of notepaper.

Harry Pratt took the letters, checked the addresses, and how many sheets of paper each letter comprised.

'That'll be a shilling and thruppence for the Cheltenham, and a shilling each for the Brummagems. Plus sixpence each for the Brummagems' sheets and nine pence for the Cheltenham's.' Harry Pratt grinned wolfishly. 'So I make that to be five shillings in total you got to pay.'

'Five shillings?' The man protested angrily. 'That's bloody daylight robbery, that is! I aren't going to pay that!'

Harry Pratt's grin widened. 'Then I aren't going to take 'um. I don't set the prices, does I? That's the work o' the Parliament, that is. It's a shilling each for the distance to Brummagem, and a shilling and thruppence for the distance to Cheltenham, plus thruppence a sheet for each letter, and you got two sheets each in the Brummagems, and three sheets in the Cheltenham. So if you don't want to pay, then you can deliver the buggers yourself.'

He offered the letters back, but the other man shook his head in scowling surrender, and counted out coins which he handed to Pratt. The Bellman grinned triumphantly, pushed the letters through the bag-slot and marched smartly onwards ringing his bell and shouting, 'Bring me your letters! Bring me your letters!'

Phoebe Creswell was waiting outside the village tavern and when she heard the shouts and bell she hurried to meet the Bellman.

'Good morning, Master Pratt.'

'Good morning, Miss Creswell.' He smiled pleasantly at this woman who always greeted him with the utmost courtesy.

'I want to send this letter to Redditch, Master Pratt.'

He took the letter. 'That'll be sixpence for the distance and thruppence for the single sheet o' paper, Miss Creswell.'

She drew a sharp breath of distress. 'Oh, I've only a sixpence with me, Master Pratt. Could you be so very kind as to wait by the inn while I go home and get the rest of the money?'

He looked at the address on the letter and his eyes glinted with curiosity, then he winked at her. 'I'll tell you what, Miss Creswell, seeing as it's you, you can just pay me the tanner and I'll make sure that Master Bromley gets this letter this very day.' He raised his forefinger to his lips and winked again. 'Don't breathe a word to nobody of this though, or else I'll have every Tom, Dick and Harry in the village demanding the same favour.'

Phoebe gratefully thanked him as he took the coin and slipped the letter into his coat pocket.

It was late afternoon and darkness had fallen when Harry Pratt came into the lamplit premises of 'Bromley's Stationery Emporium for All Articles of Stationery, Rare and Antique Books and New Literature', which was located in the High Street of Redditch Town.

The middle-aged, pot-bellied proprietor's magnified eyes blinked in surprise behind his bulbous-lensed spectacles. 'Hello, Harry, why aren't you in the Horse and Jockey at this hour? Have you given up the drink?'

'There's no danger o' me ever doing that, Charlie.' Pratt laughed and produced Phoebe Creswell's letter. 'I'm doing a favour for somebody and making a special delivery o' this.'

Bromley took the letter and held it up to the hanging lamp to read the address. 'I've fetched a half-dozen or more of these from the Post Office this last week. Not that I'm complaining, mind you, I get paid well for fetching them.'

'That's a bloody queer name, "XYZ". Who the fuck is that when they're about?' Pratt questioned.

'I can't tell you that, Harry, I'm sworn to secrecy,' Bromley demurred.

'And so is my arse.' His friend scoffed. 'Come on, spit it out.'

'I can't be telling you the man's name, Harry, and that's the God's truth. All I will say is that he's a rich and honourable gentleman. He came to see me a few weeks past and told me that he wanted to have some private, post-paid letters addressed to my shop. But it has to be a strictly confidential arrangement, that's why he pays so well. So don't you go blabbing about what I've just told you.' He paused and raised his eyebrows interrogatively. 'Who gave you this one?'

Pratt grinned mockingly. 'It's more than my job's worth to tell you that, Charlie. You know very well that as one of His Majesty's Bellmen, I'm sworn to secrecy on all matters concerning the Royal Mail. Now I'm off to the Horse and Jockey to quench me thirst and enjoy meself. Like you'll be doing a bit later wi' your fancy woman, no doubt.'

As the door closed behind his friend, Charles Bromley dolefully shook his head and muttered, 'I don't think so, Harry.'

THREE

Feckenham Village, Worcestershire
Sunday, 13th January
Morning

As the service ended in the ancient church of St John the Baptist, Walter Courtney immediately left his seat and went out into the churchyard. The air was cold and still and a spattering of snowflakes were drifting gently earthwards. The numerous worshippers coming out of the church were not lingering to make conversation with the clergyman who was bidding them farewell outside the church door – a fact which suited Courtney's purpose as he moved slowly among the ancient gravestones nearest to the door, halting at length at each stone, feigning to study it closely.

The last parishioners departed through the churchyard gates, and from the corner of his eye, Courtney saw the clergyman coming towards him, made an instant valuation of the man's threadbare clothing and turned to greet him heartily.

'Good morning, Reverend Mackay. It lifted my heart to hear Isaiah Fifty-five this morning. It's one of my favourites and your reading of it was superbly done.' He began to intone sonorously, 'Ho, everyone that thirsteth, come ye to the waters, and he that hath no money; come ye, buy and eat.'

Horace Mackay visibly preened, and he immediately joined in. 'Yea, come, buy wine and milk without money and without price. Wherefore do ye spend money for that which is not bread? And your labour for that which satisfieth not? Hearken diligently unto me, and eat ye that which is good, and let your soul delight itself in fatness.'

They beamed at each other and shook hands in mutual congratulation.

'Allow me to introduce myself, Sir.' Courtney bowed. 'Geraint Winward, who is, like yourself, a humble, thrice blessed servant of our Lord and Master.'

He proffered an ornate calling card, and the other man was visibly impressed by its expensive quality.

'I'm honoured to meet you, Reverend Winward.'

'As I am to meet you, Reverend Mackay,' Courtney assured fulsomely. 'During my very brief sojourn in your parish I have already heard much praise of your diligence in the service of our Faith. I shall most certainly do my utmost endeavours to bring these most favourable opinions to the attention of our Lord Archbishop, at the earliest opportunity.'

He produced two rolled scrolls of vellum from his pocket and handed them to the other man.

'Will you please read these very carefully? They are my identification and authorization from His Grace, my Lord Archbishop of the Ecclesiastical Province of Canterbury. I am currently acting as a confidential secretary and personal aide to His Grace, and am touring his province to ascertain the structural condition of our churches and the ministries of our clergy.'

Mackay quickly read the documents, and gasped with awed respect. 'His Grace has added a footnote affirming that you are his trusted friend, and has appended his personal signature, Charles Manners-Sutton. What an honour he does you, Reverend Winward!'

'Indeed he does; and I have been greatly blessed by his trust and friendship for these many years. But of course, because of the highly confidential nature of the investigative task His Grace has currently entrusted to myself, concerning in part your own possible advancement in position, I would request that you do not speak of our present conversation to anyone. There are certain parish incumbents in this diocese who are sadly lacking in true Christian charity, and who bitterly resent the advancement of those whom they consider to be of more lowly status than themselves.'

'I am most gratified by your high opinion of my work here, Reverend Winward.' Horace Mackay, a lowly penurious curate, was simultaneously astounded and delighted. 'And of course I do assure you that not a word about our conversation will ever fall from my lips. I can only say that although I am unworthy, I do my very best to serve our Lord. And if in my own humble way I can be of any service whatsoever to yourself, Reverend Sir, I beg you to demand it of me.'

'Indeed I do have one demand to make on you, my dear Reverend Mackay. I've taken lodging at the Old Black Boy Inn here in the village. My demand is that you will come there to take refreshment and break bread with me this very day, and also permit me the pleasure of sitting beneath your pulpit during Evensong.'

Mackay felt near to weeping with joy at this invitation, and could only gasp in gratitude. 'It will be a great honour to accept your proposals, Reverend Sir.'

'Here is my arm, Reverend Mackay. We will walk to the inn, as befits Brothers in Christ.'

As they left the churchyard conjoined in arms and pace, Courtney was complacently certain.

'Before this simple fool goes to his bed tonight, I'll have him eating out of my hand.'

FOUR

Redditch Town, Parish of Tardebigge, Worcestershire
Monday, 14th January
Midday

The solitary bell of St Stephen's Chapel rang out across the flat central plateau of Redditch Town as the newly wedded couple exited the chapel's main door. In the skies the louring grey clouds suddenly rifted and a shaft of sunlight illumined their smiling faces as they were brought to a standstill by the small crowd of cheering and clapping wedding guests.

'There now, what better omen could there be that these two am going to have a happy wedlock!' a woman proclaimed. 'When the sun shines on a new-wed couple it's a certain sure sign that they'm going to be blessed wi' good fortune!'

The woman beside her frowned and shook her head. 'Oh no, they'll not! They sat together and heard their banns called at least once to my knowledge, and everybody knows how unlucky that is. Their kids 'ull suffer sorely because they did that. The first-born will be an idiot and all the rest 'ull be deaf and dumb.' She nodded emphatically. 'You mark my words, because they sat together to hear their banns called, they'll know naught but sorrow now they're wed.'

'Don't talk such bloody rubbish.' Her husband sneered contemptuously. 'Me and you never sat together and heard our banns called, did we, and the bloody sun shone bright on our wedding day. But all we've ever known is hard times and misery.'

'That's only because you'm such a miserable useless bugger, Will Tyrwhitt!' She rounded on him furiously. 'And I should have wed Harry Jakes when he begged me to, instead of being fool enough to believe all your lies!'

'And I wish to God that you had taken the sarft bugger. And when I next sees him I'll tell him that he's more than welcome to take you now!' he retorted.

The pretty young, petite, blonde new bride tugged on her older, exceptionally tall and lanky husband's hand and he bent low, gazing adoringly into her sparkling blue eyes.

'What is it, Amy?'

'I just want to tell you how happy I am that I'm now Mrs Thomas Potts 'til death do us part.'

Tom Potts felt overwhelmed with joy, and tears stung his dark eyes as he told her, 'You've made me the happiest man on God's earth, Amy, and I swear by all that I hold holy that, 'til death do us part, I'll be the best husband to you that any girl ever had.'

Josiah Danks, father of the bride, intervened. 'Come on, you two, the wedding breakfast 'ull be ready and waiting.'

Pretty, buxom bridesmaid, Maisie Lock, also urged the bridal couple. 'Yes, be quick and lead on, you two, I'm starving hungry.'

'I'll wager you don't have the ale money, Tom?' the handsome, elegantly dressed best man, Doctor Hugh Laylor, accused jokingly.

'You know very well that he never has money when it's his turn to buy.' The pleasantly ugly, remarkably muscular wedding curate John Clayton grinned.

Tom patted his pockets and frowned in mortification. 'Dammit! I've clean forgotten to pick it up when I came out.'

'There now! What did I tell you!' Hugh Laylor exclaimed. 'Now you see how tight-fisted he is with his money, Amy. You'll be spending your married life on very short commons, I fear.'

Both he and John Clayton proffered Tom coins, but Tom laughingly refused.

'No, thank you, I've plenty with me. I was merely testing your readiness to be good Samaritans.'

Led by Tom and Amy, with Hugh Laylor and Maisie Lock directly behind them, the procession of guests crossed to the chapel yard gateway, which had a chain stretched across it as a barrier.

The guardian of the barrier, a sandy-haired, broad-shouldered, scar-faced man, stepped forward to block the way.

'Hold hard, Constable Potts, do you have money enough to pay the toll to pass through this gate?'

Tom grinned happily. 'Yes, I do, Deputy Constable Bint.' He counted gold coins into the guardian's hand.

Ritchie Bint returned the grin, waved the fistful of coins above his head, and shouted, 'Thanks to the good heart of Constable Potts, we'll all go home as drunk as Lords from this wedding.'

The procession cheered lustily as with a flourish Bint unfastened the chain, dropped it to the ground and with a bow invited, 'Please to pass through the gate, Constable and Mistress Potts!'

In the roadway outside the chapel yard gate a fiddler and drummer, long ribbons streaming from their antiquated tricorn hats, struck up a lively tune.

Tom Potts blinked in surprise, and Hugh Laylor laughed at his expression and told him, 'This is my contribution to the festivities, my friend. We can't let this happy occasion pass without music and dance, can we?'

The loud beating of the drum carried on the air and brought curious onlookers peering through windows and exiting from the doors of the nearby rows of buildings.

* * *

Some forty-five yards eastwards, standing outside the main entrance of the Fox and Goose Inn, florid-faced, fat-stomached Tommy Fowkes saw the exodus and hurried back into the large Select Front Parlour where his florid-faced, fat-stomached, panting and sweating wife and daughter were frantically laying the trestle tables with soup bowls, plates, cutlery, glasses, tankards and bottles of wine and stout.

'Great God Almighty! What in Hell's name have you been about?' Fowkes shouted angrily. 'This should all have been done and dusted by now. And where's the bloody cake? Why aren't you put it out ready?'

'Don't you come bawling at us, Fowkes, or I'll be giving you something to make you wish you hadn't.' Gertrude Fowkes brandished a knife threateningly at her husband.

'That's right, Ma, you tell him!' Her daughter Lily launched into a petulant tirade of her own. 'It's all his fault that we'm run off our feet like this. It's not fair to me, is it, him giving our skivvies days off to get wed and be bridesmaid. It's not fair him making me slave like this! I'm the daughter of the boss, not a bloody skivvy!' Tears of chagrin glistened in her eyes as she finished plaintively, 'And I wanted to be bridesmaid instead of bloody Maisie Lock. It's not fair.'

'God save me! I'll fetch the bloody cake meself.' Tommy Fowkes groaned resignedly and stamped from the room.

Charles Bromley was at this moment a very troubled man. He sat, head bowed, at his kitchen table, sucking noisily on his crudely fashioned bone false teeth, fingers toying with his bulbous-lensed spectacles.

'Well, Bromley, how many times must I repeat myself?' The squat, grossly overweight woman standing in the doorway demanded. 'Why have you not come for me?'

The room was dank and cold but Bromley's pink bald pate shone with nervous perspiration.

'Damn you, Bromley! Look me in the face and give me an answer!' She shouted in fury, and his hands jerked in fright, spilling his spectacles on to the table.

His normally egregiously mellifluous tone was now a reedy whine as he begged, 'Please don't be angry with me, my dearest one. Today's event had merely slipped my mind.'

'Today's event had slipped your mind?' Widow Gertrude Potts' eyes, normally mere slits in puffballs of fat, widened in exaggerated incredulity. 'Slipped your mind? This day which you know well is a day of heartbreak for me! A day of purgatory! A day of bitter humiliation! This day is the worst day of my life! And you dare to say that it slipped your mind?'

He sighed heavily, put on his spectacles and rose to his feet. 'I'll make ready to go with you, my dearest one.'

'And be quick about it, or they'll all be too drunk to even hear what I mean to say.'

In the Select Front Parlour of the Fox and Goose, Tom and Amy had ceremoniously cut the cake, and all present had eaten a little of it, because not to do so would bring ill-luck upon both the abstainer and the bridal pair. Several toasts had been proposed and drunk and now the breakfast menu was being consumed amid a hubbub of talk and laughter.

On the top table two chairs were conspicuously empty, and Josiah Danks grimaced at Tom.

'It don't look as if your Mam and her fancy man are coming, Tom. Why's that, do you suppose?'

Tom flushed with embarrassment, and could only mumble, 'She's maybe sulking. We had high words last night, and she refused to speak to me this morning.'

'I guessed as much when she didn't come to the chapel. She thinks that you've married beneath you, don't she? You being the son of an officer and gentleman, and my Amy being only the daughter of a common gamekeeper.'

Before Tom could reply the door of the room crashed open and black clad, thickly veiled Widow Potts limped ponderously across the threshold and halted, leaning heavily upon her two walking sticks.

The hubbub of talk and laughter stilled, curious eyes stared, and a man's voice questioned loudly, 'Why's she come dressed for a funeral? Didn't anybody tell her that this is a wedding party?'

Charles Bromley entered, flicking nervous glances about the room.

Tom rose and went to them. 'I'm so glad that you and Charles are come, Mother. Your chairs are waiting.'

He reached out to take her arm but she lashed at his hand with her walking sticks.

'Don't touch me, you cruel, ungrateful wretch!' She turned to address the room at large. 'I'm come here to tell the world how my unnatural beast of a son intends to treat me. He intends to cast me out from my own home, now that I'm too old and feeble to be of any use to him. He intends to put me into the Parish Poorhouse, and see me end my days as a penniless pauper.'

Here and there in the room sounded exclamations of shocked disapproval.

Tom stared at her in shock and gasped out, 'That's not true, Mother! How can you say such things?'

'I can say such things because they *are* true. I've heard you and that skivvy you've wed laughing together about what you're going to do with me. So for once in your miserable life act like a man, and confess to it.'

Amy's blue eyes flashed with temper. She jumped to her feet and shouted, 'Tom's got naught to confess! He's got no intention of throwing you out of the lock-up, much as I'm dreading living there with you, because you're naught but a nasty-natured old bitch!'

'There now, just hear her threatening and insulting me!' Widow Potts appealed to the room. 'Insulting and threatening a poor, defenceless, crippled old woman!'

Mortally embarrassed, Tom tried to calm the situation. 'Amy's not threatening you. Please will you and Charles come and sit with us and enjoy this wedding day. We both want you to be happy for us.'

'You're inviting me to sit and enjoy the day in the company of you and that common trollop who hates and abuses me! And you're telling me that you both want me to be happy for you!' Widow Potts shook her hanging jowls and declaimed incredulously, 'I cannot believe I'm hearing such hypocrisy. I would sooner sit a year in the company of fiends from Hell rather than spend another moment in the company of you pair!'

She swung about and limped from the room.

Charles Bromley wrung his hands and blurted apologetically, 'I fear she is not in the very best of humours this morning, Tom.'

'Bromley! Get out here this instant!' Widow Potts shouted, and with a final despairing ringing of his hands Charles Bromley scuttled to obey her command.

Tom's heart sank as he looked at Amy's furious expression and he could only desperately beseech her, 'Now please don't upset yourself, sweetheart. Don't let our day be spoiled because of this unfortunate occurrence.' He turned to the guests. 'I do apologize to you all for what has happened. Please, let us all put this unfortunate incident from our minds and continue with the festivity.'

'I'll second that most heartily, Tom.' Hugh Laylor rose to his feet and lifted his glass high. 'I propose a toast, ladies and gentlemen. Pray charge your glasses and join me in drinking to the bride and groom's future happiness, and to wish them long life, good health and good fortune throughout their marriage.'

With cheers and stamping feet the guests applauded and behind his serving counter, Tommy Fowkes' eyes glistened with satisfaction as glasses were filled and gulped empty. More toasts and good wishes followed in rapid succession amid laughter, cheering and the stamping of feet, as the festivities continued.

At the top table, Maisie Lock was exultantly telling Amy, 'Jimmy Slater can't take his eyes off me, so I'd best start preparing me bottom drawer this very week in case he asks me to wed him.'

Amy's rosy cheeks were still flushed with anger. 'Never mind the bottom drawer,' she hissed. 'Just make sure that you've got a door you can bolt against your bloody ma-in-law, whoever she might turn out to be. To tell you the truth, Maisie, I've a good mind not to step foot into the bloody lock-up until that evil old bitch is gone from it for good.'

'Don't be daft, my duck. The lock-up's your wedded home and you're the mistress there now, not that rotten old cow. And Tom 'ull be heart-broke if you don't share his bed this night, and he's too nice a man to do that to, aren't he?'

'That's his trouble sometimes,' Amy complained ruefully. 'He's too soft-hearted for his own good, and for mine as well.'

'You won't be thinking that when you're in bed with him tonight, wi' you still being a virgin, and wanting him to be all soft and gentle and patient wi' you.' Maisie puckered her lips suggestively. 'I'm sure he'll give you a sweeter breaking in than that bugger who took my maidenhead give me. Bloody hell, it hurt!'

Amy's angry mood dissolved into blushing, giggling protest. 'Breaking me in? You're making it sound as if I'm a horse!'

Her friend laughed and whispered, 'Well you'm certainly a

proper nag at times, my wench. But for your sake I hope that Tom is hung like a stallion so that's he's able to really pleasure you. That's what I'll be looking for in my husband when I gets one.'

As always on such festive occasions, urchins, idlers and curious passers-by had collected on the street outside to peer through the latticed bullseye windows at the noisy gathering within.

One passer-by had spent a considerable time studying the glass-distorted features of the people in the room. Now with a satisfied smirk he hurried away, and entered a narrow alleyway at the far end of which stood a small alehouse.

In the alehouse two men were sitting at a table intent upon their hands of playing cards. The incomer pulled up a three-legged stool and sat down with them.

'How's your luck, Rimmer?' one of the players greeted him, and pitched his cards down on the table with a disgusted growl. 'Because mine's fuckin' terrible.'

'Well now, Porky, me old mate, come nightfall that's going to change.' Rimmer smirked.

'How so?'

'Because I've just been taking a close gander at that wedding party in Fatty Fowkes' place.'

'Taking a gander at a fuckin' wedding party, how's that going to change our luck? You'm getting puddled in your old age, you am, Rimmer,' Porky jeered derisively.

Rimmer was unfazed by this reception of his news, and smirked confidently.

'The bloke who's just wed Amy Danks is Tom Potts, aren't it; and Ritchie Bint and Josiah Danks am there in the Fox with him, aren't they. So it's certain sure that none of them will be out on the prowl later because they'll all be pissing it up at the party. So the Grange job is on for tonight. And on our way up there we can lift that one from Willie Tyrwhitt's place as well.'

'What about Willie Tyrwhitt? What's to stop him coming out to see why the dogs am barking?'

'I'll tell you what's going to stop him coming out. I spotted him and his missus sitting in the Fox as well. So they'll be in there pissing it up while we're doing the business.' Rimmer paused and bared rotting, greenish-brown teeth in a triumphant grin. 'Like I told you, Porky, your luck's just turned.'

FIVE

Redditch Town
Monday, 14th January
Midnight

The festivities were ended, the guests dispersed. The newlyweds, both very tipsy with wine, were being escorted by some of their equally tipsy friends towards the lock-up at the eastern point of the triangular Green.

When they reached the compact castellated structure that served as the Parish prison, with cells on the ground floor, and living quarters of the Parish Constable on the floors above, Amy tugged Tom's arm.

'Why aren't the lamps lit, Tom? I thought Ritchie had gone ahead to let your Mam know that we were coming.'

Even as she spoke Ritchie Bint came hurrying up to them from the rear of the black-shadowed building.

'There's no lights showing anywhere, Tom. I've rung the bells, and hollered and hammered loud enough to wake the dead, but there's no answer from your Mam. She's got to be in there because the door's barred from the inside.'

'She's done it on purpose!' Amy flared in angry accusation. 'Your Mam's done this to spite us!'

'We don't know that, Amy!' Tom protested weakly, although in his mind he was despairingly certain that his bride was right. 'Perhaps she was nervous to be there on her own, that's why she might have barred the door for fear someone might break the lock and come in while she was upstairs.'

'Don't make daft excuses for her.' Amy gritted out the words.

Tom desperately clutched at straws. 'She may have taken a dose of laudanum to ease her pains? Or even, God forbid, have been taken ill and can't rise up to answer the door? That must be it! She's either taken laudanum and is deep asleep, or she's lying ill in her bed.'

'Well, if the latter is the case we need to get inside without delay.'

Drunkenly swaying, Hugh Laylor declared, 'We'll break the door down.'

'That's easier said than done, Hugh.' John Clayton blearily demurred and indicated the iron-studded door, the iron-barred cell windows and frontal arrow slits of the ground floor. 'The place is built like a fortress. We'll need fifty men and a battering ram to break that door down, or a barrel of gunpowder to blow it in.'

The drizzling rain abruptly turned into a downpour.

Amy burst into tears, and cried out, 'It's ruined! My wedding night's ruined!' She furiously berated Tom. 'This is all your fault, Tom Potts! I begged you to find that old bitch somewhere else to live, didn't I! And you promised me that you would! But you haven't, have you! And now my wedding night is ruined! And my new bonnet is getting soaking wet and ruined as well! And it's all your fault, Tom Potts!'

'Oh, Amy, please, I beg you don't say this.' Tom pleaded and moved to embrace her, but she struck his hands away.

'Don't you dare touch me! And don't even try to speak to me until you've got rid of that rotten old bitch for good! Come on, Maisie, we'll be sharing our bed again tonight.'

She lifted her long skirt and petticoats and ran headlong back towards the Fox and Goose.

'I could bloody well swing for your bloody Mam!' Maisie Lock shouted at Tom, and hurried after her friend.

Tom went to follow but Hugh Laylor pulled him back. 'Leave them go, Tom. You'll only make things worse if you try to drag Amy back here.'

'He's right, Tom.' John Clayton also blocked Tom's way, saying sadly, 'If you try to fetch her back by force it'll cause a ruction at the Fox and just make everything harder to heal between you both.'

'Force?' Tom blurted despairingly. 'Force? I would never ever use force against my little Amy! But I can't let matters lay between us like this, can I? It's our wedding night and it's a disaster!'

The final sentence was more like a long drawn-out wail of utter dismay.

Two miles distant from the lock-up another man, Willie Tyrwhitt, was also wailing in dismay.

'Me Newfoundland's gone, Missus! Me bloody Newfoundland's gone! Some bugger's pinched me Newfoundland!'

SIX

Redditch Town
Tuesday, 15th January
Morning

The dark grey bleakness of the dawn matched Tom Potts' mood when after sleepless hours spent tossing and turning in bed and pacing the floor, he came downstairs.

'What will you have for breakfast, Tom? Ham and eggs? Kedgeree? Toasted muffins and cheese?' his host, Hugh Laylor, invited genially. 'Black tea? Green tea? Brazilian coffee? Or perhaps a few drams of something a little stronger?'

'Nothing, I thank you, Hugh, and I'm more than grateful for your kindness in giving me a bed. But I really must be about my business without any further delay.'

There was concern in the doctor's eyes as he looked at the pallor of mental strain on his friend's features, the stooped posture of the narrow shoulders, the rumpled untidiness of the wedding suit, and thought ruefully, 'By God, Tom Potts, you've always been plain in looks and string-bean in body, but this morning you look positively wretched in all aspects.'

Aloud he urged, 'At least stay a little while and have tea or coffee and smoke a morning pipe with me, Tom. We can discuss what's best to do, because I don't doubt that the news of what's happened is already spreading far and wide across the parish.'

Despite his outward abject appearance, Tom's dark lucent eyes radiated determination as he said quietly, but very firmly, 'This isn't the first time by a long chalk that I've been made into an object of mockery in this parish, Hugh, so I'm well able to bear it. But I need to speak with Amy without further delay, and to reassure her that all will be put right in very short order.'

Laylor frowned and shook his head. 'No, Tom, you need to speak with Amy after, not before, you've put this situation to rights. You need to show proof that you've acted, not merely say that you will act.'

Knowing his new wife's fiery temper as he did, Tom was forced to agree.

'I fear that you're right, Hugh. I'll go directly to the lock-up and get that sorted, before I go to see Amy.'

'I'll come with you,' Laylor offered.

Tom shook his head. 'No, it's best that I go alone. So thank you again for your hospitality, Hugh, and I'll keep you informed of events.'

Laylor's house was situated near to the northern point of the Green's broad triangular expanse, and as Tom made his exit the bells of the various Needle Mills and factories began ringing their final warning summons to the workforce.

He grimaced ruefully, knowing that men, women, youths, girls and children would now come swarming from the courts, alleys and streets which radiated outwards from the central Green, and that dressed in his dishevelled wedding finery he would attract curious stares and jeering gibes. Among the labouring classes there were very few who looked upon any Parish Constable as a friend and protector of the poor. The vast majority saw the constabulary as the willing instrument of the rich, powerful, land-owning gentry, Needle Masters and factory owners, and the harsh enforcer of these same ruling classes' self-serving laws.

The first raucous bellows came from a group of workmen. 'Look at Jack Sprat over there! Don't he look a picture!'

'Oh, where did you get that hat, Jack Sprat, wi' all them luverly flowers? Oh, where did you get that hat, Jack Sprat, wi' all them luverly flowers?' A gang of factory girls mocked in song.

Tom inwardly cursed himself for neglecting to remove the wedding rosettes from his tall hat as he strode through the oncoming stream of grimy, unshaven, malodorous, shabby-clad humankind.

'That wedding didn't last long, did it! His missus has buggered him off already!'

'Can you blame the poor little wench? Her must have thought her was in bed wi' a long bag o' bones.'

Tom looked straight ahead, stoically enduring their jeers and mocking laughter.

'That's right, that is! Her must ha' thought her was being shagged by a bloody skeleton!'

'I'll bet it didn't half hurt her when her got a length o' bone up her cunt instead of a nice warm prick!'

'You should know, Charlie; you've had enough bones shoved up your arse in your life, aren't you! But you liked it, didn't you!'

Another man shouted at the previous jeerer, and a furious fist fight instantly erupted between the pair which drew the passing stream's attention and enabled Tom to walk on without further insult.

His first clear sight of the lock-up, with its Gothic-arched front door wide open but no light coming from within, or from the upper window above it, shocked him into fearful suspicion that there might be intruders in the building, because it was the paramount rule that this door at all times be kept securely locked. He covered the remaining distance at a run, halted at the door and peered inside.

Flanked by closed cell doors the murky-shadowed passage which bisected the ground floor appeared empty. At the far end of the passage there was another door which opened into a rear yard enclosed within high, spike-topped walls. To the inner side of this door a narrow, sharply angled flight of stone steps led up to the living quarters on the second floor.

Tom stepped into the building and halted, listening nervously for any sounds of movement or voices. All was still and silent and the only sound and movement he could actually hear and feel were the thudding pulse of his heartbeat, and rapid rasping of his breath.

'Goddamn you, Thomas Potts, for being such a despicable coward!' He angrily castigated himself for what he always perceived as his physical cowardice when faced with any prospect of violent confrontation. 'Now go forward!'

As silently as possible he moved along the passage, checking each cell in turn to make sure that it was locked, lowering the door hatch and looking inside to ensure it was empty.

Tom reached the end of the passage, found that the rear door was also locked, turned to go up the stone stairs, and heard the sudden heavy metallic clatter of hobnailed boots from above. He recoiled in shock and emitted a strangled shout.

'This is Constable Potts. Come down here and show yourself!'

'I'm already coming down, aren't I?' a hoarse shout replied as hobnails clattered on the stone steps and the burly figure of Willie Tyrwhitt appeared. Scarlet-faced with anger he bawled, 'The bloody bitch has gone! And I wants to know what you'm going to do about it, Tom Potts?'

'What?' Tom was completely taken aback. 'I'll thank you not to speak so disrespectfully of my mother!'

Tyrwhitt gaped at him in astonishment. 'Your Mam? Who's said anything about your Mam? What's her got to do with anything?'

'Is my vile beast of a son insulting me yet again, Master Tyrwhitt?' From upstairs the Widow Potts' shriek carried clearly to both men's ears. 'I thank the Good Lord that you are here to protect me from him, Master Tyrwhitt! I'm sure he intends to do me grievous harm!'

Despite his dislike of her as a person, Tom could not help but feel relief that no harm had befallen his mother. He lifted his hands in a rueful gesture, and told the other man, 'Please ignore her accusations, Master Tyrwhitt. I do assure you that they are without foundation. Now tell me clearly, why are you here?'

'My Newfoundland bitch. You've got to search and find it afore any harm comes to it.'

'I beg of you, Master Tyrwhitt, don't let that beast of my unnatural son come up to my room! He means to do me grievous harm!' Widow Potts shrieked.

Bodily weary through sleeplessness, distraught with worry about Amy, Tom's control momentarily snapped, and he shouted back, 'If you don't keep silent, Mother, then I swear I *will* do you a grievous harm!'

'Never mind blarting at your Mam! You needs to get out there now and find my Newfoundland! It's worth a bloody fortune as a breeding bitch!' Tyrwhitt scowled threateningly. 'And if any harm comes to it I'll be laying charges against you for neglecting your lawful duty!'

Tom took a deep breath, and struggled hard to answer quietly. 'It is not part of my lawful duty to go searching for straying dogs, Master Tyrwhitt. But, if you'll give me a description of the animal, then if I do see it I'll do my best to catch it and return it to you.'

'It aren't a bloody runaway,' Tyrwhitt spluttered indignantly. 'It's been stole! Pinched from my kennels while me and my missus was at your wedding party last night! The back yard gate's been broke open and there's a bloody great hole in the kennel fencing, so it's been stole. Now what am you going to do about it?'

Tom considered briefly and, despite all the troubles that were besetting him, experienced the onset of the atavistic hunting instinct that always pulsed through him when told that a crime had been committed.

Now in his thoughts he told Amy, 'I'll come to see you just as soon as I'm able, my love.' Aloud he said quietly. 'Give me a full description of your dog, and I'll make investigation into the robbery, Master Tyrwhitt.'

'It's a heavy-coated, black-furred Newfoundland bitch with no other markings. Two years old, standing twenty-six inches at the shoulder and a good four and a half feet from head to tail, and answers to the name o' Judy.'

With the description implanted in his memory, Tom nodded. 'Very well, Master Tyrwhitt. Might I suggest that you have this same description cried throughout the parish with the offer of a reward for information about any sightings or present locations of it?'

Tyrwhitt nodded in his turn. 'I'll go directly and tell Jimmy Grier to start the crying this very morning. Good day to you, Constable Potts.'

'Good day to you, Master Tyrwhitt.' As Tom watched the burly figure go out of the main door he steeled himself for the inevitable heated confrontation with his mother.

'I'll make it plain that after the way she behaved yesterday I'll no longer tolerate her bad humours and behaviour . . .'

As he went up the stairs his resolution hardened, and he knew that he was fully prepared to do exactly what he intended. He knocked on the door of his mother's room and entered.

She was sitting in the armchair by the window. She glared at him and opened her mouth, but before she could utter a word, Tom pointed his finger and warned grimly, 'Stay silent and listen. Or I swear that I'll throw you out of the window!'

She blinked several times, her mouth closed, and there was a wariness in her eyes.

'Amy is now my wife, and the mistress of this household. You will behave towards her with respect and address her with politeness. If you do not, I'll drive you from this house, and be damned to what people will say of me!'

He paused to give her opportunity to reply, but none came, and so he continued, 'I'm going to fetch my wife home now. Are you going to make any objection to her coming?'

She shook her head, causing her hanging jowls to wobble violently.

'Do you give me your word that you will behave towards my wife with respect and politeness?'

She nodded.

'Good! So let us all try our best to live peacefully together.' Tom turned on his heels and left her glaring after him, hissing beneath her breath, 'You may have got the better of me for now, you vile beast, but you're forgetting that I know of more ways than one to kill a cat!'

Tom walked across the Green towards the Fox and Goose Inn, his trepidation increasing with every step he took.

'Please God, let her agree to come back with me!'

Still wearing her wedding finery, after a sleepless night Amy was staring despondently out of the window of her attic bedroom. She was bitterly regretting her drink-heated tantrums of the previous night, and wished desperately that Tom would come to her. She saw him approaching and her heart began to pound. When she judged that he was in earshot she opened the casement and called down to him.

'Are you coming to see me, Tom Potts?'

He came to an abrupt standstill, his own heart pounding, his throat constricting so painfully that his voice sounded mangled as he shouted back, 'I'm coming to beg you to come home with me, Amy, because I love you more than life itself, and cannot face a life without you.'

She giggled with delighted relief, and beckoned. 'Then come up here and help me pack my things again.'

He broke into a shambling run and Amy opened her door and shouted downstairs. 'Tom's coming up to help me pack, so don't you lot delay him down there.'

When he came into the attic, stooping under the low ceiling, tears of relief and happiness brimmed in her eyes. She clasped her arms around his neck and rained kisses upon his lips and cheeks and his own tear-wet eyes.

Tom returned her kisses in joyous relief that they were reunited.

Then guilt and dread flooded through him, and he drew back his head and confessed, 'I'm very sorry, Amy, but I have to tell you that my mother's still at the lock-up. But she'll not trouble you, because I've warned her that I'll not tolerate one iota more of her rudeness towards you, and I swear upon my poor father's grave that I'm going to move heaven and earth to find her other lodgings, so that we can live by ourselves—'

She clapped her hand over his mouth, and ordered sternly, 'Shush now! I don't give a fig where the old cow is or will be, just so long as she'll not be sharing our bed. And you just make sure that when you share it with me tonight, you'll be fresh shaved. Because your bristles are rubbing my face raw.'

He looked stricken with mortified shame, and began to babble apologies, but she only giggled mischievously and told him, 'Be quiet now and kiss me again, then we must go.'

When the couple came downstairs, Tom's muscles and lungs straining beneath the heavy weight of the large, iron-bound chest containing his wife's 'bottom drawer', Gertrude Fowkes, Maisie Lock and Lily Fowkes were waiting by the front door.

'We'm all coming wi' you, Master Potts. To get our dear girl settled in nice and snug.' Gertrude Fowkes waved both hands in emphatic rejection of any demurral. 'No! I'll not be gainsaid! I wouldn't be able to get a moment's peace if I didn't come and help you both get settled in. Amy's been like a daughter to me these many years, and I loves her as if she was my own blood.'

Tom racked his brain for words to dissuade the woman, but none would come and he could only shrug in helpless acceptance.

Maisie Lock's eyes glinted with amusement at Tom's discomfiture. 'Yes, we'll not be denied, never mind what your Mam might say in objection.'

Tom reddened with embarrassment, and flustered hastily, 'I'm sure that my mother will raise no objections. We're both sure, aren't we, Amy my dear?'

He looked apprehensively at Amy, dreading a contradictory reaction to his assertion. But to his relief she only nodded calm agreement with his words.

Inwardly Amy was savouring this imminent triumphal entry

into the lock-up at the head of her supporters, and how it would demonstrate to all and sundry that she was its new mistress.

'This is going to shoot you right up your fat arse, you evil old bitch,' she thought, relishing the sweetness of victory over her bitter enemy, the Widow Potts.

As always in Redditch, gossip-mongers, some sympathetic, some malicious, had widely spread their varying accounts of the events at Tom Potts' wedding feast and the subsequent debacle of his wedding night. Curious eyes had noted that morning's shouted exchange on the Green between him and Amy and his subsequent lolloping entry into the Fox and Goose. Tongues had busily wagged, and housewives had suddenly decided that it was time to fetch their husbands' jugs of supper ale from that same inn.

When Tom emerged, a sizable audience of mainly women were eagerly awaiting the next act of the drama, and he groaned in dismayed apprehension.

'Dear God, what are they going to do?'

The four women who followed him out on to the Green reacted differently.

Amy walked with preening pride, waving and smiling graciously to the onlookers like a newly crowned queen regnant. The onlookers in return were clapping, cheering, and shouting salaciously ribald advice on how she was to behave towards her husband.

Maisie Lock and Gertrude Fowkes were thrilled to be at the centre of such exciting attention.

Lily Fowkes was consumed with jealous envy, moaning over and over again, 'It's not fair! It's just not fair! It should be me who's new-wed, and getting cheered at! Not one of our bloody skivvies!'

The onlookers moved en masse to follow the small procession towards the lock-up.

Behind the closed upper window of her room, the Widow Potts glared hatred at her approaching son and daughter-in-law.

Leaning heavily on her walking cane she shuffled from the room and made her laborious way down to the front door, opened it wide and stepped onto its threshold.

Tom saw the squat gross figure framed in the Gothic-arched doorway, and misgivings struck through him. He called on his last remaining dregs of muscular strength and lung capacity to quicken his progress. When he reached the shallow steps which led up on to the lock-up's narrow front platform he lowered the chest to the ground and, struggling to draw breath, demanded, 'What do you intend doing, Mother? Because I warn you I will do as I threatened if you upset my wife in any way whatsoever.'

'I'm here to apologize to your wife, and to beg her to let me make amends for the wrong I did her yesterday.'

'What?' Tom could not believe that he had heard correctly.

His mother repeated what she had said.

Tom shook his head in amazement, still unable fully to credit what he was hearing.

Widow Potts repeated the exact sentences yet again, only this time added waspishly, 'Dear God! Surely even a dolt like you can understand such plain English!'

'What the bloody hell is that old bitch saying to Tom, I wonder?' Maisie Lock exclaimed in loud indignation.

Amy's temper fired and she ran to Tom's side. 'What's she saying to you, Tom?'

'I'm saying that I'm waiting here, daughter-in-law, to humbly beg your forgiveness for my behaviour yesterday; and to beg you also to give me opportunity to make amends for all the times I've been rude and cruel in manner or word towards you.'

It was Amy's turn to gape in astonishment, and to doubt her own hearing, but in the next instant she was also doubting the evidence of her own eyes.

Widow Potts dropped her walking cane, slumped down on to her knees and, lifting her gaze and hands heavenwards, shouted at the top of her voice, 'Let the Lord above strike me dead this instant, if I do not truly and bitterly repent of all the hurt I've done to my daughter-in-law! Let a thunderbolt of lightning cast from His hand crash down on me this instant and strike me dead if I'm lying!'

'I'll second that!' Maisie Lock gibed.

Tom instinctively reached down to lift his mother, but she struck his hands away, shouting, 'No, Thomas, no! I want the whole town to witness my repentance.'

Those among the avid spectators who in the past had felt the lash of Widow Potts' bitter tongue, jeered and mocked. Other more tender-hearted individuals voiced sympathy for her.

Tom's face reddened with embarrassment, and he pleaded desperately, 'Please, Mother, let me help you to get up.'

'No, I'll not rise from this spot until your wife tells me that she will forgive me! Let this terrible humiliation I'm suffering be my punishment for how I behaved yesterday.' She covered her face with her hands and vented loud sobbing shrieks. 'I deserve to suffer. I deserve it! But I only behaved so badly because I was being abandoned by my only son!'

A woman ran up to Tom, and angrily berated him. 'You ought to be ashamed of yourself! How can you cause your poor old Mam to suffer so! If any one of my kids did this to me, I'd hang myself for the grief and shame of it!'

From here and there among the spectators came cries of agreement, and other women came aggressively hurrying towards Tom.

Amy was seething with fury against Widow Potts, but realized that there was only one way to save Tom from more verbal assaults. She went to Tom's side, and told his mother, 'I forgive you for what you did yesterday, Mrs Potts. Come now, let me and Tom help you back to your room.'

Hidden behind her hands, Widow Potts' eyes gleamed with satisfaction. She vented more sobbing shrieks. 'Oh, bless you, my dear daughter-in-law. Bless you for your tender heart! But I beg and beseech you to call me Mother! Because that is what I shall strive to be towards you. A fond and loving mother!'

'Oh, bless the poor old soul. She just wants to be a loving mam to both of them, bless her!' Tom's initial attacker cried out to the crowd, and many of them applauded and echoed her sentiments.

Amy mentally bit the bullet and deliberately spoke loud enough for the crowd to hear her. 'Please, Mam, let me and Tom help you back to your room.'

'Her's calling the poor old soul "Mam". That's being a good girl, that is!' the nearest woman shouted, and plaudits for Amy rippled through the crowd.'

To her own surprise, Amy drew ironic amusement from the plaudits and couldn't stop herself loudly telling Tom, 'Come now, Husband, help me lift our dear Mam up.'

Widow Potts kept her face buried in her hands, and vented loud sobs but allowed the couple to lift her to her feet and support her weight back into the lock-up, being closely followed by the Fox and Goose trio carrying Amy's chest between them.

Maisie slammed and barred the heavy iron-studded front door, and couldn't resist calling teasingly to Amy, 'Take care you don't let your dear old mam fall down the stairs, Amy. Not now you've grown so fond of her.'

Amy detached one hand and surreptitiously forked its index and middle fingers at Maisie in the ancient derogatory salutation of the English archers towards their battlefield opponents.

After they had settled the Widow Potts comfortably in her room, Tom and Amy joined the three women in Tom's room.

'What are you going to sleep on tonight, Amy?' Maisie questioned. 'There's no bed in here and this floor 'ull be cruel hard to lie on, because it's just bare boards. Your arse'll be surely black and blue with bruises tomorrow.'

Gertrude Fowkes gestured lasciviously. 'Yes, and if your man is only half as rampant as my bugger was on our wedding night, you'll no doubt end up wi' an arse full o' wood splinters as well, judging by the state o' these floorboards.'

As the two women uproariously laughed at their own sallies, Amy turned to Tom in bewilderment.

'But what have you done with the bed, Tom?'

He smiled happily and pointed above his head. 'I've had the garret converted into our bedroom, sweetheart. Come and see it. I promise you won't be disappointed.'

He grabbed her hand and led her out of the room and down the landing to the short flight of narrow wooden steps that led up into the room directly beneath the eaves of the gabled roof. He gently positioned her at the foot of the steps and urged, 'Go on up, sweetheart.'

He followed her up the steps, and grinned with relief when he saw her delighted reaction to the newly painted and expensively furnished room, its air redolent with the scented herbs garlanding the walls.

The door and corridor bells began to ring and Tom told his wife, 'I'll have to answer that.'

Amy kissed him and called to her friends, 'Come up here, girls, and see my bedroom, it's like a palace.'

The caller at the door was the man-servant of Joseph Blackwell Esq.

'My master wants to see you straight away, Constable Potts. He said to tell you that the business is urgent.'

'Very well, I'll come directly.' Tom nodded and hurried to call upstairs, 'Amy, I've to go out on urgent business.'

'Don't you stay out all night, Tom Potts,' Maisie Lock shouted back. 'This new bed of yours looks prime for making babbies.'

The other women laughed and added their own risqué opinions on the bed.

Tom was smiling as he hurried over the Green towards Joseph Blackwell's large house standing at the top of the long steep Fish Hill which fell away northwards into the broad valley of the River Arrow.

Blackwell rose from his desk when Tom was ushered into the book-lined study by the man-servant. Middle-aged, small and thin, with a pallid, deeply lined face, Blackwell's physical appearance belied the power he possessed. Trained in the Law, he held multiple positions of authority: Coroner, Clerk to the Magistrates, Clerk to the Select Vestry, Senior Overseer to the Poor, Director of the Parish Constabulary. He was also the trusted confidant and legal advisor to many of the aristocrats, Needle Masters and minor gentry who constituted the ruling class of the extended Needle District.

Now he smiled and held out his hand. 'Many congratulations on your wedding, Thomas Potts. I was sorry that I was unable to attend, but I was unavoidably detained in Worcester and only returned late last night. I'm glad that you and your wife are reconciled with your mother.'

Tom shook the proffered hand. 'The previous difficulty has now been dealt with to our mutual satisfaction, Sir.'

He felt no surprise that the other man appeared to be fully conversant with what had happened at the wedding and this morning. He knew that Blackwell had myriad secret sources of information about what was happening throughout the parish and much further afield. Tom always visualized him as a spider at the centre of a very large web.

'I've a task for you, Constable Potts, which needs to be undertaken immediately. Claude Blair, who's the newly appointed Factor at Hewell Grange, came to see me this morning. During the night some of the Hewell Grange dogs were stolen.

'His Lordship, who is expected to be returning to the parish next month, apparently values these particular beasts most highly. So, we must ensure that we do our utmost to recover them and apprehend the thieves before His Lordship's homecoming.

'Therefore you must give it priority above all other matters, no matter what they be, until you have brought it to a satisfactory conclusion. You will have the use of the bay mare from my stable until this case is concluded. I bid you good day, Constable Potts.'

Blackwell gestured in dismissal, returned to his seat at the desk and immediately began to pore over a sheaf of documents.

'Good day, Sir.' Tom was frowning as he exited the room. He had met His Lordship, the Earl of Plymouth on several occasions, and knew how arrogantly that nobleman behaved towards his inferiors in wealth and position.

As on so many other occasions during his life, Tom was battling with an inner conflict between his love and loyalty for his country, and his resentment for the contempt displayed by the vast majority of its ruling caste towards the ordinary people of England.

'No matter what else might happen in the parish, I'm now to disregard it and concentrate on solving the case of this bloody Noble Fop's missing dogs! If only I had the power to alter such a state of affairs!'

Then from the deep recesses of his mind a voice sounded wearily. 'I beg you yet again, Thomas, to please stop your pathetically futile sniveling and set about solving this case. Then you will be free to deal with other crimes as and when they need your attention.'

Tom grinned wryly and his anger subsided.

SEVEN

Tuesday, 15th January
Midday

John Mence, proprietor of the Unicorn Hotel and Inn, the largest hostelry in Redditch Town, always took great interest in any new customers. This morning he was taking a close look at the quality of the horse belonging to the guest who had arrived very late on the previous night, and who was now partaking of a solitary late breakfast in the dining room.

'What d'you reckon to this nag and its tack?' Mence asked his stable hand.

'The bugger's ready for the bloody knacker's yard, and the tack's naught but patched-up rubbish!' the elderly hand judged scathingly.

'I'll second that.' Mence nodded agreement as he left the stables.

In the dining room the guest had finished eating and was now savouring the fragrant smoke of a cheroot and taking sips from a steaming cup of coffee.

John Mence went into his small office adjoining the dining room and through a hidden peephole studied the powerfully built stranger, taking inventory of his fashionably styled riding clothes and boots, his elaborately curled hair and the French-style whiskers which met under the chin of his florid features. He also noted that the man's fashionable clothing appeared somewhat threadbare in places, the riding boots down at heel, and this, coupled with the state of the horse and tack, confirmed his earlier opinion.

'I'll need to keep close watch on this bugger.'

Mence closed the peephole, made his way into the dining room and bowed.

'Good morning to you, Sir. I'm John Mence, the proprietor of this establishment. I regret I was not present to receive you upon your arrival.'

'Pray do not distress yourself, Master Mence. I took no offence at your absence. It was of no consequence.'

The guest dismissed the apology with a lordly wave of his be-ringed hand. Then he rose and bowed in return. 'Permit me to introduce myself; I am Archibald Ainsley. My name may not be entirely unknown to you since I am led to believe that I possess some degree of repute as a luminary of the theatrical profession.'

Mence smiled and said smoothly, 'I do believe that I've heard your name mentioned in that connection, Sir, and I'm honoured to have you beneath my roof. But may I make so bold as to enquire why you're visiting Redditch? We've no theatres here; we're only country bumpkins sadly lacking in any such citified entertainments.'

Archibald Ainsley resumed his seat, took a long pull at his cheroot and slowly dribbled out the resulting mouthful of smoke before declaiming unctuously, 'This is the very reason I'm here, Master Mence. I know only too well how lacking in civilized culture these industrial districts are, and I've long harboured a dream of bringing the same civilized culture to these same sadly unenlightened districts.'

He paused, took another long drag on his cheroot, slowly dribbled the smoke through his lips and continued, 'Thanks to my success in the theatre I can now make that dream a reality. I have engaged a cast of the most accomplished actors and actresses in the kingdom, and I intend to present the works of our finest playwrights for the delectation of the inhabitants of these cultural deserts. Currently I'm scouring the Midlands for venues which can be utilized for the staging of those entertainments, and I'm wondering if you could suggest any such likely places in this vicinity?'

'If you can wait here for a few minutes, I'll make out a list of possible buildings and directions to them,' Mence offered.

'I take that very kindly, Master Mence. Very kindly indeed. And while I'm waiting I'll enjoy a bottle of your very finest brandy.'

'Certainly, Sir. I'll have it brought to you immediately.' Mence bowed and exited, telling the waiter hovering outside the door, 'Bring a bottle of the best brandy to this gentleman, and look sharp about it.'

Next he went to the stables and told the hand, 'There's every chance the flash bugger who booked in last night might try and do a runner, so tell me straight away if he brings any baggage out here.'

For his part, Archibald Ainsley would most certainly try to decamp without paying his bills should it prove necessary, but his present intention was to fully explore what opportunities for profit this vicinity might hold for him. So, before studying the list John Mence gave him of possible venues and their locations, he followed his usual practise of going out on foot to familiarize himself with the town, its immediate environs and best escape routes should he need to make a hurried departure.

When Ainsley left the Unicorn he turned eastwards and strolled up to the town's central crossroads then went southwards along the High Street. At this hour of the morning with most of the townspeople and their children in their workplaces there were few pedestrians and sparse traffic and Ainsley made leisurely progress, halting at intervals to peer though the bullseyed casements of a shop or workplace.

A smart-looking covered gig with a glossy-coated horse was tethered outside one shop front which bore an ornately lettered sign proclaiming it to be 'Bromley's Stationery Emporium for All Articles of Stationery, Rare and Antique Books and New Literature'.

As Ainsley neared the gig a man dressed in clerical clothing came from the shop carrying letters in his hand. He halted by the side of the gig, opening and scanning the letters.

Ainsley's eyes widened in shock.

'Surely it can't be! Can it?' He quickened his pace and called. 'Walter Courtney? Is it you, Walter?'

Walter Courtney froze motionless as the other man reached him exclaiming, 'As I live and breathe, it is you, Walter! Godammee! It must be nigh on five years since we last parted! What brings you here?'

By now Walter Courtney was fast recovering from his initial shock, and his mind was racing as he stepped back from the gig and faced his questioner. He forced a smile.

'There's no need to shout, Archie. I still have my hearing. Now where the devil did you spring from?'

'Never mind that! Have you not got so much as a handshake for an old friend?'

Ainsley reached for the letter-holding hand, and as Courtney jerked that hand away two of the opened letters dropped to the ground.

Ainsley bent and lifted them, swiftly scanning their addresses.

'Both post paid, and addressed to "XYZ".' He grinned, gave an exaggerated wink and tapped the side of his long nose with a forefinger. 'You're still on the "Lonely Hearts Lay", I see.'

'And you're still minding everyone's business but your own, I see,' Courtney snarled and tried to snatch the letters back.

Ainsley fended him off. 'Take care! There's a fellow in the shop staring through the window at us.'

Courtney's eyes flicked to the distorted image of Charles Bromley's face staring through the bullseyed panes of glass.

'It wouldn't do for us to engage in fisticuffs, would it now, Walter?' Ainsley grinned. 'That nosey fellow might run and fetch a constable, might he not. And coming to any unwanted attention of the constabulary wouldn't benefit either of us, would it?'

'Is all well, Reverend Winward?' Charles Bromley was now standing in the shop doorway.

Walter Courtney forced a smile and turned to face the shopkeeper. 'All is very well, I thank you, Master Bromley. This gentleman and myself are old friends who have not had the good fortune to encounter one another for many years. It has come as a most welcome surprise for both of us.'

'It most certainly has, Master Bromley. Pray allow me to introduce myself. I am Archibald Ainsley, sole proprietor of the London Theatrical Company.' Ainsley smiled and bowed with a flourish. 'But alas! I fear that the Reverend Winward and myself must now take our leave of you, since we have many matters to discuss. So we must bid you Adieu for the present, Master Bromley.'

He took Courtney's arm. 'Come, my old friend. Time is pressing.'

'Indeed it is,' Courtney assented. 'Good day to you, Master Bromley.'

The pair got into the gig, and Courtney set the horse into motion.

Ainsley was chuckling to himself.

'What's so fuckin' amusing?' Courtney snarled.

'You were always brilliant at playing the God Botherer, Walter. What is it this time? Parson? Rector? Vicar? Deacon? Archdeacon? Canon? Or have you risen through the ranks to become a fuckin' Bishop, no less?'

Courtney only grunted sourly.

Ainsley's smile didn't falter. 'Now listen to me, my old friend. Just cast your mind back to when we worked together. Haven't I always been brilliant at ferreting out all the details of any "mark"? And didn't I always steer a safe course and make sure that we never hit any submerged reefs?'

He went on at great length, but underlying his apparent easy confidence and bonhomie was the note of desperation.

Courtney remained silent, his features dourly expressionless. But now that he had fully recovered from the shock of this totally unexpected reunion, he was beginning to realize that he could turn it to his great advantage.

'So what do you say, old friend? Have you got anything for me?' Ainsley finally ended.

Courtney stared hard into Ainsley's eyes for several seconds, then queried, 'What's your cover story here?'

Seized by a rush of hope, Ainsley almost babbled the words. 'It's ideal for your present purpose. I'm a prominent figure of the

London Stage who is currently looking for suitable venues for my touring troupe to play in. Which means I can go anywhere and ask a deal of questions, because I'm the potential bringer of good fortune, ain't I?'

Courtney again pondered silently for a considerable period, slowing the horse to a walk and circuiting the limits of the town's broad central plateau. He finally reined to a halt, and asked, 'Where are you lodging?'

'At the Unicorn, just down from the crossroads where the chapel is.'

'I know where it is. Now how well lined are your pockets?'

'Lined well enough for me to carry off my role to perfection, and to obtain all the information you'll be needing.'

'Give me those letters.'

Ainsley's tension was now palpable as he handed back the two single sheets of notepaper.

There was a long silent pause, then Courtney nodded. 'I'll give you a trial run, Archie.'

Ainsley gusted a sigh of relief. 'You'll not regret this, Walter. It'll be just like old times, you'll see! I'll not fail you, I swear on my life!'

Courtney's tone was now avuncular. 'I'm confident, Archie, that the next time we meet, you'll be able to tell me all that I need to know about this lady. Her name is Miss Phoebe Creswell, and she lives at Orchard House in the village of Beoley, which lies about four miles to the east of here.'

He returned one of the opened sheets to Ainsley, who blustered confidently, 'I'll ferret out everything you need to know about her, Walter, never fear. How long have I got?'

'I'll contact you in a few days. Should you satisfy me, then you shall have other letters to keep you busy.'

'I'd best waste no time in getting to work then,' Ainsley grinned.

They parted with a hearty shaking of hands, both now well satisfied with this course that events had taken.

Ainsley returned directly to the Unicorn and immediately sought out John Mence in his office.

'Well, Master Mence, I find that your establishment has many excellent amenities which truth to tell I did not expect to encounter other than in a city hotel.' He took a small, well-filled leather coin bag from his pocket and handed it to Mence. 'I intend therefore to make this my base while I am in these parts. Here is an advance payment for my board, lodging and stabling. When it is near spent please inform me immediately so that I may replenish it.'

This was most definitely a gesture that Mence had not expected from this particular guest, but his long experience in the trade enabled him to mask his shock.

'I'm most gratified to hear your words, Sir. Be assured that I shall do my utmost to ensure that my establishment continues to deserve such pleasing approbation.'

As Ainsley left the office, Mence shook his head in self-reproof. 'There now, Johnny boy, that's a lesson for you, aren't it? You can still be mistaken about somebody even after all your years in the trade.'

A few minutes later the stable hand came to tell him, 'That flash bugger's just come into the stable, Master, and told me to ready his nag for riding. What d'you want me to do about it?'

Mence grinned wryly. 'Ready his nag for him. For the time being he's a guest in good standing.'

EIGHT

Parish of Tardebigge
Tuesday, 15th January
Late evening

Hewell Grange, the family seat of the Earl of Plymouth, the Right Honourable Other Archer Windsor Clive, was two miles to the north-west of Redditch. Tom had hastened to get there, only to find on his arrival that the Factor was not present at the Grange, but had left strict instructions that Tom was to wait at the stable block until his return.

When over the course of several hours Tom attempted to question the butler and other assorted house servants, stable hands and gardeners about the missing dogs, he was answered with shrugs and denials of any knowledge about any dogs.

Now, hungry and frustrated, he was being forced to marshal all his remaining stores of patience to continue waiting beside his horse in the chill darkness of the stable-yard for the Factor's return. The clatter of hobnailed boots upon the cobbles was immediately followed by the shout, 'Tom, I've only just been told that you're here.'

It was Josiah Danks' voice and Tom went towards the oncoming figure.

'I'm waiting for Claude Blair, Josiah. I'm come about the missing dogs.'

'He's still out searching for the buggers,' Danks answered.

'Can you describe the dogs to me, because I've been told nothing about them or even how many are gone? In fact nobody would tell me anything.'

'That's because Blair's threatened that he'll give their sacks to anybody who speaks of this. He's shit scared of His Lordship finding out that the dogs got pinched.' The gamekeeper's rugged, weather-beaten features creased with contempt. 'Anyway, there's three beasts gone. All Bernese Mountain dogs. His Lordship bought 'um in Switzerland and sent 'um back here. Big buggers they are . . .'

Danks went on to describe their appearance in minute detail and Tom listened and stored the information to memory, and also the further details he was hearing.

'I've found what looks to be three separate sets of boot and paw marks going easterly around the lake, but once they'd reached the woods there was no more tracks to be followed. I'd brought along me best hound as well, but the rain put paid to any chance of him picking up a scent.'

Tom shook his head regretfully. 'The woods to the east also stretch for miles to the north and south, don't they?'

'Yes, and there's a good few bridle paths running through 'um. So if they'd got a packhorse hid away they could have slung the dogs across it and been gone double quick to wherever they was heading.

Josiah Danks also gave a regretful shake of his head. 'The thieving bastards are clean away, Son-in-law.' Then he grinned salaciously. 'And the hour is getting nigh to bedtime, so shouldn't you be getting back to your new missus and start making some grandkids for me and my missus to make a fuss of?'

With a guilty shock Tom realized that he had been so engrossed in this new investigation that he had not thought of Amy since leaving Redditch.

'You're right, Father-in-law. She'll be wondering where I've got to! Will you please tell Blair that I'm making all possible enquiries into this thievery?'

'I will. Now go on home and start making me a fine grandson!'

Tom rubbed his heavily bristled chin, and grinned ruefully. 'Before I can head home and begin that task, I've another urgent task to do, or Amy won't let me near her. Can you find me a razor, please? I must shave and wash properly.'

By the time Tom rode back into Redditch the town was still and quiet, the taverns closed and only here and there a window showing light. But despite his burning desire to be with Amy, Tom had to return the horse to Joseph Blackwell's stables and to bed the animal down for the night, which delayed him still further.

As he finally hurried back across the Green towards the lock-up he saw that though its upper-front windows were dark, there was a long vertical slit of light glimmering down one side of the front door. The door which at all times should be kept securely locked was slightly ajar.

'Are there intruders?'

Anxiety for Amy struck through him and he broke into a lolloping run. But when he reached the lock-up he abruptly slowed and halted. Hard and painfully gained past experience would dictate his actions from this point.

He crept up to the door and paused there, listening for any sound coming from within. All was silent. He cautiously pushed the door further open and saw his yard-long, crowned and painted Constable's staff of office propped against the inside wall within his reach. Despite its garish appearance it was a formidable weapon. Its crown and top shaft were filled with a weight of lead which, when directed with deadly intent, would crush the skulls and shatter bones.

He grabbed it, dragged in a deep breath, pushed the door wide and stepped inside ready to strike. But the dimly lit passage was empty and silent, the cell doors closed and bolted.

He closed and locked the front door behind him and moved as quietly as he could to the far end of the passage to find that the rear door was also locked and bolted. He craned his head into the recess of the foot of the stone steps and saw a glow of light from above.

Suddenly as he slowly mounted the narrow flight a succession of loud snores pierced the silence.

He expelled a gusty sigh of relief. 'She's sleeping. That's why everything's like it is.'

Then he thought disconcertedly. 'I never knew Amy snored so loud! In fact I never knew she snored at all! How could I? I've never seen her asleep, have I!'

The doors on the landing were closed and the light was being diffused from the open door of the garret bedroom above, from where the snores were also coming.

Tom looked into his sitting room and could see several bottles spread about the floorboards. He checked and found that they were empty.

Next, he went up into the lamplit garret and found his new wife and her friend, Maisie Lock, lying asleep on top of the bed. Clutched in Amy's fingers was another empty bottle, which he gently prised from her grip and sniffed at.

'Gin!'

For brief seconds annoyed resentment dominated Tom's mind. Then another series of loud snorting snores erupted from Maisie Lock and he couldn't help but think ruefully, 'Well, I suppose I should at least be relieved to find out that it's not Amy who's snorting like a pig!'

He returned to the sitting room below and settled himself as comfortably as he could in the wooden armchair, sadly resigned to spending this second night of marriage deprived of such eagerly anticipated newly-wedded connubial bliss.

NINE

Redditch Town
Wednesday, 16th January
Morning

Tom had spent a virtually sleepless night and he actually welcomed the jangling of the bells in the first grey light of approaching dawn as a distraction from his sombre thoughts.

He used flint, steel and tinder to light his candle lamp and went downstairs. The bells jangled again as he neared the front door and he shouted, 'This is Constable Potts. Who's there?'

'It's Rimmer and his lads come for the shit, Constable Potts!' a gruff shout answered.

'Alright.' Tom unlocked and unbarred the door and as he opened it wide ordered, 'Stand fast until I call for you.'

He went quickly along the passage to the rear door and carried out the same operation then stepped out into the rear yard shouting, 'Come through now!'

Three men clad in filthy smocks, faces half hidden by droopy-brimmed slouch hats, each carrying a broad bladed shovel, large jug and rope-handled wooden cask, shuffled down the passage and into the rear yard.

Even in the open air their combined foul stench was miasmic. It filled Tom's nostrils and, accustomed though he was to the normal unpleasant smells which were part and parcel of daily life, he could not help involuntarily stepping further back from them as they passed and went to the hutted triple-holed privy in the corner of the yard, where they quickly jugged and shoveled its odorous contents into the casks and loaded them on to the horse-drawn cart outside the front door.

As Tom handed over the four pennies collection fee, Rimmer grumbled sourly, 'Not very good pickings for me today, Constable Potts. It's plain that you aren't had no buggers in the pokey this last week. This shit I got from you won't feed more than a single fuckin' cabbage.'

Tom couldn't help but chuckle in reply. 'I can only offer you my sincere apologies for that, Master Rimmer. I'll certainly do my utmost to fill the cells this coming week.'

As he stood outside the door watching the trio moving away, he mentally compared his own lot in life with theirs and reached a grimly ironic conclusion: 'We lead a similar existence in one sense. They earn their living scavenging and disposing of evil smelling faeces and assorted rubbish, and I earn my living in major part by dealing with the after effects of the evil that some rubbishy, faecal-type humans do to others.'

Once they were out of earshot of the lock-up, Ezekiel Rimmer sneered contemptuously, 'That fuckin' beanpole don't know his arse from his elbow, does he. Not like that crafty bastard Cashmore.

He used to have the bloody cells filled to busting, didn't he, and filled his pockets through it.'

'Don't remind me of bloody Joe Cashmore!' Porky Hicks spat out angrily. 'I lost count o' the times he banged me inside, and I had to pay him not to lay charges against me. Same for you, warn't it, Dummy?'

The third of the trio, a dumb mute, bared his teeth in a snarl and nodded emphatic agreement.

'Where shall we go next, Ezekiel?' Hicks asked.

'You two go and clear the Horse and Jockey, and then deliver all the load straight to Bordesley Farm. I'll go back home and do them dogs. The sooner I gets 'um skinned and scraped the sooner we can have a decent piss-up for a change.'

The isolated cluster of buildings on the eastern edge of the town centre comprised a large cobbled yard containing a towering, stinking rubbish heap enclosed by festering hovels. Polite members of local society called it by its traditional name of 'The Old Laystall', the archaic name for a dung heap. The impolite members of society called it 'Shit Court'. But both the polite and impolite of the town were united in their low opinion of its inhabitants. Even the roughest, scruffiest slum dwellers in the rest of the parish regarded those unfortunates who lived in Shit Court as being far beneath them in social standing.

Ezekiel Rimmer had been born and bred in the Old Laystall, and had risen to become its undisputed ruler. Now as he entered his domain, his subjects hastened to greet him. He graciously returned the salutations of those who were currently high in his favour. Those who were not he scowled at, or ignored completely.

Rimmer's present dwelling place reflected his status here. Standing twice the height of the adjoining hovels, it was stone-built and was once the lay brothers' living quarters of a grange farm belonging to the nearby Cistercian Abbey of Bordesley. The un-partitioned ground floor was strewn with assorted rubbish, noisy with the voices of the women and children busily pawing through that rubbish, and the mewling cries of rag-swaddled infants. The air was fetid with assorted odours and thick with smoke from the smouldering fire in the huge inglenook set into one wall.

'What brings you back, Master Rimmer?' his corpulent, raggedly dressed, toothless wife questioned.

'Just shurrup and get on wi' your work! Or I'll be giving you a dose o' this.' He growled and lifted his fist, and she cowered back, shielding her face with handfuls of rags. Rimmer hawked up a gob of phlegm and spat it on to her bowed head, then went out of the back door to unlock the padlocked bar on the door of the big windowless wooden shanty at the rear of the house.

As the shanty door opened the mingled reeks of nauseous excretions and rotting flesh swirled out from the dark interior.

Rimmer stepped inside and closed the door behind him. Reaching above his head he pulled a lever which opened a shutter in the roof. Daylight spilled through to disclose the row of cages along one wall, and several wooden frames of varying sizes, some with animal pelts stretched flesh side up across them.

The light also bathed the thick roof beam from which four large dead dogs hung by nooses around their necks. Rimmer closely examined each in turn, carefully checking the elasticity of their hides. Then he made his selection, lifted a sharp knife from a stretching frame, lowered the chosen beast to a convenient height and began to expertly skin it.

The subject of dogs was paramount in Tom's mind as he completed his morning ablutions at the pump in the rear yard, and dried his head and upper body on rough towelling. Then he brushed his teeth with fine-powdered wood ash, swilled out his mouth and chewed a fresh sprig of parsley to freshen his breath.

'The Newfoundland breed is becoming fashionable, and no doubt a good young bitch might find a ready sale. But Bernese Mountain dogs? They're a different matter altogether, and I doubt there's a ready market for them. This is the first time I've heard of them even being in this country.'

His train of thought was broken by Amy rushing into the yard, and he hastily spat out the parsley and dried his lips.

'Tom! Oh, Tom, I'm so sorry about last night! I'm so sorry and ashamed! Say that you forgive me! Say that you do!'

She pulled his head down and kissed him passionately before relating her tale.

'Gertie Fowkes went home and then came back with the bottles, and I only intended to have a single glass of wine, but they all pressed more on me and kept on calling more toasts to our marriage, and said I must drink the toasts and be making merry because I'd finally moved into my new home with my new husband, and it was only fitting to celebrate.'

Again she pulled down his head and kissed his lips, then went breathlessly on, 'I didn't like to be so churlish as not drink the toasts to our marriage and our new life together. But I must have been so carried away with all the excitement of finally being here together with you, that the drink went to my head, and the next thing I knew I was waking up in our bed.'

Her voice became a sob of distress. 'But it was Maisie who was beside me, and not you! When I realized what I'd done, I wanted to die of shame! I swear it will never happen again! I swear it on all that I hold holy!'

Witnessing her distress the sole emotion pulsating through Tom was the desperate need to comfort her. He clasped her close, cradling her in his arms, softly crooning to her over and over again.

'You've done nothing wrong, my darling! Nothing at all! There is nothing to blame! I'm not in the very least annoyed at you having a little party and drinking a few toasts with your friends. I'm only sorry that I wasn't here to enjoy those toasts with you. It's me who should be begging your forgiveness for going out and leaving you for all those long hours as I did. You've done nothing wrong! Nothing at all!'

Snuggled against him, Amy's eyes danced with mischievous delight, and in her mind she silently told him, 'I'm going to be very happy with you, my darling Tom. Because I know that I'll always be able to have you eating out of my hand. It's one of the reasons I love you so much.'

TEN

Warwick City
Wednesday, 16th January
Mid-morning

For the previous hour Walter Courtney had been sitting in his hooded, two-wheeled gig some distance from the forbidding walls of Warwick Gaol, watching people entering and leaving through the small wicket gate set into the great main gates.

The closed wicket opened again and a woman wearing the black veil, bonnet and clothing of full mourning emerged into view. Courtney grunted with satisfaction and waited until she had walked further away from him before he drove his gig to the gates, dismounted and rapped on the wicket.

A small shutter opened and a face appeared at the barred grill, a gruff voice demanding, 'What's your business here?'

Courtney held a gold sovereign up to the grill. 'Tell me what you know about the woman who just left here, and this is yours.'

Iron bolts squealed, the wicket door opened slightly and a grimy, black-nailed hand appeared through the gap.

Courtney clenched the coin tightly and laid his closed fist upon the upward palm.

'Let's be hearing what you know.'

'Her calls herself Mrs Peelson and her's been visiting her man, Terry Peelson. He's to be topped this coming Saturday for "bit faking". Her said her hadn't set eyes on him for the last ten years and never knew where he was or what he'd been a-doing until her read in a newspaper that he'd been sentenced. So her come here to see him, and make sure it was really him. Been here six days on the trot, so her has.'

'Terence Peelson, you say. I read of his case. From all accounts he must have done very well for himself from the bit faking.' Courtney probed casually.

'Some of the lags in here reckons so. They reckons he's got a pile o' rhino hid away. You can bet that's why his missus has come looking for him. She's bound to be hoping he'll tell her where he's hid it. But her can't have been having much luck if her's had to keep coming back here these last six days.'

Fingers pressed on Courtney's fist. 'That's all I knows, so let's be having it.'

Courtney released the coin on to the palm and walked quickly away.

The grimy hand disappeared, the grill shutter snapped down, the wicket slammed shut, iron bolts squealed.

Courtney remounted his gig and set the horse to a brisk trot, humming contentedly to himself.

The black-clad woman was still in view as she walked up the

long sloping road into the town. When Courtney neared her he slowed the horse and kept his distance until he saw her enter the same house in the tall-storied, opulent-looking terrace that he had watched her leaving from earlier that morning.

Beaming with satisfaction he congratulated himself. 'This really does look most promising.'

An hour later he was in a small tavern on the other side of the town waiting to meet with Sylvan Kent.

When Kent eventually arrived he was displaying the bloodshot eyes, hoarse voice and foul breath that denoted the after-effects of a bout of heavy debauchery.

'What news do you have for me, Walter?'

'Surprising news, Cousin.' Courtney beamed jovially. 'Our widow, Mrs Adelaide Farson, who claims to be in deep mourning for her recently departed Mamma, is apparently wedded to a coinage counterfeiter, Terence Peelson by name, who is to be hung this coming Saturday at Warwick Gaol.'

'Bloody hell!' Kent ejaculated in surprise. 'This has been a wasted journey then.'

'Not at all.' Courtney chuckled, waving his hand in dismissal of that claim. 'I've a notion that this will be a quick and easy bit of business for a change. Now I want you to get yourself fit and ready to do what you do best, my boy.'

Kent held his hand out. 'I'm in sore need of some readies, Walter. When I woke up yesterday morning the little bitch I was with had done a runner with what pennies I'd got left, and my watch and chain as well, not to mention my new cravat pin.'

Courtney frowned angrily. 'By God, Cousin! I pray for the day to dawn when you'll keep a sober head, not be so spendthrift of our money, and make wiser choice of the whores you sleep with.'

He gave the other man some coins, and ordered him brusquely, 'Now stay away from the whores, and start practising sobriety. Your drinking's getting out of control.'

As Courtney was leaving through the door, Kent mouthed silent defiance to his back.

ELEVEN

Thursday, 17th January
Morning

In the darkness before dawn Amy Potts awoke in the bed beside her slumbering husband and explored her emotions.

'Well that's it! That's my cherry gone! I liked it well enough at the start when we were kissing and feeling each other, but when he pushed into me, it bloody well hurt! Good job that part of it was over quick!

'I know Maisie says that after I've done it a few times it won't hurt any more, and that it'll feel so good that I'll be shouting for him not to stop. Well it don't feel like that to me at this minute! But I'll just have to grit my teeth and bear it, won't I! That's what a wife has to do.'

She tentatively felt between her legs and her fingers encountered the stickiness there and on the sheet beneath.

'Bugger it! I've bled! I'll need to get the bedding washed straight away.'

She threw back the coverlets, slipped from the bed and fumbled on the floor for her clothes, muttering irritably as the cold air goose-pimpled her soft skin.

Her movements had roused Tom to drowsy wakefulness and he turned over, reaching for her. The empty space beside shocked him fully awake and he sat up, calling, 'Amy? What are you doing? Amy?'

'I'm trying to find my clothes,' she snapped curtly.

'But it's still only dead of night. Why are you rising at this hour? Come back to bed.'

'Just light the candle, will you?' she demanded impatiently.

'Are you unwell, my love?' he questioned anxiously.

'Will you stop asking me stupid questions, and just light the bloody candle!' Her temper flared.

It was his turn to throw aside the coverlets and with goose-pimpled skin to fumble upon the small bedside bench for the tinder box, flint and steel.

In short moments the candle flame cast its glow enabling Amy to sort out her clothes and get dressed.

Guilt struck through her as she saw Tom's anxious stare.

'Oh, don't pay me any mind, Tom. I'm always a snappy bitch when I first wake up.'

She knelt on the bed and kissed him, then ordered, 'But you must get up as well, because I need to wash the bedding. There's blood on it from last night. Go down to the wash-house and fire up the copper.'

He moved to take her in his arms, but she pushed him away. 'I'm in no mood for that now. You must wait until tonight.'

He accepted this rebuttal without protest, but couldn't help asking anxiously, 'Are you happy, Amy? Are you content that I'm your husband?'

'Of course I am, you great lummox. But if you don't get up this instant and see to that copper I'll not be!'

When dawn came the soiled bedding was in the bubbling water of the wash-house copper, and the couple were eating their breakfast of salted oat porridge and fried onions in the lamplit warmth of the ground-floor cooking range alcove.

'There's been no sounds from your Mam. She must be still asleep,' Amy said, then giggled. 'It wouldn't surprise me because the noises I was making when you were breaking me in would have woken the dead! I'll bet the old cow will be moaning and blarting about it when she does wake up.'

'Amy! You shouldn't say such things.' Tom was shocked at her earthiness.

'Why not?' she challenged.

'Well . . . Well it's . . . it's not . . . it's not . . .' Tom desperately sought for words. 'Well, what happens between man and wife in their bed, shouldn't be made a joke of. It's a very private and sacred thing between themselves.'

'Phooo!' She blew a dismissive raspberry. 'There's naught sacred about what a man and wife get up to in their bed! It's what God put us on this earth to do! To make babbies! Are you trying to tell me that when you were a kid you didn't never hear nor see what your mam and dad were doing in their bed?'

'No, I didn't ever see or hear them doing such things!' Tom stated firmly. 'How could I? I was in my bedroom and they were in their bedroom, and I was never allowed to go into their bedroom unless they specifically told me that I could.'

Amy's mood abruptly changed, and all trace of levity disappeared from her manner.

'That's the big difference between you and me, isn't it, Tom?' she stated very quietly. 'You were brought up as a gentleman, by parents with money and nice houses with rooms to spare. And you had years of schooling, and being taught your fine way of speaking and your gentlemanly manners.

'But people like me have to work from the day we have strength to do anything at all to earn a wage. My mam and dad have always had to struggle to survive. They've never had any money to spare for their kids' schooling. They've never owned nice houses with lots of rooms. Until my dad got the job as Head Gamekeeper we always lived in hovels. So us kids always had to share beds with each other, and with our mam and dad as well when we were tiny. So of course there were times when they thought we were all sound asleep that we heard and saw what men and women do with each other in their beds.'

She paused, head bent as if searching for words, and then with a catch in her voice told him, 'If me talking about it as I do upsets you, then I'm sorry for being so rude-spoken, and I'll guard my tongue in the future.'

While she had been speaking Tom's feelings of guilt and shame had burgeoned unbearably, and now he shook his head and blurted vehemently, 'No, Amy! No! It's me who needs to guard my tongue, not you! I'm truly sorry for what I said, and for behaving like a pompous, arrogant moron! And if I should ever again take you to task for your manner of speech, then kick me as hard as you can. All I can beg for now is your forgiveness!'

The loud clanging of the bells intervened, and Tom instinctively reacted to their summons, turning his face to the sound and starting to rise from his chair. Then he stiffened in an awkward half-risen posture, and flustered.

'I'm so sorry, Amy, the bells took me by surprise!'

Magnanimous in victory, Amy smiled. 'Go and answer them before they deafen me. And yes, I do forgive you.'

Tom grinned with heartfelt relief, stretched across the small table-top and kissed her, then hurried to the front door.

'Good morning, am I addressing the Constable?' The caller was a short, stocky man dressed in military-style riding clothes, with a peaked cap on his head.

'Yes, I'm Constable Thomas Potts.'

'Honoured to meet you, Constable Potts.' The caller snapped off a smart salute. 'My name is Elias Bradshaw, late Troop Sergeant in His Majesty's Sixteenth Light Dragoons; but now the Captain of Bradshaw's Mountebanks.' He indicated the group of mounted men and women and the trio of long-based covered wagons on the Green behind him. 'They're the finest trick-riders in the Kingdom, Constable. Every man and woman of them trained in the equestrian arts, by me personally.'

'Are you intending to give displays around the Needle District, Master Bradshaw?' Tom asked.

'That's my intention, Constable, should weather permit, but for now I need to water and rest my horses; and I was wondering if you could direct me to a suitable camping ground. It needs to be flattish, with access to fresh water, and I'm ready to pay a fair rent for the use of it.'

Tom thought briefly, then stepped out of the lock-up and beckoned for the other man to come with him around the corner of the building.

'Follow this road eastwards, Master Bradshaw. But take care not to let your horses drink from the Big Pool a hundred yards down there where the road bends north-east, because it's a foul cesspit.

'Continue on until you reach an inn called the King's Arms where the road forks and runs downhill. Take the right-hand fork, which is called the Hollow Way, and continue to the bottom of the hill. At the bottom you'll see on your right some wide flat meadow land stretching up to a farm called the Millsboro Lodge Farm. James Houghton is the farmer and there's plenty of good clean water on his land. Tell Master Houghton that I've sent you, and I'm confident he'll be prepared to accommodate you.'

'Many thanks, Constable Potts.' Bradshaw pointed down the road and shouted, 'There's our route, Corporal Taylor. Lead on.'

Led by the mounted party the wagons lurched into a line of march, and as they did so there sounded a loud deep-baying chorus.

'What's that noise?' Tom queried curiously.

Bradshaw grinned. 'You'll see what's making it if you look there behind the rear wagon.'

As the last wagon neared him Tom saw a pack of both large and small dogs secured by long leashes to its tailboard, and was stuck by the unusual and varied colours of the large dogs' coats.

'Those are my Otterhounds belling out. Those big buggers.' Bradshaw announced proudly. 'The finest scent-hounds for water in this world. They can smell and track an otter in water it's passed through hours before, and they swim like bloody fishes, so they do. My hounds track the otters and keep them bottled up, and then my little terriers go down into the holts and kill the buggers off.'

Bradshaw mounted his horse. 'Many thanks again for your help, Constable Potts. I hope you'll come and see my Mountebanks perform some day, and have a drink with us as our guest.'

He saluted and rode away. Tom sighed wistfully. 'I wish I could sit on a horse like that man does; he could pass for a centaur.'

The deep baying of the hounds grew fainter and Tom shrugged ruefully. 'Now I've got another day on horseback to look forward to, which most probably will only gain me a red-raw backside and no trace of any stolen dogs again.'

In the rear yard of the King's Arms, Ezekiel Rimmer and his helpers were shoveling the contents of the privy into their casks when the breeze-carried sound of baying hounds reached them.

'Is that a fuckin' fox hunt?' Porky Hicks straightened from his odorous labour to listen hard.

'Could be, but it don't exactly sound like foxhounds.' Ezekiel Rimmer also stopped work to listen.

The noise ceased, and the two resumed work, only to stop and straighten up again when the baying resumed some seconds later.

'They'm coming this way by the sound of it.' Rimmer left the privy and went out of the yard gate, followed immediately by Porky Hicks and Dummy.

The trio stared up the road at the approaching convoy of horses and wagons.

'What's this lot then?' Porky Hicks asked. 'Is it a circus, d'you reckon?'

'Could be,' Rimmer grunted.

Elias Bradshaw was riding several yards in advance of the troupe and when he came abreast of these spectators he reined in and sought confirmation.

'Is this the road called the Hollow Way?'

'That's its name, Master.' Rimmer nodded.

'And Millsboro Lodge Farm, where's that exactly?'

'When you gets on to the flat at the bottom of the hill, Master, you'll see it way off to your right where the land rises again.'

'Thanks.' Bradshaw dropped a few pence at Rimmer's feet. 'Have a drink on me, and spread the word that Captain Bradshaw's Mountebanks, who've performed their displays of dare-devil horsemanship before all the Crowned Heads and Aristocracy of Europe, are come to Redditch, and will be performing all over the Needle District during the next few weeks, should weather permit.'

Rimmer snatched up the coins and doffed his hat. 'I'll do that, Master. I'll spread the word all across the town, so I will.'

The trio stood and watched the convoy pass, and Rimmer drew a sharp hiss of excitement when he saw the dogs following behind the rearmost wagon.

'Take a close gander at that lot. Them big 'uns am Otterhounds. See their colours. I'll guarantee all the flash lads 'ull go fuckin' mad for them colours and we'll get top prices.'

He took his friends and pulled them with him back into the yard. Then he told Dummy, 'Cut through Millsboro Wood, Dummy, and watch where they makes camp, and take close heed o' where them dogs are stowed. Don't let any fucker get a sight of you, or I'll cut your fuckin' bollocks off!'

TWELVE

Warwick City
Saturday, 19th January
Afternoon

Ella Peelson, still wearing her nightdress and bed cap, was sat at the dressing table sipping a glass of gin and water when the knock sounded on the bedroom door. She frowned irritably.

'What is it?'

'If you please, Ma'm, there's a man at the door who's wanting to see you.' Milly Styke's voice was muffled by the baize-covered door panels. 'He asked me if Mrs Adelaide Farson was at home, and when I told him yes, he give me this card to bring to you. He says it's very important and private business he's come on.'

'What does he look like? How's he dressed? Is he rough spoken?' Ella Peelson hurled questions.

The girl answered excitedly. 'He's big and fat, wi' a big fat red face; and he's a parson wi' a tie-wig on his head, and a black coat and black breeches, Ma'am! And he speaks like the gentry!'

Ella Peelson frowned thoughtfully. 'Bring me the card.'

The child hastened to obey.

The calling card bore only one line of print: *The Reverend Geraint Winward DD*.

But beneath this written in ink was the brief statement: *I am here on behalf of XYZ*.

Ella Peelson fingered the card, noting that it was made of the finest vellum, and expensively embossed with intricate gold filigree.

'There could be rhino here. I might have struck lucky.' She smiled with satisfaction.

'Show the gentleman into the drawing room, my dear, and tell him that I'll join him shortly.'

As Walter Courtney followed the diminutive, neatly clad maidservant through the entrance hall and into the drawing room, his shrewd gaze evaluated the expensive furniture, draperies, wall-hung paintings and numerous and varied ornaments.

The maidservant bobbed a curtsey. 'Me mistress said to tell you that she 'ull join you shortly, Sir.'

'Hold there a moment. What's your name, child?' Courtney's manner was avuncular.

'Styke, Sir. Milly Styke.'

He produced a silver sixpence which he held out towards her. 'Well this is your reward, Milly, for receiving me so graciously.'

'What does that mean, Sir?' The girl's features showed interest. 'That last big word you said?'

Courtney chuckled. 'It means that your mistress is very lucky to have such a good and clever girl serving her. How long have you been with her?'

'Nigh on two years, Sir. She took me out from the Feckenham Parish Poorhouse in Worcestershire, Sir. She chose me because

I've had some schooling, and me Mam and Dad brought me up proper afore they died.'

'And a very good choice she made, my dear, because I can see that you're a very well-brought-up girl,' Courtney congratulated, and quickly asked more questions until, satisfied that he would learn nothing more, gave her the sixpence, and whispered with a broad wink, 'This must be our little secret, Milly, or your mistress will surely take this sixpence from you. So we won't tell her that we talked together, will we, my dear? It shall be our own little secret.'

'Yes, Sir.' The girl bobbed a curtsey and left him alone.

He sat down on an elaborately brocaded, tall-backed chair, placed his top hat on the floor beside him, and listened hard. The instant his sharp ears heard the rustle of movement outside the closed door he bowed his head, closed his eyes, clasped his hands before his face in an attitude of prayer and began murmuring the words of a psalm.

He sensed the almost noiseless opening of the door, but remained motionless until he heard a soft warning cough.

He opened his eyes, lifted his head and, gasping in feigned dismay, jumped to his feet and bowed low.

'I beg you to accept my humblest apologies, Ma'am. I was seeking the guidance of our Lord, and as always at such times I fear that I lost all awareness of this material world about me. I beseech you to forgive my ill manners!'

'There is nothing to forgive, Reverend Winward; I beg you not to distress yourself. I also lose all awareness of this world when I am communing with our Lord. Please, resume your seat.'

The woman's voice was husky and low pitched, and Courtney could detect an underlying Irish accent. He took this first close-up opportunity to make a rapid inventory of her appearance. She looked to be in her mid-thirties, with dark eyes and hair, and a handsome, fresh-complexioned face. She was of medium height, wearing a fashionably styled, black silk mourning gown which accentuated her full breasts.

She seated herself opposite to him on a similar type of chair and stared expectantly at him.

'I trust, Ma'am, that I am addressing the same Mrs Adelaide Farson who has recently replied to an advertisement placed by

XYZ in the *Birmingham Aris Gazette*?' Courtney smilingly sought confirmation.

'Indeed you are, Sir.' She smiled back, and he noted that she had good teeth.

'Then let me begin, Ma'am. I am come here on behalf of my friend, Major Christophe de Langlois, of the Madras Native Infantry, Honourable East India Company Army.'

From an inner pocket he produced the finely executed miniature portrait of Sylvan Kent and handed it to her.

'This was painted recently, Ma'am, and I can verify that it is a true likeness. He stands near two yards in height, and has the physique of a warrior . . .'

He continued at length, verbally creating an image of a gallant soldier of Huguenot descent, who had amassed wealth and property in India. Who was a bachelor, but now desired above all else to find a suitable wife to share his life in India and enjoy the benefits of his good fortune.

Ella Peelson, wife of the convicted 'coiner' Terence Peelson, sat silently gazing at the miniature, while committing her guest's words to memory. A product of the rancid slums of Dublin, she had survived the sexual abuse and maltreatment of her childhood by utilizing her sharp wits and acute intelligence to escape from there. These same attributes had served her well throughout her life in the underworld of criminality, enabling her to enjoy the considerable profits of crime and evade the gallows which had claimed the lives of so many of her varied confederates.

'. . . and so that brings my account of Major Christophe de Langlois to its end.' Courtney smiled. 'With the utmost respect, Ma'am, may I make so bold as to request to hear some account of your own antecedents and passage through life that I may carry back to him? Who naturally is most eager to learn more about you.'

Ella Peelson returned the miniature, smiled and requested: 'Before I relate such antecedents and personal experiences, Sir, may I be permitted to spend some time in reflecting upon what you have told me about this gentleman? I'm sure that you will appreciate my delicacy of feelings concerning this matter. I am a widowed lady with limited experience of the wider world. Having spent my life in somewhat cloistered surroundings, I need to consider very carefully my decision on this matter.'

'But of course, Ma'am! Your wish is my command!' Courtney immediately rose and bowed. 'I'll take my leave now, Ma'am. Will you permit me to call upon you again at this same hour on Monday next to receive your decision?' He smiled warmly. 'I pray that you will forgive my boldness. But now that I have met you, I must confess that in my opinion my friend will have true cause for regret if you should decide against furthering your acquaintance with him.'

'Oh, Sir!' She reacted with girlish flutters of her hands to shield her blushing cheeks and with head bowed murmured shyly, 'I shall expect you at this hour on that day. Good morning to you, Sir. My maid will show you out.'

As soon as she heard the outer door closing upon her departing visitor, Ella Peelson shouted, 'Milly, bring me a bottle of gin, a jug of water and a glass.'

Within seconds the child had brought the articles and placed them on the table at her mistress's side.

'The man who just left, did he ask you any questions?' Ella queried.

'Oh yes, Ma'am.' The girl related all that had passed between herself and the visitor. 'And he give me this sixpence to keep it all secret from you, Ma'am.'

Her mistress chuckled and stroked the girl's cheek. 'What a treasure you are to me, Milly. You shall have whatever treat you want tomorrow, and two more sixpences to spend with that one. But leave me now, my dear.' She jerked her head in dismissal, mixed gin and water into the glass and, deep in reverie, began to sip the drink.

'Madame Adelaide de Langlois. I like the sound of that, and if he looks half as well in the flesh as he does in his picture, and is half as rich as the parson tells me he is, then he'll make a real good catch. If I play my cards right, I could be living like a queen in India for the rest of my days. There'll be no danger of my fuckin' husband's brothers ever pestering me there.'

The mental vision of Terence Peelson's haggard death-cell features suddenly intruded, and she gloated.

'He'll have been buried by now, and with a bit of luck I'll be an Officer's Lady well before he's rotted to nothing under the jail yard.'

Driving his gig away from the house Courtney chuckled appreciatively. 'You're a fly bitch and no mistake, Ella Peelson, but now you've come up against an even flier old dog. I'm going to enjoy furthering our acquaintance.'

THIRTEEN

Warwick
Friday, 25th January
Afternoon

Ella Peelson had spent long hours on her toilette and now, as she examined her reflection in the bedroom's full-length mirror, was not unhappy with the result.

'You're still good-looking enough, girl, and I doubt he'll be even half as handsome as his picture.'

She turned her thoughts to her present situation and the course events had taken.

On the day before his execution Terry Peelson had finally relented and told her where his cache of coinage and die stamps were hidden, and she had lost no time in retrieving them. Even though the majority of the coins were counterfeit, there was still a very large sum of genuine coinage, and the die stamps were worth a great deal of money to any Coiner.

The meeting with the Reverend Winward on the day of her husband's execution had gone better than she could have hoped; and had been followed by meetings on the following Monday, Tuesday and Wednesday. He had told her it was a matter of urgency that Langlois should return to his regiment in India, and therefore should they find that they were a suitable match, his friend wanted to be married immediately by Special License.

As for her own land and property, the Reverend himself would be remaining in England, and if she so wished would undertake the care and administration of it, as he did for that of Langlois.

'Therefore, Ma'am, if you would be so kind as to now furnish me with the particulars of your property it will save much time should the marriage take place and the necessarily hasty departure for India.'

Ella Peelson had been happy to comply with that request.

Now, after a final examination of her mirrored refection, she went down to the drawing room and spent some minutes in altering the positioning of the lighted candelabras in order to illuminate the chair in which she intended her visitor to sit, so that she might clearly read his facial expressions.

That task completed she seated herself and awaited the arrival of her visitor, exerting all her self-discipline not to surrender to her pressing need for a strong mix of gin and water.

The clock struck the hour and she readied herself for the imminent arrival of Major Christophe de Langlois.

Sitting in the stationary gig around the corner from the terrace of opulent houses, Walter Courtney was briefing Sylvan Kent.

'I found out from the house agents that she's renting this place here by the month, and it's costing her plenty, so she's definitely got money to spare. Her cover story is that she wed very young. Her husband was a lot older than she, and he died very soon after they wed. She and her mother had always lived together and she's temporarily renting the house here because to remain at her family home at this time is too painful for her after her mother's death last year.'

'And where does she say this family nest is?'

'A hamlet called Bradley Green. It's close to Feckenham Village where I have my lodgings. But it'll take me a little time to check out her story, because I'll need to tread very carefully. These country yokels are always suspicious of any stranger making enquiries. But if she does own the property there, and she really is on her own now, then it could be very good business for us, and quickly completed.'

Kent chuckled. 'And if she's as toothsome as you say she is, then I'll enjoy the work for a change.'

'Just don't mess up,' Courtney warned. 'And keep off the drink, because you'll need to keep a clear head to handle this one. She's a fly bitch, not a gormless old maid.'

Kent stepped down on to the road, unhitched the saddled horse from the rear of the vehicle and mounted it as his companion drove away.

He trotted around the corner and along the terraced street and reined in before the house he sought. Dismounting, he tied the horse's reins to one of the bollards that fronted the pavement and rapped the highly polished lion's head door knocker. From the corner of his eye he glimpsed the slight movement of the lace curtain in the bow window.

When the diminutive maidservant opened the door he smiled down at her. 'I take it that you are Milly.'

Her eyes widened in shock and she bobbed a curtsey and blurted, 'That's me name right enough, Sir.'

'Well, Milly, will you be so kind as to tell your mistress that Major Christophe de Langlois has come to see her.'

'Major Cristo—' She screwed her face with the effort of trying to repeat his name.

Still smiling, he enunciated slowly, 'Major Christophe de Langlois.'

'Major . . .' A pause. 'Christophe . . .' A pause. 'De . . .' Another pause. 'Lang . . . Lang . . . Langos, Sir?'

He chuckled jovially. 'I trust that will do well enough, Milly.'

Before she could reply Ella Peelson came to the door herself and gently directed her maid. 'You may go to the kitchen, Milly; I'll receive this gentleman myself.'

Kent swept his top hat from his head and bowed. 'Have I the honour of meeting Mrs Adelaide Farson?'

She curtseyed. 'You have, Sir, and I trust that I have the honour of meeting Major Christophe de Langlois.'

They smiled at each other.

Sylvan Kent was telling himself, 'This bodes well! If all goes to plan, I'm going to thoroughly enjoy fucking this one.'

Ella Peelson, taking in his handsome face, fine teeth, well-groomed thick dark hair, powerful physique, elegant clothing, scented emanation of expensive pomade, was telling herself exactly the same.

FOURTEEN

Redditch Town
Saturday, 26th January
Morning

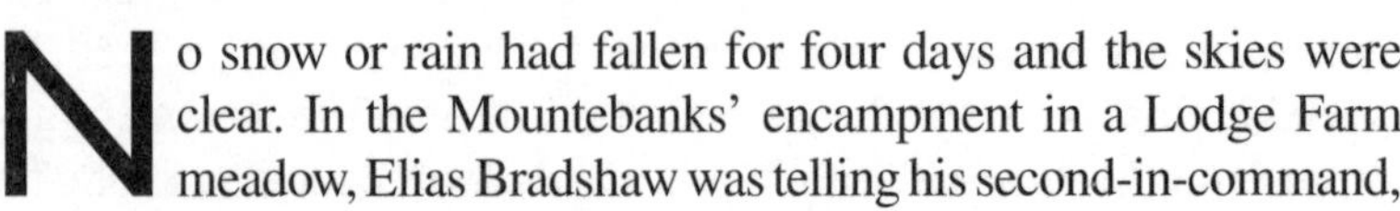

No snow or rain had fallen for four days and the skies were clear. In the Mountebanks' encampment in a Lodge Farm meadow, Elias Bradshaw was telling his second-in-command,

Corporal Taylor, 'It's market day, and the ground's firm enough now for us to drum up some trade. I'm going to see the Constable and find out if we can make use of the Green.'

In the slum-filled cul-de-sac known as Red Cow Yard, Ezekiel Rimmer was in discussion with a swarthy-featured itinerant pedlar.

'You'm trying to make a cunt out o' me, Yakob Weiss. Half a dozen prime cat furs, and a dozen rabbit, all fresh and washed with never a scrap o' meat on 'um and you'm offering me a measly two shillings. I knows full well that I could get double that if I took 'um up to Brummagem.'

'You take 'um up there then, and just see what price you'll get,' the pedlar challenged. 'Because the most I'll give you is three shillings, and that's me final offer.'

'Oh, alright then, you bloody Shylock,' Rimmer accepted. 'I'll have 'um ready for you in the Cow's back room when you're done with the mart. But you giving me such a rotten price means that I'll be taking me prime goods up to Brummagem to sell.'

The pedlar stared questioningly at the other man. 'Come on, Rimmer! Spit it out! What other stuff have you got?'

'The best you can get,' Rimmer announced triumphantly. 'The sort o' fur that's fuckin' wind and weatherproof. The rain just jumps off it, so the skin don't need oiling, tarring or lining. The sort o' pelts that any other cap-maker'd bite me hands off to get hold of 'um. That's guaranteed, that is!'

The pedlar frowned and tugged on his long straggly beard. 'What pelts are they?'

'Massive big dog pelts. A Newfoundland and three Bernese Mountain dogs.'

'Where did you get hold o' them? Because I know for a fact that Bernese Mountain dogs are bound to be few and far between in these parts.'

'That's very true, my friend,' Rimmer agreed equably. 'You don't come across many o' the buggers round these parts. But that's the very reason that any cap-maker 'ull be mad keen to get hold o' them, because all the flash lads 'ull be mad keen to be flashing off such a kicksy-upsy titfer and be ready to pay through their noses to get one.'

'Well, just supposing I did take a look at them, and just supposing I might be persuaded to take them off your hands, what sort of price are we looking at? Because I'm thinking that these Berneses weren't dumped on a rubbish tip and left to die there by a cruel master.' The pedlar winked meaningfully. 'Not that I mind how they come to stray and get lost.'

Rimmer grinned and winked back. 'I'll have them with me tonight, Yakob. I'm double sure we'll agree a fair price after you've seen them.'

Sitting in the cooking alcove of the lock-up, toying with his breakfast of onion porridge, Tom Potts was also thinking about a price. But in his case it was the mental price he was paying for having his wife and his mother living under the same roof. The mutually reluctant truce between the two women had endured for only a few days, and for the past week Tom had been the hapless recipient of blame from both of them for this unhappy domestic arrangement.

What was lowering his present depressed spirits still further was his failure to find any trace whatsoever of the missing dogs, despite searching almost the entire length and breadth of the Needle District for news of them.

'I'll have to tell Blackwell that I think my time could be better spent here at the mart today,' he decided. 'There's been no dealer's licenses checked yet this month, and there was a robbery and at least three bad fights last week because nobody was here to keep order with Ritchie and me away looking for those bloody dogs.'

He pushed the plate of half-eaten porridge away and rose to his feet, just as Amy came down to the ground floor complaining pettishly, 'Your Mam's snoring is driving me mad! Kept me awake half the night it did! That's why I've overslept again this morning! I can't get a decent night's rest with the rattle she makes. It's enough to raise the dead!'

Tom drew a long breath, and invited wearily, 'Why don't you sit down, my love, and I'll make you a pot of tea before I go to work.'

In the drawing room of her home, Phoebe Creswell was experiencing greatly mixed emotions as she listened to Doctor Hugh Laylor, while Pammy Mallot stood protectively by her chair.

'I deeply regret, Miss Creswell, that in the type of apoplectic seizure such has stricken your father, I am not able to predict the outcome with any great degree of certainty. His condition is . . .' Laylor hesitated, seeking the words.

'Pardon me for being so forward, Doctor,' Pammy Mallot intervened. 'But Miss Phoebe is well able to bear the truth. Nothing's worse for her than not knowing what the likeliest thing is that's going to happen to Master Creswell. So you do her the kindness of speaking out straight and true. I'm here to look after and care for her no matter what is coming about for her dad.'

Laylor considered briefly, then sighed and told Phoebe, 'Regretfully, Miss Creswell, I fear that your father is never going to fully regain his former robust health or clarity of intellect. Also I'm unable to foretell just how long it may be to recover some degrees of both physical and mental recovery. However, you may rest assured that now I have bled him, and thus weakened the malignant humours which have caused this seizure, his physical and mental condition will undoubtedly begin to improve.'

He hesitated momentarily before admitting, 'But to what extent, only the Good Lord above can know. I shall of course be ready to respond instantly to any further need you may have of my services during this unhappy period.'

He added his customary words of condolence. 'In this time of trouble, Miss Creswell, perhaps you may draw some comfort in the knowledge that your father has enjoyed a long and happy life, and has been blessed by spending much of that life with such a loving and dutiful daughter as yourself.'

Now he fell silent and waited watchfully. Despite his long experience of telling people their loved ones were gravely ill, or in fact dying, he knew that he could still be surprised at how some individuals could react to such dread news.

Phoebe Creswell lifted her hands to her mouth, and remained rigidly still for several seconds. Then she dropped her hands, and with a slight frown told Laylor quietly, 'I must accept what you have told me without complaint, Doctor Laylor. All things are ordained by God, are they not? I shall be most grateful if you will continue to do what you can to help my father, and to ensure that he suffers no pain. I thank you for your kindness, and now must bid you good day, Sir. I feel overwhelmingly the need to be alone with my thoughts.'

'Let me see you out, Doctor.' Pammy Mallot bustled to open the door.

'Good day, Miss Creswell. You may rest assured that I will come at your summons and ensure that your poor father will not suffer any bodily pain.' Laylor bowed in farewell.

He went to the rear yard of the house where his horse was tethered, thinking commendably about Phoebe Creswell's reception of the bad news.

'She took it damn well. Like a true English gentlewoman.'

He mounted and took the horse at a walk around on to the forecourt of the house. As he passed the large drawing-room windows he glimpsed movement within the room, and turned his head to look.

'Great God above! That's a strange reaction to such bad news!' He gaped in astonishment as for brief seconds he clearly saw Phoebe Creswell and Pammy Mallot locked in a close embrace. The younger woman's features were hidden from him, but on Pammy Mallot's face there was a broad grin of delight.

FIFTEEN

Redditch
Saturday, 26th January
Afternoon

The skies were still clear and although the pale sunlight did nothing to temper the icy chill of the wind, the market stalls, which stretched the full length of the south side of the Green, were doing good business, as were the shops, inns and taverns throughout the town.

Tom Potts moved at a leisurely pace along the Market Place, resplendent with a brand new beaver top hat on his head, and wearing his wedding coat, waistcoat and trousers, white linen shirt, and silk cravat. His crown-topped staff sloped like a musket on his shoulder, as he halted at intervals to check the Trading Licenses of varied stall holders and pedlars, hucksters and basket-women.

As always for the majority of the inhabitants of the Needle District this hour of a Saturday was the end of their working week's grinding toil. The mills, factories and workshops were, in the main, closed until Monday morning. Wages had been paid, coins jingled in pockets, and the air was pervaded with a holiday atmosphere.

On the Green three of Elias Bradshaw's Mountebanks were performing riding feats in front of a crowd, while Bradshaw himself was selling raffle tickets for the prize of what he claimed to be a solid silver horseshoe.

In the Market Place outside the Fox and Goose an outburst of vociferous anger necessitated Tom Potts' attention.

'This is a piece o' shit, this is, and I wants me money back!' A burly, smock-clad young countryman was bawling furiously as he brandished a fur cap before the swarthy features of Yakob Weiss. 'This fuckin' thing is rubbish, so it is!'

'What's the problem here?' Tom intervened between the pair.

'This is the fuckin' problem!' The young man now brandished the cap before Tom's face. 'I paid a whole crown piece for this piece o' shit, because he told me that it was made o' Russian bear's fur and not wind nor water could pass through it. Well water and wind does get through it, and now it's falling to bits as well, so it is. The stitches has broke and the peak's come off, and I aren't been wearing it for more than a month!'

'Constable, my own dear childrens sew my caps, and they do good works. Please, take a close look at my goods for yourself, Constable! Please, lift them and look at them very careful.'

Weiss spoke so volubly that flecks of spittle sprayed from his pendulous lips as he dramatically gestured towards the wooden frame on which rows of fur headgear were hanging.

'And I sells them very cheap as a favour to the poor peoples who have to work very hard for little monies. I have never ever cheated any man, woman or child in my life! And it wasn't me who sold this man his cap.'

'It was you, you fuckin' liar,' the young man shouted. 'And I bought this off you in Bromgrove mart, not more than a month since! Now give me my money back!'

'Please, will you calm down?' Tom requested politely. 'Losing your temper and shouting will not solve anything.'

'There's fuck all needs solving. Here's the fuckin' proof of what I'm telling you!' Again the fur cap was brandished and the young man's beer-laden breath gusted against Tom's face as he threatened, 'And if this cheating bastard don't give me my money in two seconds flat, I'm going to ram this up his arse and rip up every cap he's got, and then take every penny he's got off him.'

As always in such potentially violent situations Tom's heart was pounding and he was struggling to master his apprehension. He shook his head and managed to keep his voice firm as he warned, 'You'll not rip up anything, and you'd best stop making these threats.'

'And you'd best fuck off right now, you lanky streak o' piss!' the young man warned in return. 'Or I'll make fuckin' mincemeat out of you at the same time as I does this cheating bastard!'

Tom drew a long, deep breath, and gabbled, 'If you keep making threats against me, I shall be forced to arrest you. So just go away now and come back next week in a calmer frame of mind to discuss this matter with this gentleman – which discussion I promise to preside over.'

The young man instantly punched Tom in the face, sending his top hat flying, and Tom himself staggering backwards to collide with an onlooker, who cried out in protest and pushed Tom violently, sending him staggering helplessly forward to be met with another heavy punch from the initial assailant. Tom's knees crumpled under him, but at that same instant he flailed out with his staff. Its lead-filled crown thudded into his attacker's temple, sending him reeling and collapsing limply on to the cobbles.

Tom was on his knees, shaking his head to clear his scrambled senses, and trying to focus his eyes on the young man. He levered himself painfully upright and realized to his immense relief that his opponent was unconscious.

Pointing his staff at different men among the onlookers, Tom panted, 'In the King's name I'm calling on you, and you, and you and you, to help me take this man to the lock-up.'

He next selected a woman who was carrying a large covered basket.

'Do you know where Doctor Laylor lives, Ma'am?'

'Indeed I do.'

'Then I would ask you please to go to Doctor Laylor's house and request him from me to come to the lock-up and examine the prisoner.'

None of those selected raised any objections to being summoned to do their lawful duty in the King's name. To be so actively involved ensured that they would have colourfully embroidered stories to tell, which would arouse envy in those unfortunates who had missed this dramatic incident.

The return to the lock-up resembled a bizarrely triumphal procession, with Tom, the victor, at its head, his defeated foe borne on the shoulders of the four men directly behind, and a noisily excited crowd following them.

Amy came out on to the lock-up steps, calling anxiously, 'What's happened, Tom? Are you alright? Are you hurt?'

He hurried to her. 'It's nothing for you to worry about, my love. I'm perfectly well. There's just been a dispute in the mart, that's all.'

'Look at the state of your clothes, they're filthy dirty!' she exclaimed in annoyance. 'And where's your hat?'

'It fell off, and I haven't had time to look for it.'

'Is he dead?' She pointed to the senseless countryman, her eyes widening with alarm. 'Did you kill him?'

'No! Of course not! He's merely stunned! Now please, Amy, just allow me to get this man into a cell. I'll tell you all about it later.'

'And I pray that you'll also be telling her to stop thieving my finest green tea leaves to put on airs and graces in front of her skivvy friends!' Widow Potts screeched furiously from the upper window. 'My caddy was full, and now it's empty, and I've not had even the taste of a tisane for days! That's what comes of marrying beneath you, Thomas Potts! You've brought her and her low cronies, who're the very dregs of humankind, into my home to take tea as if they were gentlefolk like myself!'

The crowd immediately erupted with jeering cheers and catcalls.

'That's what you all are!' Widow Potts screeched as she shook her fists at the crowd. 'The dregs of humankind, the very scum of the earth!'

She was answered with even more jeering cheers and catcalls, and instantly countered with another screeching diatribe.

From bitter experience Tom knew that all he could do now was to get the prisoner into a cell as quickly as possible, and hope that his mother and the crowd would soon tire of their mutual entertainment.

He beckoned the bearers into the lock-up and they laid the unconscious man on to the raised stone slab sleeping bench in the nearest cell, then despite their obvious reluctance to leave were shepherded outside by Tom. As they separated one of them gave Tom the offending fur cap.

Tom thanked him, then took Amy's arm, led her into the lock-up and barred the door.

Inside the cell the prisoner's features became animated, his arms and legs twitched jerkily, and he began moaning loudly.

'I'll need to manacle him in case he becomes violent again,' Tom told Amy. 'Will you wait by the front door and let Hugh Laylor in when he comes.'

Amy frowned anxiously. 'Why not just lock the cell and wait for Hugh Laylor to come and help you? That bloke might have another go at you while you're chaining him up!'

It was an unwelcome possibility, and Tom was very tempted to agree to this suggestion. But, unwilling to display any hint of timidity before her, he shook his head.

'I'm well able to deal with him, sweetheart.'

He took manacles, chains, keys and padlocks from the wall hooks and went into the cell. The prisoner was still lying on his back, limbs jerking, but now his eyes were open and he was mouthing sentences which to Tom sounded like gibberish.

For several seconds Tom was paralysed by foreboding. 'Will I be able to master him if he fights with me again? Wouldn't it be wiser to wait for Hugh to arrive? If this one was to get the better of me, what evil might he do to Amy?'

Then self-disgust coursed through him. 'What a bloody coward you are, Potts! Why must you always shiver and shake like a frightened old woman? For God's sake get a grip on yourself, and act like a man for once in your miserable life!'

Dominated by the impulsion of self-directed anger he warned the prisoner, 'Don't try to resist, or it will be the worse for you.' And within a very short space of time he had secured the man's arms and legs with the padlocked, manacled chains.

The bells clanged as Tom completed the task, and he told the prisoner, 'I'll take these off you when I'm satisfied that you'll behave yourself.'

The man only went on mouthing unintelligibly, his limbs jerking spasmodically. Tom could only hope for the doctor's quick arrival.

The crowd outside was watching intently as Amy opened the door to the woman who had gone to the doctor's house.

When Tom joined the pair, the woman informed him, 'It don't look as that there's anybody at Doctor Laylor's house, Master Potts. I rung the bell and hammered on the door real loud, but nobody come.'

Because of the condition of his prisoner this was unwelcome news for Tom. 'Very well, Ma'am, I'm most grateful to you for your help. I thank you for it.'

She craned her neck trying to stare past him into the passageway. 'Is there aught else I can do for you, Master Potts? I can come in and help if you wants me to.'

'No, thank you, Ma'am, everything is done. But thank you anyway.'

Tom tried to close the door but she pressed her hand against it.

'I'm Mrs Maud Harman. I'm a neighbour of Alfie Bennett.'

Tom was puzzled. 'Ma'am?'

She smiled amusedly at his reaction. 'Alfie Bennett, Master Potts. He's the bloke you've just took in. He's a neighbour of mine.'

Tom moved to allow her access. 'Will you be kind enough to step inside, Ma'am?'

There was a concerted groan of frustration from the onlookers as the door closed behind Maud Harman.

'What can you tell me about Alfie Bennett, Ma'am?' Tom asked.

'The first thing I can tell you is that he's telling the truth about his cap. I was there in Bromsgrove mart when he give that robbing Jew bugger a full five shillings' worth for it.'

Tom grimaced ruefully. 'I wish I'd known that fact before I intervened in their argument. It might have saved a deal of trouble.'

'It would have saved us the cost of losing a brand-new beaver, and your best clothes from being ruined! You great fool!' Amy scolded him.

'Yes, Amy, I accept that,' Tom told her wearily. 'But I'm on official duty now, and engaged upon more pressing matters than my own hat and clothing. So would you please go away and allow me to talk with this lady in private.'

'Humph! I'll be happy to do just that, you great fool!' Amy tossed her head, and flounced off.

Tom reddened with embarrassment. 'I do apologize most sincerely, Mrs Harman. My wife has been under much stress of late, and this is causing arguments between her and myself.'

Mrs Harman waved his apology away. 'Don't give it another thought, Master Potts. Now, like I said, me and Alfie Bennett lives nigh to each other on Merry-Come-Sorrow Hill, above Feckenham village . . .'

A loud wailing sound caused her to stop speaking and cock her head to listen.

Tom hastened to tell her, 'I fear that's Master Bennett. I'd best make sure he's alright.'

Maud Harman shook her head. 'Oh, don't bother with him, Master Potts. He'll just be having one of his funny turns. He fell out of a tree and landed on his head when he was a nipper, and ever since he has these funny turns regular. Especially when he's been on the drink. Just leave him be and he'll soon go to sleep; and when he wakes up he'll be as right as rain. If you goes moithering him now, it'll only make him play up worse.'

'Well . . .' Tom was hesitant to accept. 'Well, perhaps if I just . . .'

'There's no perhaps about it!' She frowned sternly. 'I knows him, don't I. You just leave him be, and he'll quieten down and go off to sleep.'

Tom decided that discretion was the better part of valour, and accepted meekly. 'Very well, Ma'am, as you say, you know best in his case.'

'Indeed I do.' Mollified by her victory she smiled pleasantly. 'And now if you'll allow me, Master Potts, I'll tell you all about poor Alfie . . .'

She spoke at length, and Tom mentally docketed the salient facts.

Alfie Bennett lived with and was the sole support of his aged parents, and without that support they would be forced to go into the Poorhouse. Totally illiterate, he made a meagre living by catching rabbits and vermin, and whatever casual labour he could obtain.

Maud Harman emphasized that she was convinced that when he struck Tom, he was already suffering a funny turn. She ended by pleading with Tom not to bring charges against Bennett, for the sake of the man's aged parents, describing in heart-rending detail how hideously that innocent, harmless, fragile couple would suffer if their beloved son was taken from them and cast into prison.

When she fell silent, Tom mulled over what he had heard. Remembrance of something she had said much earlier caused him to ask curiously, 'When you spoke about Alfie paying for the fur cap, you said he paid a "full five shillings' worth for it". Why did you use that particular term?'

For a moment she seemed puzzled by his question, but then smiled and nodded. 'Oh, I see what you're asking. What I meant was that Alfie paid the Jew in skins. Moles and rats and suchlike. You see when Alfie goes rabbit and vermin catching for the farmers and others, they gives him a few pence and lets him take the dead vermin and some of the rabbits. So then Alfie sells all the skins and him and his Dad and Mam eats the rabbit meat. And if truth be told when times is hard and they're getting desperate hungry, they eats the vermin meat as well.'

'Ah, yes I understand now.' Tom nodded, then the vivid memory of Alfie Bennett's angry shouting came back to him.

'I paid a whole crown piece worth for this piece o' shit, because he told me that it was made o' Russian bear fur and not wind nor water could pass through it.'

And the unbidden voice that dwelt in the depths of Tom's mind suggested, 'Could that be why the dogs were stolen? Would their fur be weatherproof enough for it to be worth going to the trouble of stealing them to make fur caps?'

'No, surely that can't be,' Tom muttered aloud, and then became aware that Maud Harman was staring curiously at him, and hastily apologized.

'Pray excuse me, Ma'am, I was thinking aloud.' Even as he spoke the unbidden voice was urging him, 'Go and ask the pedlar if he ever deals in fur caps made from dog skins. Go now and ask him.'

'What about Alfie, Master Potts?' Maud Harman pressed.

Tom made an instant decision. 'I shan't bring him before the magistrates, Ma'am. You may tell his parents that he'll be released as soon as he's recovered from his funny turn. You may see him now and reassure yourself that he isn't severely hurt, and then I have to go out again.'

After Maud Harman had inspected Bennett, she and Tom left the lock-up together. As they walked across the Green he remarked casually, 'That's a large basket you have, Ma'am. When it's filled it must be heavy for you to carry back to Feckenham. That's a longish walk when bearing a load.'

'And don't I know it,' she agreed, smiling happily. 'But I'll not be bearing the load today. Parson Winward brought me here in his gig and is taking me back in it.'

'Parson Winward?' Tom shook his head. 'He's not known to me, I'm afraid. I understood Reverend Mackay was the curate at St John's church.'

'He is. But Parson Winward is come to the village on some church business or other, and he's lodging at the Old Black Boy. I works there, you see, that's how I've come to know him. He's ever such a kind and charitable gentleman, so he is.

'Like you am yourself, Master Potts. I shan't be forgetting how kind you've been about poor Alfie. If I can ever do you a good turn, then you only need to ask it of me, because I'll be more than glad to do it for you.'

At the Market Place they parted company with mutual good wishes and Tom went to speak with Yakob Weiss, but the space the pedlar had occupied was empty.

'Do you know where the fur cap man has gone?' he asked the nearest stall holder.

'No idea, mate; he packed up his stuff and went off while you was taking that bloke to the lock-up, and the next time I saw him he was beating his donkey and going like the clappers over the crossroads there.' The man laughed. 'I reckon he thought that one unhappy customer was enough for the day and scarpered afore another 'un got hold of him.'

'Are you sure the donkey was his?' Tom queried.

'O' course it's his. He's too fuckin' idle to backpack his wares about wi' him. I've seen him with the bloody thing at Worcester and Bromsgrove markets. You must have known he keeps it tethered behind the Red Cow when he's here.' The man nodded.

'Oh yes, so he does,' Tom concurred. 'Well I'll leave you to keep on selling.'

He continued his patrolling of the market and the nearby inns and taverns, calling in at the Red Cow tavern to verify that the pedlar did indeed customarily tether a donkey in its back yard. An hour later as he was checking that the shops and taverns along the High Street were not having trouble with any obstreperous drunken customers, he noted in passing the exceptionally fine quality of a horse and gig parked outside Bromley's Emporium. Some short time later he was coming out of a tavern when the same gig came past at speed, and he saw its passenger, Maud Harman, talking animatedly to the fat, florid-featured driver who was dressed in clerical clothing.

'That'll be the Reverend Winward,' Tom told himself, and without any conscious reason thought casually, 'He'll certainly be easy enough to recognize again, should I ever have need to speak with him.'

SIXTEEN

Redditch Town
Sunday, 27th January
Early morning

It was raining hard when Elias Bradshaw tugged on the lock-up bell-rod in the darkness before dawn to interrupt Tom Potts' breakfast.

Tom took the lamp and went to the door calling, 'Who's there?'

'It's Elias Bradshaw, Master Potts. I've got a job for you.'

Tom unbarred the door and invited, 'Step in out of the rain, Master Bradshaw. What can I do for you?'

'You can find the thieving bastards who stole my dogs during the night, Master Potts,' Bradshaw growled angrily.

'All of them?' Tom queried.

'No, not the terriers. But they've took all six of my Otterhounds.'

'Is there a ready market for the hounds?'

Bradshaw shook his head. 'Not a ready market, no. They're no good for general hunting, or as guard dogs, and caring for them don't come cheap. There are only a few packs of them in this part o' the country and we all knows each other, so there's questions asked when it comes to the buying and selling of them.'

As Tom listened he felt impelled to seek a confirmation. 'Their coats are proof against wind and water, are they not, Master Bradshaw?'

'O' course they are. They'd be no use for hunting in water else.'

'Can you furnish me with a description of each dog's colouring and markings, Master Bradshaw?'

'I've already written them down.' Bradshaw took a sheaf of paper from his inside pocket and gave it to Tom. 'And I've already sent one o' my lads to go round the nearest packs with descriptions, so I'll hear pretty quick if anybody tries to sell my hounds to them.'

'Very well, Master Bradshaw, I shall begin making my enquiries as soon as it's daylight.'

'And me and my people will be doing the same, Master Potts. So with any luck I could have my hounds back safe and sound before nightfall.'

'Indeed you might,' Tom encouraged, but in his mind there was now a hardening conviction that the hounds had been stolen for their hides and fur, and they might well be dead already.

Somewhat tentatively, Tom told the other man what was in his mind, then added, 'I give you my word, Master Bradshaw, that if this is the case, I will nevertheless still continue to hunt for the perpetrators. How can I get in contact with you to let you know my progress in this matter?'

'My brother, Clem Bradshaw, keeps the Union Jack tavern in Dudley. You need only send word or letter to him and he'll be able to pass it on to me in short order, because he keeps note of my travels.'

After some further discussion they shook hands and parted.

Tom went up to the bedroom, where Amy was still asleep. He woke her gently, and as she blinked drowsily at him, he thought tenderly how beautiful she was in the soft glow of the lamplight.

'What hour is it, Tom?'

'Not yet six o'clock, sweetheart.'

'Then why did you wake me so early? The only chance I get of a lie-in is Sabbath morn,' she complained pettishly. 'And if you're wanting kisses and canoodles you've come to the wrong shop. I'm not in the mood for them.'

'You rarely are,' he thought ruefully, but only told her, 'Elias Bradshaw's Otterhounds were stolen in the night, and I have to make investigation. I may be gone for some time.'

'Well, if you intend to leave me by myself for God knows how long, then I'll go to the Fox and spend the day with Maisie and the others. Your bone-idle Mam can cook her own meals for a change.' Amy huffed and, pulling the sheet over her head, ordered curtly, 'Now take that lamp away and leave me go back to sleep.'

As Tom returned to the ground floor he couldn't help but wryly think, 'The old adage is right, isn't it? Marriage isn't always a bed of roses.'

He went to Alfie Bennett's cell and found him sitting on the side of the sleeping bench. Bennett's face was drawn and tense and as soon as Tom entered the cell he blurted out fearfully, 'What did I do? I can't remember what happened. I must have been having one o' me funny turns. I aren't killed anybody, has I?'

The man appeared so genuinely distraught that Tom couldn't help but feel pity for him.

'No, Alfie, you've not killed anyone. But you did assault me.' He pointed to his bruised and swollen cheekbone.

'Oh my God! Was it me did that to you?' Bennett wailed, and his manacle chains rattled as he clutched his head in despair. 'I'm going to prison for it, an't I? Oh my God! What'll become o' me Mam and Dad when I'm in prison? Oh my God!'

'Now just be quiet and listen to me, Alfie!' Tom told him sternly. 'I might let you go free and not bring any charges against you. But if I do that, you've got to tell me all you know about the fur cap man in return. Do you understand what I'm saying?'

'Does you mean that, Master? Does you? You'll let me go free if I tells you about the fur cap man?' Bennett beseeched.

'I do,' Tom assured him firmly. 'You have my word on it.'

'God bless you, Master! God bless you!' Bennett rung his hands in gratitude, but then choked out in dismay: 'Trouble is, Master, I don't know all that much about him, excepting the marts he says he goes to. And that he never asks me how I comes by me furs. He always says that that's between me and the Devil, and then he winks and laughs, so he does.'

'Don't worry, just tell me what you know, and I'll keep my word,' Tom reassured him.

'God bless you, Master! You'm a true Christian, you am!' Tears shone in Bennett's eyes as he frantically babbled out a list of markets at which the pedlar claimed to do business.

Tom listened intently, committing the information to memory, and when the other man fell silent and stared anxiously at him, immediately unlocked the manacles and removed the chains, then ushered him from the lock-up.

Standing at the doorway watching Bennett scurrying away across the Green, Tom grimaced unhappily as he considered the widely dispersed locations of the markets, and the varying and sometimes conflicting days they took place.

'I'm going to be spending a lot of nights away from home, and get a very sore backside jaunting around this lot. Amy's not going to be best pleased, is she?'

He sighed as he visualized her reaction when he told her what he was going to have to do. Then decided: 'Coward that I am, I'll wait until she's had breakfast and is in a good mood. I'll go first and report to Joseph Blackwell, then go and tell Ritchie Bint what's to happen.'

Joseph Blackwell had just finished his own breakfast when Tom called to make his report. As always he listened silently, sitting at the dining table, forefingers steepled beneath his chin, until Tom had finished speaking. Then he carefully considered what he had heard before requesting clarifications.

'Are you absolutely sure that the dogs have been stolen for their coats to be made into fur caps?'

'I am, Sir,' Tom replied firmly.

'But as of yet you have no actual proof that this particular pedlar is stealing the dogs himself, or buying their coats from the thieves?'

'No, Sir. But I've got full descriptions of every dog, and their individual colours and patterning are rare and very distinct. I'm confident of recognizing a fur cap that is made from any of their skins.'

'And on the grounds of your suspicion you want me to ask the Justices to issue a warrant for this pedlar's arrest? I'll tell you frankly, Master Potts, that in this case mere suspicion is not sufficient. These are only dog hides, not rare and costly furs. If it wasn't for the fact that the Earl is one of the losers, I'd not have had you waste a moment of your time investigating this case; and I'll not have the Justices issue any arrest warrant until you bring me better reason to. Good day to you, Master Potts.'

He waved his hand in dismissal.

'But, Sir . . .' Tom protested, and Blackwell immediately cut him short.

'But nothing, Master Potts! Even if you should find the man selling such caps, he would immediately claim that he found the skins abandoned with other rubbish. Or bought them in good faith from a travelling gypsy, or some other story, and it is impossible to prove otherwise.'

Knowing very well that to rouse his employer's wrath could bring unfortunate consequences for himself, Tom summoned all his resolve and doggedly stood his ground.

Blackwell's pallid features scowled warningly. 'I have no more time to waste on this matter, Master Potts. I say again, good day to you.'

'With respect, Sir, I don't want the warrant to be issued on these particular grounds. I want to be in possession of a warrant for his arrest on the grounds that he is defrauding the Commissioners of the Treasury.'

Blackwell's eyebrows raised in surprise, as Tom continued without pause.

'Yakob Weiss holds the four pound per annum Pedlar's License, which as you know, Sir, entails that he backpacks his goods to market and between markets. I have solid proof and witnesses that in fact he uses a donkey to transport his goods. Which means that he should be in possession of the eight pound Hawker's License for his use of beasts of burden in the pursuit of his business.

'Therefore, Sir, he is currently defrauding the Treasury of four sovereigns per annum. For which offence he can be imprisoned, or fined very heavily, and his goods be confiscated.'

Tom paused to allow Blackwell to digest this information.

A fleeting smile momentarily quirked Blackwell's thin lips, and he said quietly, 'I do not need a lesson in Law, Master Potts. But knowing you as I do, I am sure that you have more to add to what you have just told me.'

'I do, Sir.' Tom's nervous tension dissolved instantly. 'What I propose is that I wait until I catch Yakob Weiss selling fur caps made from these particular dog pelts. I then arrest him for the license offence. But during the hours following that arrest I imply that should he give me the identity of the people he obtained the dog pelts from, and bear witness against them in the courtroom . . .'

'. . . Then he will be treated very leniently by the magistrates for defrauding the Treasury!' Blackwell finished the sentence, and chuckled dryly. 'Your seemingly bottomless well of deviousness never fails but to surprise me, Master Potts. Come back here at noon; I should have the warrant by then.'

'Very well, Sir. In the meantime I'll go and tell Ritchie Bint what's afoot.'

Traversing the long narrow slum alleyway of Silver Street where Ritchie Bint lived, Tom was the target of resentful scowls and hissed jibes and insults, but he knew that there was very little danger of physical assault. His tough, much-feared Deputy Constable was also his close friend, and the denizens of Silver Street were in no doubt that should any of them lift a hand against Tom Potts, then Ritchie Bint would come after them seeking retribution.

Ritchie Bint's hovel was distinguished from the vast majority of its neighbours by having its windows intact and dressed with curtains. Its sparsely furnished interior was also in stark contrast to the majority, being clean and neat, the fetid faecal odours of the alley kept at bay by the bunches of fragrant herbs festooning the freshly limewashed walls.

A slatternly young woman opened the door to Tom's knocking and scowled.

'If you'm after Bint, the rotten bugger's still abed.'

'Then I'm sorry for disturbing you, but can you please tell him that I urgently need to speak with him?'

'Tell the rotten bugger yourself, and you can tell him as well that I'm shagging him no more unless he weds me, and I bloody well means it this time!' She pushed past Tom and went away along the alley.

Tom smiled wryly. Ritchie Bint was a bachelor who, because he earned exceptionally high wages as a Needle Pointer, plus his Deputy Constable's fees, was considered to be a very good catch by the many girls who continually tried to inveigle him into marriage. An added attraction for these girls was that, unlike a sizeable number of the local males, he didn't abuse and beat his women, but instead invariably treated them with kindness and generosity.

'Is that you, Tom?' Bint shouted from upstairs. 'Come on in, I'll be down directly.'

Tom stepped inside as the other man came downstairs barefoot dressed in only his shirt.

Bint grinned and held up his hand. 'There's no need to pass on Tilly's message. I heard it loud and clear. Now what can I do for you?'

Tom quickly explained about his projected journeying to the markets. 'I'll have to be away most nights until I find Weiss selling the fur caps I need to catch him with. So starting this evening will you be able to stay and sleep in the lock-up after your work and cover for me? I'll make sure of a good stock of food, drink and tobacco for you there.'

'O' course I can.' Bint grinned. 'To tell the truth I'll be glad to get away for a bit from Tilly's nagging me about wedding her every time she shares me bed. Don't get me wrong, I likes her well enough and if I ever babbied her, or any other wench for that matter, then I'd wed 'um and give the babby me name. But I aren't in any rush to get wed. I likes being single and living on me own.'

Tom grinned ruefully. 'Yes, there are occasionally moments when I wouldn't mind too much being single again either. Anyway, I have to get going now, so thank you very much for covering for me.'

Tom returned to the lock-up to find, much to his relief, that Amy appeared to be in a better mood, so he immediately told her, 'This afternoon I'm going to go in search of the pedlar Yakob Weiss, to arrest him. I'll have to search the Worcestershire marts for him so I could be away for three or four nights on this trip.

'I'll be getting a bed in Evesham tonight because it's a good twenty or more miles' journey. And I need to inform the local constables there what I'm going to do, and to be in the market at dawn tomorrow. Then I shall be at the Pershore Mart on Tuesday, and Worcester Mart on Wednesday.'

'What's your plan exactly when you're at the marts?' she queried, and stayed silent until he had finished explaining.

'What do you think of my plan?' he asked her.

'I'm thinking that it'll fail,' she replied bluntly.

'Why so?'

'You can be sure that if he's been buying stolen pelts and using them to make fur caps with, then he'll have been doing it for years, and has learned very well how to get away with it. I don't think that you've any chance of catching him out about the dog-robbing with this half-baked plan of yours.'

'Why do you call it half-baked?' he demanded indignantly.

'Because you're forgetting that the pedlars and hawkers are mostly as thick as thieves with each other, and they sound the alarm when one of them spots a constable coming who's not the local man.

'Most of the ones that work the Worcestershire marts come here for our Redditch marts as well, don't they? So they'll all know you, and because you're so tall and lanky they'll see you coming a mile off, and send the warning around the market like lightning. Then any one of them who's got something to hide will be away like a shot, and you won't see their heels for the dust.'

Tom could only stare at her in discomfiture as acceptance dawned that she was possibly right.

'Well, what have you got to say to that, you great booby?' she challenged belligerently. 'The cat's got your tongue now, hasn't it, you useless fool!'

Tom's own resentment rose against this undeservedly aggressive attack, and he told her sharply, 'We'll see who's the useless fool when I bring back the pedlar; and I hope for once you'll be in a good temper when I return.'

SEVENTEEN

Redditch Town
Saturday, 2nd February
Morning

It was snowing when Tom Potts, travel-stained and bone-weary, came limping painfully across the central crossroads of Redditch Town leading his limping horse behind him. The market stalls were already open for business and thronged with early shoppers. A stall-holder spotted Tom and bellowed.

'Bloody hell, look what the cat's dragged in! It's Constable Potts again! And he looks like he's on the Retreat from Moscow!'

Instantly catcalls and mocking laughter sounded along the line of stalls and people hurried to see the target of this attention.

'Watch out for them Rooshian Cossacks, Constable; there's a gang of 'um down by the Fox there.'

'Where's Napoleon? Has he buggered off and left you by yourself again, like he did at the other marts?'

'When am you going to eat your horse?'

'It don't look as if there's enough meat left on the poor nag's bones to feed any bugger!'

'You'd best jump into the cooking pot wi' it, Master Potts; it'll need you two bags o' bones together to make even a single drop o' gravy!'

Tom gritted his teeth, turned to his left, and keeping his gaze fixed straight ahead grimly limped northwards past the front of St Stephen's Chapel towards the top of Fish Hill and Joseph Blackwell's house, where he was dreading the reception he would get from his de-facto employer.

To Tom's relief the serving man who received the horse from him said that his master was not at home, and with barely veiled chagrin enquired, 'What's you done to this poor mare? Her was in fine fettle when you took her from me. Now her looks ready for the bloody knacker's yard.'

'We had a mishap yesterday morning at Droitwich Mart. She threw me and bolted, then collided with a cart.' Tom was feeling very guilty. 'Believe me, I'm truly regretful that she should be hurt in any way whatsoever.'

'My master 'ull be a bloody sight more than regretful when he sees her, you mark my words! He'll go bloody mad, so he 'ull.' The man appeared to relish that prospect.

'When will your master return?' Tom asked.

'Some time Tuesday next, and I shouldn't like to be in your shoes when he does.'

Tom wordlessly un-strapped his leather bag and constable's staff from the rear of the saddle and limped away across the Green.

At the lock-up it was Amy who opened the door to him, and seeing his bedraggled appearance and depressed expression could not resist telling him before he had even greeted her, 'I can see by the sight of you that it's all gone awry! Well it's your own fault! I told you it would, didn't I?'

He sighed heavily, and held up his hand to ward off any further recriminations.

'Yes, Amy, it has! Yes, Amy, it was! Yes, Amy, you did! Now can you please stand aside and let me enter!'

She giggled and stepped aside, but when he entered she saw his limp and instantly cried out in distressed concern.

'You're hurt, sweetheart! Why didn't you tell me? What's happened? What have you done to yourself?' She snatched the bag and staff from him and put them on the floor, then clasped her arms around his waist, shouting back over her shoulder, 'Ritchie! Ritchie! Get here quick! Tom's hurt!'

Ritchie Bint came running from the kitchen alcove, and Tom hurriedly told them both, 'It's nothing to worry about, I'm only bruised! There's no harm done! The horse bucked me off, that's all. I'm only bruised!'

Amy dragged him into the kitchen alcove and forced him down on to a chair.

'You sit there until I tell you to get up again, and while I'm making your breakfast you can tell us where you've been and what you've been doing since last Sunday.'

Ritchie Bint handed Tom a flagon of ale. 'Get this down you. You looks like you needs it a sight more than I does.'

Tom drank deeply, relishing the sweet nutty taste, and once his thirst was eased he began to relate his sorry story.

'I reckon I've covered well over a hundred miles. I started off at Evesham Mart, then went on to Pershore, Worcester and Kidderminster Marts. Yesterday I was at Droitwich. I only saw Yakob Weiss once and that was at Kidderminster, and he had nothing of what I was looking for laid out for sale. Then, of course, yesterday the horse went lame so I've had to walk back here this morning.' He grinned wryly. 'But truth to tell, by then my backside was so sore that I preferred walking to riding; and I do believe that the poor mare was that sick of having such a clumsy rider as me on her back she deliberately made herself lame so as not to carry me any further.'

Now he spoke directly to Amy, who was frying bacon in a cast-iron skillet.

'You were right about the traders recognizing me straight off and passing the word around. I should have listened to you, sweetheart.'

'Of course you should.' Amy smiled smugly.

He could only nod in rueful agreement, then asked Ritchie Bint, 'How have things gone here? Have you needed to put anybody in the cells?'

'Not a soul! It's been very quiet and dull. All that's happened was Old Widow Darke from Fish Hill come last night to complain that Porky Hicks had poisoned her cats.'

'Very well.' Tom nodded indifferently, and then asked, 'Have you and my mother agreed well enough?'

'Have we buggery!' Bint grinned. 'After two nights she told me that it was too demeaning for a high-born lady like her to be sleeping under the same roof as a slum rat Needle Pointer from the Silver Street. So she packed her bags and went to stay wi' her fancy man. And she told me to tell you that you've got to give her a sovereign and a half a week for the costs of her keep at Bromley's.'

'Dear God!' Tom exclaimed in shock. 'Thirty shillings! That's double the week's wage for skilled Needle Makers!'

Bint's laughter pealed. 'Well, you can draw comfort from the fact that you've no cause to worry about me taking any offence at her insulting me so, Tom. And you needn't worry about your Mam losing her good name either, for going to live in sin wi' her fancy man. It's all very respectable at Charlie Bromley's. His sister has come over from Brummagem to chaperone 'um.'

'And long may they all stay there!' Amy wished with heartfelt emphasis. 'This is the best bargain I've had in years, and well worth the price.'

Tom sighed, and wryly agreed. 'Well, after the week I've had, the last thing I needed was my mother shrieking abuse at me, and there's money enough in my reward trust fund to pay for her keep without causing us hardship.'

'What's you going to do about the dogs, Tom?' Bint wanted to know.

Tom could only shrug wearily. 'That all depends on what Joseph Blackwell has to say to me when he comes back.'

In the rear yard of the Red Cow tavern, Yakob Weiss was unloading and sorting his packs of wares from his donkey's back, and so engrossed in the task that he was unaware of the other man's approach until the harsh voice bellowed.

'I'm arresting you in the King's Name, Yakob Weiss!'

The pedlar cried out in shocked alarm and swung round to confront the grimed, unshaven features of Ezekiel Rimmer, his rotting teeth bared in a delighted chortle.

'You blutty *scheisshund*! You nigh on scared the shit out of me!' Weiss shouted angrily.

Rimmer laughed uproariously, then told him, 'Be easy now, you windy cunt. I've got summat real good for you. Just take a gander at this.'

He glanced quickly around to make sure that no one else was watching, then furtively produced a bundle from inside his clothes and displayed it to Weiss.

The pedlar's eyes gleamed as he realized the quality of what he was seeing. 'That's an Otterhound's pelt. Where did you come by that, Rimmer?'

'Ne'er mind that now. I'se got another five like this, and all of 'um am in top condition, wi' colours that you'd fuckin' well die for. The flash lads 'ull be biting your hands off to get ahold of any caps made from these, won't they just?'

Weiss's immediate reaction was to instigate the bargain haggling, and he shrugged deprecatingly. 'Maybe a few might, but a lot more might not. But Otterhound pelts are uncommon, so I need to know where you got them from before we talk of doing any business.'

Rimmer pondered a moment, then nodded. 'Fair enough. They was with the Mountebank show. And from what I hears, it'll be moving on up to the north country next week, so then you'll be safe enough selling the caps in the marts you deals at.'

It was Weiss's turn to ponder for a few moments before nodding. 'Let's talk prices.'

EIGHTEEN

Feckenham Village
Saturday, 2nd February
Mid-morning

Walter Courtney had just eaten a hearty breakfast, and was sipping a glass of Madeira wine in the select parlour of the Old Black Boy Inn when the landlord came to tell him that a man was asking for him.

'I'm ever so sorry to disturb you at your breakfast, your Reverence. But he says you knows of him. Here's his card, your Reverence. He's one o' they actor blokes from what it says on the card.'

'Oh yes, I've had some correspondence with him concerning a charity for decayed theatrical people to which he has requested me to donate.' Courtney smiled graciously. 'You may show him in, Master Blake; and please see to it that I'm not disturbed while he is with me. I prefer to keep my charitable works as discreet as possible.'

'Alright, your Reverence. But I'm forced to say that ever since you come here the news of your good heart and kindness has been spreading. You must take great care that you'm not taken advantage of by these Thespians nor none o' the local ne'er-do-wells. Else you could end up wi' sadness in your heart for having been deceived by some scoundrel.'

Courtney nodded and answered softly. 'I thank you from the bottom of my heart for your concern for me, Master Blake, but remember what the Good Book tells us.'

His tone became sonorous. 'Every man according as he purposeth in his heart, so let him give; not grudgingly, or of necessity: for God loveth a cheerful giver. Second Corinthians. Chapter Nine: Verse Seven.'

His smile broadened. 'Now how can there ever be sadness in my heart, so long as I have Our Lord's love, Master Blake?'

'You'm a true man o' God, your Reverence.' The landlord exclaimed admiringly. 'I'll show the gentleman in right away and make double sure you aren't disturbed.'

'Good morning, Reverend Winward, I hope I find you well?' Archibald Ainsley doffed his dandified broad-brimmed hat and bowed with an elaborate flourish.

'I am indeed well, for which I give thanks to Our Father in Heaven.' Courtney rose and bowed in return, then invited, 'Please, sit down.'

The landlord was hovering expectantly in the doorway, and Courtney smiled. 'Master Blake, could I please trouble you to bring a fresh bottle of your fine Madeira and another glass for the use of my guest.'

'It'll be a pleasure, your Reverence.' The man bustled away.

Courtney whispered, 'Archie, you're begging me for money for decayed Thespians.'

Ainsley winked broadly, and when the landlord came back was telling Courtney, 'So far this year, Reverend Winward, the charity has relieved more than thirty poor benighted souls, who were in some cases in the very last extremities of want and hardship. Indeed, it is not too much to describe them as being literally standing at Death's doorway, needing only days more before they passed through it . . .'

Blake placed the opened bottle and the glass on the table between the seated men and withdrew, closing the door behind him.

Courtney signaled with his finger and Ainsley continued speaking, gradually lowering his tone until satisfied that it could only be a indistinct murmuring to the ears of any eavesdropper, then changing the subject.

'Now, I've been investigating this lot. The Widow Joyce. Old Hundred House, Withybed Green, Alvechurch. Owns her house and twenty-three acres of pasture which is rented out. About twenty-eight years old. Was married at twelve years of age and has five kids under twelve years still living with her.

'Miss Tabitha Haden. Ipsley Green. Both parents dead, but several living relatives with whom she has little contact. Is thirty-two years old. Dresses well, of good character, neat cottage and garden. Considered comfortably off, but is a ranting Methodist who spends all her time at prayer meetings.

'Miss Susan Carr, Salters Lane House, looks to be about sixty years old . . .'

Courtney signaled him to be silent, and leaned nearer. 'You've done well, Archie. But for the time being I'm going to concentrate on that Beoley mark, Phoebe Creswell. So there's no need for you to further investigate these others.'

'Oh, I see!' Ainsley snapped in disgruntlement. 'So you've no further use for me? Is that what you're going to tell me?'

'Not at all, Archie.' Courtney smiled benevolently. 'Our current relationship is going to be one of long duration and mutual benefit. It's just that I need you to do other urgent tasks for me at this time. Now listen very carefully. You will remember my cousin, Sylvan Kent, who used to play the lead Beau parts.'

'Oh yes.' Ainsley frowned. 'A gambling fool, and can be a nasty piece of work when he's in drink, especially with women. Which is a pretty frequent occurrence, as I recall, having had to teach him his manners a couple of times myself.'

'True! And eventually you might well have to teach him his manners again.' Courtney smiled. 'But he's still a honey-pot for the women and very useful to me. He's currently paying court to a mark in Warwick. She's a bitch who calls herself Adelaide Farson, but her real name is Ella Peelson, whose husband, Terence Peelson, was topped very recently at Warwick for bit-faking.

'I need to know all about the Peelson family, who apparently are well known among the Birmingham swell-mobs. Tread very carefully as you go about this particular job and be extra fly because we don't want them breathing down our necks.'

NINETEEN

Warwick City
Sunday, 3rd February
Midday

Ella Peelson was in her bed, tipsily enjoying a glass of gin, when Milly Styke knocked on the door and called, 'The Major's come, Ma'm. He's in the drawing room.'

'Fuckin' Jasus! What's he doing here! He's not supposed to be coming today! Fuckin' Jasus! I hope he's not getting cold feet!' Ella Peelson swore worriedly to herself. Then she gulped down the remainder of the gin and instructed, 'Tell him that I'm at my morning prayers, and will join him shortly.'

She scrambled from the bed and went to her dressing table, opened a small silver box, took small, hard-sugared caraway cachous from it and crammed them into her mouth, chewing forcefully on them to release the pungent anise oils which would mask the smell of the gin on her breath. She dressed hurriedly in black mourning clothes and arranged her unruly hair in neat coils upon her head. Lavish applications of lavender water on her neck, wrists and hands completed her hasty toilette, and she made a carefully stately descent to the drawing room.

Sylvan Kent rose from his chair and bowed as she entered the room, then went to her with outstretched hands.

'Please forgive me for intruding upon you without invitation, my dearest Adelaide, but I confess that spending an entire day without seeing you was too much hardship for me to bear.'

She played the bashful lady to perfection, allowing him to clasp her hands in his while blushingly protesting, 'But we have spent much time together every day since our first meeting, Christophe; and it has been my custom since my tragic loss to spend the Sabbath without company, so that I may think solely of my dearest Mamma and pray for the repose of her soul.'

He detected the whiff of anise upon her breath, spotted the slight wavering of focus in her eyes, and instantly recognized with resentment, 'She's lushed up! And here's me been dying for a fuckin' drink all the fuckin' week and not took a drop!'

He played the contrite suitor. 'Oh, my dearest Adelaide, I beg you to forgive this intrusion. I know that I'm behaving like a callow, love-sick boy, but I cannot help myself. Every time I am with you I feel complete, but when we are apart I feel as if some part of me is missing. I've never experienced such depth of feelings towards anyone in my life, as these tender feelings I have for you.'

She disengaged her hands and sat down, head bowed, eyes downwards, hands clasped together on her lap. But behind the demure mask she was silently urging him, 'Stop fucking about, and get on with it. Propose to me! Propose to me!'

'Adelaide, I have this very morning received a messenger sent by the Court of Directors of the Company instructing me to return to Madras by the earliest possible sailing date.'

He went down on one knee and held a ring towards her. 'My dearest Adelaide, this betrothal ring was my own beloved mother's, which she entrusted to me on her death bed, making me take an oath before God that I would only ever offer it to the woman I love and wish to spend all my life with.

'That woman is you, my darling, and you will make me the most fortunate, the most blessed, and the happiest man in this entire world if you will accept this ring, marry me, and return with me to India.'

Triumphant, alcohol-intensified satisfaction coursed through Ella Peelson. 'I've done it! I've got him!'

From under her lashes she peeped at the ring, and the sight of the glittering diamond and gleaming gold increased her elation. 'It's fit for a queen, so it is! By Jasus, Ella! You've won the first prize this time, girl!'

Kent took her hand and urged fervently, 'Say it, my darling girl! Say yes! Say that you'll marry me, my darling!'

Ella Peelson was being engulfed by an emotion she had never experienced before. She was being overwhelmed by a rapidly burgeoning feeling of trust in this, the first man who had only ever behaved towards her, and treated her with courteous and tender consideration. She was asking herself over and over again. 'Is this love that I'm feeling? Is it? Is it?'

She heard his voice gently begging her.

'Marry me, my darling. I love you more than life itself. Please, I beg you to say that you'll marry me.'

'I will. I will marry you, Christophe.'

Kent slipped the ring on to her finger, drew her close and kissed her. Gently at first, but his lately enforced and unwelcome period of celibacy had its inevitable effect and his kisses became increasingly passionate. His hands began to roam, to touch, to caress, to seek and fondle ever more insistently the soft warm flesh of her neck, her silk-covered breasts and thighs.

Ella Peelson was a sexually needful woman who had also been celibate for some time, and her certainty that this handsome virile man was now her own possession to have and keep, coupled with the effects of the gin she had drunk, made her throw all caution to the winds.

She let him undress her, and when his naked body crushed down upon her she hungrily opened her thighs to receive him, and cried out with pleasure as he thrust into her.

Milly crouched on the other side of the door, her eye pressed against the keyhole, avidly watching the writhing and gasping couple, giggling delightedly to herself.

'They'm having a proper "Do", like I seen the Master and the big girls in the Poorhouse. They'm having a proper "Do"!'

TWENTY

Orchard House, Beoley Village
Monday, 4th February
Afternoon

'Phoebe, it's a parson at the door who's asking for you, here's his card,' Mrs Mallot announced excitedly. 'His cloth and linen looks to be of the very best, and he's come in a real fine horse and gig, and his speech is that of a gentleman. It wouldn't surprise me to find that he's high-born gentry.'

Phoebe Creswell's own excitement kindled as she took the expensively embossed calling card and read the single line of print and the brief handwritten statement beneath it.

The Reverend Geraint Winward DD
I am here on behalf of XYZ

'It's to do with that letter I sent, Pammy. That letter to the officer who placed the notice in the *Herald*. This gentleman states he has come on that officer's behalf.' Phoebe's sallow features flushed hotly as she flustered. 'What shall I do, Pammy? What shall I do?'

'You'll have the sense to see him, o' course, you silly besom,' Pammy Mallot told her firmly. 'This could be just the chance that you needs of finding a decent husband! Now catch your breath and pull yourself together while I fetches him in.'

'But what can I say to him? I'm not witty enough to entertain a gentleman or even to make polite small talk. He'll think I'm just a country frump, with no brains in my head!' Phoebe protested nervously.

'You just act natural and be your own sweet self, my girl.' Pammy Mallot smiled fondly. 'And if this parson's got even an ounce o' good sense he'll soon see what a good person you are, and what a wonderful wife you'll make for any man on this earth.

'Now just take some deep breaths and calm yourself down. Remember, even though this parson might be high-born, you'm the sole heiress of as good and worthy a family as ever lived in England.'

She bustled away to return very quickly with Walter Courtney, who bowed with courtly grace, and fervently apologized, 'It is an honour to meet you, Miss Creswell. I do most humbly apologize for calling upon you without previous introduction. I beg your forgiveness for doing so, and beseech that you will be gracious enough to hear my explanation for approaching you on behalf of Major Christophe de Langlois.'

He waited for her reply, quickly evaluating her gauche lack of poise and self-confidence.

'She's a timid, woefully plain country mouse, right enough,' he told himself with satisfaction. 'I do believe I've dropped lucky with this one.'

Phoebe's hands were trembling with nervousness, and her mouth so dry that she could not help but stammer when she answered. 'P-p-please, Sir, there is no need for any apologies, I am honoured to receive you in my house.' She gestured awkwardly at a fireside chair. 'P-p-please, be seated. W-w-would you c-c-care for some refreshment?'

He bowed his head as he sat down, and his eyes flicked momentarily towards Pammy Mallot, who was staring like an anxious mother at Phoebe Cresswell.

'It's not mistress and servant, but mother hen and her chick! That's the way of it between this pair!' He recognized the situation instantly, and made equally instant use of that recognition, rising and bowing to Pammy Mallot.

'That is most kind of you, Miss Creswell, but I cannot bring myself to trouble this good lady with my bodily appetites.'

'Oh, it's no trouble at all, Sir.' Pammy Mallot beamed. 'You just tell me what's your fancy, and I'll have it here for you in two shakes of a lamb's tail.'

Courtney beamed back at her. 'I doubt not, Ma'am, it is already plain to me that your competence is a match for your good heart. But I feel that we should first discuss the purpose of my visit, and then perhaps take some refreshment and be merry together.'

He sensed that already both women were quite taken by his avuncular smile and manner, and, gesturing at another chair he invited Pammy Mallot, 'Please will you be seated, Ma'am, and do me the honour of taking part in these discussions.'

'O' course I will, Sir, and I'm real pleased to be so invited.' Pammy Mallot placed a chair at the side of Phoebe Creswell's and seated herself, but Courtney remained standing.

He produced the two rolls of vellum, which he opened to display the ornately scrolled writing and several imposingly embossed seals. He handed them to Phoebe Creswell and said to both women, 'Will you please read these very carefully. They are my identification and authorization from His Grace, my Lord Archbishop of the Ecclesiastical Province of Canterbury. I am currently acting as a confidential aide to his Grace, and am touring his province to ascertain the structural condition of our churches, and the ministrations of our clergy.

'But of course, because of the highly confidential nature of this investigative task my Lord Archbishop has currently entrusted to myself, I would request that you do not speak of what I have told you of my current task to anyone. There are certain parish clergy in this diocese who are sadly lacking in their duties towards their parishioners, and if they were to hear of my presence they would hide their true characters behind a facade of charitable zeal.'

He paused to allow the women to study the scrolls, and noted with satisfaction their awe-struck expressions. Then he went on, 'For many years I was in India and it was there that I met my good friend, Christophe de Langlois. As you may know the military officers of the East India Company are but poorly paid; they are allowed however to earn money by trading for themselves and also by the rendition of services to the various native rulers.

'It was by these means that my friend has accrued his monetary fortune, and the ownership of a considerable amount of land and property within the Madras Presidency. Quite a remarkable achievement for such a comparatively young man.'

He smiled as he produced the portrait miniature of Sylvan Kent and handed it to Pammy Mallot, who exclaimed, 'Oh, just look at him, Phoebe! Aren't he beautiful!'

Phoebe Creswell's sallow features flushed as she stared at the miniature, and then muttered despondently, 'Indeed he is, but he'll not think that of me, will he?'

'Come, come, Miss Creswell!' Courtney chided gently. 'Knowing my friend as I do, I can affirm with the utmost certainty that he will find you most pleasing to his sight; and on meeting you will be as charmed by your manner and deportment as I am myself.'

'O' course he 'ull, and so 'ull any man who's got an ounce o' sense in his noddle!' Pammy Mallot emphatically agreed, then asked, 'But where is this gentleman now, Sir?'

'He is unavoidably detained at the East India Company Military College in Addiscombe. He sends his sincerest apologies for not having been able to come and meet you in person at this time. The reason being that the Court of Directors of the Company are having a series of most important discussions with him.'

Courtney winked roguishly. 'What I am going to tell you now must remain strictly confidential between ourselves, until he tells you of this himself. Although Christophe is far too modest to boast of his achievements, I have it on excellent authority that he will be advanced to very high office within the Company upon his return to India. He and his bride will be the virtual monarchs of their own realm within the Madras Presidency.'

'Well now, aren't that something wonderful to think on!' Pammy Mallot's expression verged on the awe-struck.

'But mind now!' Courtney placed his forefinger across his lips. 'Not a word about this must pass your lips until Christophe tells you of it himself. Otherwise he'll be most displeased with me for divulging his private affairs.'

'You can rest assured about that, Sir,' Pammy Mallot told him solemnly. 'Not even the cruellest torture 'ull make us breathe a single word about what you've just told us.'

'I have implicit faith in you both, Ma'am.' Courtney smiled and bowed to her, then took his seat and chuckled. 'And now I would greatly appreciate a small glass of whatever refreshing beverage you may have available, and after that I will answer any questions you wish to ask me.'

Pammy Mallot jumped to her feet. 'Name your fancy, Sir, and I'll have it in your hand in two shakes of a mare's tail.'

'I'm exceedingly partial to a small glass of Madeira wine, Ma'am.' He gave her his roguish wink. 'But that is another thing that must be kept strictly between ourselves. Otherwise, His Grace, my Lord Archbishop, may come to regard me as a shameless old reprobate.'

Both women gurgled with laughter, as Pammy Mallot hastily placed a small table at his side, and a bottle and glass, and told him, 'Now you drink the whole bottle if you've a mind to, and another dozen after that if you wants 'um, Sir, and your boss 'ull never get to know nothing about it.'

The atmosphere in the room was now verging on festive, and their three-way conversation flowed more and more easily as, with the ease of long practice, Courtney regaled the women with colourful stories of Christophe de Langlois, and his own experiences in India.

When the clock chimed the hour, Courtney reacted with an exclamation of concerned surprise.

''Pon my word, is that the time! My dear ladies, what must you think of me? I've been babbling away like a garrulous old fool, and have unforgivably intruded upon your most generous hospitality for far too long I fear.'

He rose to his feet. 'I shall take my leave this instant, dear ladies; and can only beg for your forgiveness and express the fervent hope that you will allow me to call upon you again?' He shook his head and reproached himself. 'I've been such an ill-mannered bore. Monopolizing the conversation and not allowing you to tell me more of yourselves. I do apologize most sincerely for having done so. But it is rare for me to encounter such charming ladies, and I could not resist the temptation to tell you about my dear young friend, Christophe's daring exploits in India, and my own much less adventurous years in that far off place.'

'And we've loved hearing them, Sir, haven't we, Phoebe?' Pammy Mallot's rosy face beamed with pleasure. 'And we could sit and listen to you talking 'til the cows come home, couldn't we, Phoebe? And you, Sir, must come again tomorrow so we can listen to some more stories about you and Mr Langlois.

'Reverend Winward must come early tomorrow, mustn't he, Phoebe? And he must have food and drink with us, and make a day of it, mustn't he, Phoebe? We won't take no for an answer, will we, Phoebe?

'You're to be here nice and early, Sir, and have breakfast with us, mustn't he, Phoebe? Then we can talk all morning, then have another bite to eat, can't we, Phoebe? Then we'll have all afternoon to talk in, shan't we, Phoebe?

'Come dinnertime we shall have a feast fit for a King, shan't we, Phoebe? And after dinner we'll have the whole night to talk in. It'll be lovely for us, won't it, Phoebe? And some time in the day, Sir, you must meet the Master hisself, mustn't he, Phoebe? Although I fear the Master 'ull not be much for talking, him being in such sore straits and bedridden like he is, aren't he, Phoebe? But we've accepted his sad condition as being God's Will, haven't we, Phoebe?'

As Pammy Mallot went on, and on, and on, Phoebe Creswell, unable to find a momentary pause in the other woman's excited dialogue to actually voice her own agreement aloud, could only repeatedly blush and nod, and blush and nod, and blush and nod.

TWENTY-ONE

Redditch Town
Wednesday, 6th February
Morning

In the early hours Tom took great care to slip from the bed and dress in the darkness to avoid disturbing his softly snoring wife, then fumbled his way downstairs to the alcove kitchen.

He carefully raked the top covering of ashes from the still-glowing embers in the cooking range fire hole and, topping them with wood chips and small coals, blew hard to rekindle the flames. When the fire began to give off heat and spread warmth through the freezing cold air he sat on a low stool staring into the leaping flames. His mood was made sombre by the prospect of the coming meeting with Joseph Blackwell.

'What excuse can I offer for failing so miserably in this investigation?' he thought glumly. 'And not only that, but I've also injured one of his favourite mares, and presented him with a damned stiff bill from the horse doctor.'

Tom's mental focus abruptly changed direction, and he angrily growled aloud. 'Now stop feeling so sorry for yourself, you sniveling moping oaf! Get off your backside, and get yourself cleaned and groomed. Then go and see Blackwell and don't make excuses for your failure. After that think very carefully about how you are going to solve this case, and then set about doing it.'

'So, Constable Potts, on top of the fee for the horse doctor to tend my injured mare, the Parish is now expected to pay the exorbitant fees of your deputy, Richard Bint, for carrying out your official duties, plus the cost of his candles, coals, drink and food during his nightly sojourns at the lock-up.' Joseph Blackwell's tone was grimly accusatory. 'And I dread to think what amount the Parish is to be expected to reimburse you with for the maintenance of yourself during these fruitless promenades around the county.'

The memory of freezing cold days, hard travelling, hard beds, little rest, poor quality food and drink, plus the constant pain of his sore backside, stung Tom into resentfully countering his employer's accusatory attitude.

'Do not forget, Sir, that it was yourself who insisted that I abandon my normal duties, and instead concentrated all my time and efforts in trying to recover the Earl's dogs.'

'And you have singly failed in that task, Constable Potts!' Blackwell immediately counter-attacked.

'Not yet, I haven't!' Tom declared doggedly. 'I'm fully confident that I shall solve this case, and sooner rather than later!'

They stared unblinkingly into each other's eyes for long, long moments, until Blackwell's thin lips parted slightly and a reedy chuckle issued from between them. Then he nodded and said quietly, 'And I'm fully confident that eventually you will solve it, Thomas Potts. Fortunately for both of us I've been informed that the return of the Earl to Hewell is to be much later than was thought. So to save the Parish unnecessary expense you may also attend to your normal duties while still continuing with this investigation. I bid you good day.'

TWENTY-TWO

Redditch Town
Monday, 18th February
Morning

During the twelve days since his last interview with Joseph Blackwell, Tom had made no progress in his investigation of the stolen dogs, and now had just left Blackwell's house after making another report of his continuing failure.

Drawing deep draughts of the frosty air, he stood gazing northwards down the long steep slope of the terrace-lined Fish Hill and across the broad snow-covered pastures of the Arrow River valley bordered by the long ridges of higher ground beyond.

Suddenly he remembered Richard Bint telling him about the Widow Darke's complaint concerning her poisoned cats, and guilt assailed him.

'Dear God, I'd completely forgotten about that poor old soul. I'd best go call on her now and make my apologies.'

The terrace of thatched cottages on the Fish Hill was set some twenty yards back from the road and even before Tom had traversed that short distance the door of Widow Darke's home was flung open and she came scurrying to meet him.

Although she was tiny, bent nearly double, and her face and body shriveled with age, Tom was shocked by the strength and deep timbre of her voice.

'Where's you been this last weeks, Constable Potts? You'm supposed to be at the lock-up when we needs you! Not going off gallivanting around the county like Lord Muck!'

'I'm very sorry I've not visited you before, Ma'am,' he told her. 'But I'm here now, and at your service.'

'This is a terrible thing, and you aren't done nothing about it, you Jackanapes!' she scolded furiously. 'I've had three o' me cats murdered! And I wants the bugger who done it, brought to trial and hung for being a bloody-handed murderer!'

'Murdered, you say? In what manner?' Tom asked.

'Poisoned! By that evil devil, Porky Hicks!'

'Do you have proof of this, Ma'am?'

'Proof! Proof! What d'you mean by asking me if I've got proof?' Flecks of spittle sprayed from her toothless mouth as she bellowed indignantly, 'I'm a respectable, God-fearing, Chapel-going Methodist, who was wed to a respectable, God-fearing, Methodist Chapel Elder for forty years. During which time I birthed and buried ten kids and laid each one of 'um in hallowed ground. And you've got the sauce to ask me if I've got proof? May our sweet Lord turn his gaze away from you, and fling you into the fiery pits of Hell for ill-using me in such a way!'

Her furious rant brought curious faces to stare from windows and doorways all along the terrace, and shouted questions.

'What's he want wi' you, Widow Darke?'

'Has he come about your cats?'

'He's took his bloody time in coming, aren't he!'

Tom hastily suggested to the irate old crone. 'Let us both go inside and discuss this matter, Ma'am. You can then voice all your suspicions to me without fear of interruption.'

'It aren't only Widow Darke who thinks that it's Porky Hicks who killed her cats. The bugger's done such before, all over the place.' Another woman came up to Tom. 'And I saw him feed 'um something the day him and the rest of the gang from Shit Court come down our backyard to empty the privies.'

'Yes, and that same night my poor beautiful darlings was shitting and spewing all over the place, and dead by next nightfall!' Widow Darke was near to tears. 'And the very day after that Porky Hicks and his Dummy mate come back down here scavenging our rubbish, and he asked me if there was any dead animals lying around here which needed to be shifted.'

'And how did you answer?' Tom asked.

'Well, Mistress Kings here had told me that she saw Porky Hicks give summat to my beautiful darlings, so I was suspicious of him. And I answered him, no there wasn't no dead animals. I said my darlings had been a bit poorly, but that they was as right as rain again. And does you know summat, Constable Potts! He looked really shocked when he heard that.' The old crone nodded emphatically. 'I knew for sure in that very instant, that that evil devil had murdered my poor beautiful darlings!'

Tom briefly considered what he had heard, and then asked, 'If they were assailed with diarrhoea and vomiting, might it not have been that they had contracted a virulent form of the distemper, Ma'am? It's a common enough cause of dog and cat deaths after all.'

'Oh no!' She vehemently dismissed this suggestion. 'I knows distemper when I sees it. It wasn't any distemper that killed them. It was poison!'

Again Tom briefly considered his options, and decided. 'Very well, Ma'am, I shall make further investigation into this matter. Have you buried the cats?'

'No. I've got the poor darlings covered wi' ice and snow to keep 'um fresh. I wants somebody who knows what they'm doing to look close at 'um and find out what's killed 'um.'

'Let me see them, Ma'am.'

'Cummon then, I've got 'um round the back.'

She led him through her cottage into the rear yard, where a heap of snow and ice was piled high. She burrowed into the heap and one by one drew out the stiffened bodies of three cats and laid them in a row.

Even in their present condition they were recognizable as exceptionally fine feline specimens.

'Their coats would make very handsome fur caps.' The thought came instantly into Tom's mind, followed almost simultaneously by the instinctive conclusion that this was why they had died.

'Scavengers make their profit from collecting rubbish and then selling on anything amongst it that has some sort of market value . . . Human urine and animal skins to tanners! Human and animal shit to farmers! All types of animal furs to furriers! Of course Porky Hicks could see a profit to be made from these three beasts for the outlay of a pennyworth of rat poison.'

As these thoughts flooded his mind, aloud he requested, 'Will you let me take them with me, Ma'am? I can discover what killed them. But I must request you to refrain from making allegations against Porky Hicks until I've completed my enquiries.'

After he repeated that request twice more she reluctantly acquiesced, and Tom picked up the cats and walked away leaving her glaring after him.

A short time later, as Tom entered the entrance drive of Hugh Laylor's house, its front door opened and the doctor came out accompanied by a clergyman Tom recognized as the one who had been in the gig with Maud Harman.

'Good morning, Tom,' Hugh Laylor greeted warmly. 'You've come in the nick of time; I was just about to set out for Beoley with the Reverend Winward here.

'Reverend, allow me to introduce my dear friend, Thomas Potts, Constable of this parish. Tom, this gentleman is the Reverend Geraint Winward.'

The two men bowed cordially to each other.

Then Laylor asked Tom, 'What can I do for you, Tom?'

'I'm come to ask a favour, Hugh. Would you please allow me to have the use of your dispensary for a few hours?' Tom answered and indicated the dead cats he carried in the crook of his arm. 'I've some specimens here that I need to dissect and examine.

Their owner thinks that they've been deliberately poisoned, and I'd like to try and verify if that is the case.'

'Any ideas as to what the poison might have been?' Laylor asked.

'The owner said that they'd been given some scraps to eat, and within a short space of time they were violently vomiting and defecating, and died within another short span of time. So it could well have been arsenic. If it was a large dose then the hydrogen sulphide test will show it very plainly.'

'And if it was only a small dose, what can you do then, Tom?' Laylor asked with interest.

Tom shook his head. 'I really don't know. My father once spoke of a correspondence he was having with a brilliant chemist employed in the Woolwich Arsenal who was engaged upon a series of experiments which would discover even the slightest traces of arsenic.' He grinned. 'But I can only hope that these poor cats contain very noticeable traces.'

'Well I wish you success, my friend,' Laylor declared. 'I'd like nothing better than to assist you in this task; however the Reverend and myself must make haste to Beoley, so you go on inside. Mrs Blakely, as always, will be eager to fuss over you.' He turned his head to tell his companion, 'Tom is a particular favourite of my housekeeper, Reverend. Every time she sees him she behaves like a mother hen with her chicken.'

The trio parted and Tom went inside the house to be warmly welcomed by the motherly Mrs Blakely.

On the road to Beoley, as Laylor rode close alongside the gig, Walter Courtney remarked, 'I've never before in my life encountered a Parish Constable who carries out dissections and scientific examinations, Doctor Laylor. It must be a unique situation.'

Laylor chuckled. 'I do believe it is, but Tom is of gentle birth and highly educated. His father was a wonderfully talented physician and surgeon who chose to spend his life in the army. Tom became his father's apprentice at a very early age, so has had many years of medical training and practice in both military and civil hospitals.

'Tragically in the final stages of Tom's medical studies his father died very suddenly, leaving his family virtually destitute. Tom being an only child, he was forced to abandon his studies before gaining his degree and to seek other work in order to support his mother. His leaving the medical profession was our loss, because he has a far greater aptitude for surgery than I possess.'

'And now he is a lowly Parish Constable, subjected to constant verbal insult and physical abuse by the very dregs of our nation. Poor unfortunate fellow!' Courtney murmured sympathetically. 'I have to confess, Doctor Laylor, that there are times when I am driven to question why our Blessed Father in Heaven places such heavy loads upon the shoulders of such meek and goodly people as your friend. As Jesus, our Saviour, has told us, God does indeed move in the most mysterious of ways.'

'Indeed he does, Reverend!' Laylor agreed wholeheartedly. 'Ironically, Tom now has an independent income from a trust fund a wealthy family established for him after he had rescued their relative from grave danger. But the local Chief Magistrate, Reverend the Lord Aston, has very spitefully used his power and influence to ensure that Tom must continue in the post of Parish Constable for several years to come, thus preventing Tom from completing his medical studies and becoming a practising doctor.'

In Hugh Laylor's dispensary Tom laid the cats side by side within the broad shallow stone trough, and again was struck by what fine feline specimens they were in size and the quality of their black fur.

He quickly set up a round-bottom flask, the cork stopper of which was threaded through with a long, slender, stop-cocked glass thistle funnel and a much shorter delivery tube. Then he dropped a few small pieces of ferrous sulphide into the flask and in a smaller flask diluted some sulphuric acid with water.

Next he took up a knife, deftly opened the first body and carefully dissected from it the organs he required. Finely slicing and dicing a portion of them into a small pan of water, he took it into the kitchen and with the housekeeper's permission, set it down to boil on the cooking range.

Mrs Blakely clucked her tongue disapprovingly. 'Is that your breakfast you're cooking, Master Tom! Well all I can say is that your wife ought to be ashamed of herself for letting you leave the house wi'out feeding you a nice breakfast!'

'No, Mrs Blakely, this is most certainly not my breakfast,' Tom hastened to assure her. 'It's to do with the experiment I'm conducting. I'll be back directly.'

This time he returned with a spirit lamp.

After several minutes he judged the pan mixture had boiled long enough. He lit the lamp and took it together with the pan back into the dispensary, where he sieved the pan's contents to remove the solid tissues and poured some of the remaining liquid solution on to the ferrous sulphide in the round-bottom flask. Next he inserted the flask's cork stopper and extended the protruding curved end of the delivery tube with a further longer piece of tube, under the middle of which he positioned the wavering bluish flame of the spirit lamp.

He picked up the small flask of diluted sulphuric acid and prayed as he poured its contents down the thistle funnel. 'It's a long time since I last tried this experiment, Lord, and it failed miserably on that occasion. Please be merciful and let it work this time.'

He twisted shut the stop cock and held his breath, silently counting the seconds, waiting for the acid to react with the ferrous sulphide to form hydrogen sulphide gas, which in turn should react with any arsenic present to create yet another gaseous mixture.

Tom's explosive gasp of relief broke the silence as the mixture began to emit tiny bubbles and wraiths of visible fumes which snaked up and along the delivery tube. Now he focused all his attention on the section of the delivery tube extension being heated by the flames of the spirit lamp.

At first it looked to be steam coating the inner surface of that section, but as the seconds passed that initial coating disappeared and Tom could clearly see the yellowish-white layer of precipitation caused by the heat discomposing the gases. Unable to control his impatience, he detached the tube extension and sniffed both its ends. A smell which resembled garlic filled his nostrils, and he punched the air in triumphant recognition.

The yellowish-white layer was composed of minute crystals of yellow arsenic trisulphide.

As Tom Potts was smiling in triumph, his friend Hugh Laylor was standing at the bedside of George Creswell, frowning in chagrined bafflement.

The sick man's turgid breathing was an irregular weak rasping, his heartbeat was slow, his skin pale and clammy, and although he was to all intents comatose, yet his hands still moved restlessly, fingers scratching at his nightdress-covered skin.

'You said that he was vomiting severely during the night, Reverend, but was not afflicted with the diarrhoea. What did he eat prior to that – I mean the last things he ate?' Laylor sought clarification.

'Well he ate his breakfast before my arrival here this morning, Doctor,' Walter Courtney replied. 'I assume that it was the special broth that Mrs Mallot prepares for him.'

'Mrs Mallot's special broth. Could that have provoked the vomiting?' Laylor mused aloud, as he stared down at the sick man's deathly pallid face. Suddenly an unbidden memory rose in his mind: the joyful smile on Pammy Mallot's face after he had first told the two women about the gravity of George Creswell's condition. That unbidden memory brought with it a sense of uneasiness.

Courtney shook his head and spoke hesitantly. 'Regretfully, I'm not medically qualified. Also I've only been visiting the family for a few weeks, so can make no judgement on what may have caused such a severe bout of vomiting.'

'Is it always Mrs Mallot who prepares the broth?' Laylor pressed.

'I don't know.' Courtney shrugged. 'But she appears to do all the cooking here and may I say she is a very fine cook indeed. I've eaten dishes that she has prepared and they have been without exception among the most toothsome I have ever tasted.'

He shook his head dismissively. 'No, I cannot believe it is Mrs Mallot's broth that is causing these attacks of the vomit. I've eaten that very same broth myself on more than one occasion and experienced no pangs of discomfort.'

The uneasiness in Hugh Laylor's mind goaded him to question further. 'Does Master Creswell feed himself?'

'Apparently he's not able to do so without spilling the broth over himself and his bedding, so I assume Mrs Mallot or Miss Phoebe normally feed him.'

'How much time elapses between Master Creswell's taking food and his attacks of the vomit?' Laylor probed.

'I really can't say.' Courtney shrugged, and went on, 'It's unfortunate that Miss Phoebe and Mrs Mallot will not be returning home until tomorrow afternoon. Perhaps you might call then and ask if they have taken notice of the times elapsing.'

It was Laylor's turn to shrug. 'I shall have to see what other demands are made on my time before I can give you an answer to that, Reverend. However, I would request of them that for the time being Master Creswell's sustenance must be solely white bread soaked in milk, and a glass of port wine four times daily.

'What is imperative is that the next time Master Creswell vomits, then that vomit must be saved and delivered to my house as quickly as possible, and also any bowel excretions.'

'They most certainly will be, Doctor, because I shall take that task upon myself,' Courtney stated gravely.

A little later Courtney was contemptuously sneering as he stood at the window watching Hugh Laylor ride away.

'He's just another stupid yokel quack, isn't he?'

It was late in the afternoon and Tom Potts was finishing the cleansing of the instruments and equipment he had used when Hugh Laylor returned to the dispensary.

'How goes it, Tom, have you had success?'

'Oh yes. All three cats were definitely poisoned with arsenic. And if Widow Darke's neighbour is to be believed, it was Porky Hicks the scavenger who fed it to them on scraps of food.' Tom grimaced wryly. 'Unfortunately I fear that proving his guilt in a court of law will be nigh on impossible, because we have none of the original scraps of food as evidence that they were impregnated with arsenic.'

Laylor frowned thoughtfully and muttered, 'Yes indeed, that's what is needed above all else.'

Tom finished cleaning the final glass tube, and picked up the sack containing the bodies of the cats.

'Well, many thanks for letting me use your dispensary, Hugh. I'm truly grateful.'

'You know that you're welcome to use it whenever you wish, Tom. In fact, I might have cause to request the help of your expertise in this field some time soon.'

'Why so?' Tom asked curiously.

'George Creswell, the patient of mine at Beoley that Parson Winward fetched me to see today, has some symptoms which are puzzling me. Should the poor fellow be attacked with any further vomiting fits, I'd greatly appreciate your assistance in analyzing his vomit and bowel excreta.'

'I'll be happy to help.' Tom readily agreed. 'Now I must give these poor creatures a decent burial, so with thanks once more I'll bid you a good day.'

But as Tom walked away from Laylor's house a fresh idea occurred to him. He came to a standstill and mulled over this new idea. Then he changed direction and tramped the several miles to the hill known as Merry-come-Sorrow above the village of Feckenham. He called at the cottage of Mrs Maud Harman and spent some considerable time talking to her. When he left the cottage he was no longer in possession of the dead cats, and there was a smile on his face.

TWENTY-THREE

Feckenham Village
Saturday, 23rd February
Morning

When Walter Courtney halted his gig outside the Old Black Boy, Archibald Ainsley hurried to greet him.

'Is it him there, Walter?'

Courtney nodded grimly. 'Oh yes, it's him alright, he exactly fits the description you gave me. He's looking for the Irish bitch, without any doubt.'

'What shall we do about him?'

'Nothing at this time. But we'll cut all connection with her this very day. I'm meeting Sylvan in Redditch at noon, then I shall go on to the Creswells' house. I want you to go straight to Birmingham now and arrange bed and board for him at this address.'

Courtney passed over a slip of paper, and drove off.

Among the bustle and noise of Redditch mart day the two soberly dressed men attracted no attention as they joined company.

Walter Courtney frowned as he saw Sylvan Kent's bloodshot eyes, and the dark shadowed bags beneath them.

'Goddammit, Sylvan, didn't I tell you to lay off the drink!'

The other man only smiled. 'Don't upset yourself, Cousin. I've merely been enjoying bed and board at my newly betrothed sweetheart's house! She's a prize lush who can drink you and I both under the table! And she's mad keen to wed me, so all you have to do is to hand over the Special License now, and I'll be a married man within the week.'

Courtney shook his head. 'No you will not.'

Now it was Kent who frowned. 'Why? What have you found out? Aren't she got any property then?'

'Oh yes, she has a fine property in Bradley Green; and some old cow by the name of Farson was indeed buried in Feckenham churchyard a few months past.'

'Well that's what we were hoping for, isn't it?' Kent's handsome features were puzzled. 'Now we can do the business in short order.'

'Oh yes, we most certainly could have done so,' Courtney agreed equably. 'But there's an unforeseen snag cropped up.'

'And what might that be?'

'There are people searching for her. I went to the house to have a mooch about and it looked to be shuttered up. But as I drew in on the forecourt a hard-looking cove, sporting a fine "Chiv Ribbon" knife scar, came out of the house and asked me if I'd come there to call on the Widow Farson. He said he was a close relative and needed to see her most urgently on family matters. But unfortunately she had unexpectedly gone away for a brief stay with friends of hers, and he didn't know their address. Might I be able to help him in this matter?'

'And what did you say?'

'That I'd never met the lady, and I was seeking for a property to rent in the neighbourhood, and had wondered if this one might be available? To which he answered me very positively that it was not. I thanked him for his information, insisted on shaking his hand and took my leave.'

'I wouldn't have bothered to shake his fuckin' hand,' Kent grunted sourly.

'No, you wouldn't, would you, Cousin? And that's one of the many reasons why I call the tune, and not you,' Courtney sneered. 'You see, I can tell a great deal about a man when I shake his hand, and one of the trademarks of bit fakers' hands are acid scars and brown patches of skin.'

Kent instantly understood the implication. 'You think he's one of her husband's coining mob.'

'You've got it in one, Cousin! By God, what a fly cove you are!' Courtney mocked. 'But he's Terence Peelson's brother, Billy, and not just one of the gang.'

'How do you know that?' Kent demanded.

'Never you mind,' Courtney scowled.

'Well, even if he is, I don't see why that should stop me doing the business with her,' Kent argued.

'You don't see why, because you're too stupid to see past the end of your prick!' Courtney snorted in disgust. 'Well all you're going to need to see now is the new bride that I've found for you. She's a spinster living with her father.'

'Living with her Pa! That's got to be a recipe that'll make bad eating!' Kent scoffed challengingly.

'Her father is currently bedridden with illness, and when he dies she'll inherit a great deal of money, and property.'

Courtney produced the letter sent by Phoebe Creswell, which Kent scanned and then queried, 'How have you come by the information, because there's no mention of a sick father, land or property in this?'

'At this moment, how I've come by this information is no concern of yours, Sylvan. What you'll do now is break off all connection with the Irish bitch this very day. Tell her you've been called back to Addiscombe, but will be coming back to her as soon as possible. Tell her the Directors are making difficulties about you getting wed, but that you're not going to stand for it, and that you'll marry her no matter what their objections may be. Make sure the parting is sweet and you leave her believing all will be well. Then go to Birmingham and wait in this lodging house until I come for you.' Courtney passed over a slip of paper with an address on it.

'Well if that's the case, then I'll need some rhino,' Kent grunted sullenly. 'Paying court to the Irish bitch has fairly skint me.'

'And paying for your drinking and gambling and whoring is fairly skinning me,' Courtney scowled. 'So I've already arranged for you to be fed and watered at the lodgings. You won't be having any more of my money to waste until you earn it.' He hesitated then gritted out, 'I'm warning you now, Cousin, that if you don't keep away from the drink and stop gambling and whoring, then you and I will be parting company. I can easily find a replacement for you, but without me you would starve.'

He turned and walked away.

After a few seconds Kent went in the opposite direction, seething with impotent anger.

'I've had a bellyful of his arrogance. Who the Hell does he think he is, lording it over me as he does. I'm his kinsman, not a hired hand. He's got the easy role in this work. It's me who has to suffer being wed to ugly old bitches. And now, the first time I'm actually enjoying fucking a mark, he's telling me that I've got to split from her straight away, and sit twiddling my thumbs in some stinking lodging house with no money in my pockets! Well, fuck him!'

TWENTY-FOUR

Beoley Village
Saturday, 23rd February
Afternoon

Since their first meeting, Walter Courtney had visited the Creswell home almost daily. During each visit he and the two women had prayed fervently at George Creswell's bedside; and he was now regarded as a dear friend and trusted confidant by both Phoebe Creswell and Pammy Mallot. He had garnered many details of the money, properties and land that Phoebe Creswell would inherit on her father's death, and had now decided that it was time to progress to the next stage of his plan.

It had snowed intermittently all through this day and, with the hour of darkness imminent, Walter Courtney rose up from his fireside chair and announced to the two women sitting with him, 'It's time I was leaving, my dears, before full nightfall is upon us.'

Phoebe pointed to the snow-flecked window, and protested, 'You can't go out into that weather, Geraint, it's snowing hard again. You must stay here for the night.'

'Regretfully I can't do that, my dears; I have charitable tasks to complete in Feckenham this evening.'

'But the roads will all be blocked by the snow, Geraint,' Phoebe insisted.

'You could get stuck and freeze to death,' Pammy Mallot declared.

'I know that is a possibility, my dears, but I have trust in our Lord. He will undoubtedly keep me safe as I struggle through the snow and ice.'

'But He cannot prevent us from worrying ourselves half to death about you!' Phoebe Creswell seemed near to tears.

'Geraint! How can you be so heartless and unfeeling as to put us through this worriting over you? You'd oughter be ashamed o' yourself!' Pammy Mallot was driven to heated protest at the sight of her beloved Phoebe's distress.

An expression of distress creased Courtney's features and he uttered brokenly, 'Indeed at this moment I truly am bitterly ashamed that I could have upset either of you in any way whatsoever! I beg you both to forgive me! It's only that I cannot bear the thought of causing the extra work and trouble in caring for me to be added to all your other terrible burdens.'

'But it's not trouble at all, Geraint. It'll be our pleasure, won't it, Pammy?'

'O' course it 'ull! Now I'll not hear another "No" from you, Geraint. You'm stopping here with us this night, and that's all there is to it.'

'Then with all my heart I most gratefully accept your kind invitation, my dears. Let us kneel and give thanks to the Lord for our friendship, which is most surely blessed by Him.'

They all knelt and Courtney's sonorous tones filled the room as he thanked God long and passionately for blessing them with their close friendship. As he uttered the final 'Amen', the clock chimed and Pammy Mallot exclaimed in dismay, 'Oh my word, is that the time? The master needs to have his food! And his ointment rubbed in for his sciatica. I'se got a score of other jobs needs doing as well!' She clambered stiffly to her feet and the others rose with her.

'Thanks be to our Lord!' Courtney declaimed joyfully. 'For vouchsafing the selfish wretch that is myself this opportunity to be of some use to you, my dears.'

The women stared at him in puzzlement, and he chuckled warmly as he told them, 'It shall be my great pleasure both to feed the master, and to apply his sciatica salve, and by doing so, to free your good selves to carry out your other tasks.' He waved his hands in the air as if to fend off any protests. 'No! I'll not be gainsaid in this matter. You and I shall go to the kitchen this instant, Pammy, and you shall equip me with the necessary items to give the master his sustenance, and apply his sciatica salve. Please don't stop me doing this for you; it will give me so much happiness to be of some service to my two newest and dearest friends.'

Within scant minutes Courtney was carrying a laden tray into the sick man's bedroom.

George Creswell appeared to be sleeping, lying on his back, eyes closed, toothless mouth gaped wide, breath rasping.

Courtney quietly placed the tray on the bedside table and took a small pot and a pair of leather gloves from his pockets. While he stared down at the other man's gaunt, grey-skinned, stubbled features, he pulled on the gloves and opened the pot. Smiling broadly he gently shook the sleeping man's shoulder, and equally gently exhorted him, 'Wake up, Master Creswell. Wake up now. I'm come to give you your supper, my dear Sir, but first I shall soothe the pains of the sciatica that afflicts you.'

TWENTY-FIVE

Warwick
Saturday, 23rd February
Night

Sylvan Kent had called in at several wayside taverns on his way back to Warwick, but the copious drinks he had imbibed had done nothing to soothe his foul mood. He was penniless and aggressively drunk when he rode into the yard of the livery stable where he was keeping his horse. As he dismounted a stable-hand came and took the horse's reins from him.

'My boss wants a word wi' you, Sir.'

'What about?' Kent slurred.

'Oh, he'd sooner tell you that hisself, Sir.' The stable-hand spoke over his shoulder as he led the horse away. 'He's in the office.'

Kent went to the main building and, without knocking, entered the lamplit office to find the owner sitting at his desk.

'Your man told me you wanted a word.'

'That's right.' The owner rose to his feet and came past Kent to shout out of the door. 'Get in here, lads!'

With a clattering of iron-shod boots on the cobbles men came running across the yard.

'Listen, I've got important business to attend to, so make haste and tell me what you want,' Kent snarled.

Two big, tough-looking men came through the office door as the owner said, 'I want my money.'

'What the fuck are you talking about?' Kent demanded aggressively. 'I paid you three sovereigns in advance for stabling and feed this very morning, didn't I!'

The owner cast three coins at Kent's feet. 'You paid with shoful, you bloody macer!'

Kent was taken aback. Shoful! Counterfeit money!

The previous night, when Ella Peelson had fallen into a drunken slumber after their love-making, he had searched through the drawers of her room and discovered a purse full of gold sovereigns. Expecting to get money from Courtney with which to replace them he had taken six of the coins.

'I didn't know it was counterfeit!' he blurted. 'I swear I didn't!'

'Don't give me that shit!' the owner growled. 'If just one of them had been shoful, I might have believed you. But all three of them is too much for me to swallow. I've a mind to send for the constables and turn you in, you cheating bastard.'

The threat roused Kent to desperation, and if he and the owner had been alone he would have turned violent. But he knew he would stand no chance against three men, so he tried to bluff his way out of his predicament.

'Look here, I'm a senior officer in the army of the East India Company, and I really am telling the truth about not knowing this money was counterfeit. But to atone for this unfortunate incident, I'll compensate you for your trouble!'

The other man's eyes narrowed as he considered this offer, and emboldened by the fact that the man was considering it, Kent went on.

'I don't fear facing the constables because I am an officer and gentleman of the Honourable Company, and its Court of Directors will vouch for my unblemished character. What troubles me is the fact that I am so dreadfully embarrassed not to have realized that these coins were counterfeit at the very moment I received them. It makes me appear to be an absolute donkey.' He managed to force a rueful smile. 'In fact I *was* an absolute donkey, wasn't I; and to punish myself for my own stupidity, I'll give you ten sovereigns in compensation.'

The owner held out his palm. 'Alright.'

'I'll have to pay you on Monday.' Kent again forced a rueful smile. 'I've been enjoying a day of reunion with old comrades and have spent all the money I had with me. Unfortunately the nearest offices of the agents of the Honourable Company are in Birmingham, and there will be no one there until Monday next. But I can draw from my account there on that same morning and make my payment here on that same afternoon.'

'Make sure you do.' The owner frowned. 'Or from first thing Tuesday morning your horse and tack will be up for sale to the first buyer, whether it's a fair price or not.'

He paused to let Kent absorb that information, then jerked his head in dismissal. 'Now get off the premises, and I'd best warn you that my night-watchman uses his blunderbuss against intruders, and he don't stop to ask if they're officers and gentlemen.'

'Then I shall take care only to return here in the broad daylight of Monday afternoon. Good night to you all, gentlemen.' Kent smiled confidently, and the men stepped aside to let him go through the door.

As he exited the yard and was enveloped in darkness, his smile metamorphosed into a worried grimace.

'Fuckin' shoful! How could I have been so fuckin' stupid? I should have expected that being wed to a bit-faker she'd have some fuckin' shoful in the house! What do I do now? What?'

The memory of his cousin's warning sharpened his desperation.

'He'll go mad if I lose the horse. It could be the finish for me and him, and then what will I do to earn a living?'

By the time he reached the house his desperation was at fever pitch, his nerves strained to their utmost, and his craving for more drink all-consuming.

It was Ella Peelson who answered the door to his knocking and he asked, 'Why are you come to the door? Where's Milly?'

'She's not here. Where have you been all day? Have you got the license?' Her words were slurred, her breath stank of gin, and aggression was seething in her.

'No.' He shook his head.

'Why not?' she demanded.

'Don't keep me standing on the doorstep, woman!' he snapped curtly and an urge to smash his fist into her face almost overcame him. 'I need a drink.'

'Don't you take that tone with me; I'm not one of your nigger soldiers!' Her voice shook with rage. 'You've got some questions to answer, my fine bucko! Why haven't you got the license?'

'Just let me pass, damn you!'

He pushed her aside, strode into the drawing room, poured himself a full glass of gin from the bottle on the sideboard, and drained the glass in two gulps.

She slammed the front door shut and came into the room and he decided that the best course of action would be to try and mollify her. Exerting all his willpower he managed to modify his tone.

'I will explain about the license if you'll allow me, my love. There's no call for you to be so angry.'

'Try explaining about this first!' She threw the ring he had given her at his feet. 'I took it down to the jeweller this morning to get it valued and he told me that it's pinchbeck, not gold, and the diamond is naught but leaded glass!'

The shock of her making this discovery caused him to fumble for words. 'Pinchbeck? That jeweller's a damn fool! It was my mother's betrothal ring! I swear on her grave that it's gold and diamonds.'

'And are you going to swear on her fuckin' grave that you didn't take money from my purse, you fuckin' macer?' Her gutter-devilry exploded. 'Six sovs, that's what you took, and that's why I took the fuckin' ring to be valued! And don't try to deny it, because Milly was looking through the keyhole and she saw you going through the drawers and taking money from the purse.'

He still tried to bluff his way out. 'She's telling lies, and you're a damn fool for believing her.'

'I was a damn fool for being taken in by a fuckin' Fancy-Dan like you,' she screeched.

His own temper again erupted and he bawled back at her, 'Well I was never fooled by you, you fuckin' whore. I've known from the first that you're naught but a fuckin' bog-rat whore whose husband's just been topped for bit-faking. And his mates are looking for you right now. So unless you do exactly what I say, I'll be letting them know where you are, you fuckin' whore!'

She suddenly hurled herself at him, hissing and spitting like a wildcat, raking at his face with her long fingernails, tearing skin and fetching blood.

He bellowed in shock and pain and, grabbing her wrists he forced her back as she screamed and struggled. They collided with a small table and fell with her underneath. As she lay winded, he scrambled to his feet and lost all control, kicking and stamping on her body and head, smashing her nose, breaking teeth, mercilessly battering her into senselessness.

Then as the red haze of fury cleared from his sight he stood for long moments dragging in gulps of air, staring down at the bloody wreckage of her face, threatening worms of encroaching panic wriggling in his mind.

'Fuckin' hell! Now I'm really in the shit!'

He went to the sideboard, lifted the gin bottle to his lips and took several swigs, gasping as the liquid burned its way down his throat.

Ella Peelson's breathing was an erratic snorting and spraying of blood.

Kent could only stare at her, telling himself over and over again, 'Now think! Think! What's best to do now? Think, dammit! What shall I do! The girl could come back at any moment!'

That realization tipped the balance and panic overwhelmed him. He rushed upstairs and made a frantic search for money. To his relief he found a satchel containing coins, and an assortment of coinage die-stamps.

He slung the satchel over his shoulder, exited the house by the rear door and, furtively dodging from shadow to shadow, made his escape.

TWENTY-SIX

Droitwich, Worcestershire
Friday, 29th February
Late afternoon

Dusk was fast approaching and the stallholders' lamps were shining as they chaffered and bargained with the shoppers, their mingled breaths cloudlike in the cold, still air. Yakob

Weiss's hands were deep in his capacious pockets, his fingers turning, fondling, expertly evaluating the coins within. As he finished totalling the amount he grunted with dissatisfaction. Business had been very slack at this market.

A poke-bonneted, shawl-swathed woman approached him. 'Can I have a word wi' you?'

'You can, Mistress. If it's a fine fur cap you want, then you've come to the right man, and I'll do you a very good deal.' He grinned ingratiatingly.

'Well, yes, I do want to buy a fur cap. But first, I want to know how much you'll give me for these?'

From her capacious shopping basket she produced three black pelts. 'They're cat furs, and they aren't got no mange nor nothing else wrong with 'um. Beautiful cats they was. I raised 'um from kittens, so I did, and it fair broke me heart when they died a week past. All at the same time, it was. I reckon me neighbour, who don't like me because she's jealous o' what a fine-looking man my husband is, I reckon she fed 'um poison. The evil cow!'

Weiss took the pelts and briefly handled them, then gave them back and told her, 'I'll tell you what I'll do, Mistress. You choose the cap you wants, and then we'll sort out the prices. I'm a very fair man, I am. As anybody who's ever had dealing with Yakob Weiss will tell you. So now . . .' He moved to run his hands across the dangling rows of fur caps on his display stand. 'Which one of these fine caps do you want? They're proof against the worst wind and snow, and hail and wet, that the Gods above can throw down upon us!'

Maud Harman came to stand beside him and closely examine the wares before shaking her head.

'I don't mean you no offence, Pedlar, but these sort o' furs aren't what I'm looking for. You see, like I told you afore, me husband is a very fine-looking man, and he likes to wear only the best of everything. Well, it's the anniversary of our wedding day in a couple of days, and I wants to buy him a real special-looking fur cap, so that everybody who sees him in it 'ull be real jealous of him for having it on his head. I've been saving up me bits o' money for ages, so I can afford to pay a good price for the sort o' cap I wants to buy him.'

Weiss audibly sucked his tongue, and stared speculatively at her for some moments before replying.

'Well, Mistress, I do have some very special caps which I keeps for my very special customers among the fine gentry and nobility. If your husband was wearing one o' them on his head, why then, all who saw him would swear on oath that he was a nobleman himself, so they would.'

'Show me them caps then,' Maud Harman demanded.

Weiss spread his hands wide and with a troubled expression answered. 'Them that I got with me have already been ordered by a Noble Lord, Mistress. I can show them to you, but I don't know what the Noble Lord would say if I was to sell you one of them. He wouldn't like to think that a common working man was wearing the exact same fur cap as him.'

The woman reacted indignantly. 'I'll have you know that my husband aren't no common working man! He's a Master Tradesman, so he is, and he's got dozens o' common working men at his beck and call. My husband is as great a man as any nobleman in this land, and fit to wear any fur cap that he wants to wear.'

'I'm sorry, Mistress! I'm sorry! I mean you no offence, I swear I don't. O' course you shall see these caps; and o' course your husband's as good as any Lord in this land.' Weiss volubly sought to soothe her as he delved into the small bag slung across his shoulders and pulled from it a fur cap which he flourished in front of her face.

Her eyes widened, and she exclaimed as if in awe. 'God strewth! That's a rare looking colour, aren't it? I've never seen a fur cap that colour afore. What sort o' beast does that come from?'

'One o' the rarest beasts in the world, Mistress. The fur that this cap is made of is from that same rare breed of beast that the King himself demands to have his own fur caps made from.' He paused, and then whispered reverently, 'This is the fur of a Royal Iceland Otterhound. If a man had one o' these on his head, he could stand under the fiercest waterfall in the world for a hundred years, and not a drop of water would ever pass through this cap to touch his head. A man could be closed into a solid block of ice for a hundred years, and his head would stay as warm as toast, because no cold could ever get through this fur. A man could walk for a hundred years in boots made of this fur, and never need a cobbler, it's so hard wearing.'

He reached out to take her hand and gently enclose it with the cap.

'There now, Missus. There's the proof that what I'm telling you is the God's honest truth. Feel the softness, feel the warmth, feel the comfort and luxury of it.'

'I can! I can!' Maud Harman gasped out and closed her eyes. 'I can feel all them things! I wants to buy this 'un for me husband.' She opened her eyes. 'What's the price?'

'Three guineas!' Weiss tested.

'What?' Maud Harman's horrified reaction. 'I daren't pay that. Me husband would break me neck for spending that much!'

'Well, that's what my noble gentlemen pays me for a wonderful cap such as this one,' Weiss gently explained as he took the cap back into his own safe-keeping. 'And they think it to be a bargain at that price.'

'Well that may be, but my husband has never paid more than five shillings for any fur cap he's ever wore!' Maud Harman argued.

'Then he's only ever wore rats skins and the like,' Weiss riposted firmly. 'The Royal Iceland Otterhound is worn by Kings and Emperors. Just imagine how splendid your fine husband would look in such a Royal fur cap as this one. He would feel like worshipping the ground you walk on for giving him such a magnificent proof of the love you bear for him.'

Maud Harman appeared to be holding back tears of distress. 'I just can't pay that much for it. I haven't got nowhere near three guineas.'

'Oh, my dear lady, I cannot bear to see your terrible disappointment,' Weiss murmured sympathetically. 'How much money do you have with you?'

She rummaged in her purse and choked out, 'A sovereign, a crown piece, and three pennies. But there's me cat furs as well. They'm worth something, aren't they?'

He shrugged regretfully. 'No more than a few pennies, dear lady.'

'Oh my God!' she wailed in despair. 'I aren't got no more money in me house either, so I can't buy the cap, can I! And I wanted to buy it with all me heart, so I did.'

Weiss held his hand up to signal for silence. 'Allow me to think for a moment or two.'

She stood gazing anxiously at him until he lowered his hand, and smiled encouragingly at her.

'It's Leap Year Day today, and it only comes once every four years, don't it? It's a very special day to me because it's the day I wed my beloved wife. What better way could I give thanks for this day, than to do a good turn for a good woman who loves her man, like my wife loves me.

'So, I'm ready to sacrifice my own profit on this cap. I'll sell it to you for two sovereigns and five shillings only. Now, you already have the sovereign and the crown piece. Is it possible that you might have a friend close hereabouts who will loan you the second sovereign?'

'Well, my sister-in-law lives just a mile or so along the road towards Bromsgrove. I'm sure she'll lend me the other sovereign and gladly, because she owes me a couple of big favours. I'll go and get it off her straight now.' Maud Harman began to hurry away.

After doing such poor business that day, Weiss wasn't prepared to let this prize fish slip his hook, and he shouted desperately, 'Wait, dear lady! Wait!'

She halted and turned to face him.

'I'm finished my trading here for the day,' he hastily explained. 'And I'm going back to Bromsgrove myself, so we can go together to your sister's house. I just need to take my goods to where my donkey is and then we can be on our way.'

Flanking the road to Bromsgrove, just over a mile from the outskirts of Droitwich Town, the sign of the Robin Hood Inn swung and creaked in the cold wind.

When the lights shining from the inn's windows came into view, Maud Harman told her companion, 'There's the Robin Hood, me sister-in-law's house is right behind it. We'll be there in no time at all.'

'And you will then become the lucky owner of one of the finest fur caps in all of England.' Weiss smiled. 'And your husband will be made a very happy and loving man.'

'He will indeed!' Maud Harman happily declared, and quickened her pace. 'I can't wait to get there!'

'No more can I, dear lady,' Weiss chuckled.

Maud Harman led the way up to the frontage of the inn, and told Weiss, 'You wait here, because I don't want me sister-in-law to know that I'm buying this present. I wants to keep it a secret until I give it to me husband. Here, hold this basket for me. I'll be back in two ticks.'

She handed him her laden basket and scurried round the side of the inn out of his view.

Weiss hummed contentedly to himself. 'There now, Yacob, this day's ended well after all.'

Within scant seconds Maud Harman was back, triumphantly brandishing a gold sovereign. 'There now, didn't I tell you that I'd get the money? Come into the light so we can see what we're doing.'

They stood bathed in the light shining from the window, from where the voices and laughter of the people within came clearly to their ears. Maud Harman carefully counted the two sovereigns and the five-shilling piece into Weiss's hand, and in return he un-strapped the small bag from the donkey's load, opened it and handed her the fur cap.

He re-strapped the bag on to the donkey and told her, 'Your man's going to love the cap, dear lady. And now I wish you goodbye.'

He started to lead the donkey away but had only taken a few paces when a voice shouted.

'Stand still, Pedlar! In the King's name! Stand still!'

Dark-shadowed figures loomed at each side of him.

'I'm Constable Potts, and I'm arresting you, Yakob Weiss, in the King's name. If you try to resist we shall use force.'

Deep in shock, Weiss could only blurt, 'I've done nothing wrong! I've done nothing!'

The second man snatched the donkey's lead rope from Weiss's hand, as Tom Potts gripped the pedlar's arm and pulled him back into the light from the window.

Tom produced a vellum document and showed it to the bemused man, and then requested, 'Please will you, Ma'am, and Master Bennett also take heed and bear witness to what I am now going to say? This is the warrant authorized by Reverend the Lord Aston, Justice of the Peace. It's for the arrest of Yakob Weiss on the grounds that he is defrauding His Majesty's Commissioners of the Treasury . . .'

'No! No! I'm doing no such thing! I'm an innocent man! An honest man!' Weiss shouted in continual protest.

Tom continued in a steady voice. 'Yakob Weiss holds the four pound' per annum Pedlar's License, which entails that he back-packs his goods to market and between markets. I, Thomas Potts, Constable of the Parish of Tardebigge, have solid proof and witnesses that in fact he uses a donkey to transport his goods, which means that he should be in possession of the eight pounds per annum Hawker's License for his use of beasts of burden in the pursuit of his business.

'Therefore, Yakob Weiss is currently defrauding His Majesty's Treasury of four sovereigns per annum. For which offence he can be imprisoned, or fined very heavily and his goods be confiscated.

'I am arresting you, Yakob Weiss, for this license offence, and I warn you that any attempt at resistance will be very severely dealt with.'

'And it's me that'll be doing the dealing!' Tom's companion, Alfie Bennett, brandished his cudgel in menacing threat.

'But you got no right to arrest me here,' Yakob Weiss argued desperately. 'You're only the Constable of Tardebigge Parish, and we're in the Droitwich Parish, so you've got no power of arrest here. And that bugger there aren't a constable, so he's breaking the law by robbing my donkey from me by force, and I shall lay charges against him for horse thieving.'

Tom smiled grimly. 'This warrant empowers me to arrest you in any parish of this kingdom, Master Weiss, and this Gentleman with me is obeying the law by giving me the assistance I demanded from him in the King's name.'

Tom turned his head to speak to Maud Harman. 'I regret, Ma'am, that I must regretfully confiscate the fur cap you have just purchased from this pedlar as material evidence. Also you will be called upon to testify at his trial, both as witness and victim, in that he has taken your money under false pretence.'

'What false pretence?' the pedlar shouted indignantly. 'I've sold her honest goods! That fur cap is genuine Otterhound!'

Hearing this admission, Tom experienced a moment of pure elation. Then he attended to the business of taking chains and manacles from his satchel and securing Weiss's hands behind his back.

'Now, Master Weiss, if you behave yourself I will carry you pillion back to Redditch, and save you the labour of walking there. Master Bennett, will you please fetch my horse, while I obtain this good lady's particulars.'

He drew Maud Harman aside and they whispered together so that Weiss could not overhear what passed between them.

When Tom was mounted with Weiss riding pillion, and the laden donkey secured to his saddle by a long leading rein, he bade Maud Harman and Alfred Bennett goodbye and rode away towards Redditch Town.

Alfred Bennett led a second horse from the rear of the inn, Maud Harman climbed on pillion behind him, and they made their own leisurely way homewards.

TWENTY-SEVEN

Redditch Town
Saturday, 1st March
Dawn

Tom Potts unlocked the cell door and shone his bulls-eye lantern on the snoring, blanket-covered prisoner within.

'Master Weiss,' Tom called loudly. 'It's time to rouse yourself and eat your breakfast.'

The man didn't stir, so Tom went into the cell, put the chunk of bread and cheese and pitcher of ale on the floor beside the stone pallet, and shook the sleeper's shoulder until he was roused to wakefulness.

'What did you have to wake me up for?' Weiss complained. 'I've only just got to sleep.'

'You are Jewish, are you not, Master Weiss? And Saturday is Shabbat, your Holy Day, is it not, Master Weiss? I thought that you might want to be at your prayers, so I've brought you an early breakfast. But I need to ask you about your customary diet. Do you eat only Kosher food, with all meats prepared by the melihah method, and no pork, hare, camel or hyrax meats whatsoever?'

Weiss pushed himself up to a sitting position and stared at Tom as if he could not believe what he was hearing.

Tom frowned impatiently. 'Come now, Master Weiss, you know well that it's mart day here and I have much to do and little enough time to do it in. So kindly give me your answer.'

Weiss answered with a question. 'Are you telling me that if I eat only Kosher food, you will have my meats prepared in the melihah way?'

'Of course I will.' Tom nodded.

The pedlar shook his head. 'I don't bother with the Kosher these days. I like a bit of bacon for my breakfast.'

'Well tomorrow you shall have bacon for breakfast. And while you're here you'll be eating the same good food as myself and my wife,' Tom assured him, then added, 'But I fear that when you're in Worcester Jail you'll be eating the same slops as the rest of the convicts. I have no influence there.'

Weiss gulped hard. 'Worcester Jail? Do you think that I'll be sent to prison then?'

Tom sighed. 'Regretfully, you undoubtedly will be imprisoned, Master Weiss. And I say regretfully because I don't believe that you're a wicked man. But our Parish Vicar, Reverend the Lord Aston, is the chief magistrate, and he's a very harsh judge. Personally I don't blame you for trying to avoid taxes. Everyone does their best to avoid them. Your misfortune was that you were informed upon.'

'By who?'

Tom shook his head. 'I can't tell you his name. It's more than my life's worth to divulge such secrets.'

Weiss broke into sobs. 'Oh God, what about my poor wife and my innocent children? What will become of them when I'm in the jail! Oh God!'

'I have to go now, Master Weiss. I'll come back later and talk with you.' Tom stepped back out of the cell and relocked the door, and the pedlar's sobs and wailing lamentations followed him as he went upstairs.

Amy was on her knees raking the overnight covering of ashes from the glowing embers of coal in the small living-room grate and adding woodchips and fresh coals, her rosy cheeks bulging as she blew hard upon the embers to rekindle the flames.

When Tom came into the room she sat back upon her heels and grumbled.

'What have you done to that man to make him caterwaul so? It's an awful racket! And another thing, how long are these bundles going to be cluttering up the place and making it look like a rubbish tip?' She pointed to several packs of the pedlar's goods.

'Not long,' Tom told her. 'I just need to examine all of them very closely and compare them to the descriptions I wrote down about the colourings and patterns of Elias Bradshaw's Otterhounds, the Earl's Bernese mountain dogs and Will Tyrwhitt's Newfoundland bitch.'

'Well get them shifted out of my way because I need to tidy up,' she ordered.

Tom did as he was told.

TWENTY-EIGHT

Redditch Town
Saturday, 1st March
Afternoon

When Tom Potts returned to the lock-up from his patrolling of the market, Amy was singing to herself in the alcove kitchen, but there was no sound coming from the pedlar's cell.

Tom opened the door's drop-flap and peered inside. Weiss was lying on the stone pallet, blankets pulled over his head. Tom closed the flap and went to join Amy, who proffered a platter of hot mutton stew.

'This is for the bloke in the cell, and there's fresh bread in the cupboard.'

Tom took the food to the cell and as he unlocked the door called, 'Wake up, Master Weiss, I've got your dinner here.'

The blankets moved and the pedlar's swarthy face appeared over their edges.

Tom held the platter towards him. 'You'd best eat this before it gets cold, Master Weiss.'

Weiss cast the blankets completely off and stood up to declare brokenly, 'As God is my judge, Constable Potts, I'm too sick in my heart to be able to eat anything. I can only think of one thing, and that is what is going to happen to my helpless wife and children when I am sent to the jail. It will be the death of them, Constable Potts!'

'I'm truly sorry to hear that, Master Weiss,' Tom replied gravely. 'But the Law is the Law, and you have broken it. So it must take its course, and you must go to jail.'

'But please, I beg you, Constable Potts, please to hear what I tell you. I am just like you are. I am an honest man, who keeps his word. A man of kind heart and charity. A dutiful and loving husband and father . . .' Tears brimmed and fell from Weiss's eyes and sobs tore from his throat as he went on, and on, and on expounding his multitudinous virtues.

At length, Tom lifted his hand and ordered grimly, 'Be silent, Master Weiss, and listen very carefully to what I say, because it may well be that I can help you to stay out of jail.'

The pedlar's eyes instantly narrowed, his sobbing voice hushed, his hands rubbed frantically together.

Tom lowered his voice conspiratorially. 'Now, Master Weiss, what I'm going to say will be strictly private between you and myself. And you will make reply only when I give you my permission.'

Weiss hissed sibilantly, nodding agreement and cocking his head to place his hairy ear in closer proximity to Tom's mouth.

'Otterhounds, Master Weiss? Bernese mountain? Newfoundland dogs? In your packages you have fur caps made from the pelts of all these breeds. Who sold these pelts to you? Tell me this, and I shall do my utmost to ensure that you will not go to jail.'

Tom allowed time for the other man to consider what he had heard, then told him, 'You may now speak, Master Weiss.'

Weiss's tongue snaked out to lick his lips, his entwined black-nailed fingers rubbed and kneaded furiously. He cleared his throat and whispered hoarsely, 'And the fine, Constable Potts? What about the fine? I am a very poor man, and a heavy fine would drive me and my sorrowful, innocent wife and children into the Poorhouse.'

Tom frowned and hardened his tone. 'If you go to jail, your wife and children will certainly be forced into the Poorhouse, will they not? And you may never come out of jail alive, Master Weiss. Very many prisoners die of the Gaol Fever.'

He let the implied threat sink fully home, then added in a softer tone. 'However, if you were to turn King's evidence, I'm sure that the magistrates would be prepared to take my word that you deserve another chance to buy a Hawker's License and trade legally in the future. You may answer now.'

Weiss groaned despairingly. 'These men will cut my throat if I give such evidence against them.'

'These men you refer to will not be able to cut your throat, because they will be in jail. And these same men could be the ones who informed on you. So, do you say yes or no to my offer? You may answer.'

Once again Weiss emitted a long, drawn-out groan of despair, but then nodded and whispered, 'I'll do it, Constable Potts. I'll turn King's evidence.'

'A wise decision, Master Weiss,' Tom congratulated. 'Now give me their names.'

'You won't break your word to me, will you, Constable?' Weiss begged tremulously. 'You'll not let them send me to jail?'

'No, I won't, Master Weiss. I swear that I shall keep my word to you,' Tom assured him.

'Then I believe you, Constable Potts. And the men you wants are Ezekiel Rimmer, Porky Hicks, and the one called Dummy.'

Half an hour later Tom was in Joseph Blackwell's study, relating what had happened between himself and Yakob Weiss.

As was customary Blackwell sat impassively in his chair, fingers steepled beneath his chin, and listened without comment until Tom had finished, but then snapped curtly.

'You have once again exceeded the bounds of your authority, Constable Potts, by promising this pedlar exoneration from the serious crime of defrauding the Treasury in return for his evidence against Rimmer. The Lord Aston will be greatly angered and I fear you will have good cause to regret your misconduct.'

Tom gasped in shocked disbelief at what he was hearing, and protested, 'But I told you that I was going to do that, and you had Lord Aston sign the arrest warrant for Weiss that very same day.'

Blackwell frowned and retorted, 'That same warrant was for defrauding the Treasury, and Weiss's guilt is beyond doubt. He must also answer to charges of receiving stolen property, and again for that offence his guilt is beyond doubt. He is an incorrigible villain, and deserves to be punished with the utmost severity that the Law provides for. Which I am confident will be demonstrated in the sentence my Lord Aston will pass upon him.'

Tom stood silent, as in his mental vision there rose the features of his own father. The man he had respected, loved and honoured above all others. 'I'll not dishonour your name, Father,' he vowed silently. 'Please God, Amy will understand, and forgive me for doing this.'

He fought to master his fear at what was to come, then swallowed hard, shook his head, and declared firmly, 'No, Master Blackwell! I'll not be a party to this! I gave Yakob Weiss my word that he would be shown the utmost leniency if he agreed to turn King's evidence against Rimmer and his confederates; and I told you what my intentions were, and you accepted everything I said without demur.

'Now you accuse me of misconduct, and threaten me with the consequences of Lord Aston's anger! Well, I'm prepared to tell Weiss what betrayal is in store for him, and for myself to suffer the consequences of Lord Aston's anger for doing so!'

Tom fixed his stare upon the wall behind Blackwell's head, and waited for the figurative fall of the axe.

'Do not be a fool and bring ruin down upon your own head, Master Potts, for the sake of keeping your word to scum like Yakob Weiss. Were your positions reversed he would not hesitate to tell any lie that would secure his profit and would happily bring you to the gallows by doing so. You know that to be a simple fact.' Blackwell gritted out his words.

Tom met the other man's challenging stare, and chose his own words carefully. 'I don't do this for Yakob Weiss, Sir. I do this for the son I hope to have one day. I want my son to have just cause to respect, love and honour me, as I respect, love and honour the memory of my own father.'

Blackwell's eyes gleamed, and he clapped his hands.

'Bravo, Thomas Potts! You have once again justified my faith in your honourable character. But, as I said previously, you have once again exceeded the bounds of your authority in the matter of Yakob Weiss. However, your transgression shall be overlooked on this occasion. The Earl will undoubtedly be most gratified to learn that the rogues who stole his precious dogs have been finally laid by the heels; and I am relieved that you will at last be free to concentrate on solving other more serious crimes as and when they occur.

'Lord Aston will be on the bench next Tuesday to hear the case against Rimmer and his confederates, and I am confident he will be happy to accept Weiss as King's evidence and remand Rimmer's gang to the Assizes.

'As for myself, I have the utmost confidence that you will ensure Yakob Weiss purchases a Hawker's License and no longer defies the Law by defrauding the Lords Commissioners of His Majesty's Treasury. I bid you a good day, Constable Potts.'

Tom mentally sagged with relief, and assured his employer, 'I'll make certain that Weiss buys a Hawker's License. I bid you good day, Sir.'

As Tom left the house the bell of St Stephen's Chapel began to toll. Because of the day and hour Tom knew that the tolling bell signified a death.

The bell fell silent for a brief interlude then tolled three separate strokes, and Tom grimaced in recognition that these chimes signified it was a child who had died. If the bell had tolled the nine strokes known as the 'Nine Tailors', it would have signified an adult man. For a woman it would have tolled six strokes. Now, after another pause the bell tolled four more strokes, to signify the dead child's age.

He saw his friend John Clayton coming out from the vicarage further down the Fish Hill and went to meet him.

'It's a sad day for some poor parents, John. Who are they?'

The curate's pleasantly ugly features displayed his sense of resignation to what was a very frequent occurrence, since throughout the parish more than a third of children died before reaching their fifth year.

'They live in the Old Laystall, Tom. The father is Ezekiel Rimmer the scavenger. The girl died last night, and the mother sent for me to go down there and pray for the passing of her child's soul.'

'Oh my God!' Tom exclaimed in shocked dismay. 'This is very unfortunate!'

'Of course,' Clayton agreed. 'But I have to bury a child from the Old Laystall virtually every week. May God forgive me, but when I witness the degradation and sufferings of the people who live in that cesspit, then the thought strikes me that the child who dies is perhaps more fortunate than those who survive.'

'That may be, John, but my concern is that I have to arrest

Ezekiel Rimmer this very day. It's going to be a hard-hearted thing to do, to arrest a man who has just lost his child.'

Clayton shrugged his broad shoulders and smiled grimly. 'While her child was dying, Mrs Rimmer was yet again sporting freshly inflicted black eyes, and Rimmer was out carousing with his cronies. So you may draw comfort in the knowledge that you'll be giving his wife and surviving children a most welcome respite from the ill-treatment they constantly receive from him.'

Tom could only nod in wry acceptance of the truth of that statement.

TWENTY-NINE

Warwick
Monday, 3rd March
Morning

Sitting bolt upright in her bed, Ella Peelson's fingernails dug deep into her palms, and she vented a strangled cry of pain as the elderly doctor unwrapped the final length of bandage from around her head and peeled away the thick pads of ointment-impregnated dressing which had stuck to her face.

The doctor then adjusted his pince-nez and carefully studied the grotesquely swollen, bruised features, the flattened spread of the smashed nose, the torn disfigured lips, the bulbously lumped eyes, and announced with a satisfied air, 'I do declare, Ma'am, that thanks to my treatments, your injuries are now on the mend.'

He held up his hands before her eyes and asked, 'How many fingers are extended? Which fingers on which hand?'

'Three. The forefinger and ring fingers on the left hand, and the little finger on the right hand.' Her voice was weak and her diction badly distorted by her tongue impacting against her jaggedly broken teeth, and the difficulty of moving her lips.

'And how many, and which fingers are extended now, Ma'am?'

'The second and little fingers on the right hand. Forefinger and thumb on the left hand.'

'Excellent, Ma'am! Excellent! Now tell me, how is your ability to swallow the liquid sustenance progressing? Does it pain you as much as it did?'

'No, it's becoming easier.'

'And the sleeping draughts, are they enabling you to enjoy some periods of unbroken sleep?'

'Yes. Some.'

'Excellent, Ma'am! Excellent! What I now propose is that you leave your injuries exposed to the atmosphere for the remainder of this day. I will return this evening and dress them afresh. I shall also bring you more sleeping draughts, and my new Sedative Elixir, which will serve to soothe the discomfort of your injuries, and also have a most salutary effect upon your total bodily and spiritual well-being.'

'Thank you so much, Doctor Rainforth, I'm very grateful for the wonderful care you're lavishing upon me. Might I impose upon your kind heart even more shamelessly, and request a further service of you, Doctor?' Ella Peelson lifted a sealed packet from her bedside table and proffered it to him. 'Would you be so kind as to have this delivered to this address in Birmingham by special courier this very day? I will of course recompense you for the expense.'

He took the packet from her. 'It will be my pleasure to do so, Ma'am. I know a most reliable man, and you may be assured that it will be delivered well before nightfall.

'Now, do not finger your wounds, and try to rest until my return. Also, I would advise you not to look at yourself in a mirror. It will only cause you unnecessary distress, because you will not be able to perceive, as my medical experience enables me to, the signs of the healing process which will in due course restore your features to their previous unblemished state.'

As soon as the doctor had left the house, Ella Peelson called her maid to her bedside.

'Milly, bring me a looking glass.'

The child frowned doubtfully. 'But I heard the doctor say that you warn't to look at yourself, Ma'am.'

'Snooping at the keyhole again, were you?' Ella Peelson gingerly shook her head. 'One of these days, my dear girl, you might be seeing or hearing something that you wouldn't wish to. Now bring me a looking glass.'

'But it'll only upset you, Ma'am.'

'Bring it this bloody instant!' Ella snapped irritably.

The child recognized the warning signs and hastened to obey.

Ella Peelson waited until Milly had left the room before she looked at her reflection.

She drew a sharp intake of breath, and cursed virulently. 'Bastards! Fuckin' bastards! I'll pay you back for this! You're going to wish that you'd never been born when I catch up with you!'

THIRTY

Redditch Town
Saturday, 8th March
Early evening

The rain clouds which had been gathering in the skies throughout the day finally began to shed their loads. The first spatterings quickly developed into a steady downpour which drove the late shoppers from the market place and forced the remaining sellers and assorted loafers and hangers-on to decamp and go their various ways.

Tom Potts was able to abandon his patrol and hurry back to the shelter of the lock-up to find Ritchie Bint waiting for him there.

'We're in luck, Tom.' Bint grinned with satisfaction. 'They'm all three of 'um going to be playing in tonight's money-match down in the Horse and Jockey skittle alley. Couldn't be better, could it! Only the one door which we'll be blocking, and barred windows. They'm bloody rats up a drainpipe!'

As always the prospect of confronting and arresting offenders against the Law evoked in Tom the conflicting tremors of excited anticipation and physical fear.

Amy was at her mother's house and would not return until morning, and loud snoring was sounding through the locked door of Yakob Weiss's unlit cell, so there was nothing to further detain Tom here.

He nodded. 'Just as you say, Ritchie, they're rats up a drainpipe, so let's go and root them out of it.'

He stared out through the open door. 'It looks as if the rain's stopped so let's get them in here before it starts again. I'm quite wet enough already.'

The Horse and Jockey tavern was situated on the eastern side of the fetid reeking Big Pool. Its skittle alley was housed in a long narrow wooden shed situated in a broad swath of enclosed pasturage a few yards from the rear of the tavern.

Tom and Ritchie Bint went around the outside of the tavern and, from a concealed vantage point, watched for a while the haphazard comings and goings of men, women, youths and girls through the door of the shed's lamplit interior.

The thumps and clattering of wooden balls and skittles punctuated by shouts of acclamation and howls of exasperation signified a contest in progress.

The clatter of wood ceased and there was a louder outburst of cheers and volleys of chagrined oaths followed by a sudden stream of bodies exiting the shed and ranging along its outside walls, the males unlacing their breeches flies and urinating, the females lifting their skirts and squatting to do the same.

Tom nudged his friend. 'There's Rimmer and Hicks. I can't see Dummy though.'

'He'll not be far away,' Ritchie Bint hissed. 'But we've got the two bastards that matter most. Shall we take 'um now?'

Even as he asked the question Rimmer and Hicks finished relieving themselves, and fastening their flies headed back to the door.

'It's best we wait and take them inside,' Tom judged. 'If they spot us coming they can bolt across the pasture and we could lose them in this darkness.'

They waited until everyone had returned through the door and then walked slowly across the intervening space. From inside the shed the voice of the Bellman, Harry Pratt, was bawling.

'My Lords, Ladies and Gentlemen, the next contest is a Western Alley Rules of nine turns apiece. It's a money-match challenge for three guineas, between the Red Lion Needle Pointers . . .'

A roar of cheering greeted this name.

'. . . And the Old Laystall Court Gentlemen – better known to all present as the Shit Court Shit Eaters.'

A cacophony of jeering hoots and whistles greeted this name followed immediately by Ezekiel Rimmer's furious bellowing.

'I knows all your fuckin' names and where you lives, and you'd best watch your backs, all of you!'

His voice was drowned out by an even louder cacophony of jeers.

Tom couldn't help but grin and say to Ritchie Bint, 'I've a notion that Rimmer's not going to have many people fighting to set him free when we arrest him.'

'Order! Order! Let's have some order!' Harry Pratt bellowed, and as the crowd hushed he announced, 'By the special request of both teams I shall referee this match. And my word will be the final judgement. Laystall Court won the toss for first go, so first thrower step up to the line.'

Tom Potts and Ritchie Bint stepped into the shed to be enveloped by clouds of tobacco smoke, rank-smelling body odour, stinking breaths reeking of alcohol, foodstuffs and rotting teeth and gums. Barrels of varied sizes stood on trestles against the wall directly opposite to the door and a tapster was hastily filling quart pots from them, which two serving girls were pushing through the dense crowd to deliver to the buyers.

Tom and Ritchie kept their staffs concealed and stood shielded by the crowd with their backs to the shadowed wall, studying the scene before them, noting that Dummy was now in company with his friends Rimmer and Hicks.

The actual skittle alley, lit by overhead lamps, ran lengthways down the middle of the shed, with the spectators flanked on either side. Bordered by foot-high planking the alley was three feet wide and twenty-four feet long. At its far end nine barrel-shaped, ten inch-high skittle pins were arranged in a symmetrical group. At its near end closest to the door was the line from where the players made their throws at the target.

Grinning confidently, Ezekiel Rimmer stepped up to the throwing line, tossing a wooden ball from hand to hand, while among the noisy spectators wagers were being agreed by the gamblers by spitting on hands and exchanging of loud slaps of palm against palm.

'Remember now, Master Rimmer, we're playing by Western Alley Rules, so your ball must bounce a single time only before hitting the pins,' Harry Pratt instructed. 'And my decision on any throw will be final.'

'Let's just get on wi' it, for fuck's sake!' Rimmer retorted. 'I'm going to show these Red Lion cunts how to win a match. Then

I'm going to have the greatest o' pleasure pissing their money up against the wall!'

'You fuckin' wish!' Harry Pratt exclaimed scornfully, then bellowed, 'My Lords, Ladies and Gentlemen, on the count of three, Master Ezekiel Rimmer will make the first throw of this match. Onnnnnne! Twooooo! Threeeee!'

Rimmer bent low to one side and hurled the ball with all his strength. It bounced once, smashed into the grouped pins, rebounding at tangents creating multiple collisions, thumped into the padded end wall and dropped to the ground.

There was a momentary hush, followed by multiple shouts from the crowd.

'He's dropped all the fuckin' pins!'

'Lucky bastard!'

'It's a bloody fluke, that's all!'

'It's a bloody good throw, that's what!'

Harry Pratt marched down to the fallen pins and set them in position once again. Then returned to the top of the alley and declared, 'Nine pins dropped, nine points scored. Take your second throw when you're ready, Master Rimmer.'

Rimmer's rotting teeth bared in a triumphant snarl at the three disgruntled faces of the Red Lion team, and he baited them as he tossed his second ball from hand to hand.

'Does you cunts want to double the stake? I'm more than willing to oblige if you've got the stomach for it.'

They scowled threateningly back at him, and he laughed, turned and hurled the ball.

All nine pins again went tumbling over. His supporters roared their applause and even some of those who had wagered against him couldn't help but grudgingly acknowledge his skill.

The crowd was now seething with excitement, and the spitting and slapping of palms were sounding throughout the entire shed.

Tom bent to whisper in his colleague's ear. 'If we try to take them in before the end of the match we'll have a riot on our hands. I think we must bide our time for a while.'

Ritchie grinned and rattled some coins in his hand. 'Too true, Tom. We'll wait 'til it's finished, and meanwhiles enjoy ourselves. Here, take me staff for a bit, I'm going to place a bet on the Shit Eaters winning this match, and then get us a drink. Shall I bet on 'um for you while I'm at it?'

Tom shook his head. 'If they were to win me some money, I'd feel awkward about arresting them.'

Ritchie laughed. 'I won't, because we'll be doing the parish a service taking these scumbags off the streets.'

'Har har har! That's shot you lot from the fuckin' Red Lion up your fuckin' arses, aren't it!' Ezekiel Rimmer bawled exultantly as Porky Hicks scored the winning strike with the final throw of the match.

'Let's be having the stake-money, Pratt.' Rimmer confronted Harry Pratt, who scowled contemptuously as he handed over the six sovereigns and six silver shillings stakes.

'Let me collect me winnings and then we'll take the buggers in and wipe the grins off their ugly mugs.' Ritchie Bint grinned happily. 'You should have put a bet on 'um, Tom, like I told you to.'

'I've no regrets.' Tom shrugged. 'But just be quick, Ritchie, because the sooner we make the arrests, the better. The way the Red Lion team are looking, we could have a full-scale riot on our hands if we leave the Shit Eaters here to crow over them for much longer.'

Ritchie looked across at the glowering Red Lion group and instantly replied, 'You're right! I'll collect me winnings tomorrow. Let's take 'um in now!'

Holding their staffs high so that all could see them, Tom and Ritchie pushed through the crowd and confronted their quarry.

'Ezekiel Rimmer, Porky Hicks, Dummy, you're all under arrest, in the King's name!' Tom shouted. 'For the offence of dog-stealing!'

The three men stared blankly at him in utter shock.

Voices in the crowd hushed, but they still elbowed and pushed against each other for better vantage points of this drama.

'Put your hands behind your backs!' Tom ordered.

Rimmer was the first to recover his senses. 'What the fuck's this about? Am you out of your fuckin' mind, you lanky bleeder?'

Instantly Ritchie Bint's crowned staff cracked down upon Rimmer's skull and he dropped to his knees, and toppled forwards on to his face.

'Get your hands behind your backs,' Ritchie Bint snarled, and the two remaining men hastily complied.

Then Ritchie changed his mind. 'No, stretch 'um out in front of you.'

Tom hastily manacled the proffered wrists, while Ritchie bent over and manacled the prostrate Rimmer's wrists and ankles, then ordered the other two men, 'Pick him up! You're going to carry the bugger to the lock-up, and I don't care how many times you drops him on the way. You'll still have to pick him up again and carry him! Now get moving, or I'll break your fuckin' skulls!'

To a chorus of jeers and cheers, Tom led the way out of the shed.

THIRTY-ONE

Birmingham City
Sunday, 9th March
Morning

Archibald Ainsley reined in his horse in front of the closed theatre, and scanned the playbills which plastered its façade, paying close attention to the varying dates of presentation, and the names of the players. Then he smiled with satisfaction and kneed the horse onwards. At the stage door at the side of the building, he dismounted, tethered his mount to a wall ring, rearranged his flamboyant cravat, tilted his wide-brimmed hat at a dashing angle and entered the building, calling out, 'Doorman, where are you, Sir?'

The bent-bodied old doorman came scurrying, shouting hoarsely, 'You shouldn't be in here! Nobody's allowed in here wi'out permission. What's you want? You'd best have good reason for coming in like this, or you'll be paying a sore price for it!'

Ainsley stared haughtily down at the old man's heavily stubbled, small-pox pitted face, and produced a large silk handkerchief which he wafted through the air and then held to his nose.

'Gad, Sir, you stink like a polecat! Now hold your insolent tongue, and take me to Charles Channing.'

For brief seconds the old man seemed inclined to stand his ground, and Ainsley lowered his handkerchief, glowered menacingly and warned, 'Do not delay me an instant more, or I guarantee that within the hour you will no longer be employed here. Now lead on, Sir!'

The doorman's toothless gums bared in a defiant snarl, but he turned and shuffled into the shadows, shouting hoarsely, 'Master Channin', there's a bloke wanting to see you. Master Channin'? Where be you?'

Ainsley followed the other man along dark winding corridors and up and down flights of rickety stairs, their passage punctuated by the doorman's shouts, until finally another shout answered.

'I'm here, Tonky, I'm here! Moderate your noise, there's a good fellow! You're making my head positively ring!'

A pool of lamplight glowed from a doorway and by its light Ainsley could see a rotund, bald-headed figure swathed in a long dressing gown.

'Good morning my old friend,' he greeted. 'Archie Ainsley, at your service, Sir.'

'Archie Ainsley! Well by God, as I live and breathe, you are the very last person I was expecting to see.'

'Then I trust that I am a shaft of most welcome sunshine come to lighten your sombre day.'

'Indeed you are, my dear old friend. Come in! Come in!'

Ainsley shoved the doorman aside and embraced Channing.

As the pair went into the sparsely furnished, damp-smelling room, Ainsley smiled, produced a silver flask from his pocket and proffered it to the other man.

'Here, my old friend, I've brought you a small gift. It's the very finest *uisge beatha* that money can buy. I'm confident it will be greatly to your discerning taste.'

The fat man immediately unscrewed the flask cap and took a gulp of its contents, then gasped breathily.

'Ahhh! It's nectar, Archie. Heavenly nectar!'

'No more than you deserve, Channy!'

They both perched gingerly on rickety wooden chairs, and Ainsley came straight to the point.

'I'm currently circuiting in Warwickshire and Worcestershire, doing a spot of barn-storming with a small cast of virtual amateurs that I've taken under my wing. Tonight I've arranged to stage "The Honest Thieves".'

'Terry Knight's farce in two acts. I staged it here not a fortnight since,' Channing put in.

'Did you indeed!' Ainsley exclaimed in mock astonishment. 'Then by Gad, I do believe that you may be able to help me. My damned fool of a wardrobe man has mislaid the Nolly Careless parade uniform.

'Well, normally of course while barn-storming to audiences of pig-ignorant, unlettered yokels I wouldn't give a damn about the niceties of production and would let Nolly Careless play in plain civilian rig. But for the next four nights, by special invitation, we are performing for Sir Francis Godericke and his family and friends at Studley Castle. And I have it on good authority that the noble gentleman regards himself as an expert on all things theatrical, and is a stickler for totally exact presentations of any work. I also have it on very good authority that the noble gentleman is particularly fond of and very familiar with Terry Knight's farces. So, I'm prepared to pay a generous rental for the loan of the Careless uniform, or even to buy it outright from you.'

He paused to allow his friend to consider what he had explained.

Channing took another extended pull at the silver flask, then belched and replied.

'This may be your lucky day, my friend, since I'm prepared to sell it to you. But whether it will suit your purpose is dependent on the size and build of your player.'

'He's about two yards high and strongly built.'

'Well, my player is somewhat shorter, but he's strongly built. So if your fellow wears high boots or gaiters when dressed in it the uniform should fit well enough to pass muster.'

'Excellent!' Ainsley exclaimed, and the pair shook hands in mutual satisfaction.

An hour later Ainsley called at the large lodging house on the outskirts of the city where Sylvan Kent was staying and had his man fetched to the door.

Kent frowned in surprise when he saw his caller. 'What the fuck do you want, Ainsley? What in Hell's name brings you here?'

'By Gad, Kent! I see that your manners haven't improved since our last meeting.' Ainsley grinned. 'But that's no matter, because when you find why I'm here, you'll realize that you must dance to my tune. Here, read this. It's from your cousin, Courtney.' He handed the other man a note.

As he scanned its contents Sylvan Kent's face reddened in anger.

Ainsley's grin broadened as he saw Kent's reaction, and he jeered. 'Going to throw one of your temper tantrums, are you? Well nothing would give me more satisfaction, my bucko! I'm not one of the weak little women that you take such pleasure in knocking about, am I? You and I both know very well that I can quite easily give you a thrashing, and thoroughly enjoy doing so.'

Ainsley turned away and calmly took several parcels from his large saddlebags.

'Here, you can carry these yourself, my bucko. They contain your uniform. Courtney intends for you to meet Phoebe Creswell tomorrow.'

THIRTY-TWO

Beoley Parish
Monday, 10th March
Midday

The skies were clear and the wind blew strongly. Harry Pratt was marching along the narrow straight Roman road known as the Icknield Street when the shouts came from behind him.

'You there! Bellman! Hold hard! God dammit, are you deaf?'

Pratt halted and turned to face the questioner, then conditioned by his long years as a soldier instinctively stiffened to attention, saluted smartly, and shouted back, 'Sorry, Sir, this wind is making it hard to hear anything.'

The mounted military man came at a canter, and reined in some feet distant. A voluminous grey riding cloak hid most of his uniform, but Pratt instantly identified the bugle badge and the green cockade topping the front of the black-bodied, gold-banded, bell-topped shako.

'Officer of the Light Company of a Line Regiment, this 'un.' He saluted again and asked respectfully, 'How can I be of service to you, Sir?'

The horseman frowned. 'You salute as if you're a soldier?'

'That's it, Sir. Twenty-five years' service, Sir. Went to pension as Colour Sergeant, Sir.'

'I see.' The officer nodded brusquely. 'Now can you direct me to Beoley Village, and the house of the family Creswell?'

'Certainly, Sir. You goes straight on down this road until you comes to the crossroads. Take the left-hand turn and go up and over the hill that's topped by the church. From the top o' the hill you'll see the village directly beneath you.' He continued to give directions for reaching the Creswell house.

When Pratt had finished speaking, the horseman made no acknowledgement and spurred his horse on ahead.

'Now why's an officer wanting to go to the Creswell place? Sour-faced bastard that he is!' Pratt mused curiously, and was suddenly struck by a thought. 'Is it anything to do wi' that letter Phoebe Creswell asked me to post for her, I wonder?'

Phoebe Creswell was sitting gazing out of the window of her father's bedroom when she saw the mounted officer coming towards the house.

'Oh my goodness!' she gasped, and clutched both hands to her mouth.

Sitting at the bedside of the comatose George Creswell, Walter Courtney questioned, 'What is it, my dear?'

Phoebe's heart was pounding hard and her breathing so rapid that she could only choke out, 'It's a soldier! He's on the road. He's coming this way!'

Courtney came to the window and exclaimed, 'Now God be praised! It's himself! It's Christophe come to visit you, my dear!' He smiled down at her and patted her shoulder reassuringly. 'I'll go downstairs and greet him, my dear, and allow you time to compose yourself, and so be completely at ease when you meet him.'

'But how can I be at ease?' Her sallow face was haggard and tears were glistening in her eyes as she wailed, 'He looks so handsome and splendid, and I'm so dowdy and ugly. He'll turn on his heel and leave as soon as he catches sight of me. I know he will!'

Courtney frowned sternly, and waggled his forefinger reprovingly at her.

'This is nonsense! I know Christophe as well as if he were my own son, and I can state with absolute certainty that he will find you as sweet-faced and charming as I do. Now calm yourself, my dear, and listen carefully.' Courtney lowered his voice conspiratorially as he smilingly stroked her shoulder. 'These are the first moments of the first day of the life that, within a very short span of time, you will most certainly be spending as the beloved wife of Major Christophe de Langlois.'

The front door bell jangled, and Phoebe drew a long, shuddering intake of breath.

Courtney chuckled fondly. 'I'm going to greet my friend. Take all the time you need to compose yourself, my dear Phoebe, and then come downstairs and meet your husband-to-be.'

Night had long fallen when Phoebe Creswell and Pammy Mallot stood in the roadway outside the house calling their goodbyes to the gig and its accompanying horseman disappearing into the chill windy darkness.

Even after that disappearance Phoebe Creswell still lingered there, until Pammy Mallot urged her, 'Come on, my wench, we needs to get back inside a bit sharpish, else we'll be catching our deaths o' cold if we stays out here any longer.'

She took Phoebe's arm and led her back into the drawing room of the house.

'Now you set yourself down by the fire, my wench, and warm your bones.'

'Oh, Pammy, I can't believe this is happening to me. Isn't he the most handsome, most charming gentleman you've ever met in your life?' Phoebe was glowing with happiness. 'Did you see him whispering to me as we went outside?'

'O' course I did!' Pammy Mallot smiled fondly. 'What did he say?'

Phoebe blushed and told her excitedly, 'He said that he could hardly bear to part with me so soon after we'd met, and that he'd be impatiently counting the minutes until he was with me again tomorrow.' She buried her face in her hands and giggled excitedly like a child. 'I can't believe that this is happening to me, Pammy. I'm feared that I'm asleep and that at any moment I shall wake up and discover it has all been a dream!'

'Oh no, it aren't any dream.' The older woman nipped Phoebe's cheek between her finger and thumb. 'Did you feel that?'

'Yes, of course.'

'Well that proves that you'm awake and this is no dream, don't it?'

'Oh yes!' Phoebe exclaimed fervently. 'And I shall be counting the very seconds until he returns.'

One of the bells on the board beside the door began to ring, and Pammy Mallot tutted resentfully. 'I see he's woke up! I hope he aren't started bloody spewing and shitting himself again. I had enough of that to last me for a lifetime over the weekend.'

Phoebe frowned worriedly. 'I'll come up and help you with him, Pammy.'

'No you will not, my pet!' the older woman stated firmly. 'You'll not have this lovely day spoiled by him. You'll stay here, and keep your mind on your intended. And I won't have any argufying about that!'

As the gig horse slowly laboured up the steep incline of the Beoley Mount, Walter Courtney heartily congratulated Sylvan Kent.

'Well done, Cousin! She is well and truly entranced by the glitter of your military garb! There's nothing more romantic than the scarlet coat of a dashing warrior to win a maiden's heart. That's why I insisted on you wearing a uniform this time. The little country mouse has never before met such a dashing hero in all her dull life.'

Kent had been mentally contrasting Phoebe Creswell's physical charms with those of Ella Peelson, much to the detriment of the former, and he snarled in reply.

'Well I'm not in the least entranced by the prospect of shagging her! She's ugly, has no tits and her breath stinks!'

'Then you must feed her with some very strong cachous before you consummate the match,' Courtney chuckled.

'What about her Pa? What's your plan for him?' Kent queried.

'It's progressing in a most satisfactory manner, and that's all you need to know for the present.'

'And what about Miss Stinking-Breath, No-Tits?'

'I shall decide upon the date of her demise as and when it suits me, Cousin.'

'Well, that date had better come sooner rather than later. Because I'm not prepared to spend months sharing her bed and being poisoned by her breath, just for your benefit. I can assure you on that fact! And I'll be wanting my full share of the profits, have no doubt on that score. You can pay that cunt, Ainsley, out of your own cut. I'll not stand for him having anything from mine.' Kent grunted sourly.

Courtney stayed silent, but in his mind warned, 'If you try my patience too far, Cousin, you may well be accompanying your bride on her journey, when the time comes for her departure from this life.'

THIRTY-THREE

Redditch Town
Wednesday, 12th March
Afternoon

The front door bell of Bromley's Stationery Emporium for All Articles of Stationery, Rare and Antique Books and New Literature signaled the entry of a burly, well-dressed man, who had a long scar running from temple to chin on the left side of his face.

Charles Bromley rose from his low stool at the side of the counter and eagerly enquired, 'How can I be of service, Sir?'

'Are you Charles Bromley, Sir?'

'I am, Sir.'

'I'm a debt-collector acting on behalf of the *Birmingham Aris Gazette*.' The man took a folded newspaper from his pocket, opened it out, held it close to Bromley's eyes and tapped his forefinger on one of the advertisements. 'This notice ran for nine editions and only the payment for the first printing of this notice has been received by the proprietors of this newspaper. I'm employed by those same proprietors to recover the debt you owe for the succeeding eight printings.'

Bromley bent forward and scanned the advertisement. His jaw dropped in shock and he vociferously protested.

'This is no debt of mine! I personally haven't placed this or any similar notices! I'm merely acting as a collection point for the letters that are addressed to this XYZ, and I've no knowledge of who sends the letters, or for what purpose they send them.

What's more I've never subscribed to the *Aris Gazette* anyway, so the only time I sight it is when such a subscriber might give me a lend of it.'

'Who collects the letters from you?' the other man demanded.

'A gentleman, who I can assure you is not a military man.'

'What's this gentleman's name, and where can I find him?' The scar-faced man scowled threateningly. 'And if you've any letters you're still holding for him, then you'd best hand them over to me!'

'Hold your tongue, Bromley! Don't you dare give him any answer!'

The screeched command brought both men's heads jerking round towards the squat, fat, black-clad figure standing in the doorway which led into the rear room.

'Who might you be?' the scar-faced man questioned.

'I'm the betrothed wife-to-be of Master Bromley; and I've been listening to everything that's been said.' Gertrude Potts stepped fully into the shop and brandished her walking stick at him. 'How dare you come in here and order Master Bromley to give you a gentleman's private property? How dare you try and force him to break the Law?'

'Because I'm acting within the Law,' the man grunted sourly. 'And you'd best keep your big snout out of my business if you knows what's good for you.'

'And you'd best apologize to me this instant for that insult, if you know what's good for you, you ruffian! I'm not like this timid milksop!' Gertrude Potts pointed her cane to indicate the blanched-with-fright features of Charles Bromley. 'My son is the Head Constable of this Parish, and also a personal and trusted friend of Reverend, the Lord Aston, the Chief Magistrate of this parish and Justice of the Peace for this County.'

The doorbell tinkled and a woman ushering three small children entered the shop.

The scar-faced man grinned mockingly as he bowed to Gertrude Potts. 'I fear I must reluctantly take temporary leave of you, Ma'am. It's been a great pleasure to meet you.'

He then bowed to Charles Bromley. 'And we shall most definitely be resuming our interesting conversation in the very near future, Master Bromley. Good day to you both.'

The man sauntered casually out of the shop and Gertrude Potts glared and hissed at Charles Bromley. 'When you've finished attending to this lady, Bromley, you and I will also be resuming a most interesting conversation. Is that understood?'

Bromley gulped hard and reluctantly nodded assent.

THIRTY-FOUR

Feckenham Village
Wednesday, 12th March
Evening

In the private parlour of the Old Black Boy, Horace Mackay and his host Walter Courtney had enjoyed the best meal that the tavern's kitchen could provide, and now were savouring the pleasures of pipes of fragrant Turkish tobacco, and their fourth bottle of Madeira wine.

Because of the enforced frugalities of living on a lowly curate's stipend, Horace Mackay only enjoyed such munificence when he dined with Courtney, and he was continually voicing his appreciation and fervent thanks to his host, and reiterating each time, 'You have become such a dear friend to me, Geraint. I just wish with all my heart that I could be of some service to you. You're always so kind and generous towards me.'

Each time Courtney smilingly responded, 'Your companionship is more than enough reward for any hospitality or small acts of kindness I may render towards you, my dear friend. Be assured that when you're enjoying the very advantageous Benefice I have in mind for you, I intend to inflict myself upon your own hospitality very frequently indeed.'

As he refilled his guest's empty glass he added casually, 'I've just recalled that there is a small favour you might do for me.'

'Name it, and count it as done,' Mackay slurred.

'His Grace, my Lord Archbishop, has had conveyed to me a Special License for Marriage Certificate for an officer in the East India Company Army. The officer is known to me, and is a very fine young man indeed. His future wife is fortunate to be entering into matrimony with such a gallant and honourable fellow. I wonder if perhaps you might perform the ceremony in your church? I will act as one of the witnesses.'

'I'll be delighted to do so, Geraint. When do you wish me to perform the ceremony?'

'Oh, I'm not absolutely sure at present, but apparently he must shortly return to India to take up a most important position there—'

There came a knock at the door and the innkeeper's voice requesting, 'Sorry to disturb, your Reverences, but can I have a private word wi' you please, Reverend Winward?'

'Of course, Master Blake,' Courtney consented, smiling, and told his companion, 'I'll be as quick as possible, Horace. I beg you to empty this particularly fine bottle during my absence because upon my return there will be others of its ilk to follow.'

When Courtney went into the passage, closing the parlour door behind him, the innkeeper whispered, 'There's a bloke waiting outside in the back yard, who says his name is Bromley, and he needs to spake wi' you urgent-like. I told him you wasn't to be disturbed but he said it was a matter o' life or death, and he must spake wi' you this very minute.' Blake nodded his head towards the front rooms of the inn where the babble of voices and laughter resounded. 'If you want, Reverend, I'll get a couple o' the lads to run the bugger off out of the village, and see to it that he don't come back again to annoy you.'

'Thank you for your care of my welfare, Master Blake. Your constant acts of kindness toward me warms my very heart and soul.' Courtney's smile was avuncular. 'But there's no need for any concern. The poor fellow is known to me, and is frequently in need of my counsel. While I talk with him, could you please uncork another couple of bottles of your very fine Madeira and take them into the parlour?'

'I certainly can, Reverend.' Blake bustled away, and Courtney went into the rear yard and greeted his visitor with a stern frown.

'What brings you here, Master Bromley, despite my specific request that our personal intercourse must be solely confined to your Redditch premises? I am extremely displeased that you have seen fit to so blatantly disregard my express wishes.'

Sweating heavily despite the chill of the air, Charles Bromley quailed inwardly as he regarded the angry glare of the bulky man before him. But then another angry, glaring face filled his mental vision, and he stammered plaintively, 'I beg you to forgive me,

Reverend Winward! But I've been forced to come here by my wife-to-be! In all truth, I feel trapped between the Devil and the deep blue sea, and I hope and pray that the "Deep Blue Sea" will prove to be the more merciful to me.'

Courtney snorted contemptuously. 'I take it that I am that "Deep Blue Sea"? So tell me what is the problem? And keep your voice low so that you are not to be overheard.'

Bromley hurriedly related his account of the Debt Collector's visit, and finished with impassioned assurances.

'I was ready to pay the money he was demanding myself, but Mrs Potts, that's the lady I'm betrothed to, wouldn't let me. She said that I must come directly here to speak with you, and to receive your instructions on what I'm to do about this Debt Collector. I swear to you, Reverend Sir, as God is my Judge, I haven't told him your name, or breathed a word about you being in lodging here.'

Bromley's breathy voice stilled and he waited fearfully for several seconds. Then he gasped with relief as the man before him metamorphosed back into the genially smiling, kindly spoken Reverend Winward of previous experience.

''Pon my soul, Master Bromley, I am greatly indebted for this present service you have done me. May I add how gratified I am that my trust in your honour and probity has not been misplaced. That honour and probity shall be rewarded this very instant.'

Coins clinked as they were transferred from Courtney's hand to Bromley's.

'Oh, thank you, Sir! Thank you!' Bromley stammered gratefully.

'Now listen carefully, Master Bromley. This Debt Collector is plainly in error concerning the agreement I made with the proprietors of the *Aris Gazette*. However that error can be easily rectified. I ask of you only one thing, and that is that you will continue to exercise the utmost discretion concerning our own arrangement.'

'Of course I will, Sir.'

'Good man!' Courtney approbated. 'Oh, by the way, what does this fellow look like, so that I may recognize him if I should by chance meet up with him. Because in that event I shall most sternly advise him that he should conduct himself in a more polite manner.'

He listened impassively to Bromley's description. Then smiled and congratulated the man.

'You have a very observant eye, Master Bromley.'

When they finally parted and Bromley hurried away, Walter

Courtney's genial smile of farewell metamorphosed into an angry scowl.

'Long scar on the left side of his face. That fits Billy Peelson!'

He went back inside the inn and upstairs to his room where he wrote a brief note and sealed it. Then he returned downstairs and spoke with the landlord who immediately assured him, 'I'll send my boy wi' it straight away, your Reverend.'

'Thank you, Master Blake.' Courtney smiled and handed over the note together with three pennies. 'The boy must have these for his trouble.'

'That's too much, Reverend. A penny will be more than enough for him,' Blake objected.

'Well, let me err on the side of generosity this once, Master Blake. Please give him the three pence.'

'I will, Reverend, and God bless you for your kindness to all of us, is what I say.'

THIRTY-FIVE

Feckenham Village
Thursday, 13th March
Morning

Walter Courtney and Horace Mackay had come to sit in the church vestry to discuss Mackay's glittering prospects for career advancement.

'A thought occurred to me as I was at prayer this morning, Horace, which I would like to confide to you. I know that what I now tell you will go no further,' Courtney began.

'You honour me by sharing such confidences with me, Geraint.' Mackay's eyes shone with hero-worship. 'And I would suffer all the agonies of Hell, and still not divulge one single word of what you tell me.'

'I know you would, my dear friend.' Courtney smiled benevolently, and paused meaningfully before continuing. 'Well now, the thought that occurred to me was that although rectorship of a Parish can be lucrative, time spent as an Archdeacon in a Diocese would stand you in much greater stead, as regards your future high-advancement.

'His Grace has often told me of his strong belief that such experience gained in the practicalities of administering a Diocese better prepares a man for the highest offices in the service of the Church. I think that I might be able to arrange for you to serve in that capacity in a suitable Diocese within our province of Canterbury, if you so wished it.'

Mackay drew a sharp breath, and Courtney took full note of the instant gleam of excitement in his companion's eyes.

He was about to continue speaking when the slamming of the outer door and the hurried thumping of boots upon the flagged floor of the nave was followed by a pounding upon the vestry door, and a voice calling, 'Are you there, Reverend Winward? It's Archibald Ainsley! I need to speak with you most urgently about a tragedy that has befallen one of my poor old people.'

Courtney instantly shouted, 'Calm yourself, Master Ainsley. I will join you in a moment!'

He shrugged expressively, and told his companion with a smile of resignation, 'Christian charity is a duty which at times I can't help but feel makes undue demands upon me. However, that same duty now compels me to deal with whatever is disturbing Master Ainsley so grievously. But our present discussion will be continued when possible, I do assure you. Until then I must love you and leave you, my friend.'

As he opened and passed through the vestry door, Courtney saw the worried expression on Ainsley's face, and nodded towards the outer door.

Out in the rain-drizzled churchyard Courtney led his companion towards the lych-gate and when they were beneath its arched roof snapped curtly, 'It seems that Billy Peelson was making enquiries about XYZ at Bromley's yesterday. He was claiming to be a Debt Collector, and he put the shits up Bromley, I can tell you.'

'Sweet fuckin' Jesus!' Ainsley exclaimed in disgust. 'So Bromley's put him on to us!'

Courtney shook his head. 'No, Bromley swears that he's not told anything to anyone, and I believe him.'

'Then what happens now?' Ainsley questioned anxiously.

'Don't fret yourself, Archie.' Courtney smiled grimly. 'Billy Peelson has done us a great favour. The only way he could have got on to us, is for the Irish bitch to have told him about the notice in the *Aris Gazette*. So there's a chance that he and her are staying together at the house in Bradley Green. If that's the case we can kill two birds with one stone this very night.'

Ainsley's relief was palpable as he declared fervently, 'I never even thought of that aspect of it. You're a bloody wonder, Walter! I do believe that you possess true genius!'

Courtney shrugged and demurred. 'No, I'm not a genius. But circumstances have this tiresome habit of continuously changing, Archie; and I possess the necessary flexibility of mind to instantly adapt my order of battle to deal with these changing circumstances.

'Firstly I want you now to go directly to Bradley Green and check the house. When you're satisfied that they're there, then come to the Black Boy and ask for me.'

Ainsley hurried away, and Courtney frowned as he considered the implications of this latest development. He now accepted it was almost a certainty that Ella Peelson had put her late husband's gang on to his and Kent's trail.

'Sylvan must have fucked up the parting from her!' A murderous lust coursed through him. 'When the time comes, Cousin Sylvan, I'm going to relish sending you back to your fuckin' Maker.'

THIRTY-SIX

Bradley Green
Friday, 14th March
Earliest morning

Beneath the cloud-shrouded skies the only visible light was the faint candle-glow from a ground-floor window of the house. Concealed by the surrounding hedgerow, shrouded in their travelling cloaks, Courtney and Ainsley had been watching the building for several hours, stoically enduring the cold air and the frequent bursts of wind-driven rain.

'I'm sure that the bastard's on his own,' Courtney hissed in chagrin. 'He's the only face we've spotted, and that's the only room that's shown a light. If the Irish bitch and her maid or anyone else were in the house, we'd have seen lights in other rooms by now.'

'Then let's do the business. I can shoot though the glass and put a ball in his skull,' Ainsley urged impatiently. 'If we stay here much longer I'll be catching my own death from wet and cold.'

'You're talking like a fool, Archie!' Courtney reprimanded sharply. 'We need to find out where the bitch is, and if there are others who're in the know about us. Now listen carefully. I'll draw him out of the house and you'll club him down. Then we secure him and ask him a few questions.'

Billy Peelson was shocked out of his drunken stupor when the casement rattled under sharp impacts and the voice screamed frantically, 'Sir! Sir! Can you help me? Please help me! Help me!'

Peelson lurched to his feet and came towards the window.

'Please help me, Sir! My carriage overturned and my wife is trapped beneath it. Help me! Please! She could be dying, Sir. Help me, I beg of you!'

Peelson squinted through the latticed window panes at the bulky black shape screaming out for help, and shouted back. 'Come to the front door!'

'I will, Sir, but please help me! I beg of you! My wife is trapped beneath the carriage. She could be dying. Help me, Sir. Help me!'

Peelson lumbered unsteadily from the room and along the passage. He fumbled with the bolts and tugged the door open. The black shape was some yards distant from the door, still screaming for help.

Peelson stepped outside, took three paces forward, and the lead weighted bludgeon smashed into the side of his head, and crumpled him to the ground.

'Leave him to me, Archie! Get inside and search the house,' Courtney ordered as he came to the side of the fallen man.

Ainsley produced a pair of pistols from beneath his cloak, cocked them and went inside.

When he returned to report that the house was empty, and virtually all the furniture dust-sheeted, he frowned in surprise to find his friend standing staring down at the motionless Billy Peelson.

'What's up, Walter?'

'The bastard's dying on us, Archie. You hit him too hard. His skull's crushed right in.'

'But I only used my normal force! He must have a bloody thin skull!' Ainsley protested, and then questioned anxiously, 'What do we do now?'

'Hush, Archie, and allow me to ponder the situation.' Courtney was very calm, and after a few moments instructed quietly, 'He's still wearing his outdoor clothes, so go to the stable, saddle his horse and bring it out here. It'll stay near him without a doubt. Then we shall close that front door and quietly leave. When he's found, it'll be believed that he was thrown from his horse, and smashed his head on the ground.'

Courtney stretched out his hand to pat the other man's shoulder. 'We've nothing to worry about, Archie. Should anyone happen to enquire about our late whereabouts tonight, we've been carrying out highly confidential charitable work together.'

Ainsley stared at Courtney with an expression bordering on awe, and declared passionately, 'I've said it before, Walter, and I'll say it again. You're a bloody genius!'

When everything had been arranged to Courtney's satisfaction, Ainsley asked him, 'What now, Walter?'

Courtney shook his head and sighed regretfully. 'It looks as if my cousin made a mess of the parting from the Irish bitch. So there's only one choice left to us, Archie. You'll have to deal with her as soon as possible.'

'Me? Deal with her?' Ainsley frowned doubtfully. 'What do you mean by that, exactly?'

'Exactly what I say! We can't risk leaving her alive,' Courtney rejoined harshly. 'You're to go back to Warwick, and close her mouth for good! And to make sure that there's nothing in her house that bears Bromley's address, or any mention of Christophe de Langlois or the Reverend Geraint Winward, you'll have to burn the place down. That way you'll cover your tracks, and she'll be thought to be just another tragic victim of a fire.'

Ainsley shook his head. 'I don't think that I like the sound of this, Walter. It's your fuckin' cousin's mess, and you want me to risk my neck to clear it up.

'In fact, I don't relish this plan one little bit. Because it's me who takes all the risk, and after the wedding to the Creswell woman it'll be that bastard Kent who'll doubtless be getting a much larger share of the gravy than I shall!'

Courtney's manner changed abruptly, and now his smile was

avuncular. 'I haven't finished telling you what's in my mind, my old friend. Very soon after their wedding, Major Christophe de Langlois and his bride will be leaving for India, never to return. I shall be remaining in this area to wrap up all the financial and property affairs of the happy couple as quickly as possible. So of course you'll receive your rightful share of the profits.'

'And then what?' Ainsley demanded.

'I visualize you as Joseph Manners Esq. A Gentleman of independent means. Who has recently returned from Canada, where you were a very successful merchant. And as soon as you are installed in a suitable venue, I visualize us embarking upon our next venture.'

Ainsley grimaced unhappily. 'I'm not sure that I want to work with your cousin again, Walter.'

Courtney's avuncular smile didn't falter. 'Haven't I already told you, Archie, that soon after their wedding, my cousin Sylvan and his new bride are going to India.' He paused, then added with emphasis, 'Never to return!'

As the full import of the emphasis dawned on Ainsley, he grinned, tapped the side of his nose with his forefinger and breathed admiringly. 'By God, Walter, I'll take good care never to get on the wrong side of you!'

THIRTY-SEVEN

Bradley Green
Friday, 14th March
Dawn

Joey Sparks pushed out of the pile of hay where he had spent an uncomfortable night, and groaned as he stretched his stiff, cold body, and drew his ragged layers of clothing tighter about him.

Another head pushed out of the hay, and Joey Sparks scowled down at it and growled. 'Come on, you lazy cow, we needs to get going.'

'I'm fuckin' starving,' Maggie Sparks complained.

'We'll try our luck at the next house we comes to. And I'm going to ask if they got any old boots, because me feet am bloody killing me.'

Her husband wrapped his bare feet in pieces of rag and limped haltingly out of the barn, hissing with distress each time his red-raw soles met the hard ground. She snatched up the wrapped bundle she had rested her head on, and followed after him.

A half-mile from the barn Joey Sparks pointed. 'We'll try that one.'

They went slowly up the winding, hedged lane towards the secluded house, and Maggie Sparks exclaimed, 'What's that fuckin' nag doing up front there?'

'Am you blind as well as stupid? It's fuckin' eating the fuckin' grass. That's what nags does. And that's what we'll be doing again today unless our fuckin' luck turns.'

'Well why aren't it tethered like it should be?' she questioned and ran on ahead of her husband until she reached the grazing animal, then turned and shrieked.

'Come quick, Joey, there's a bloke laying on the ground over here.'

She disappeared around the bend.

Joey Sparks limped after her and as he rounded the same bend found her standing in front of the house looking down at a prone man.

'I reckon he's dead, Joey.'

Joey Sparks bent close to search for signs of life, but after a few seconds nodded. 'That's right enough.'

He hobbled to the front door and hammered on its panels, shouting out, 'Answer the door! Answer the door!'

His wife went to peer through the solitary window which was un-shuttered.

'I can't see nobody, Joey.'

He continued hammering and shouting for a short while, then shook his head. 'I reckon there's nobody here.'

He turned the door knob and pushed, and as the door swung open, bent forwards and cocked his head, listening intently and shouting several times.

'Is anybody here?'

Then he turned and told his wife, 'It's fuckin' empty right enough.'

'Let's get away from here, Joey!' Maggie Sparks was darting anxious looks about her. 'If somebody comes now and catches us here, they'll blame us for him being dead! Like we gets blamed for everything else bad that happens!'

He closed the door and nodded. 'You're right! We'd best get well clear!'

He went back to the dead man. 'I've got to have them boots though. I'll be crippled for life else, if I walks another step in these fuckin' wraps.'

He tugged the boots off the dead man's feet, and hissing with pain unwrapped his bloodied foot rags and pulled on the boots. He clambered to stand and gingerly press each foot in turn on to the ground, then grinned at his wife.

'It don't hurt half as much, Maggie. Let's see what else he's got in his pockets.'

Then a shout came from somewhere close, and Maggie panicked.

'Fuckin' 'ell! There's somebody seen us!'

'Cummon quick!' Her husband grabbed her hand and they hurried away from the house.

The grazing horse briefly lifted its head as they passed, then went back to its meal.

As the hours passed the horse slowly moved further away from the house and reached a junction in the lane where a hedge-layer was working.

'Now then, my beauty, where's your rider? Has you bucked him off?' The man crooned as he secured the dangling reins and stroked the animal's neck.

'You'd best come along o' me, my beauty, and we'll have a look-see for your rider.'

The hedge-layer led the horse back up the lane and when he came in sight of the secluded house muttered, 'Have you come from there, my beauty? Let's go and find out, shall we?'

THIRTY-EIGHT

Beoley Village
Monday, 17th March
Morning

Bearing large jugs of hot and cold water, Pammy Mallot used her foot to tap on the bedroom door and called, 'Geraint? Geraint? Are you awake?'

'I am indeed, Pammy,' his sonorous voice called back.

'I've brought your water, Geraint, can I bring it in?'

'Please do, Pammy. I'm newly risen from bed but I can assure you that I am fully garbed and shall not cause you any shock or offence.'

When she entered she found Walter Courtney sitting in the armchair before the window.

He smiled roguishly at her and indicated the voluminous dressing gown that swathed him from neck to feet.

'There now, did I not tell you that I was fully garbed, my dear? There is naught to shock you in my appearance, is there? Everything is well covered.'

She cackled with laughter and retorted, 'I've been wed and widowed three times, and it takes more than the sight of a man's bits and pieces to shock me these days.'

He joined in her laughter. 'I do declare, Pammy, your quick wit pleasures me so much, that should you choose not to accompany your mistress to India, then I shall offer you a position as my housekeeper.'

'And if I hadn't got Phoebe to care for then I'd have jumped at your offer, Geraint, because in all my days I've never met a more agreeable gentleman than yourself. It's a pleasure to serve you, so it is. But truth to tell I shall never leave Phoebe's side, and shall go with her to India come Hell or high water. And if Joey Stokes wants to wed me he'll have to come to India and live there as well.'

'Of course he will come to India, Pammy, and I'm positive that you will both be very happy there.'

She put the jugs on the wash stand and asked him, 'What would you like for breakfast? I've got lamb chops, pork chops, ham, bacon. Eggs, new-baked bread, butter and cheese. Barley porridge, oat porridge, curds and whey. Plenty of fine onions. Sweet pickled pears, apples and gussgogs. And there's tea and coffee both, and fresh milk and sour or fresh cream.'

He beamed at her. 'I do declare you sorely tempt me with such riches, my dear. And I fear that I am perilously near to committing the sin of gluttony.'

'I'm sure the Good Lord will forgive you this once, Geraint. Now what's it to be?'

He sighed and shook his head dolefully. 'Miserable sinner that I am, I shall force myself to have a bowl of barley porridge mixed with some pickled pear. Then a platter of pork chops with fried onions, to be followed with bread, butter, cheese, coffee and fresh cream.'

He mock-scowled and pointed to the door. 'Now get thee behind me, Satan!'

Giggling delightedly she hurried away.

An hour later Courtney and the two women had just finished eating breakfast and the conversation turned to the day ahead.

'You'll be feeling hungry after your shopping, Phoebe, but I doubt that Master Fowkes' establishment will be able to furnish you with any repast as wonderfully palatable as Pammy's always is?'

'O' course it 'ull.' It was Pammy Mallot who answered the question. 'The grub there is fit for a king, because it's me sister who cooks it, and she won't let Fatty Fowkes interfere with that side o' the business. She's cooked for more Lords and Ladies than I can remember, and they all praised her dishes to high heaven, so they did.'

Phoebe Creswell joined in, blushing girlishly as she told them, 'I'm longing to see what progress has been made on my wedding gown and bonnet.'

'They're both going to be lovely!' Pammy Mallot declared. 'I'se known Lizzie and Sarah Henbath since they was nippers, and there aren't a finer pair o' dressmakers in this kingdom. Does you know 'um, Geraint?'

Courtney smiled. 'I've not met them, but I know of them, my dear. I've frequently passed by their establishment and read their splendid signboard.' He paused then intoned sonorously, 'Mesdames

Elizabeth & Sarah Henbath, Mantua Makers & Milliners To The Nobility.'

He winked roguishly. 'Such credentials lead me to believe that their names will be emblazoned upon the annals of mantua making and millinery, and their fame will resound down through the centuries.'

'What a wicked tease you are! I've a good mind to box your ears for you!' Pammy Mallot cackled with laughter.

'If you do, I shan't loan you my gig to go to Redditch,' he mock threatened. 'Because I shall undoubtedly need it myself to go in search of a doctor to repair the injuries you will have inflicted upon my defenceless head.'

Both women laughed delightedly, and Pammy Mallot chortled. 'Well I won't box your ears for you this time, because Joey Stokes has just gone past the window and he'll have the horse in the traces in no time. So we'd best make ready to go, Phoebe.'

'Are you sure that you'll be able to drive safely, my dear Pammy? My horse is a high-spirited beast,' Courtney asked with a concerned look.

'Drive safely? Me? I been driving all manner o' teams since I was a young 'un, Geraint. Ask Joey Stokes how good a driver I am, and he'll tell you that he's never seen a better one.' Pammy Mallot jumped to her feet and, taking Phoebe's arm, pulled her upright as well. 'Come on now, Phoebe, let's make haste and get ready. I'll clear this lot away and wash up when we gets back.'

'And I shall now make haste to go up to the Master and take him some breakfast.' Courtney rose to his feet.

'His bread and milk is in the bowl on the dresser, Geraint, and there's an opened bottle of port in the pantry. I've put the new rubbing potion you brought us on the table by his bed,' Pammy Mallot informed as she and Phoebe were leaving the room. 'We'll be back well before nightfall, but if we're a bit later there's no call for you to worry about us.'

A little later in the bedroom Courtney smiled down at the almost comatose George Creswell.

'Now before I feed you, my dear Master Creswell, I shall rub some potion into your back to ease the pain of the sciatica.'

He pulled on a pair of leather gloves, stripped back the bedclothes, gently turned the sick man over on to his front, lifted the long nightshirt and rubbed layer after layer of the potion into the shriveled skin of Creswell's lower back.

THIRTY-NINE

Redditch Town
Monday, 17th March
Midday

'Pammy, Miss Phoebe, come on through and set yourselves down. This is a nice surprise.' Gertrude Fowkes led her visitors into the rear parlour of the Fox and Goose, and told the man seated in front of the fireplace, 'Shift your backside over, Harry Pratt, and let these ladies see a bit o' the fire.'

The Bellman jumped to his feet and immediately dragged two other chairs nearer to the flaming coals.

'Good morning, Miss Phoebe. Morning, Pammy.'

'Good morning, Master Pratt.'

'Morning, Harry.'

When the visitors were seated, Gertrude Fowkes questioned curiously, 'What brings you to Redditch on such a freezing day?'

Phoebe Creswell blushed and looked down at the floor.

Harry Pratt saw her embarrassment and offered, 'Perhaps I'd better go. These ladies might want to talk in private with you, Gertrude.'

'You can stay where you am, Harry Pratt,' Pammy Mallot told him firmly. 'What we'em come to Redditch for aren't nothing we needs to hide from anybody. More like the opposite. We've just been having a look at Phoebe's wedding gown and bonnet.'

'Well I never!' Gertrude Fowkes' plump red face mirrored her utter astonishment. 'Who is it you'm going to wed, Miss Phoebe? Is he a local chap? One o' the Needle Masters? Does I know him?'

'No fear!' Pammy Mallot preened triumphantly. 'My Phoebe's marrying a sight higher up in the world than some Needle Master or other. Her's getting wed to an officer in the East India Company's army, and when him and Phoebe goes back to India, they'm going to live in a palace, and be like a King and Queen ruling over thousands and thousands o' them blackies.'

'India, you say! Royal palace! Well I never!' Gertrude Fowkes was astounded. 'And you'm going to be a Queen there, Miss Phoebe! Well I never!'

'What part of India am you going to, Miss Phoebe?' Harry Pratt wanted to know.

'To the Madras Presidency, Master Pratt,' she told him. 'My betrothed Major Christophe de Langlois is presently serving in the Madras Native Infantry. But he is to be promoted to a much higher position in the administration department upon our return there.'

Pratt's eyes narrowed fleetingly, but he nodded and smiled. 'Does you know, I reckon I might ha' met with the gentleman last Monday week. He asked me directions for the Creswell house. A fine, handsome-looking gentleman as well, so he was, and wearing a grand uniform.'

'Last Monday week, you say,' Pammy Mallot put in. 'That's got to be him then.'

'The officer I met was wearing a gold-banded black shako wi' a green cockade on its front, and a big shiny bugle-horn cap-plate,' Pratt offered. 'Would that be him? Or might I have spoken to another soldier who was wanting to call on you as well?'

'Oh no, there's no other soldier called on us. And that was the hat our Major had on his head alright, no doubt about it,' said Pammy Mallot.

'You was a soldier, warn't you, Harry?' Gertrude Fowkes joined in. 'Didn't you tell me that you'd been in India for a good many years?'

The clock on the mantle shelf whirred and chimed, and Harry Pratt exclaimed in dismay, 'My oath! Is that the time? I'm running very late!' He jumped to his feet. 'I beg your pardon, ladies all. I'd love to stay, but I've got to attend to me rounds, else my boss 'ull be having my guts for garters. Good mornin' all.'

As he exited, Lily Fowkes, Maisie Lock and Amy came into the room, more greetings were exchanged and when that was done, Lily immediately went into the adjoining kitchen, heated a skillet on the range and began to cook a pancake.

'I'd best get back to the lock-up and do my housework,' Amy smiled.

'Not before you've ate some of my pancakes, my wench,'

Gertrude Fowler told her and ushered them all back into the parlour. 'And while we'em eating 'um, I wants to hear everything there is to know about your intended, Miss Phoebe. And what you means to do when you'm living like a queen in India.'

When Amy finally left the Fox and Goose more than two hours had passed. Walking across the Green towards the lock-up, she sighed enviously as she compared the mundane household tasks awaiting her with the exotically glamorous life awaiting Phoebe Creswell in India.

In the lock-up, Tom was sat by the kitchen range fire, rummaging among his father's large chest of files and medical records. Amy stared at his uncombed hair, stubbled chin, workaday shirt, breeches, gaiters and boots, made a mental comparison of his appearance with the miniature portrait of Major Christophe de Langlois, and clucked her tongue disparagingly.

Tom looked up and smiled uncertainly. 'Is anything amiss, my dear? You're looking rather grimly at me.'

'I don't mean to look grim,' she told him. 'I was just trying to picture you in Scarlet and Gold, that's all.'

'Scarlet and Gold?' he queried. 'You mean you were trying to picture me as a soldier?'

'Yes, I was. Phoebe Creswell is to marry a Major in the East India Company's Army, and she showed me a miniature of him in his uniform. Oh, he's ever so handsome and dashing looking! And she's going to India with him as soon as they're wed, and they're going to be living in a great big palace and ruling over thousands and thousands of blackies, just like a King and Queen.

'And you should see the betrothal ring he's given her! It's all diamonds and gold and worth a fortune. He's told Phoebe that it's been in his family for centuries, and that their tradition is that the first-born son must always present it to his wife-to-be. And now it's been presented on to Phoebe.'

A note of wistfulness entered Amy's voice. 'He went down on his knees when he asked her to wed him and gave her the ring. Isn't that truly romantic, Tom? It would have been lovely if you could have done that when you asked me to wed you.'

These reminders of his own self-perceived inadequacies as a romantic lover did nothing for Tom's morale, and he could only sadly reply, 'Yes, it was truly romantic, Amy, and I truly regret that I wasn't able to do such. But I do truly love you.'

Instant remorse struck through her as she saw the sadness in his eyes, and she rushed to clasp his head and kiss his lips and tell him, 'I know you do, my darling! And I love you truly, and I wouldn't change you for the world.'

It was some time later before Tom gave any more thought to Phoebe Creswell's forthcoming marriage, and knowing by repute the secluded life her domineering, tyrannical father had enforced upon her, his curiosity was roused.

'How did Phoebe Creswell come to meet this Major in the first place?' he asked Amy.

She shrugged and shook her head. 'I don't know. When I asked her, she only blushed and dithered and looked down at the floor. And Pammy Mallot just laughed and said that was for them to know and for us lot to wonder about.'

'Well of course, it's Phoebe Creswell's own personal business after all,' Tom accepted, but the faint nagging of curiosity would reoccur at intervals during the hours that followed. 'How ever did a put upon little mouse like Phoebe Creswell ever come to meet and get betrothed to such an exotic figure as a Major of the East India Company?'

Throughout the afternoon, curiosity had also been nagging at Harry Pratt as he walked through the outlying areas of the town ringing his collection bell. Time and time again he mentally pictured the mounted officer who had asked for directions to the Creswell house. Time and time again he shook his head in frowning negation.

'That shako warn't no Major's titfer of John Company's Army. That shako was definitely Light Company officer of a King's Line regiment. That letter Miss Phoebe give me was addressed to XYZ, warn't it? Was that him, this Chris-bloody-summat de Lan-bloody-summat-else?'

'Bellman? Bellman, I've a letter for you!' a man shouted from a nearby house, and Harry Pratt had to turn his mind to the business in hand.

FORTY

Beoley Village
Tuesday, 19th March
Afternoon

Harry Pratt was in the taproom of the Village Inn taking a break from his round and enjoying a flagon of ale, when the innkeeper drew his attention to the couple passing by on the road outside. The woman was resting her hand familiarly on the man's crooked arm, smiling radiantly up at him as he leaned his head towards her, appearing to be telling her something.

'Look there, Harry. That's the Creswell wench and that bloke who's courting her, arming it together. He's a Dandy, aren't he? Them clothes must ha' cost him more than a few sovs.'

Harry Pratt frowned thoughtfully as he took note of the passing man's expensively fashionable clothes, then asked, 'What's the talk of him in the village, Dick?'

'That he's a high-up officer in the East India Company's Army, and that him and Phoebe Creswell am to be wed and go out to live there like bloody royalty.'

'Is he lodging local?' Harry Pratt questioned.

'No, I don't think so. They says that he rides in from the direction of Brummagem every day, and goes back that way of a night time.'

'Have you spoke to him at all?'

'Only the once. He come in one night, bought a bottle o' gin and stowed it away in his saddle bag, then rode off out of the village. Ne'er said more to me than to ask the price and chuck the money on to the counter. The very next day I was standing in me doorway when he come riding past, and I wished him a good day, and he ne'er so much as looked at me.

'I reckon he's a arrogant, sour bastard! But when I asked Pammy Mallot about him, her said he was one o' the nicest gentlemen her'd ever come across in her life.'

'Ah well, officers can be nice down-to-earth blokes, or nasty, high and mighty cunts like him! I've soldiered wi' plenty o' both sorts,' Harry Pratt observed philosophically. He drained his flagon of ale, shouldered his mail-bag, and picked up his bell. 'I've got to be off, Dick. See you next week sometime.'

Outside the inn Pratt stared speculatively after the couple who were walking towards the steep slope of the hill leading up to the Parish Church, and muttered, 'I reckon I'll test you out, my fine Bucko!'

At a slow pace he also began to walk towards the hill, his left hand firmly clutching the clapper of his bell.

At the base of the hill Sylvan Kent gently drew Phoebe Creswell to a halt and asked her, 'Can we now speak of more serious matters, my dearest girl?'

Her radiant smile faltered. 'Is there something amiss, Christophe?'

'Nothing can ever be amiss between you and I, my love.' He hastened to reassure her. 'But I have to tell you that my Court of Directors strongly pressed upon me the necessity of my returning to India as quickly as possible. Now I've made the Allegation and posted the Bond for our Special Marriage License.

'Geraint has submitted the application to the Archbishop himself, and assures me that he will be receiving the License within a matter of days. He will then engage a clergyman acquaintance to perform the church ceremony. So with any luck we can be wed and within a month set sail for India on a Company ship.'

For the first time that day Phoebe Creswell's brows creased in a troubled frown.

'There's nothing in this world that I want more than to be wed to you, Christophe, but what about my father? I fully confess that he and I have never had the most loving of relationships, and that there have been many times when I have resented his manner towards me. But he is still my father, and I feel so very guilty at thinking of leaving him, while he is so ill and helpless.'

'I share that guilt, my dear, but Geraint will ensure that your poor father receives the very finest medical treatments and care that money can buy; and when he is sufficiently recovered in health he can come out to India and live with us. He'll be treated like a king there, and will undoubtedly enjoy life to the very fullest.'

'But Doctor Laylor holds out virtually no hope of my father

ever fully recovering his health. I want with all my heart to become your wife, Christophe, but I have a duty of loyalty to my father.'

The flush of happiness had now completely drained from Phoebe's cheeks, and her sallow face was drawn with strain.

Sylvan Kent's expression was one of deep concern. 'You must remember, my dearest girl, that Doctor Laylor, although a man of good intentions, is merely a country physician lacking the qualifications and experience of the medical specialists that we will be engaging to treat and care for your father. Geraint has already written to the very men he has in mind for this task. They've achieved almost miraculous cures in cases which were seemingly far more hopeless than your father's.'

Before Phoebe could reply their conversation was interrupted.

'Good afternoon, Miss Phoebe, I thought it was you when I was still at a distance.' Harry Pratt came up to them beaming broadly.

As they swung round to face him, he came to rigid attention, snapped up a quivering salute to Sylvan Kent, and began to babble excitedly.

'And a very good afternoon to you, Sir. Miss Phoebe has told me of you being a Major in the Madras Regiment. I was at the Battle of Assaye wi' my regiment and I saw the Madras Regiment win the badge of the Elephant Crest for their bravery. Their war cry on that day sent the shivers down me spine, I can tell you, Sir. No wonder the enemy turned tail and ran away from them. I can hear that cry sounding in me ears this very moment, Sir.'

Pratt drew a deep breath and bellowed, '*Veera Madrassi! Adi Kollu! Adi Kollu!*'

Then he immediately went on. 'You no doubt were there yourself, Sir. Correct me if I'm wrong, but it means, "Brave Madrassi! Go Forwards! Go Forwards!" Don't it?'

Taken totally aback, Sylvan Kent was momentarily at a loss, and could only nod and grunt. 'It is as you say, Bellman.'

'And their motto, Sir. Does you know I reckon I can still remember what it was, but for the life o' me, after all these years I'm not sure if I remembers rightly the exact full meaning of it in English. Please tell me if this is right though, Sir? *Swadharme Nidhanam Shreyaha*. That's the motto, aren't it, Sir?'

Kent was recovering from his initial shock, and managed to answer calmly. 'Yes, Bellman, but of course your pronunciation is dreadfully mangled.'

'Well, it would be, wouldn't it, Sir? Because I'm just a lowborn soldier wi'out your schooling, aren't I, Sir? I aren't clever enough to speak the same way as one o' them Bengali warriors your regiment is recruited from, am I, Sir?'

'No, of course you're not,' Kent acknowledged stiffly.

'And the meaning of it in English, Sir. Isn't it summat about your regiment being the "First into battle, and the last out of it"?'

Kent coughed several times, and gasped. 'I've something catching in my throat.'

'Oh, I'm dreadful sorry for that, Sir. I'll leave you in peace. Good day to you, Miss Phoebe. Good day to you, Sir.' Pratt saluted in farewell and walked away, but then came to a halt and called back plaintively, 'I'm dreadful sorry for pestering you again, Sir, but could you please put me mind at rest and tell me if I'm right about the meaning in English of your motto?'

Conscious of Phoebe Creswell's adoring gaze, Kent felt forced to call back. 'You're near enough, Bellman. Now be off with you. Myself and Miss Phoebe wish to continue our conversation without further interruption.'

'Certainly, Sir, and thank you for your kindness.' Harry Pratt came to ramrod attention, snapped up another quivering salute and smartly marched away up the hill, scornfully muttering under his breath.

'Cris-bloody-summat de Lan-bloody-summat-else, or who-some-ever you might be! You'm no more a fuckin' Major o' the Madras Regiment than I am!'

FORTY-ONE

Redditch Town
Wednesday, 19th March
Midday

The weekly magistrate's hearings in the Select Room of the Fox and Goose had taken place on Tuesday. The Right Honourable and Reverend Walter Hutchinson, Lord Aston, Justice of the Peace, Vicar of the Parish of Tardebigge, had remanded Ezekiel Rimmer and his friends to Worcester Jail. Tom and Ritchie Bint had taken them there in Richard Humphries' coach that same evening, and then stayed overnight in the city.

It was just past noon when Humphries' coach arrived back in Redditch and halted in the Market Place to allow Tom and Ritchie Bint to alight.

'Will you collect me money from Joe Blackwell, Tom? I've got to get back to me pointing, there's a batch needs finishing a bit rapid,' Ritchie Bint requested.

'Of course, Ritchie.' Tom nodded and, as his friend hurried away, Hugh Laylor came along.

'This is very well met, Tom. I've a favour to ask of you. I have a sample which needs to be analysed as quickly as possible.'

'Alright, but first I have to go and tell Amy I'm back; and also report to Blackwell. What's the sample, and what am I to look for in it?'

'It's George Creswell's vomit. I was called to see him yesterday night. I think the man is dying, Tom. All I can do is to try and prolong his life for a while.' Laylor's handsome features displayed some discomfiture. 'But I've no real idea what's causing him to repeatedly vomit so. I wondered if it might perhaps be arsenic. God knows there's enough domestic uses of it, so he could well be ingesting it accidentally. If that's so, then at least I may be able to relieve that aspect of his sufferings.'

They discussed the matter for a brief while longer then parted company.

Tom went on to the postal office and deposited a letter to be forwarded to Clem Bradshaw at the Union Jack tavern in Dudley, informing him about the capture of the men who had stolen Elias Bradshaw's Otterhounds.

Next Tom hurried to the lock-up where Amy greeted him with a hug and kiss.

'Has Weiss behaved himself?' he asked.

'He's been as quiet as a lamb.'

'Is that you, Constable Potts?' the pedlar's voice sounded from the locked cell.

'It is, Master Weiss, I'll come and speak with you directly.' Tom kissed Amy again, then moved to open the hatch in the cell door.

'What is to happen to me now?' Weiss questioned anxiously.

'Because you've turned King's Evidence and also now paid for a Hawker's License, Lord Aston has decided to show mercy, but warns that should you offend in any other manner, he will ensure that you'll be hung. So I'm releasing you now.'

Weiss gusted a sigh of relief, and exclaimed, 'You've kept your promise to me, Constable! I'm very grateful to you!'

As they parted at the front door of the lock-up, Tom remarked, 'Your wife and children will be very happy to see you, I don't doubt.'

'They'd be very surprised.' The pedlar winked slyly. 'You have a saying in this country about the rolling stone gathering no moss. Well I'm the rolling stone, and they were the moss. I rolled away from them more than twenty years ago in Krakow!'

Tom could only grimace wryly and close the door.

He went upstairs to where Amy was tidying the room.

'I need to go and report to Joseph Blackwell now, sweetheart. Then I've got to go to Hugh Laylor's dispensary and analyse a specimen. So I might be away for two or three hours.'

'I'd really like to watch you doing that analyse thing,' she told him. 'That's when you look for poisons and stuff, isn't it? What are you going to look for today?'

'Arsenic,' he told her. 'Hugh thinks that one of his patients might be swallowing it accidentally. So there's a bowl of vomit for me to delve into.'

'Whose is it?'

'A man named George Creswell.'

'Is that Phoebe Creswell's dad? From Beoley?' Amy questioned excitedly.

Tom was surprised at her eager reaction. 'Yes, it is. Do you know him?'

'Only by sight. But yesterday night, me and the girls was talking about Phoebe Creswell and that bloke she's going to wed.' Amy's blue eyes sparkled with amusement and she giggled. 'And Gertie Fowkes and Old Harry Pratt nigh on come to blows over it, and if Harry hadn't cleared off the very moment that he did, Gertie swore that she'd have boxed his ears for him.'

'For what reason?' Tom's lively appreciation of gossip was sparked.

'Well, Gertie Fowkes reckoned that Phoebe Creswell was very lucky to be wedding a Major of the East India Company Army, and

Harry Pratt reckoned that the bloke's not a Major at all, and not who he says he is neither. Harry said that that very afternoon he'd tested Phoebe's bloke with some questions about the Madras army, and that Phoebe's bloke knew bugger-all about the Madras army.'

'Tell me all about what was said.' Tom was keen to hear more.

Amy, with many giggles and some embellishments, related the full account of that clash in the back parlour of the Fox and Goose.

Tom listened with amusement and, when she had done, kissed her.

'I've got to report to Joseph Blackwell, sweetheart. He'll know that the coach is back, and he gets very testy when he's kept waiting.'

'I want to watch you do that analyse thing.'

'Alright, you can come to Hugh's dispensary in about an hour. But don't blame me if it bores you to tears.' He smiled and left.

'Good afternoon, Constable Potts. I take it you had no difficulties while escorting the Rimmer gang to Worcester.' Joseph Blackwell stated rather than queried this.

'None whatsoever, Sir.'

'I'm pleased with your work on this case. The Earl will have no cause for criticism when he returns.' A fleeting wintry smile curved Blackwell's thin lips as he counted out the coins for the Escort Fee on his desk. 'Here are the sums due to yourself and Bint.'

Tom pocketed the coins. 'Thank you, Sir.'

'There's a matter I want you to deal with, Constable. A man whom it seems is not known locally was found dead in Bradley Green on Friday last. Apparently there appears to be something of a mystery concerning the dead man.

'Timothy Wrighton, who considers himself to be the Lord of Feckenham Parish because he owns the Old Manor House and some land there, has begged me to send you to investigate the matter. It seems that I am not the only one who holds your talents in high esteem, Constable Potts.

'So perhaps when convenient you might attend upon Master Timothy. You may take a mount from my stable.'

'I'll go over there tomorrow, Sir.'

'Excellent! I bid you good day, Constable Potts.'

'Good day to you, Sir.'

Some hours later in the dispensary of Hugh Laylor, Tom completed his analysis of the foul smelling contents of the bowl.

Amy, who had been raptly watching him work, questioned excitedly. 'Well? Is it poisonous? Has it got arsenic in it?'

Tom smilingly shook his head. 'I'm sorry to disappoint you, Sweetheart, but I can't find any traces. However, I wouldn't recommend anyone to swallow it. They'd most certainly be feeling very nauseous afterwards.'

'Let's make haste and go home, Tom.' She smiled seductively. 'I want to welcome you home properly.'

Tom drew a long deep breath. 'I'll be done here in ten seconds, sweetheart.'

FORTY-TWO

Bradley Green
Thursday, 20th March
Morning

Timothy Wrighton was a self-made man, who had gained his considerable wealth by the manufacture of buttons in a score of sweated labour workshops in Birmingham. Information that he wasted no time in sharing with Tom almost immediately after they met at Wrighton's palatial home set midway between Feckenham Village and Bradley Green.

'I started life slaving me guts out in a button workshop when I was only a Poorhouse babby. But by my own efforts I've risen in the world to my present eminence. First of all I bought the same button shop that I'd slaved in as babby, boy and man, and then I set up more and more workshops. Now I'm known through all o' Brummagem and the Black Country as the Button King.'

'You've undoubtedly been very successful in life, Master Wrighton,' Tom complimented.

'That's a fact, that is! But look at the pitiful state it's left me in.'

Wrighton gestured to his haggard, smallpox pitted features and bent-shouldered, skeletal body, and added wistfully, 'Does you know summat, Master Potts? I'd give all me wealth and success up this very second, if I could only go back to when I was a young lad.

'Because then I'd do what I always longed to do. I'd run away to sea and spend me life having adventures in all them far off lands like India and China and the Americas and Africa.'

'Well, you now have the wealth and leisure to allow you to go to those lands, Master Wrighton,' Tom pointed out.

'But I aren't got the health and strength to be able to travel any distance further than a few miles, Master Potts.' Wrighton made a chopping gesture with his hand. 'Anyway, that's enough about me! I wants you to come down to the Old Black Boy and have a look at this stiff 'un. It was one o' my estate hands who found him and the horse. I've got the horse and its tack in my stables, and I've been keeping the stiff 'un in me ice house until yesterday, when I had it taken to the Old Black Boy, because according to my knowledge the Coroner will be conducting his inquest there, it being the nearest public house to where the stiff 'un was found. Am I right? Or am I wrong?'

'Indeed you are right, Master Wrighton.' Tom couldn't help but smile in wry amusement at his companion's eccentric manner.

'Hello again, Constable Potts!' Maud Harman smiled and greeted as Tom and Wrighton entered the Old Black Boy. 'I was wondering if you'd be sent for, because this dead bloke was wearing clothes and gaiters, but had nothing on his feet. It's a bit strange to go riding like that, aren't it?

'Now Barry Blake has had to go off on an errand, but he's left the key for the cellar door wi' me. I'll open the outside trap as well, so that you'll have daylight to see the man by. We put the poor soul down there because it's the coldest place in the house, so he'll keep a bit longer before he starts stinking real bad.'

The dead man was laid on trestle boards, arms crossed on his chest, large penny coins on his closed eyes, and a peeled onion crammed into his mouth.

'What's peculiar about this stiff 'un, Constable Potts?' Wrighton questioned eagerly.

'Is it that he's fully clad and wearing gaiters, but has no boots on?' Tom replied.

'Exactly! I know that it looks to be a certainty that he was thrown from his horse and fell on his head. But why would a man get on a horse with no boots on his feet? I think it's most peculiar. That's why I asked for you to come and investigate it.'

'Has he been searched?' Tom queried.

'Oh yes, I went through his pockets to see if he had anything in them to identify him. Just look at what I found!' Wrighton took objects from his own capacious pockets and dramatically flourished them before Tom's eyes. 'This purse containing twenty-three gold sovereigns and some silver. This fine timepiece and this diamond cravat pin. All of which I now give into your custody, Constable Potts.'

Tom spent some time closely examining the wound on the dead man's head, and committing his features, height, physical build and clothing to memory. Then he told his companion, 'I've seen enough here for the present, Master Wrighton, could you please guide me to where this man was found?'

'It's my pleasure to do that for you, Constable. And what's more, I've had my blokes guarding the place ever since this bloke was found there. Because that's another thing which I find to be most peculiar.

'The house is owned by young Widow Farson, but it aren't been lived in for a good while. After her Ma's death, she went travelling on the Continent. So God only knows what that bloke was doing there, because it was supposed to be all locked up.'

'Did you have close acquaintance with the Farson family?' Tom asked.

'No, not close. They lived very secluded and kept themselves to themselves. But I saw both of 'um passing in their carriage a few times, and had occasional speech wi' the younger one. She's a very handsome woman, and it wouldn't surprise me to find out that she's met some foreigner or other and got wed again.'

At Bradley Green, Tom made a careful study of the graveled forecourt where the dead man had been found. Then he and Wrighton toured and closely inspected the shrouded interior of the house, but found nothing which could help to identify the dead man, or indeed to bring Tom any further personal knowledge about the absent Widow Farson, apart from the fact that the opulent furnishings suggested she was a wealthy woman.

When the two men finally emerged from the house, Wrighton declared emphatically, 'There now, what did I tell you, Constable! This is all most peculiar, aren't it! Am I right, or am I wrong?'

'You're most definitely right, Master Wrighton. I shall report as much to my employer, and subject to his permission to proceed, I'll investigate this matter further.' Tom was already experiencing the excitement of trying to solve this mystery.

'In the meantime, will you be so kind as to ensure that this house is kept securely locked and watched over, Master Wrighton?'

'Of course! Left in my hands it'll be as safe as the Crown Jewels, that's guaranteed that is. But in return you must guarantee to keep me in the know about how you're getting on with your investigation.'

'You have my word on that, Master Wrighton. And now I must get back to Redditch and make my report to Joseph Blackwell.'

With a warm handshake Tom took his leave.

In the Old Black Boy, Maud Harman was serving Walter Courtney with his late breakfast of ham, eggs, toasted cheese and buttered muffins accompanied by a large jug of coffee, a smaller jug of cream, and a bowl of broken lumps of cone sugar.

He smiled at her as he took his seat at the table and congratulated, 'My dear Mistress Harman, once again you have served a feast fit for a king.'

She dimpled with pleasure and bobbed a curtsey. 'Thank you, Sir. But I was feared that it was going to be a bit too late served for you.'

'Why so?'

'Well, you know we've got that dead man in the cellar. Him that was found laying outside the New Mill House at Bradley Green. Well, Master Wrighton from the Manor House sent for the Redditch Constable, Tom Potts, to come to have a look at him.'

'I expect it was just a courtesy call, Ma'am,' Courtney remarked casually.

'Oh no, I don't think so. Because from where I was working in the kitchen I couldn't help but overhear what they was saying, and Tom Potts was saying the same as Master Wrighton, about how it was peculiar that although the dead man was full-clad, he hadn't got no boots on.'

'No boots on?' Courtney's surprised reaction was involuntary.

'That's right, Sir! All dressed up and no boots on his feet; and they both thought that if his boots had been took, then why didn't whoever took 'um take the man's money and valuables and horse as well. It's a queer state of affairs, aren't it?'

'Indeed it is.' Courtney nodded thoughtfully.

'Then the constable was asking all manner of questions about the widow-woman, Mistress Farson, who owns the house where the man was found; and I heard him ask Master Wrighton to take him to the house so he could have a look around there.'

Courtney's smile was warm. 'My dear Mrs Harman, I must beg you not to talk any further about dead men at this particular time. I am longing to devour this delicious breakfast you have so kindly prepared for me. All this talk of dead men does rather deaden my appetite.'

'Oh, I'm ever so sorry, Parson Winward,' she hastened to apologize. 'I'll get off and leave you in peace.'

'But the moment I've finished my meal, I shall demand you to return here and tell me more.' He chuckled.

She laughed with him as she left the room.

Courtney sat staring down at the plate of food, evaluating what he had been told, and the possible consequences arising from it. One imperative was at the very forefront of his thoughts.

'Where the fuck has Archie got to? I need to know that he's done the business with the Irish bitch.'

FORTY-THREE

Beoley Parish
Thursday, 20th March
Afternoon

Sitting in the gig at the crossroads beneath the Beoley Mount, Walter Courtney was listening intently to what the horseman was telling him.

When Sylvan Kent had delivered his news, Courtney scowled.

'Well, Cousin. You must be losing your ability to woo the ladies. How have you made her so reluctant to wed you?'

Sylvan Kent scowled back. 'Haven't you been listening to what I've been telling you, Cousin? She says that she can't marry me and then desert her father by going to India with me, while he's in his present condition. She says no matter how deeply she has come to love me, her conscience won't permit her to do such a callous act. So in my opinion we should just forget about this stink-breathed ugly bitch and move on to some other desperate cow!'

Walter Courtney's anger exploded, his pink face almost puce as he shouted, 'I've not the slightest interest in your opinion, my bucko! We shall not be moving on anywhere! You'll continue to pay court to Creswell for as long as I want you to do so! And what's more you'll never again question any of my decisions, or you and I will be parting company. And you'll end up in the fuckin' gutter because you're too stupid to earn any sort of decent living off your own bat!'

The pair were so intent on each other that they were unaware of the man with a large bag slung across his shoulders and a brass bell in his hand who was walking down the hill towards them.

As Courtney's angry shouting carried to his ears, Harry Pratt squinted his eyes to stare at the pair, and hissed in recognition.

'It's the soldier-boy, having high words wi' somebody by the sound of it. And I reckon I've seen that fine gig and horseflesh afore, haven't I? But where was it that I saw it?'

He quickened his pace, and came into Courtney's peripheral vision.

Courtney hissed a warning to Kent. 'There's somebody coming. Ignore him.'

The two men did not return Harry Pratt's greeting as he passed them, both doing their best to keep their features averted from him.

But Harry Pratt had peered hard at the man sitting under the shadow of the gig hood.

'He's a bloody parson by the look of it. But he aren't a local, or I'd know him else. Is it him who's going to wed the soldier-boy and Miss Phoebe, I wonder?'

As he continued on his way Harry Pratt told himself. 'I reckon

I might ask Gertie Fowkes about just when and where Miss Phoebe's getting wed.'

Walter Courtney waited until Harry Pratt had disappeared from sight, before furiously rounding on his companion again.

'Now go and visit your bride-to-be, and convince her that you are going to make direct application to the East India Company, Directors of Court, to extend your furlough in England, no matter what sacrifices of the promised higher rank and wealth you may suffer for doing so. Tell her also that if they refuse this plea, you will resign from the Company, even though that will mean giving up all you have fought and endured for throughout your life. Then bid her a loving adieu, and go back to your lodging and wait there for me to contact you.'

Kent frowned, but agreed sullenly. 'Very well.'

Courtney waved his hand in dismissal, and Sylvan Kent spurred his horse up the hill.

Courtney remained still until his companion had passed from view over the crest of the hill. Then disgruntled, he muttered, 'Oh, God in Heaven, what are you trying to do to me now? I'm beginning to suspect that you're enjoying tormenting me. You spiteful old bastard!'

FORTY-FOUR

Redditch Town
Thursday 20th March
Early evening

In the study of the Red House, Joseph Blackwell had listened intently to Tom's report. When it was completed, he smiled mirthlessly.

'This is a queer kettle of fish, is it not, Constable Potts? I'd like to hear your opinions on it.'

'Well, Sir, without a full examination of the body I can't state with total certainty that the visible wound is the sole cause of death, or that it was caused by being thrown from his horse and hitting the ground head first.

'But from what I was able to discern I do think it highly possible that the wound was caused by a blow from a weighted bludgeon. The reasons being its narrow dimensions and considerable depth. If he'd been thrown violently from saddle height I would have expected to find a broader and shallower breakage of bone and also impacted gravel in the wound.

'Of course, the absence of his boots suggests robbery. But if robbery was the motive for an assault, why did the assailant not take the money and valuables, and the horse as well?

'The house is apparently owned by a widowed lady named Adelaide Farson, who's been absent from it for some time. The furnishings are of good quality. There are good-quality ornaments and some paintings and prints which would be easily portable, and easily saleable. Yet it has not been ransacked.'

Tom paused for a moment, before adding, 'I'm very sure of one thing, however, and that is that the boots were removed from his feet after he was brought to the ground. Because the soles of his stockings were unmarked by the dirt and gravel which surface the forecourt. As you said, Sir, all in all it's a queer kettle of fish.'

'Indeed.' Blackwell nodded, then asked, 'If you were taxed with investigating this occurrence, how would you commence?'

'I would immediately have the body brought to Doctor Laylor's dispensary for a post-mortem examination, which I would hope Doctor Laylor would permit me to assist in carrying out. Next I would make enquiries in the Bradley Green and Feckenham areas, and I would distribute posters issued offering a five-guinea reward for any information as to the positive identity of the dead man.'

'You echo my own thoughts.' Joseph Blackwell chuckled dryly. 'Begin your investigations into this affair, but take care that you do not bankrupt the Parish Chest. I bid you good night, Constable Potts.'

'Thank you, and good night to you, Sir.' Tom was grinning with pleasurable anticipation as he left the Red House, and went immediately to Charles Bromley's shop.

In the shop he found its proprietor sat on the stool behind the counter with a downcast expression upon his face.

'Good evening, Charles. Is my mother here?'

Bromley's expression suddenly metamorphosed into one of dawning hope. 'Have you come to fetch her back home, Thomas?'

Tom shook his head. 'No, she's found such great contentment living here, I couldn't be so hard-hearted as to drag her back to the lock-up against her will. I'm come to pay you for her board; and also to commission some posters from you.'

Behind his bulbous spectacle lenses, Bromley's eyes blinked back threatening tears as this tentative hope was yet again proven to be a false dawn, and he dolefully told Tom, 'Your mother and my sister went to my sister's house in Birmingham yesterday, Thomas. I believe they intend to stay there for a week. But they have not deigned to inform me on which exact date they'll be returning here.' He shook his head despondently. 'They treat me as if I were nothing more than their skivvy, Thomas. As if my only purpose in life were to single-handedly run this business and still find time to cater to their every whim.' He groaned wearily. 'Unhappy is the man who bears the yoke of female oppression.'

Tom placed money on the counter. 'That's my mother's next month's board fees in advance, Charles, and her personal allowance. And here is the draft of the poster I need printing as soon as possible. Thirty copies, measuring eighteen by twelve inches, should suffice. I've employed the Crier to alert the people to them.'

Bromley lifted the draft and scanned it, then shouted in shocked surprise, 'Found dead on the forecourt of the Old Mill House at Bradley Green!'

'It seems he was tossed from his horse,' Tom informed. 'And I need to know who he is. The scar on his face is very distinctive, which should strike a chord in someone's memory.'

'Five guineas,' Bromley muttered. 'That's a decent sum.'

'How soon can you have these printed, Charles? I want to distribute them as quickly as possible.'

An inner battle was raging in Charles Bromley's mind as he was beset by a quandary.

The physical description of the dead man and his clothing matched the Debt Collector from the *Aris Gazette*. But if Bromley gave this information to Tom Potts, it could mean that he would also be forced to reveal Reverend Winward's involvement with the advertisement in that newspaper; and the Reverend was paying him well for keeping that secret. Another factor was that Bromley would also forfeit his fees for posters, which would no longer be required.

Bromley forced a smile. 'Since the posters are for you, Thomas,

I'll make a start on them immediately, and all being well you shall have them come tomorrow noon.'

FORTY-FIVE

The Old Black Boy, Feckenham Village
Friday, 21st March
Morning

The moment the two men were alone in the room Courtney scowled and hissed, 'Where the fuck have you been, Archie? I expected you back long before this.'

'The job proved to be a lot harder than I expected; and the information cost a pretty penny.' Ainsley frowned. 'And that information won't please you.'

'Have we a difficulty to contend with, Archie?'

Ainsley nodded.

Courtney drew in a sharp hiss of breath. 'Spit it out, Archie. What's gone wrong?'

'Everything!' Ainsley spat in disgust. 'When I was on my way to Warwick my bloody horse cast a shoe and went lame. I couldn't get it seen to until late on the next day. When I finally got to the Irish bitch's place it was all shuttered and locked, with a bloody For Rent sign on the door. So I had to go to the letting office to find out if they had any forwarding address for her. They told me that was confidential information. After haggling for days and greasing their palms, they finally told me that some cove had called and cancelled the lease agreement they'd made with Adelaide Farson. The cove paid all that was claimed for wear and tear and the cancellation fee, and that was it! He gave no forwarding address for her.'

'Did you manage to get any description of the man who cancelled?'

'Of course I did! I'm no fuckin' flat!' Ainsley retorted indignantly. 'He gave his name as John Farson, was well dressed, and had a long scar down the left side of his face. It had to be bloody Billy Peelson.'

Courtney frowned thoughtfully and nodded agreement, then asked, 'Well why didn't you come back then and tell me what had happened?'

'Because I had a notion that there must be more I could find out, so I nosed around. But none of the tradesmen who'd been delivering food and necessaries to the house knew anything about her. They only ever met the little maid who paid them. But then I finally found out that there'd been a regular visitor of late who went into the house almost daily and stayed some time there.

'He's an old drunk of a surgeon, name of Rainsworth. The trouble is, the old bastard still believes in the sanctity of secrecy concerning the relationship between patient and doctor. Consequently I had to spend a deal of money cultivating his friendship, and loosening his tongue with the very finest French brandy.'

'Dammit! Will you get to the point, Archie!' Courtney interrupted impatiently.

'Alright, Walter, there's no call to lose your rag with me!' Ainsley protested aggrievedly.

'Get on with it then!' Courtney snapped back

'Well, it appears that the Irish bitch has been subjected to a terrible hammering, and would have almost certainly choked to death on her own blood and snot, if her little maid hadn't found her and rushed to summon a doctor – namely my new best friend, Doctor Rainsworth, who has been treating her ever since, and apparently she is making a good recovery.'

'Has she given him the name of her attacker?'

'No. She flatly refused. Furthermore she expressly forbids Rainsworth to report the attack on her to the magistrates. But he let slip, that on one occasion in her initial delirious condition she was cursing and threatening some man by name. Rainsworth couldn't quite catch the name because her speech was so mangled by her injuries. But he thought that it might have had a foreign ring to it.'

Ainsley tapped the side of his nose and winked knowingly. 'Aware as we are of our colleague's propensity for knocking women about, I do believe that we might hazard a guess at that name with a foreign ring to it.'

Courtney's features twisted in a savage scowl and he spat out, 'It was my fuckin' cousin, I don't doubt.'

FORTY-SIX

Orchard House, Beoley Village
Friday, 21st March
Evening

As Walter Courtney halted the gig in the yard Pammy Mallot came hurrying from the house, face strained with anxiety. He got down from the gig and went to meet her.

'Pammy, my dear, is something the matter?'

'It's Phoebe! She's real upset and worried about what Christophe intends to do. He says that if the Company don't agree to let him stay longer in England, he's going to stop soldiering and give up all that he's fought and slaved for all his life. He's told her that she means more to him than anything else in this world, and he'll give up everything to wed her!'

'Yes, I know. Before leaving for London he came and told me what he intended doing. I think it's our Good Lord's blessing on their union that Christophe loves Phoebe deeply enough to give up all that he has achieved in India, and make their future married home here in England. He has already asked me to find out the speediest mode for transfer of his Indian financial assets to England.'

He smiled warmly and patted Pammy Mallot's arm. 'Don't worry, my dear, he'll still have wealth enough to raise a family in comfort and security.'

'But Geraint, I've just told you that Phoebe's fretting summat awful about it!' she exclaimed irritably.

'But why should it cause Phoebe any distress?' He shook his head as if bewildered.

'Because her feels terrible guilty, that's why! Her feels guilty because he's willing to sacrifice everything that he's struggled and risked his own life to get, and now her thinks that she's unworthy of such a good man!'

'Hush your voice!' he commanded sternly. 'And if you value our friendship, then do not ever repeat those words in my hearing!

My friend Christophe worships the very ground that Phoebe treads upon. To him, she is a pure soul who personifies goodness of heart and generosity of spirit.'

He tucked Pammy Mallot's arm under his and told her gently, 'Come, let us go inside. Now you need not distress yourself any longer, my dear. I shall talk to Phoebe and bring her ease of mind.'

He took a small pot from his pocket and showed it to her. 'I've brought some fresh-made sciatica potion for poor George. At least we may draw some comfort from the fact that this is soothing his pain. I'll give him his massage after I've talked with Phoebe.'

'You've done wonders for his sciatica, Geraint. He hardly ever shows any signs of upset when I moves him about now,' she told him admiringly. 'And to think that you learned how to do all these marvelous salves and massages from them heathen blackies out in India!'

'I certainly did learn from them, my dear.' He smiled. 'In India there are so many, many wondrous things that one can witness and learn from. All the ancient wisdoms of the East!'

He smiled broadly, leaned forwards and lowered his voice conspiratorially. 'Is Phoebe within earshot?'

Pammy Mallot shook her head. 'No, her's upstairs.'

'Good! I have a surprise for her.' Courtney produced a roll of vellum tied up with bows of rose-red silk ribbon.

'This is the Special License for the Marriage of Miss Phoebe Creswell and Major Christophe de Langlois. Issued by the Ecclesiastical Office of the See of Canterbury and embossed with the personal seal of His Most Reverend Grace, Charles Manners-Sutton, my Lord Archbishop of Canterbury.'

'Ahhhhhh! Aren't that a beautiful looking thing.' Pammy Mallot's eyes became misty with emotion.

'I shall present this to Phoebe after we've had our supper.' The roll of beribboned vellum disappeared into Courtney's inner pocket, and he held his forefinger to his lips. 'And you must not breathe a word of it to her before then.'

'Wild horses couldn't drag that word from me. Me lips am sealed, and may God strike me dead if I betrays me solemn oath on it,' Pammy Mallot declared fervently.

'And I've something else to gladden both of your hearts, which I've been anxiously awaiting to reach me, and shall show Phoebe immediately I see her.'

With a flourish he produced a silver flask. 'I've received it this very morning from a courier despatched by my Lord Archbishop. It's the first delivery of a very special elixir prepared by His Grace's personal physicians, which they guarantee will over time cure Master Creswell's stomach ailment and thus enable him to partake of plain and wholesome food and drink without any ill effects such as vomiting or the diarrhoea.

'Naturally, for the time being we must continue with the low diet prescribed by Doctor Laylor. But as we witness the beneficial effects of this elixir in restoring Master Creswell's health, we shall then be able to gradually introduce good red meat and fresh vegetables back into his diet.'

He winked with boyish mischievousness. 'And in due course, the occasional cheering glass or two of fine Madeira.'

Pammy Mallot gurgled with laughter. 'Oh, you are a scamp, Geraint! I'll bet you were a real jackanapes of a boy!'

Beaming at each other they linked arms and entered the house.

FORTY-SEVEN

Redditch Town
Saturday, 22nd March
Noon

'I fully concur with you, Tom. Death is due to this skull fracture, which in all likelihood was caused by a single blow from a bludgeon type implement.' Hugh Laylor straightened his back, picked up a strip of rag off the naked torso of the dead man and wiped his bloodied hands on it.

Tom smiled wryly as he used another rag to dry his own hands. 'All I have to do now is find whoever it was that dealt that blow.'

'It's a damn strange business this!' Laylor shook his head. 'Why would anyone smash a man's head in and take his boots, yet leave his money and valuables untouched?'

Tom laid aside the towel and shrugged into his coat. 'That's what I'm hoping to find out very quickly. Amy's putting up the last of the Reward notices today, and I've already got Jimmy Grier out crying the news about them. But firstly I'll go and tell Richard Humphries that I need transport to take our friend here back to the Old Black Boy as soon as possible.'

'And I'll deliver the death certificate to Blackwell. Then I shall go to the Fox and Goose and enjoy large tumblers of brandy, and a singsong with the Apollo Club. Why don't you join us? We'll have a merry time of it,' Laylor invited.

'Sadly I can't,' Tom declined. 'It's imperative that I get to the Old Black Boy. Once the news of the reward spreads there'll be a lot of people coming there to view the body.'

On his way to Humphries' premises Tom passed through the bustling market-day crowd and heard above their noise the ringing hand bell and stentorian shouting of Jimmy Grier, the elderly town crier.

'Oyez! Oyez! Oyez! A man was found dead in the hamlet of Bradley Green on Friday the fourteenth day of March. Posters detailing his description are to be affixed in public places throughout this Parish.

'A reward of five guineas will be paid to whomsoever can truly name this dead man. All applications to view the corpse must be made to Master Barry Blake at the Old Black Boy Inn, Feckenham Village.

'God Save the King!'

FORTY-EIGHT

Feckenham Village
Saturday, 22nd March
Evening

It was late evening when Walter Courtney returned to the Old Black Boy, and he was shocked to see a noisy crowd of men, women and children clustered at the lantern-lit front door. He brought the gig to a halt and handed the reins to his companion, Horace Mackay.

'I'll go find out what is happening here, Horace.'

He went through the inn's front door to find its public rooms thronged, the air thick with tobacco smoke and the barmaids and pot men struggling to keep up with the demands of the drinkers.

Maud Harman, her tray laden with flagons of ale, pushed through the throng to tell him, 'You go on through to the private, Reverend, and I'll be with you in two ticks.' 'Why are so many here tonight, Ma'am?' he queried.

'They'm come to view the dead man, Reverend. Barry Blake's charging thruppence apiece to view and Constable Potts is taking the statements of them who thinks they can put a name to the dead 'un. I've put one o' the reward posters in the private room for you to look at.'

As Courtney held the poster up to the lamplight he noticed its bottom lines of small print.

'This Notice printed by Bromley's Stationery Emporium for All Articles of Stationery, Rare and Antique Books and New Literature, High Street, Redditch, Worcestershire.'

Courtney was instantly riled. 'Now Bromley must have recognized that this description fitted the Debt Collector who called on him. But why hasn't he already laid claim to the reward?'

His teeth bared in a contemptuous snarl. 'He obviously expects it will be more profitable to discuss the matter with me before laying any claim to it. I'll assure him that his continued discretion will guarantee him an extremely lucrative future, then allow the greedy bastard to enjoy basking in that expectancy until I close his mouth for good!'

FORTY-NINE

Birmingham City
Monday, 24th March
Midday

The bucketful of cold water impacting on his head shocked Sylvan Kent from his drunken stupor into dazed consciousness. The young prostitute sharing his bed still snored on.

'Get rid of the slut, Archie,' Walter Courtney ordered.

His companion grabbed the naked girl's long hair and dragged her on to the floor, then bent over her, slapping her face with his free hand until she came to shrieking wakefulness. Clapping his hand over her mouth to muffle her shrieks, he growled threateningly into her ear, 'Hold your noise, you whore, or I'll break your fuckin' neck!'

She subsided into terrified silence.

Archibald Ainsley released his grip and pressed coins into her hand. 'Get your clothes and go. Keep your mouth shut about this, and don' ever come back here!'

Trembling with fear she snatched up her bedraggled finery and ran from the room.

Sylvan Kent pushed himself to a sitting position and complained pettishly, 'There was no need to soak me like this, Cousin Walter. I could catch me death of cold!'

'Hold your tongue!' Courtney snapped. 'Listen very carefully, Cousin Sylvan, and commit to memory everything that I now tell you. You'll pay a sore price if you mess things up.'

He went on to give detailed instructions, making the recipient repeat those same instructions over and over again until he was satisfied that Kent had fully absorbed them.

Then he told Ainsley, 'Stay here and keep this stupid cunt sober and away from the whores, Archie. Make sure he's at the Beoley Mount crossroads, looking every inch the gallant soldier, at nine o'clock tomorrow morning.'

FIFTY

Beoley Mount
Tuesday, 25th March
Morning

The air was still, and thick fog blanketed the land. When the rattle of the gig's wheels reached the ears of the two horsemen waiting by the crossroads, Archibald Ainsley grunted with relief.

'This sounds like him now.'

'And about time too!' Sylvan Kent snarled sullenly. 'He lays down the law that we're to be here for nine o'clock and then keeps us hanging around for fuckin' ages!'

The solid dark shape of a horse and gig materialized out of the swirling greyness and came to a halt in front of them.

'I was beginning to wonder where you'd got to, Walter.' Ainsley kneed his mount forwards to the side of the gig. 'Is everything alright?'

Courtney touched his forefinger to his lips in a signal for silence, then brusquely ordered, 'Come here, Cousin Sylvan, I want to take a close look at you.'

Ainsley moved to make space for Kent, who was wearing full military uniform.

Courtney looked him up and down for several seconds, then grinned and nodded. 'Excellent, Sylvan! You're a veritable Adonis! Now listen very carefully . . .'

He gave detailed instructions, making the recipient repeat them over and over again. Then he jerked his head at the hill above. 'Get over there and claim your bride-to-be, Sylvan. I'll be joining you later.'

As Kent rode away and disappeared in the swirling fog, Courtney related the latest developments concerning the dead Billy Peelson, and the reward poster which had been printed by Charles Bromley.

As he listened Ainsley's expression displayed intensifying chagrin, and when Courtney fell silent, he cursed savagely. 'I'd best kill that bastard before he peaches on us!'

Courtney smilingly shook his head. 'Calm down, my dear fellow! I've had words with Master Bromley and ensured his continued silence concerning the Debt Collector's call upon him. I've also sworn him to secrecy concerning his future, very lucrative, employment as Printer to His Grace, My Lord Archbishop of Canterbury.'

After a moment Ainsley chuckled admiringly. 'I've said it before, and I'll say it again. You're a bloody genius, Walter! Now, what's next? Because I could do with getting back to the Unicorn and having something to eat and drink. Especially to drink!'

'Sadly your breakfast must wait a while.' Courtney was apologetic. 'I'm sorry about this, but I need you to do an errand for me which is of the utmost importance for both of us.'

Ainsley shrugged resignedly. 'Oh, very well. Where is it to?'

'Back to the lodging house. I need you to give this to the keeper.' He handed over a small canvas-wrapped, heavily sealed package, then produced a bottle. 'And here's something to sustain you on your journey.'

He uncorked the bottle and gave it to the other man. 'Try this, my friend, I'm sure you'll find it very palatable.'

Ainsley took a swig of the drink, and gasped with pleasure. 'It's powerful stuff!'

'It's the very finest French brandy!' Courtney chuckled. 'By the time you reach Birmingham you'll be riding on air.'

Ainsley took another, larger swig, and laughed. 'I feel I'm near doing that already, Walter.'

'Be off with you now, and come and see me tonight at the Black Boy. I'll have another of these waiting for you.'

'I'll look forward to that.' Ainsley saluted and rode away with the bottle once again raised to his mouth.

'Goodbye, Archibald.' Courtney bared his teeth in a satisfied smile. 'The way you're glugging that drink you could well be dead even quicker than I expected. So give my best regards to the Devil when you meet him.'

In the early hours of the morning Phoebe Creswell had risen to care for her father, and now was taking a nap in her own bedroom when Pammy Mallot rushed to wake her and proclaim excitedly, 'Christophe's come back, Phoebe, and he looks so handsome, I swear I could eat him! And he reckons that the Company has give him what he asked for. So everything's going to be alright!'

A fiery blush spread over Phoebe Creswell's thin, sallow features and she pleaded breathlessly, 'What shall I say to him, Pammy?'

Pammy Mallot hugged and kissed her. 'You'll tell him that you love him, you silly wench! And you'll tell him that you'll marry him on whatever day he cares to name!'

'But what about my father?' Phoebe's smile faltered. 'I'm all he has. What's to become of him when I wed Christophe?'

'That elixir Geraint's brought us is already making your dad better. I can tell it is. And you're forgetting what else Geraint's told us, you daft little besom,' the older woman chided fondly. 'About how he's been praying to the Good Lord for you and Christophe's and your Dad's happiness, and that the Good Lord has come to him in his dreams and told him that his prayers had been answered, and that all would be well. Now you get yourself up and put your finery on, and I'll do your hair so you looks real pretty. Because your sweetheart has already told me that he wants you to be his lawful wedded wife before this week is out!'

FIFTY-ONE

The Old Black Boy Inn, Feckenham Village
Friday, 28th March
Morning

Though the outside trapdoors of the cellar were wide open the sickly odour of rotting flesh that had assailed Tom's nostrils when he entered the building was now an all-enveloping nauseating stench as he descended the indoor cellar steps and joined Barry Blake at the side of the coffin.

'Does you see what I mean now, Master Potts? This bugger's near to driving me out of house and home, and he's already losing me trade. Some of me regulars says that they won't stay drinking here wi' this stink up their noses. He's turning green and purple all over, and the way he's blistered and all swelled up, I reckon he could bust open at any time! He's got to go!' the innkeeper stated irately, and added warningly, 'And if you don't get him shifted this very morning, then I'll have him chucked on to the nearest muckheap! And I wants his horse and tack cleared off me premises as well.'

Tom looked down into the coffin and ruefully acknowledged, 'You have good cause for complaint, Master Blake. I can only assume that he must have had some severe disorder of the internal organs to have caused such a rapid condition of putrefaction.'

He experienced a twinge of foreboding as he visualized Amy's reaction when this corpse arrived at the lock-up. But he was forced to accept that in this emergency it was his only immediate option.

'Do you know where I might obtain the hire of a horse and cart hereabouts, Master Blake? If so, I'll move this man immediately.'

Blake's mood changed instantly. 'I'm sorry if I was a bit short wi' you, Master Potts, but you can see my point, can't you?

Nobody's been able to put a name to him yet even when his face warn't so blistered and swelled up. So there aren't much chance of anybody recognizing him now, is there! And anyway, there's nobody left who wants to pay to come down here to view him.'

'The horse and cart, Master Blake?' Tom reminded.

'You go and tell Johnny Turl at the Smithy, up past the church there, that I sent you, and he'll drive you wherever you wants to go. If you wants you can leave the dead 'un's horse and tack here with me for the time being, and I'll only charge for its fodder.'

Tom left the inn, eagerly drawing in the fresh air to clear the taste and stench of the death from his mouth and nostrils, and asking himself doubtfully, 'Will it really serve any useful purpose to keep him at the lock-up? Within another day or so at this rate of decomposition he'll be virtually unrecognizable anyway, except perhaps to his own mother.'

Engrossed in his thoughts he was not aware of the woman on the opposite side of the road until she called to him.

'Constable Potts!'

He looked round to see Maud Harman coming towards him from the church lych-gate.

'Good morning to you, Mrs Harman.' He doffed his tall hat.

'Have you just come from the pub?' She smiled. 'It's a bloody vile stink, aren't it?'

'Terrible, Ma'am,' he agreed wholeheartedly, and smiled in return. 'Is that why you're here, instead of in the pub?'

'No, I've just been acting as witness at a wedding. They're strangers here and I don't know them, but they're friends of Reverend Winward and he sent for me to come in haste and do it, because the woman who was meant to couldn't come. He's promised me a new bonnet and ribbons as well for me trouble.'

'Well, that's a nice gesture on his part,' Tom observed.

'Oh, he's a lovely man, so he is.' She caught hold of Tom's arm. 'Come on wi' me. They'll be coming out in two ticks. You must see the groom; he's wearing such a splendid uniform, you'd think he was royalty to see him.'

Tom good-naturedly allowed her to lead him to the lych-gate as the wedding group were emerging from the church. But when he saw that group he did a double take. They were four in number: the bride and groom and two clergymen. He blinked in surprise as he recognized the bride.

It was Phoebe Creswell, smiling radiantly up at her groom, who stood tall, handsome and dashing in the scarlet, blue and gold uniform of an army officer. As Tom looked at the officer the memory of what Amy had related to him about the clash between Harry Pratt and Gertie Fowkes jumped into the forefront of his mind.

Because his father had been a military surgeon, Tom had spent many years of his boyhood and youth in close company with soldiers. Now he identified that the man standing beside Phoebe Creswell was wearing the uniform of an officer of a British regiment of the line.

'So, it looks as if Harry Pratt is right! But why did Pammy Mallot, and Phoebe herself, say that her husband-to-be was a Major of the East India Company Army? Were they merely egging the pudding? Or is that what he himself has told them?'

The wedding group walked round behind the church towards the vicarage and disappeared out of sight.

Tom's suspicions were now fully roused, and he decided that when he had dealt with the problem of the dead man's rotting corpse, he would be having a talk with Harry Pratt.

Walking closely behind the newly wedded couple, Walter Courtney's features were radiating smiling contentment as he reiterated constantly, 'I do declare this day has most definitely been made one of the happiest of my life, by my witnessing you two love birds being joined in Holy Matrimony, "'til Death do you part!"'

In his mind however there burgeoned an uneasy presentiment of encroaching danger.

'Why was Tom Potts in company with Maud Harman to watch us leave the church? What's behind his interest in this wedding?'

In Redditch a heavily veiled woman wearing the sombre black of mourning was reading the reward notice pinned to the outer door of St Stephen's Chapel. By her side a small girl, also clad in mourning clothes, touched the woman's gloved hand and asked, 'Did I do right to tell you about this poster, Ma'am?'

'You did indeed, Milly.' Ella Peelson caressed the girl's cheek with her fingers. 'And as reward you shall have whatever treat your heart desires, this very day.'

FIFTY-TWO

Redditch
Friday, 28th March
Afternoon

For a full twenty minutes Amy had stood blocking the front doorway of the lock-up, stubbornly declaring over and over again, 'You're not bringing that coffin in here! It smells vile!'

'But there's nowhere else I can put the poor man. It's my duty to keep him in a secure place until after the inquest.' Tom reiterated the point over and over again.

And the muscular Johnny Turl kept interrupting with ever increasing irritability, 'I've got to get back to me smithy! If you pair don't make your minds up bloody quick, I'll chuck this bugger off me cart right here on this very spot!'

As always in the Needle District a crowd of interested spectators had quickly gathered and divided into partisan divisions, vociferously applauding each repetition voiced by their chosen protagonist.

'Please, Amy, let me bring him in. It's my duty!' Tom was pleading now.

'Over my dead body!' Amy remained obdurate.

'That's it! I've had enough o' this nonsense!' Johnny Turl shouted, and with a display of tremendous muscular strength he lifted the rope-bound coffin off his cart and thumped it down at Tom's feet. 'I'm off!'

He got back on to the cart seat and whipped his horse into movement, leaving Tom staring after him in dismay.

As the partisan divisions either cheered or booed Turl's retreat, another cart accompanied by three bulky figures clad in filthy smocks, faces half hidden by droopy-brimmed slouch hats, each carrying a broad-bladed shovel, large jug and rope-handled wooden cask, came up to the lock-up door.

The cask-laden cart carried with it a rancid stench and the crowd, cursing in disgust, quickly retreated from it.

'We'em come for the shit, Master Potts.'

Tom was shocked to find himself facing the corpulent, toothless wife of Ezekiel Rimmer, accompanied by the wives of Porky Hicks and Dummy; and to his self-disgust experienced a tremor of alarm that they might be here to take violent retribution for the arrest of their husbands.

Sally Rimmer laughed raucously as she saw his reaction. 'Give you a shock, 'as we! Well you've no need to moither yourself, Master Potts. We don't bear no malice against you. In fact you did us all a favour when you took them useless, wasting, drunken bastards to Worcester Jail, didn't he, girls?'

Her companions heartily agreed.

'So, Master Potts, if you'll kindly step aside, we'll clear your privy now. It's still the same charge at fourpence. But we does a much cleaner job of it than them three bastards. Don't we, girls?'

The girls heartily seconded her.

Amy called from the doorway. 'Mistress Rimmer, do you have an outhouse or shed that you can keep locked up tight and safe from robbers?'

'I does, me duck. Me outhouse where me husband did his skinning. An army couldn't break into it when it's locked up tight, I can tell you.'

'Then how do you fancy storing this dead man in it for a few days? My husband will pay you well for doing so.'

Tom turned to her in shock at her intervention, but even as he did so he realized that it might be a very good way out of this present impasse.

He turned back again to Sally Rimmer and smiled. 'But it will have to be on the strict condition that I hold all the keys to the outhouse, Mistress Rimmer, and will have sole entry while the coffin remains there.'

'So you shall, Master Potts. You'se got Sally Rimmer's sworn oath on it. You can come down wi' us now and see it locked away. Then we'll come back up here and clear your privy. Girls, get this dead 'un on the cart.'

Led by Tom and Sally Rimmer the party and the spectators travelled towards the Old Laystall attracting attention and jeering gibes from passers-by at Tom's expense.

'Now you're doing the job you was born to do, you lanky bleeder! Body snatching!'

'Look at Jack Sprat, the new funeral mute! He's got just the right face for it, aren't he!'

'Be careful, Potts! Watch out that they don't mistake you for an extra-long turd, and shovel you up wi' the rest o' the shit!'

'They 'uddn't bother shoveling him up because there aren't enough meat on him to feed a single bloody pea!'

At the Laystall adults and children swarmed out from the hovels clamouring to know who was in the coffin, but Sally Rimmer shouted at them to make way, and her helpers carried the coffin through her house and out to the windowless shanty at the rear. She un-padlocked and flung open its door, proclaiming proudly, 'I told you that a fuckin' army couldn't break into this when it's locked up tight, didn't I, Master Potts?'

As Tom followed the coffin-bearers into its reeking interior, he thought wryly, 'They'd die of asphyxiation if they tried to stay and occupy it, that's for sure.'

Sally Rimmer demonstrated the lever-operated roof shutter.

Tom thanked her and asked for the padlock keys.

She handed them over. 'There's only these two, Master Potts, and now you can lock the door behind you and be sure that nobody can get in here unless you yourself lets 'um in.'

Tom thanked her again, closed and padlocked the door, then said farewell and made a hasty retreat from the Laystall.

'I reckon you've missed a chance of earning a few bob, Sally,' Porky Hicks' wife observed. 'I reckon a few down here who hadn't got time to walk to Feckenham 'ud probably have paid a penny or two to have a good long look at the dead bugger now he's on their doorsteps.'

Sally Rimmer's gums bared in a grin as she winked slyly and produced another rusty key. 'There aren't no flies on me, girls, apart from the ones I lets tickle me quim when I'm feeling fruity.'

Her two friends laughed uproariously.

As Tom walked back up the long slope towards the flat plateau of the town centre, the memory of the wedding party he had seen at Feckenham Church came into his mind, and with it the recollection of Amy's account of Harry Pratt's irate clash with Gertie Fowkes.

He reached the plateau and was in sight of the Horse and Jockey Inn, standing on the east bank of the Big Pool.

'That's where Harry Pratt drinks mostly, isn't it? I'll see if he's there.'

He found the half-drunk Bellman sitting by the fireside in the empty tap room and wasted no time in sitting next to him.

'I was in Feckenham this morning, Harry, and you'll never guess who I saw coming newly-wed out of the church.'

'I don't need to guess,' Pratt snorted irritably. 'Because I knows for sure who was wed there this morning. It was Phoebe Creswell and that cunt who's trying to make out that he's in the bloody Madras Regiment.'

'How did you know it was them getting wed?' Tom asked.

'Because I was in Beoley this morning, and I saw 'um setting out, so I called in at the house and asked Pammy Mallot what was going on. She was bloody narked because Old George Creswell was took very bad again first thing this morn, so she had to stop and look after him and couldn't go to the wedding.'

'Apart from the uniform, what else makes you disbelieve the man's story?' Tom queried.

Pratt scowled. 'Three simple questions that he couldn't give me answer to: the Madras Regiment's battle cry, "*Veera Madrassi, adi kollu! adi kollu!*" That means "Brave Madrassi, hit and kill! Hit and kill!" The regiment's motto, "*Swadharme nidhanam shreyaha*." That means "It is glory to die doing one's duty." And he said that the regiment is recruited from Bengal, which is in the Calcutta Presidency. When I knows for sure that the Madras Regiment is all recruited from the Nair warrior clans of the Madras Presidency.

'I was at the Battle of Assaye with 'um and saw 'um win their Elephant Crest for their bravery, and got to be good friends wi' some of 'um afterwards. So I knows one thing for certain. Cris-bloody-summat de Lan-bloody-summat-else is no more a fuckin' Major o' the Madras Regiment than I am!'

Tom fully accepted what he had been told. 'Well then, Harry, it seems very likely he's a fortune-hunter, out to get Phoebe Creswell's money.'

'That's bloody certain, that is!' Pratt agreed vehemently 'And I knows how he got to meet Phoebe Creswell in the first place. Because a few days ago I was reading a month-old *Worcester Herald*, and saw the notice put in it by an officer looking for a wife, and asking for any replies to be sent to XYZ, care of Charlie Bromley's shop. And I remembered that back in January, Phoebe Creswell give me a letter addressed to that very same XYZ, care o' Charlie Bromley's shop.'

'Do you still have that *Worcester Herald*, because if so I'd like to read it?' Tom enquired.

'I do, and I'll drop it in at the lock-up first thing tomorrow for you,' Pratt told him, then continued, 'And there's another thing that seems fishy to me as well. A couple o' weeks ago I saw that fat parson that was with 'um this morning, down at the bottom o' Beoley Mount talking ever so furtive wi' the soldier boy, and I thought then that they was hatching summat between 'um. So it stands to reason, don't it, that if one of 'um is up to no good, then they both am.'

'Let me buy you a drink, Harry.' Tom's thoughts were racing as he went to the counter and called for service. When he brought the flagon of ale back to the other man, he said, 'I'll have to leave you now, Harry, but might I ask you a favour?'

'O' course you can, Tom.'

'For the time being can you please keep what you've just told me to yourself? I'll make some enquiries about those two, and when I find out anything about them, you'll be the first to know.'

'I'll be as silent as the grave, Tom!' Harry Pratt winked owlishly and buried his nose in the large flagon.

Tom left the inn, and stood staring into the scum-floating Big Pool, pondering his next move. One name above all others was dominant in his thoughts.

'Maud Harman. What might she be able to tell me about this Reverend Winward?'

FIFTY-THREE

Merry-Come-Sorrow Hill, Feckenham Village
Friday, 28th March
Evening

When Maud Harman opened the door of her cottage to Tom's knock, she exclaimed in surprise. 'Master Potts? I thought you'd have been back in Redditch by now? Couldn't you get hold of Johnny Turl?'

'I did make use of Johnny Turl's cart, Ma'am. But I'm come

to seek your aid on another matter, which for the time being must remain strictly confidential between we two.'

'Well, me husband won't be back for a good hour, so you can speak freely, Master Potts.' She smiled. 'And if this matter profits me as handsomely as our other dealings have done, then I'm more than happy to help you.'

Inside the neat and cosy cottage, knowing that he could trust this woman's discretion, Tom came straight to the point.

'I've received information which accuses the officer who got married this morning of being nothing more than a fraud and a fortune hunter. I need you to tell me everything that you might possibly have come to know concerning him.

'Also I need to know all that I can about the Reverend Winward, his doings hereabouts, his acquaintances, any callers upon him, any information he might have given you about himself.'

At first Maud Harman's eyes widened in shocked disbelief as she heard Tom's initial words, but that wide-eyed disbelief was very quickly displaced by excited anticipation, and when Tom fell silent she exclaimed breathlessly, 'On my word, Master Potts! I do declare that since meeting you I've had more excitement than I've had in all these many years! O' course I'll help you!'

She talked and Tom listened. She knew nothing about Major Christophe de Langlois except that he was an old friend of Winward's from India. But she could relate all that the Reverend Winward had told her concerning his reasons for being here in this parish, and his charitable works. She described how he had formed a close relationship with the Reverend Mackay.

Next she described a flashy-dressed man named Archibald Ainsley who had called upon Winward several times asking for donations to a Charity for Old and Decayed Thespians, and added, 'Reverend Winward had another visitor seeking charity from him as well. I never met him meself, but Master Blake did. That one gave his name as Bromley, and I couldn't help but wonder if he was anything to do with the book shop of that name that's on the High Street in Redditch.'

Tom also couldn't help but wonder if it was indeed Charles Bromley who had called upon the Reverend Winward, and if so, for what reason?

He paid Maud Harman for her information and as he walked back towards Redditch decided how he would follow up on what he had been told. Part of his duties as Constable was to check with the innkeepers and lodging house proprietors if they might have cause to suspect any of their guests of being wrongdoers. So firstly he would make a tour of the various premises, and find out if this man named Archibald Ainsley was lodging there. Then he would call upon Charles Bromley.

As Tom was making his plans, Sally Rimmer was receiving a visitor in the Old Laystall, a small girl clad in mourning clothes who was asking to speak with her in private.

Sally led the girl out to the rear yard and questioned, 'Now what is it you'm wanting wi' me, my wench?'

'If you please, Ma'am, me mistress wants to look at the dead man that you brought here this afternoon. She said to tell you that she'll pay you very well if you lets her look at him. But that it's got to be kept secret that she's come here. She says that she wants you to come and fetch her when everybody here is asleep and that you're to make sure that nobody sees her, or comes to know that she's been here. She says that if you does this, she'll pay you very well.'

Sally Rimmer didn't hesitate. 'You tell me where I'm to come for her, and I'll be there at whatever hour she wants me. And you tell her that I'll make double sure that nobody here sees her, or 'ull ever know about her being here.'

FIFTY-FOUR

Orchard House, Beoley Village
Friday 28th March
Evening

'Worcester? They've gone to Worcester? But you told me you were all coming straight back here after the wedding?' Pammy Mallot's tone was accusatory. 'And I've been expecting you to be back hours since!'

'And that was truly my intention, my dear.' Walter Courtney lifted his hands heavenwards. 'As God is my judge, I was as shocked as you when Phoebe told me that she could not bear the thought of spending her honeymoon in the house that has been her lifelong prison; and that on this night above all others, she would insist on experiencing her first taste of freedom! So they hired a gig and went to Worcester.'

He waited to see what effect this dramatic declamation had had on his listener.

Pammy Mallot's motherly features saddened, and she shook her head regretfully. 'It's true, Geraint. That nasty old bugger upstairs did make a prisoner of the poor little soul. Her couldn't stir without him wanting to know where her was going. And how long she'd be. And why she wanted to go anywhere that was away from him.'

'While we're speaking of Master Creswell, how is he?' Courtney interrupted.

'Well, he aren't been sick or shit the bed again after I give him that dose of Elixir just before you all left. And he's took two bowls o' bread and milk and two glasses o' port and held 'um down. I've give him a little dose o' laudanum about an hour since to quiet him, so all he needs now is his back made easy wi' your special massage, and he'll be right as rain for the rest o' the week. I'se laid your gloves ready for you on the bed table.'

Courtney grinned and winked like a mischievous boy. 'Then I'll go up directly and make him as right as rain for the week. You can prepare our supper, and also select a couple of bottles of Madeira for us to toast the health, happiness and fecundity of our new bride and groom.'

'I'll drink to that, and gladly.' Pammy Mallot smiled. 'You always manages to cheer me up, Geraint, no matter how low I'm feeling.'

'And I always will do my utmost to bring that lovely smile to your lips, my dear,' he asserted fervently. 'Now let us both set to our tasks, and when they're done we can begin enjoying ourselves. But you mustn't let me get too drunk, because I have affairs to attend to tomorrow, and so must return to Feckenham tonight.'

In the shadowy, dim-lit bedroom, George Creswell lay comatose. When Courtney drew back the covering sheets and blankets from Creswell's naked body, the only sign that the man still lived was the sighing of shallow breaths which did not even noticeably lift his skeletal rib cage.

Courtney gently turned the unconscious man on to his front, telling him softly, 'Your release from all bodily sufferings is very close at hand, Master Creswell.'

A noticeable tremor shivered momentarily through the naked body, and Courtney chuckled throatily.

'By God! It seems that your hearing is unimpaired, my old Bucko.'

He used his fingernails to scratch a small patch of skin on Creswell's lower back until it wept blood. Then he took the leather gloves from the bedside table and pulled them on, produced a small pot from his pocket and opened its lid. He lightly dabbed the tip of his forefinger on to the pot's contents and tentatively touched that finger tip to his lower lip, hissing in satisfaction at the almost instant reaction of sharp tingling followed by numbness on the site of that touch.

'Bloody hell! This is powerful stuff!'

He used his fingers repeatedly to ladle salve on to the lower spine of the unconscious man, spreading and rubbing hard with both hands until the salve had been absorbed by skin and flesh.

Courtney straightened and grimaced as a twinge of pain lanced across his own stiffened lower back. 'I could do with some bugger giving me such an expert massage, Master Creswell.'

He turned Creswell over and carefully arranged him in a comfortable-looking posture, tucked the bedclothes around him and left the room.

Downstairs he joined Pammy Mallot in the kitchen.

'Come, my dear, let's have a convivial glass while we're waiting for our supper to cook.'

They sat at the table for some time drinking and talking, until Courtney dramatically slapped his hand against his forehead.

'Dammee! I do declare, Pammy, that I must be entering my dotage. I've very carelessly left the lamp burning in Master Creswell's room.'

He laid down the long pipe he was smoking. 'I'll go up now and douse it.'

'No you won't!' Pammy Mallot told him firmly. 'You've done enough for the nasty old bugger for this day. I'll go and put it out.'

Before he could protest, she was gone from the room.

Courtney grinned with satisfaction. 'She'll find the old bastard sleeping like a babe.'

FIFTY-FIVE

Redditch Town
Saturday, 29th March
Morning

'Ainsley, you say? Yes, I've had a man of that name staying here. What villainy has he been up to?' John Mence, proprietor of the Unicorn Hotel and Inn, frowned.

'Nothing that I know of, Master Mence,' Tom Potts hastened to assure. 'I'd merely like to have a word with him.'

'And so should I!' Mence spat out angrily. 'I aren't laid eyes on him for days and he owes me money.'

Tom's highly attuned instincts were aroused, and certain pieces of a mental jigsaw puzzle began to jostle for closer attention.

'You'd best give me a full description of him, and an account of anything you might know or have heard about his doings since he's been here, Master Mence.'

'Well, he claims to be a Theatrical Manager, and said that he was looking for suitable premises where his travelling troupe could stage performances. I do know that he's spoken to a lot of the local farmers about hiring their barns.

'When he first arrived I was suspicious because although he was flash clad, his horse and tack were rubbish. But then he started spending with a very free hand, and so I got a bit careless about the bills he was running up.'

Mence hissed with self-disgust. 'I should have trusted my first instincts, shouldn't I? They've been hard enough won.'

'Did he have any callers while he was here? Any clerical gentlemen, for example?'

'Not that I know of.'

'Well, if you'll now give me his physical description, I'll keep a look out for him.'

Mence gave a full description of Ainsley and his horse, and Tom stored the information to memory and took his leave.

Outside the inn Tom considered his next move. Maud Harman's

and John Mence's description of Ainsley had tallied closely, and he was satisfied that they had described the same man.

'So, here are two men of doubtful character, Christophe de Langlois and Archibald Ainsley, with a connecting link, the Reverend Geraint Winward. Who in his turn apparently has a link of some sort with Charles Bromley. I think I'd best have a word with old Charlie now, and find out what that link is.'

Tom was making his way along the High Street when he was hailed from behind. He turned to find Richard Parsons, the parish Customs and Excise Officer, hurrying towards him, radiating indignation.

'Have you forgotten our appointment, Constable Potts? I've been waiting for you at the lock-up for the past hour.'

Recollection flooded Tom, and he hastened to apologize. 'I'm sorry, Master Parsons. We are to check the traders' Weights and Measures today, are we not?'

'Indeed we are, Constable, and with the whole parish to cover I can't waste any more time, so can we commence immediately?'

'Very well, Master Parsons,' Tom agreed.

It was late evening before the task was completed and Tom was able to go to Charles Bromley's shop.

It was locked and shuttered with no lights showing, and he went around to the rear living quarters to find the same. He hammered on the door there, calling loudly for Bromley, and the next-door neighbour came out to berate him angrily.

'Will you give over making such a bloody racket! There's no bugger in! Charlie Bromley's went up to Brummagem this midday on Humphries' coach, and perhaps he's gone for good! Like I hopes you will this bloody instant!'

For the second time that day, Tom was forced to apologize and change direction.

FIFTY-SIX

Redditch Town
Sunday, 30th March
Afternoon

Intent upon their game in the comfort of the warm room neither chess player had been aware of any caller at the house until Mrs Blakely came to tell Hugh Laylor, 'George Creswell's housekeeper, Mrs Mallot, has sent a message asking you to come straight away. She thinks George Creswell is breathing his last!'

Hugh Laylor tutted in chagrin. 'Wouldn't you know it, Tom, the first time for ages I'm poised to checkmate you, and this has to happen. Thank you, Mrs Blakely; will you please tell the messenger I'll be there as soon as possible?'

'Oh he's gone, Doctor. He says he's got to go to Feckenham and inform another gentleman about what's happening.' She bustled away.

When he heard the name Creswell, Tom's instant involuntary reaction had been to picture the wedding group of Phoebe Creswell, and with mention of Feckenham, he immediately guessed who was also being informed about George Creswell's condition.

'It has to be Winward.'

'I must go to Beoley without delay, Tom,' Laylor sighed regretfully. 'But we'll leave the board as it is and finish the game at the first opportunity.'

On impulse Tom asked, 'Can I come with you to Beoley, Hugh?'

'Whatever for?' Laylor queried in surprise.

Tom forced a smile and answered casually. 'Call it a fit of nostalgia for my days spent in medical training.'

'You're more than welcome to come, my friend. I shall be very glad of your company,' Hugh Laylor smiled back.

'Master Creswell's in sore straits, Doctor. I'm not sure what you can do for him, but I sent Joey Stokes to fetch you because there's nothing more I can do,' Pammy Mallot announced calmly as she opened the door to Hugh Laylor and Tom.

'Hullo, Tom Potts, what brings you here? I'd have thought you'd have been tucked up in a nice warm bed wi' your pretty missus on a cold day like this.'

'Master Potts is here at my invitation, Mrs Mallot,' Hugh Laylor told her, and added sarcastically, 'You appear to be bearing up under this grievous burden with great fortitude.'

'It aren't no grievous burden to me, Doctor,' she stated bluntly. 'I don't like the nasty old bugger, and him likely being near to death don't alter that.'

'Is Miss Phoebe here?' Laylor asked.

'No, and truth to tell I don't know exactly where her is. Her got wed last Friday and I was told they'd gone to Worcester for a bit of a holiday. I'll take you up to him.'

In the bedroom a coal fire flamed on the hearth, and the overheated air was laden with the mingled smells of faeces, urine, vomit and unwashed flesh. On the four-poster bed the body of George Creswell was writhing and cramping, each seizure partnered by guttural groans of agony.

Tom and Laylor went to the bedside, and Laylor pulled the coverlets back to completely uncover the stricken man. His skeletal body and excreta-smeared skin was a sheen of sweat, and Tom laid his hand on the sick man's brows and chest, before remarking quietly, 'This is curious, Hugh. He's sweating freely, but his body temperature feels to be much below normal.'

Laylor was staring at the faeces and vomit strewn across the sheets. 'We'll need to collect samples of this for closer examination, Tom. Do you have a couple of crock bowls or suchlike, and a pair of large spoons we can make use of, Mrs Mallot?'

'I'll go and sort out some, Doctor. And you can chuck 'um away when you've done with 'um, because we won't be wanting 'um back.' She disappeared through the door.

Tom grinned wryly. 'I can't blame her for not wanting any further use from them, Hugh. I wouldn't relish that prospect myself.'

Creswell's body suddenly cramped violently, rolling him on to his side, doubling his knees to his chest, bringing his head ducking on to his knees, curving and straining his body like an overstretched archer's bow.

Then abruptly, a long drawn-out gusting of breath escaped from his mouth, and his straining body gently subsided into a collapsed heap of inert flesh and bone.

'He's gone,' Hugh Laylor murmured. 'And it's God's mercy on him.'

Tom was already probing Creswell's neck at the carotid artery, and with his other hand feeling for a pulse at the wrist. Next he arranged Creswell's body on its back and closely examined the eyeballs, then bent and pressed his ear between the protruding rib bones. He followed this by another check of the carotid and wrist arteries, before he told his friend, 'I don't believe there's any point in trying to resuscitate him. There's complete respiratory and cardiac arrest. As you say, it's God's mercy on him.'

While Tom spoke a pair of leather gloves lying on the small bedside table was intruding into his peripheral vision, and now he picked them up, remarking casually, 'I wonder what use the poor fellow was making of these during his illness?'

'They'm not his.' Pammy Mallot was standing in the doorway carrying two crock bowls. 'They'm the Reverend Winward's. He wears 'um when he gives Master Creswell his massages.'

'Well he'll not be needing them for that use again, Mrs Mallot,' Hugh Laylor intervened. 'Regretfully, Master Creswell is dead.'

The woman shrugged her meaty shoulders. 'I'll not act the hypocrite and say it grieves me. My hope is that God will take him to task now for being the cruel, harsh father he's been to poor Phoebe. Will you still be wanting these bowl and spoons?'

'We shall,' Laylor snapped curtly.

'I'll leave 'um with you then; and when you'm done here I'll strip the bedding and lay him out decent.'

As Pammy Mallot came and put the bowls and spoons on the bed table Tom asked, 'For what reason was Reverend Winward massaging Master Creswell?'

'To ease his back pains. The Reverend was real good to him. He brought special Elixir to soothe his stomach, and a special salve for the back pains. The Reverend used to spend hours ministering to the nasty old bugger. He's a living saint, so he is!'

She left the room as the memory of a man's death Tom had witnessed many years previously was coming back to him, and he wondered aloud, 'A special salve? What was it?'

He lifted the gloves to his nostrils and sniffed several times, then looked about him and saw the salve pot on the dresser beneath the window. He went and picked it up, opened its lid and used the tip of his right forefinger to scoop out a tiny smear of the salve, which he dabbed upon his lower lip. There were instant powerful reactions of tingling followed by numbness.

He moved quickly back to the bedside and turned the dead man face downwards, then closely scrutinized the wrinkled skin of the lower and upper back. He used the tip of his left forefinger to rub a small patch of abraded skin and once more dabbed the tip against his lip.

'Let's set to work,' Hugh Laylor invited. 'I'll collect the shit and you collect the vomit, then we'll go back to my dispensary and analyse them post-haste. From the way she's behaving it won't surprise me at all if Mrs Mallot has been feeding old Creswell here with arsenic, or some other noxious substance.'

Tom set to work using the spoon to scrape the still-damp clots of fresh vomit from the bed sheets. While he worked his memory ranged back across the years to a treatise he had once read about ancient Chinese war practices and he mused, 'I wonder if the Reverend Winward has read that same treatise?'

At this same hour in the private parlour of the Old Black Boy Inn, Walter Courtney was being informed that a man named Joey Stokes had come with an urgent message for Reverend Winward.

'Oh, I'm feeling so very tired, Master Blake. I really must rest for a while.' Courtney sighed wearily. 'So will you please tell the man that I'm not here at present, but he can entrust the message to you to pass on to me when I return.'

'O' course I will, Reverend.' The landlord bustled away to return quickly with the news that 'George Creswell is very near to death, and could the Reverend please come to Beoley as soon as possible.'

'Thank you very much, Master Blake. Now could you bring me a bottle of your very fine Madeira, and a pipe of your equally fine tobacco?'

A little later, sipping a glass of heady Madeira wine, drawing in mouthfuls of the fragrant Turkish tobacco, Walter Courtney savoured what he now deemed to be a certainty: the successful outcome of his plans.

In Worcester City, Sylvan Kent and his new bride were strolling arm in arm in the precinct of the Cathedral, and Kent's thoughts were also dwelling on the fact of George Creswell's wealth and properties.

'Now we're wed I own Phoebe's body and soul. So the moment Creswell's dead, I'll be as rich as Croesus. The first thing I'll be doing is telling that cunt Archie Ainsley to fuck off and beg for his supper elsewhere. If Walter doesn't like it, he can fuck off as well! Because I'll be holding the purse strings then, and I'll be the Master.'

'Is something troubling you, my dearest?' Phoebe asked anxiously. 'You're frowning so!'

He instantly smiled and stroked her cheek. 'I was merely frowning with regret for all the long years I've spent without you, my darling girl; and for the rest of my life I do not intend to spend a single day or night without you beside me.'

He bent to kiss her lips, and whispered urgently, 'Let's make haste back to the hotel. I'm on fire to make love to you again.'

She blushed and trembled like a shy young girl, but clasped his arm tightly, then eagerly changed direction and quickened her pace.

FIFTY-SEVEN

Redditch Town
Sunday, 30th March
Midnight

In Hugh Laylor's dispensary the final tests on the vomit and excreta had been done, and Laylor's handsome features displayed disappointment.

'No traces of arsenic whatsoever, Tom. It seems that my suspicions of Pammy Mallot are unjustified. I'll enter death by natural causes on the certificate, so there's no need for any inquest.'

Earlier that evening, Tom had gone to the lock-up and had quickly scrutinized an entry in one of the notebooks he had kept from his years of medical training. Now he pondered briefly before replying simply, 'Let's hope so.'

The clock began to strike, and Tom grimaced. 'Is that the hour already? I'd best go home. Tomorrow I shall be going back to Beoley.'

'Why?' Laylor asked.

'I want to obtain some of the salve the Reverend was using. It might soothe my own aches and pains. I'll bid you good night, my friend.'

FIFTY-EIGHT

Beoley Village
Monday 31st March
Morning

'My dear Pammy, I can only offer you my humblest apologies for not coming sooner. I was engaged on Church business and didn't return to the inn and receive your message until this morning.'

Pammy Mallot appeared to be in high spirits as she took Courtney's hand and drew him into the house.

'Don't moither yourself about it, Geraint. The old bugger died before you could have reached here anyway; and Doctor Laylor and the Constable was both here when he did croak it. All I had to do was strip the bedding and lay him out when they'd gone.'

'The Constable, you say. What did he want?'

'I reckon he just come to be nosey.' She chuckled. 'Because it aren't every day there's the chance of seeing such a nasty old bugger being sent to Hell, is it? Now, have you had any breakfast?'

'No, I set out the very moment I received your message.'

'Well then, you go and sit by the fire in the drawing room, and I'll cook you something nice and tasty.'

'No, my dear, don't begin preparing any food for me yet. It is my duty to go up to Master Creswell and to pray for the salvation of his soul.'

She sniffed disparagingly. 'It'll need a deal of praying for his soul to find salvation. He don't deserve none.'

'You must not say such,' he told her sternly. 'Our Lord is infinite mercy, and even the worst sinners can find salvation. I shall join you when I've completed my prayers.'

She looked suitably chastened as he left her.

Closing the bedroom door firmly behind him, Courtney sonorously recited the Lord's Prayer as he rifled through the drawers and chests in the room. He found a large ring of multiple keys and tried them in the lock of the strongbox built into the wall adjoining the bed on which lay the shrouded body of George Creswell. Two of the keys fitted the lock, and he took one of these off the ring and slipped it into his pocket.

He pulled out the pile of documents the strongbox contained and carefully went through them, his eyes glistening with relish as he enumerated the various bank statements, and deeds of properties and land.

'By God! This is far better than I dared hope for! It's my fuckin' dream come true! I can live out my days in luxury with this lot.'

He scanned the Last Will and Testament, and hissed with satisfaction. Apart from a couple of trifling bequests, all the money, properties and land would devolve to Phoebe. Which, now she was married, meant that in law, she, and all she possessed, now belonged to her husband.

'And when she and Sylvan are disposed of, I shall add the Last Will and Testament of Christophe de Langlois to this lot, and the job will be done.'

The vision of Archibald Ainsley's face came into Courtney's mind, and his teeth bared in a snarling grin.

'Yes, Archibald, they'll be joining you in the next life. But I don't think it'll be the Devil welcoming poor Phoebe. She'll more likely go to Heaven.'

He replaced the documents and ring of keys, picked up his gloves and the salve pot and went back downstairs.

'I'm going to burn these gloves, my dear – they're too impregnated to wear socially – and I'll throw this pot away. It's not worth keeping what's left of the salve. Then after I've eaten I shall go to Worcester and find Phoebe and Christophe. It's best I break the news to her myself, rather than send someone else with such sad tidings.'

'No, don't you dare throw that nice little pot away,' Pammy Mallot remonstrated. 'If you don't want it I'll wash it out and find a use for it.'

* * *

It was late morning when Tom rang the doorbell, much to Pammy Mallot's surprise.

'What are you doing here again, Tom Potts?'

'I wanted to ask you where I might find the Reverend Winward, Mrs Mallot. I need to talk with him.'

'Well, he lodges at the Old Black Boy in Feckenham, but he won't be there now.'

'Why so?'

'He come here first thing this morning and spent ages praying for Master Creswell's soul, and he told me he was going to go straight to Worcester to find Phoebe and tell her about her dad dying. He's a living saint, so he is.'

'Yes indeed,' Tom agreed fulsomely. 'And it's his help I'm seeking. I'm having severe pains in my joints and I wondered if he could let me have some of that amazing salve he was treating Master Creswell with; and perhaps loan me the gloves he used to apply the salve to save me having to spoil another pair because they get so impregnated with it.'

'Oh, that's a pity! He burned them gloves this morning because he said that he couldn't wear 'um any more for that very reason. But you'm in luck, because I aren't washed the pot yet and it's got a bit o' salve in it, which you'm very welcome to.'

She hurried to bring the pot and hand it to him. 'Now when the pot's empty bring it back to me because I got a use for it. And I'm sure that if you needs more o' the salve the Reverend 'ull get you some.'

'I most certainly will, Mrs Mallot. Thank you very much for your kindness, and please give the Reverend my thanks. Could you also convey my deepest sympathy for her sad loss to Mrs de Langlois.'

As they parted, Tom put the small pot into his pocket, and decided, 'Now I'll visit Maud Harman and Reverend Mackay.'

In the Olde Talbot Inn in Worcester City the newly wed Phoebe de Langlois greeted Walter Courtney with a welcoming smile, which faltered when she saw the gravity of his expression.

'Do you bring me bad news, Geraint?' she questioned anxiously.

'Alas! I do. I'm bitterly sorry to have to tell you that your dear father has passed into the care of Our Heavenly Father.'

She dragged in a long, shuddering breath and covered her face with both hands. Sylvan Kent took her in his arms and lowered her gently upon an ottoman, and sat beside her cradling her shaking body, crooning soothingly to her.

'I grieve for you, my darling wife. Try to hold it in your mind that your dear father is now freed all pain and anguish, and is safe in Heaven with our Lord and Saviour.' He kissed her forehead and whispered, 'And I shall do my utmost to soothe your pain and anguish.'

She threw her arms about his neck and clung tightly to him, burying her face against his shoulder.

The two men's eyes met. Courtney nodded and smiled approvingly. Kent stared coldly back, and told him, 'My wife and I would prefer to be alone at this sad time. You may call on us when we return to Beoley.'

'Of course. I entirely understand your need for solitude. I will await your return to Beoley,' Courtney answered smoothly, and went from the room.

He waited until he was driving his gig from the city before venting contemptuous laughter.

'Exactly what I was expecting. The cretin thinks he's the master now.'

FIFTY-NINE

Redditch Town
Tuesday, 8th April
Mid-morning

In the study of the Red House, Joseph Blackwell sat in impassive silence until Tom had finished speaking. Then he smiled bleakly and said, 'These are very tenuous grounds on which to base your suspicions of this clergyman, Constable Potts. Because he has some sort of connection with a likely fortune-hunter, and another man who leaves unpaid reckonings at an inn, does not prove that he himself is of doubtful character.'

Tom opened his mouth to reply, but Blackwell held up his hand, and snapped curtly, 'Kindly allow me to finish, Constable. As I have said, these are tenuous grounds. Nevertheless, because of the high regard I have for your talents, I shall not forbid you to abandon this investigation. With the proviso, of course, that you do not make undue demands on the Parish coffers, and should you incur the wrath of the Ecclesiastical hierarchy, then on your own head be it.'

'Of course, Sir,' Tom accepted immediately.

'But now I have a task for you,' Blackwell went on. 'I've received information that the dead man whom you lodged at the Old Laystall is now so rotted in the face as to be virtually unidentifiable, and that Sally Rimmer is using him as a penny peepshow. So have him buried as soon as possible, and arrange for the sale of his horse and tack to cover the burial costs. I bid you good day, Constable Potts.'

SIXTY

Redditch Town
Tuesday, 8th April
Night

All was quiet in the Old Laystall and only one window in a rear room of one building showed the faint glimmer of candlelight. Sally Rimmer sat in that room waiting for the tapping on that window which would announce the arrival of her visitor.

It was past midnight when that tapping came, and Sally Rimmer quickly went out of the door into the rear yard to find the small girl waiting for her.

The woman held out her cupped palm and Milly Styke placed a crown coin on to it.

'Now listen very careful, my wench, because I've got a lot o' news tonight. Tell your mistress that Old Creswell died last Sunday week, and that his daughter and that bloke wi' the funny name who's her husband, am come back to the Orchard House in Beoley. The funeral is next Monday afternoon at Beoley Church. And from what folks are saying, there'll be a lot of people going to it, because the old man was very rich and had a lot o' tenants. And tell her as well that the dead 'un her come to see is to be buried in the paupers' plot down at the old Monks' Cemetery this coming Thursday. Now, has you got all that in your noddle?'

The girl nodded, and ran off into the darkness.

Sally Rimmer went back to her chair and cackled with satisfaction as one of her friends came into the room.

'That's another five bob for us, Bessie. Just for passing on what we sees and hears when we'em out collecting shit. I reckon we knows more about what goes on in these parts than the bloody Town Crier does.'

SIXTY-ONE

Feckenham
Wednesday, 9th April
Morning

'Welcome back, Reverend. I was wondering where you'd got to these last days.' A smiling Maud Harman greeted Walter Courtney as he entered the Old Black Boy.

'I've been on the Lord's work, Mrs Harman. Giving what help and comfort I could to a young lady who has suffered a most grievous bereavement.'

'That's what I told your visitor, Reverend. That you'd most certainly be doing the Lord's work and helping some poor soul or other in their hour of need.'

'My visitor?' He raised his eyebrows questioningly.

'It was that Constable Potts from Redditch. He come on Monday and he said he needed to see you most urgent on private business. So I sent him across to Parson Mackay in case he might know where you were. Perhaps Potts told him what he wanted to see you about. Now then, what can I get you for your breakfast, Reverend?'

Courtney forced a smile and waved his hand in refusal. 'Nothing, I thank you, my dear lady, I've already breakfasted. It may be that Potts is in need of my immediate help, so I shall go and call on Reverend Mackay.'

A frown of suspicion replaced his smile as he walked out of the inn.

'Potts calls on Pammy Mallot, and takes my salve away. If he really needed a salve for his joints he knows enough about medical treatments to mix his own. Now he's poking about here. What's he up to?'

In the vicarage, Horace Mackay gave Courtney further reason for disquiet.

'Potts was asking me if that Ainsley fellow who calls on you had ever called on me. I said no, but that you had helped him several times by donating money to his charity. Potts then said that Ainsley is a charlatan, and he wanted to question him about certain matters.'

'Dammee!' Courtney evinced shock. 'I must speak with Potts about this matter without delay. Did he tell you anything further?'

'About Ainsley, no. But he wanted to examine the Parish registers.'

'Whatever for? I would think they make dull reading for a layman.'

'Not in this case, Walter. Potts was most interested when he saw the Special License for your friends' wedding. He had never before seen the personal seal of an Archbishop, and thought it very impressive.'

'Ah well, I'm glad to hear it impressed him.' Courtney smiled thinly. 'Now I must be off, Horace, I have much work to do.'

Later that day Alfie Bennett came to the lock-up to inform Tom Potts. 'Mrs Harman's sent me to tell you that she'd done what you asked her to.'

Tom gave him a shilling. 'Thank you very much, Alfie.'

'Is there any other task I can do for you, Master Potts?' Bennett asked.

'Not at this time, but I thank you for offering. Good day to you.'

Tom was closing the door when he was struck by a sudden idea. He hurried outside and called after the other man, 'Alfie, hold fast! I can offer you some employment after all. I want you to take a letter for me.'

SIXTY-TWO

Beoley Village
Monday, 14th April
Afternoon

The skies were clear and bright sunshine signaled that Spring had come. The large crowd of funeral mourners were rapidly dispersing down the slopes of the Beoley Mount in vehicles, on horseback and on foot. In St Leonard's churchyard, Sylvan Kent helped his wife and Pammy Mallot into a carriage, and told them, 'I must have a final word with Geraint. I'll be as quick as I can.'

Walter Courtney had just mounted into his gig and as Kent came to him, he hissed, 'Behave like a church mouse these next weeks, Sylvan. You're being very closely watched.'

'Of course I am. These chawbacons are naturally eager to examine the new village Squire.' Kent was radiating self-satisfaction.

'I'm not talking about the yokels,' Courtney snapped irritably. 'You need to keep your eyes and wits about you.'

'Don't use that tone to me!' Kent snapped back. 'You'd best remember that I hold the whip hand now.'

Courtney instantly replied in a mollifying tone, 'You well know that I've fully accepted that you're now in command, Sylvan. Have I not disposed of Ainsley because you wanted me to do so?'

'Disposed of Ainsley?' Kent queried.

'Just so.' Courtney winked meaningfully. 'He'd served our purpose. Now forget about him, and take a look at that great skinny lanky fellow by the gate who's showing such a close interest in us.'

Kent turned his head.

Standing by the churchyard gate, Tom Potts kept his stare directed at them, but remained motionless.

'Who the fuck is he?' Sylvan Kent demanded.

'He's Thomas Potts, the Parish Constable.' Courtney frowned. 'And he's been doing a deal of prying these past days.'

'Phooo!' Sylvan dismissed scathingly. 'By the looks of him, he's naught but a clodhopping chawbacon. You're becoming a panicky old maid, Cousin. You'll be screaming at spiders next. It's a good job for both of us that I've taken charge of our affairs. Now, repeat the instructions I've given you.'

A murderous resentment was scorching Walter Courtney, but he dutifully obeyed. 'I am to leave this district and stay away until such time as you send for me to return here. I am to follow the route and timetable you have given me. When I arrive at the designated towns I must call at the Post Office and enquire if there is a post-paid letter being held for me. When I receive it, that letter will be your summons for me to return here.'

'Well done.' Kent grinned mockingly.

'How soon might I receive that summons?' Courtney asked.

Kent shrugged and told him airily. 'Oh, that's hard to say, Cousin. Maybe two months, or three months, or even four months. It all depends on how bearable I'm finding life with this ugly, stink-breathed, no-tits you insisted on my marrying.'

Courtney exerted all his will power to smile and congratulate. 'I think it's an excellent plan, Cousin. It only remains for me to bid you a fond "*Au Revoir*".'

As the gig rattled through the gateway, Tom and Walter Courtney's eyes met and held, but no gesture of acknowledgement passed between them.

The carriage of the chief mourners next exited through the gate. Tom politely raised his hat.

'That's queer, that is,' Pammy Mallot exclaimed.

'What is?' Phoebe queried.

'Well, Tom Potts come to the house last Monday week desperate to speak wi' Geraint about the salve he was using to treat your dad; and I give him what was left of it. You'd have thought that at least he'd have come and thanked Geraint today for the use of it. Yet he didn't, did he?'

Phoebe shrugged disinterestedly and made no reply.

Sylvan Kent did likewise.

In Bradley Green, Timothy Wrighton was greeting a totally unexpected caller at his house.

'By God, Ma'am! I only wish I could have informed you that I'd had your house sealed and padlocked. It's a good job my man was making his regular check on it when you come there, else you'd have had a deal o' trouble gaining entrance.'

Clad in mourning black, thickly veiled Ella Peelson told him warmly, 'I owe you my most grateful thanks for your care of my house, Master Wrightson. I'd very much like to hear all you know concerning this intruder who was making free with my property.'

'Regretfully, Ma'am, there is nothing known about the man. No one was able to identify him, despite the offered reward bringing many to view his body. I fear it will remain a mystery.

'However, what I can do is to have my people stand guard at the house now you're in residence, and that will insure there are no further intrusions upon you. And if you need women to clean and cook, I can find them for you in the village.'

'I'm most grateful for your kindness, Sir, but I have a maid and a cook-housekeeper, and also I've taken a coachman into my employ who is more than capable of dealing with any intrusions. He's an honest, sober fellow whom I'm know very well, since his father and grandfather both gave lifelong service to my late husband's family.'

He escorted her out to her closed carriage, and when he saw the exceptionally powerful build of the uniformed coachman he exclaimed, 'By God, Ma'am! I pity any intruder who might try to get past this fellow! He looks like a champion prizefighter.'

SIXTY-THREE

Redditch Town
Wednesday, 16th April
Mid-morning

Tom bent double as his stomach heaved and he retched violently, but only a froth of saliva came from his gaping mouth because the last of his stomach contents had already been agonizingly voided minutes before.

He heard Amy's fist clumping on the privy door and her anxious voice. 'Tom, are you being sick again?'

He wiped his streaming eyes and foul-tasting mouth and gasped. 'I'm alright, my love! It must be something bad I ate, that's all. I'll be perfectly well in a moment or two.'

'What d'you mean, something you ate?' There was asperity in her tone now. 'I haven't never give you anything bad to eat!'

He opened the privy door, still clutching his painful stomach.

'This is naught to do with my breakfast, Amy. It's the result of an experiment I made last night.'

'What experiment?' she demanded. 'I never saw you making such.'

'Well it's done with now.' He grimaced in wry humour. 'And I'm very pleased to report that it's been an unqualified success.'

Even as he spoke the pain eased. 'And now I'm as fit as a butcher's dog.'

'And as mad as a March hare!' she rejoined. 'And Blackwell's man has just brought these summonses for you.' She handed him several sheets of paper.

'Then I'd best deliver them as soon as I'm washed and shaved.'

'Are you sure you're alright now?' she queried.

'Yes, I'm very sure.'

She reached up and pulled his head down, then abruptly pushed his head back and scolded. 'Oh no! I aren't going to kiss you until you've cleaned your mouth. Don't you dare to do any more experiments that makes your breath stink like it does now.'

'I can promise you that I won't,' he agreed fervently.

The previous night he had deliberately abraded a patch of skin on his lower back, and rubbed into it a portion of the Reverend Winward's salve. The resulting attacks of vomiting and diarrhoea, and his general feeling of debilitation, had convinced him that the salve had poisoned and killed George Creswell.

As was customary the coach coming from Birmingham halted at the base of the Fish Hill, and the driver, Richard Humphries, shouted, 'Everybody who aren't a cripple must get off here and walk up this hill. Me team can't draw all you lot and the baggage up it. It's too long and steep.'

Before any of the passengers could reply, he added for the benefit of an inside passenger, who was an old adversary, 'And there's no need for you to start bawling and scrawking, Widow Potts. I knows very well that you'm too fat to move your arse. So you stay seated and me poor team 'ull just have to haul their bloody guts out. But if one o' the poor buggers drops dead wi' a heart attack, you'll be to blame!'

The passengers exited the roof and inside seats to the accompaniment of a screeching tirade of threats and abuse directed at the driver by the Widow Gertrude Potts.

With straining bodies and snorting breaths the team drew the coach up the long steep hill and stopped as it reached the flat central plateau, where Widow Potts thrust her bonneted head out of the window and screeched.

'Don't stop here. Go straight on to the shop.'

'I'll do no such thing,' Richard Humphries flatly refused. 'I'm waiting here for the rest of 'um.'

'But I can't wait. They'll have to walk to the shop as well, because I can't bear another moment in this dirty, foul-smelling box.'

'Then get out and bloody well walk!'

'Alright! I will! And if I should collapse and die on the way, then may you rot in Hell, you evil, callous swine!'

'Well, if by chance I do go to Hell, I knows very well who'll be roasting on the spit next to me, don't I? It'll be you! You nasty old bitch!'

Gasping out another tirade of insults, Gertrude Potts laboriously levered her squat gross body from the vehicle, shook her walking stick at Humphries, and waddled on towards the crossroads, some hundred yards distant.

When she reached the chapel at the crossroads she decided to wait in its porch for her fellow travellers, Charles Bromley and his sister, to pass by.

'I'll teach Humphries a lesson. I'll pretend that I've collapsed and make Bromley bring a summons against the bastard for forcing me out of his coach.'

When she entered the porch she noticed the reward poster pinned on the wall and peered closely at it. Then she sucked her breath in sharply.

'That description fits that Debt Collector!' She screwed her eyes to read the small print at the bottom of the poster. 'And Bromley's done this notice! I'll wager he's pocketed the reward money as well, and he's said nothing to me about it because he's keeping all the money for himself. Well, I'll teach the sly bugger not to keep secrets from me!'

She left the porch and waddled purposefully towards the lock-up.

Carrying the summonses, Tom was exiting the building as his mother arrived, and he greeted her politely.

'Hello, Mother. Can I be of service to you?'

She didn't prevaricate. 'When did you give Bromley the money?'

Tom was momentarily taken aback. 'What money?'

She scowled and screeched, 'Don't make mock of me, you vile unnatural beast of a son! You and Bromley have shared it between you, and cheated me out of what's rightfully mine!'

Tom held up his hand. 'Pray calm yourself, Mother, and explain to me what you're talking about?'

'I'm talking about the money for naming him that was found dead at Bradley Green!'

Now Tom made the connection with the reward notice, and questioned, 'Are you claiming that Bromley told me the identity of the dead man?'

'Of course I am, you stupid blockhead!'

Excitement sparked in Tom's brain, and instantly he decided that in this matter to lie to her was justifiable. 'Very well, Mother. If you can satisfy me that Bromley was lying when he said that you knew nothing of this dead man, then you'll receive the same amount in full sum, that Bromley and I divided between us.'

As words poured from her, Tom's excitement rapidly mounted, and when she finally fell silent he immediately brought her five gold guineas from his strongbox. Then he suggested casually, 'It might well be to your advantage not to tell Bromley about this conversation we've had, Mother. Because so long as he believes that the secret he and I have shared concerning the reward money still holds, who knows what other secrets that he keeps from you, he may confide to me?'

Her eyes hooded, her mouth pursed, then she nodded and waddled away.

Tom stood still, his concentration centred on evaluating what he had heard.

His mother had confirmed for him the connection between Langlois and Winward, regarding the newspaper advertisements for a bride. Coupled with what Harry Pratt had told him, he now firmly believed that both men were frauds, and had colluded in the murder of George Creswell.

As for the Bradley Green dead man, Tom decided, 'I'll go to Birmingham tomorrow and find out if he were indeed a Debt Collector employed by the *Aris Gazette*.'

SIXTY-FOUR

Bradley Green
Thursday, 17th April
Morning

As she did every morning, Ella Peelson was sitting up in bed closely examining her reflection in a looking glass. The bruises and swelling on her features had disappeared, the scars were paling, but the flattened nose and broken snags of teeth remained to disfigure her.

This morning, as on every morning, her hatred of the men she knew as Christophe de Langlois and the Reverend Geraint Winward throbbed virulently.

'Are you awake, Ma'am?' Milly Styke called from outside the bedroom door.

'Yes, my dear, come in.'

The girl entered carrying a tray with a bottle of gin and a glass upon it. 'Dora and Sean and the other men has had their breakfasts, Ma'am, and Sean has seen to the dogs as well.'

'Tell Sean I'll speak to him presently. You and I shall go in the pony-trap to the churchyard in a couple of hours, to lay a wreath on your mother's grave. We'll go to the mason's yard after that, and you shall pick out a nice headstone for your mother.'

'Oh, that'll be lovely for her, Ma'am.' The child's face beamed with pleasure as she placed the tray on the dressing table beside the bed. 'Nobody from our family has ever had anything to mark where they lays. We've always been paupers, you see.'

Ella Peelson drew the girl to her and kissed her rosy cheek.

'Well you'll never be a pauper again, my dear. I shall make sure of that. Now go and tell Dora to come up to me.'

It was near to midday when at the end of the straggling main street of Feckenham Village a respectably dressed, middle-aged woman handed an urchin a folded note.

'Me feet am badly, me little duck. Take this to the Old Black Boy, will you, and then come back here to me and I'll give you a penny. Just give it to somebody who works there and tell 'um it's for Parson Winward.'

The urchin sped away.

Walter Courtney scanned the brief note and frowned. 'What does that holy cunt want now, I wonder. Ah well, I suppose I'd best do as he asks.'

The sun was shining as he left the Old Black Boy and walked at a leisurely pace to the church, passing a pipe-smoking, smock-clad man lounging against a wall and an untended pony and trap parked near to the lych-gate.

Courtney went through the churchyard and walked around the church, heading for the vicarage. When he disappeared from view, Milly Styke and the heavily veiled Ella Peelson came out from the high-hedged paupers' plot of the churchyard and walked quickly to mount the pony cart. As Ella Peelson drove it slowly past the lounging, pipe-smoking, smock-clad Sean Peelson, he gave her a single nod.

'Hello, Geraint. This is a pleasant surprise,' Horace Mackay greeted as he opened the vicarage door.

'What do you mean, a surprise?' Courtney challenged jocularly. 'You must know me well enough by now to know that any note from you receives my immediate attention.'

'Note? I've not sent any note,' Mackay told him.

Courtney took the note from his pocket and waved it under the other man's nose. 'Read it!'

Frowning in puzzlement Mackay did so, and shook his head. 'This note is not in my handwriting, Geraint. And it's not addressed to you by name or signed by me either. It merely says, "Please come to the church as soon as possible." It could have been sent by anyone to anyone, and obviously it's been delivered in error.'

'Yes, that must be so,' Courtney accepted, but inwardly the sense of uneasiness which had been troubling him since Thomas Potts had taken the salve from Orchard House now intensified.

'Will you take some refreshment with me, Geraint? We can make a day and night of it,' Mackay invited.

Courtney forced a smile. 'I regret I cannot, my friend. I have much work to do. So I must bid you good day.'

Instead of returning to his lodgings he walked out into the solitude of the countryside, thinking hard about Thomas Potts.

'How do I stop the bastard poking his nose into my affairs? I could kill him, but if he's confided any suspicions of me to others, his murder could bring them hotfoot after me.'

Two hours had passed before a solution finally came to him, and he smiled ironically.

'But of course! The simplest way to spike the bastard's guns before I leave is to introduce myself to Lord Aston this very day.'

SIXTY-FIVE

Redditch Town
Saturday, 19th April
Morning

When Alfie Bennet came to the lock-up both he and his horse showed the effects of long and hard travelling. Tom welcomed the man and sat him before the kitchen fire.

'Rest yourself, Alfie. Amy will cook you some breakfast, while I see to the horse.'

When Tom returned he waited until his visitor had eaten and drunk his fill, before asking, 'How did it go, Alfie?'

'Well, after I give 'um your letter I had to hang about the place for days, and sleep where I could, Master Tom; and then a bloke come and told me he'd read your letter, and he give me this 'un to bring back to you.'

He fumbled in his satchel and handed the sealed letter to Tom, who quickly opened and scanned its content, then let out a whoop of satisfaction.

'Is it what you wanted, Master Tom?' Alfie questioned.

'It most certainly is, Alfie. But this must be our secret. So tell no one where you've been.' Tom pressed gold coins into the other man's hand. 'You've well earned these, Alfie. I have to go out now, but you stay and rest as long as you wish. My wife will get you any further refreshments you'd like, won't you, Amy?'

'O' course I will, and gladly.' She smiled, and Tom hurried from the lock-up.

'What is so urgent, Constable Potts, that you must disturb my brief hours of leisure?' Joseph Blackwell demanded tartly.

'It's this, Sir.' Tom presented him with the letter. 'I've just received this from the Commandant of the East India Company, Military Academy at Addiscombe.'

Pursing his lipless mouth, Joseph Blackwell studied the letter closely as he marshaled his thoughts, and after a long pause he told Tom, 'I fully accept that this information from Lieutenant Colonel Houston proves that about seven years ago a certain Major Christophe de Langlois was cashiered from the Company's Madras Army. But if it is he who placed the advertisement which led to him meeting and marrying Phoebe Creswell, then he has committed no crime in doing so.'

'But this man is not the Major Langlois who served in the Madras Army, Sir,' Tom stated with absolute conviction. 'The Bellman, Harry Pratt, discovered that this man has no knowledge of the language and soldiers of that army. I myself have seen the man wearing a military uniform that was not of the East India Company.

'I know for certain that the dead man at Bradley Green, who claimed to be a Debt Collector for the *Aris Gazette*, was searching for the person who placed that particular appeal for a suitable lady for marriage in the *Worcester Herald* broadsheet. I've since discovered that the dead man was not a Debt Collector, and I don't yet know the reason for his search. But I'm sure that his search was the reason for his murder.

'I'm also convinced that the so-called Langlois and Geraint Winward were co-conspirators in the murder of George Creswell, and that they intend to murder Phoebe Creswell to get their hands on her wealth and property.'

'Then tell me how they murdered George Creswell?' Blackwell asked quietly.

'By poisoning him with a salve which contained the lethal poison of aconite. I know this because I witnessed his death throes, and recognized them,' Tom stated firmly.

'As a medical student, I once witnessed two men die from aconite poisoning. The roots of the common monkshood plant contain lethally toxic aconite, and the men I saw had mistaken some monkshood roots for horseradish and had eaten them.

'I was also present at their post-mortems, and the stomach contents stank of the aconite they had ingested, which proved that it was the cause of death.

'George Creswell's death throes were virtually identical. However, when Doctor Laylor and myself performed Creswell's post-mortem, there was nothing in his stomach contents or the prior vomit or excreta that smelled of aconite. This was because the aconite was administered by Winward by massaging the salve into Creswell's lower back, and the penetration of the skin by the poison was hastened by an abrasion on that area.'

Blackwell frowned doubtfully. 'On what authority do you base this theory?'

'In China, some centuries past, in time of war it was common practice to apply a thick layering of aconite impregnated grease on to the arrowheads. It ensured that the penetration of an arrowhead which might only cause a minor flesh wound would still be fatal, because the aconite would kill the victim.

'But as time passed many of the archers who rubbed the grease into the barbs and shafts of their arrows were also dying of aconite poisoning. It was eventually recognized that the poison was being absorbed through the skin of their bare hands and killing them.

'I obtained some of the salve that Winward used, and rubbed a little of it into an abrasion on my own lower back, which resulted in such dire ill effects that I'm fully satisfied that Winward's salve killed Creswell; and I still have some of it to prove its toxicity is lethal.'

Blackwell pondered on what he had been told, before asking, 'What would you have me do?'

'Have the magistrates issue me with warrants of arrest for both of them,' Tom declared.

Once again Blackwell pondered before replying. 'I will call upon my Lord Aston and put to him all that you have told me.'

'Surely I should accompany you, Sir, and explain to him myself why I want the warrants?' Tom stated forcefully.

Blackwell frowned severely. 'You know as well as I do, Constable Potts, that my Lord Aston does not like you, and that your presence never fails but to irritate him. I will call upon him by myself, and send word to you of his decision upon my return. Good day to you.'

That evening Blackwell's manservant came to the lock-up and summoned Tom to the Red House.

Joseph Blackwell appeared to be ill at ease as he told Tom, 'My Lord Aston is very displeased with you, Constable Potts. He says that he has met and talked at length with the Reverend Winward on two occasions this very week, and is more than satisfied with his credentials. He also warns that you will have good cause for regret if you persist in making these accusations against Reverend Winward.'

Tom's reaction was shocked anger, and he demanded, 'Was his Lordship drunk as usual when he met this man?'

Blackwell lifted his hand in warning and snapped curtly, 'Remember that your wife and mother are dependent on you. Would you bring ruination and misery down on their heads?'

'Of course not!' Tom retorted.

'Then I most strongly urge you to heed Aston's warning, and to bear in mind what power he wields. Because should you persist in hounding Winward, then Aston will most certainly destroy both you and your dependants' happy security of life, and I fear that I'll not be able to prevent him doing so.'

'But what if I can prove beyond any doubt that Winward is a fraud?' Tom challenged. 'You've stated many times that you have trust in my judgement, so give me this chance to justify your trust yet again.'

'How?' Blackwell frowned.

'By going myself to the administrators of the See of Canterbury and finding out if Winward is the Archbishop's appointed man, or not. Ritchie Bint can fulfill my duties while I'm away, and I'll pay his fees from my own pocket.'

Blackwell bent his head, silently pondering until Tom's tension became close to unbearable.

Finally Blackwell's head rose and his pale eyes were troubled.

'I know from past experience how difficult it is to obtain confidential information from the Church authorities concerning their clergymen, so it may take you considerable time. You must therefore apply to me in writing for a long leave of absence. You can say that the reason for this leave is that you are going to visit a much-loved relative who is on their deathbed.

'Should you fail to obtain proof of Winward's fraudulence, and should my Lord Aston discover what you have been doing, then be it on your own head. I shall not be able to save you from ruin.'

'So be it, Sir,' Tom agreed without hesitation.

The suspicion of a smile flicked across Blackwell's pallid features. 'Because of the very sad reason for your leave of absence, I shall act as a Good Samaritan. You may borrow my best horse for this journey. I wish you good hunting, Thomas Potts!'

SIXTY-SIX

Redditch Town
Thursday 8th May
Evening

The advent of the Merry Month of May had brought no merriment for Tom Potts, and his mood was one of depressed frustration as he rode back into Redditch, and went directly to the Red House.

'I judge from your general demeanour that your journey has been a waste of time, Constable Potts,' Joseph Blackwell greeted him in the study.

'It has, Sir,' Tom admitted quietly. 'I've approached the officials at Lambeth Palace, Addington Palace, Canterbury Cathedral, Saint Paul's Cathedral, Westminster Abbey and every other ecclesiastical administrative centre where I might gain information about Geraint Winward.

'There is an ordained clergyman of that name. But my request for his personal details was politely rebuffed wherever I made it. The explanation one clerk gave me was that because the Archbishop, Charles Manners-Sutton, has been taken gravely ill, and is not expected to live for very much longer, any information concerning his administrative appointments could not be divulged at this present time. The clerk's advice was for me to wait until the enthronement of Manners-Sutton's successor, and then try again.'

'And will you try again?' Blackwell enquired.

Tom grimaced wryly. 'Well, Sir, that same clerk kindly tipped me the wink that it would only be a further waste of my time. But . . .' he left the answer hanging.

'But you'll continue the hunt! So don't dare to try and deny that fact to me, because I know you too well,' Blackwell declared with absolute conviction. 'However, it seems that your bird has flown. Some days past, Winward informed several people that his work necessitated moving to another diocese, and he left this district.'

The shock of hearing this galvanized Tom. 'Then I'd best go find out straight away where he's moved to, so I'll bid you good night, Sir.'

'And I think you'd best go straight away to see your pretty little wife and ease her worries about your safe return, Thomas Potts,' the other man rejoined sternly.

Instant guilt for his lack of thought for Amy struck through Tom, and he shamefacedly agreed. 'Of course I must!'

'Then good night to you, Thomas Potts, and please convey my best regards to your wife.'

As Tom hurried across Redditch Green to be reunited with Amy, another reunion was taking place in the stable of Ella Peelson's house at Bradley Green.

'Fuckin' Hell! Didn't I tell you again and again that I wanted this bastard alive!' Ella Peelson shouted.

'He *is* alive. He's just well dosed up wi' laudanum, that's all. He'll be as right as rain when it wears off.' Sean Peelson grinned.

Ella Peelson moved in from the stable door to stand over the comatose, tied-up body of Walter Courtney and directed the beam of her bullseye lantern on to his bloodied features.

'He looks like he kicked up a bit.'

'He did. He pulled a barker and put a ball in Muttsy's leg. So I had to teach him his manners.'

'When and where?' Ella Peelson questioned.

'Three nights since on the road from Ludlow to Leominster. He'd been staying at a coaching inn in Ludlow for a couple o' days. I couldn't risk making a grab for him until I was sure he was properly on the move again, and not coming back quick to where he'd been staying.'

'What have you done with the gig and horse and his other stuff?'

'Sammy's took 'um down to Taffy Gilpin's place in Bristol, and Muttsy's gone with him to get his leg doctored. They should be back in a week or so. So tell me, what's the soldier-boy been getting up to while I've been away?'

Her disfigured face twisted with hatred and she spat out, 'I've had word that he's going out drinking and whoring of a night time. I'll find out more about that from the Rimmer woman tonight. Now let's get this fucker down into the cellars. I want to see his blood, and hear him shrieking and begging.'

SIXTY-SEVEN

Redditch Town
Saturday, 7th June
Early morning

While Tom lit the kitchen range fire and set about preparing breakfast for Amy and himself, his thoughts ranged back over the previous night, and his mood became troubled.

In the month since returning from his unsuccessful attempt to obtain information about Geraint Winward, Tom had on several occasions encountered Christophe de Langlois carousing in various inns and taverns. Every such encounter had faced Tom with a tormenting quandary. He longed to openly confront Langlois and to accuse him of being party to the murders of George Creswell and the dead man in Bradley Green. But each time he was on the verge of doing so, the mental image of Phoebe Creswell held him back.

'Since I've no solid proof of his guilt it would only cause her terrible mental anguish, and avail me nothing.'

His frustration moved to Geraint Winward. 'Where is he? What's he planning to do next?'

Amy came down to join him, and he thankfully turned his attention to her. 'Are you going to visit your mother later, sweetheart? Because if so remember to take your keys in case I'm out patrolling the market.'

'I will, and on my way back from me Mam's, I'll call in at the Fox and see what fresh gossip they've got for me.'

It was late afternoon when Amy came running up to Tom as he patrolled the market. He saw her angry expression and questioned anxiously, 'What's the matter, sweetheart?'

She took his arm. 'You've got to come to the Fox and hear what Pammy Mallot has to say.'

In the rear parlour of the Fox and Goose, Tom found Gertrude Fowkes sitting with Pammy Mallot, whose eyes were blackened and swollen.

'Oh, Tom, I'm glad you're come,' Gertrude Fowkes greeted thankfully, and urged her sister, 'Tell Tom what you've told me, our Pammy, and he'll have the bad bugger behind bars afore this day is done.'

Pammy Mallot's voice was choking with sobs as she told Tom, 'A couple of days after Reverend Winward went away, Langlois began drinking all the time and going out whoring, and when Phoebe took him to task about what he was doing, he started knocking her about all the time. Now her's too terrified of him to tell anybody what he's doing to her, and for her sake I'se had to keep my mouth shut about it as well.

'But today I'd had enough of it! He was thrashing her wi' his stick again, and her was screaming and begging him to stop. I couldn't stand it no more, so I went for him, but he blacked me eyes, and knocked me cold. I wants you to lock the evil bastard up, Master Potts, and have him sent to jail.'

Chagrin swept through Tom, since he could only tell her, 'I'd like nothing more than to do as you ask, Mrs Mallot, but in law a man has the right to physically chastise his wife, child and servant, since they are deemed to be his chattels.'

'But there must be something you can do, Tom,' Amy rounded on him.

'Oh my God!' Pammy Mallot wailed in distress. 'The bad bastard 'ull end up killing my poor Phoebe if he aren't stopped.'

'Think hard, Tom! We can't let him go on mistreating poor Phoebe like this!' Amy begged.

Tom was desperately racking his brains for something, anything he could do, and an idea came to him.

'Mrs Mallot, can you describe the stick he beats Phoebe with?'

'This long, and this thick.' She stretched her arms wide, then cupped her fingers and thumb.

Tom nodded. 'Will you be able to find and identify that stick?'

'Oh yes!' she asserted vehemently. 'The bastard keeps it in the hall stand so it's handy for him to thrash my poor Phoebe whenever he feels like it.'

'What good is having the stick going to do?' Amy questioned.

'An old law has it that when beating his wife, children or servants, a man must not use a stick which is thicker than a human thumb,' Tom said quietly. 'The stick Langlois uses is obviously thicker than a thumb. So I'll arrest him for breaking that old law, and hope that the magistrates will agree with me. Will he be at the house now, Mrs Mallot?'

'No, he's gone off out. It's mart day, aren't it, so more than likely he'll be drinking and whoring somewhere hereabouts.'

'Then I'd best start looking for him, hadn't I? When I've got him in the lock-up I'll send to you for his stick, Mrs Mallot.'

'God bless you, Master Potts. I'm going straight back to my Phoebe now to give her the good tidings.'

SIXTY-EIGHT

Redditch Town
Saturday, 7th June
Midnight

'Oh we must have it tonight
'Cos the moon is shining bright
And stars are twinkling in your
Eyes! Eyes! Eyes! Eyes!

But your old man's watching us.
He's watching you and I.
So let's go round the corner,
And have a bit on the slyyyyyyy!'

The song bellowed from a dozen throats inside the Red Cow, as Tom waited outside in the rain-soaked darkness. It had taken him hours of searching to find his quarry, and eager though he was to make the arrest, he knew from past experience that if he ventured inside this particular tavern there would be a riot. It was the haunt of jailbirds, poachers, thieves, brawlers and whores who hated the parish constabulary. He desperately wished that Ritchie Bint was here, but Ritchie Bint was on a spree in Bromsgrove six miles away.

Another hour passed before Sylvan Kent staggered out of the door and went to the horse tethered to one of the wall hitching-rings. Tom steeled himself to face possible violence and walked up to him.

'Christophe de Langlois, I'm arresting you in the King's name!'

'What?' Sylvan Kent swung round.

'I'm arresting you in the King's name!' Tom repeated, and warned, 'You'd best come quietly!'

'Do you know who you're talking to, you lanky bastard? Do you know my rank?' Kent growled.

'Yes, I do, and you're still under arrest. Now come with me.'

Unnoticed by either of them, three men wielding cudgels slipped silently from around the side of the building.

'Fuck you!' Kent growled and hurled himself at Tom, the impact bringing them both crashing down with Tom undermost.

The three men reached the pair, cudgels swung. Tom received a heavy blow to his head, and knew no more.

As consciousness gradually returned a terrible headache was pounding through his skull, and he groaningly struggled on to his knees, grasping the hitching-ring to pull himself on to his feet.

The singing was still bellowing in the tavern, but the horse and his quarry had gone.

Tom gingerly fingered his bleeding wound, and assumed he had hit his head on the cobbles when he fell backwards with Langlois on top of him.

Anger at himself for failing to arrest Langlois fuelled a grim determination. He picked up his hat, shouldered his staff, went first to the lock-up to tell Amy what had happened, then set out to walk the four miles to Beoley Village.

'He's not here, Master Potts.' Clad in a billowing nightdress and mob-cap, Pammy Mallot stared at Tom in dismay. 'Your head's bleeding! You'd best come in and let me dress it.'

'Thank you, I will.' Tom followed her into the house. 'How is Phoebe?'

'I slipped her a good dose o' laudanum in her posset, and her's sleeping like a babe.'

'Then with your permission, I'd like to remain here until tomorrow in case Langlois returns.'

'I'll be very glad for you to do that.' The woman smiled.

'When I go back to Redditch I shall raise the hue and cry for him,' Tom told her. 'And when he's captured, he'll most definitely be sent to trial for assaulting an officer of the Law and resisting arrest. With any luck he might even be sentenced to transportation.'

'I wish he might be sentenced to hang,' she retorted. 'And when Reverend Winward comes back I shall give him a bloody good roasting for bringing the bad bugger here in the first place.'

Tom made no reply, but prayed silently that Winward would indeed return.

SIXTY-NINE

Redditch Town
Tuesday, 1st July
Early morning

Tom awoke long before dawn. He lay in the quiet darkness taking pleasure in the warm sweet scent of Amy sleeping peacefully beside him. Then, inevitably, his pleasure was overlaid by the bitter frustration which for the past three weeks had dominated his waking hours.

The hue and cry, with its widespread dispersal of reward-offering

'Wanted' posters, had not produced any results whatsoever; and from past experience Tom knew that any possibility of tracking down either Langlois or Winward was by now virtually moribund.

He scowled in self-disgust. 'And I've only myself to blame for it. I should have hit the bugger over the head before telling him he was under arrest! No wonder the whole Parish is jeering at me for a fool!'

While Tom was castigating himself a closed carriage moved along the deserted streets and came to a halt on the chapel crossroads. A small girl carrying a weighted sack-bag alighted from it and ran across the Green.

When she neared the lock-up she halted and looked about to make sure that no one was abroad and no light glimmered from the neighbouring buildings. Then she darted to the door of the lock-up, dumped the sack-bag to one side of it, and ran back to the waiting carriage.

Tom went down into the rear yard at first light, doused his head and upper body under the water pump, cleaned his teeth, returned upstairs and finished dressing. With Amy still soundly sleeping, he returned downstairs and followed his usual routine, opening the front door and stepping outside to check if all appeared normal on and around the Green.

Satisfied all was well Tom turned to go back inside and only then noticed the sack-bag. Without thinking he tipped its contents out on to the floor, and found himself looking at the severed heads of Christophe de Langlois and the Reverend Geraint Winward.

He stared down at them in shock. Then he peered hard around the environs of the Green, but could see no movement or other signs of life. He crouched and pushed the heads back into the bag, stepped back inside the lock-up and closed the door. He stood deep in thought for several minutes. Finally he came to a decision and, steeling himself to instantly act upon it, he lifted the sack-bag and left the lock-up.

Two hours later the early bells of the mills and factories rang out to rouse the sleeping town, and men, women and children left their beds and readied themselves to face another long day of grinding toil.

Amy Potts opened her eyes, yawned, stretched, and called, 'Tom, where are you?'

No answer came, and Amy called louder. 'Tom? Where are you?'

This time she was answered by Tom calling from below. 'I'm making our breakfast, sweetheart.'

He stood at the cooking range stirring the savoury mess of oats and onions, his mind at ease.

'I've done the right thing, and so has whoever killed those evil bastards. George Creswell's been avenged, and poor Phoebe has been saved from a life of Hell!'

He spooned porridge into a bowl and ate it with gusto.

A mile westwards, in the deep mud-thick waters of Bridley Moor Marsh, a shoal of voracious eels was tearing into another type of breakfast with equal gusto.